Henry James THE AMERICAN
The version of 1877 revised in autograph and typescript for the New York Edition of 1907

Reproduced in facsimile from the original in the Houghton Library, Harvard University, with an introduction by Rodney G. Dennis

The Scolar *Press* 1976

Printed and published in Great Britain by
The Scolar Press Limited, Ilkley, Yorkshire,
and 39 Great Russell Street, London WC1

ISBN 0 85967 224 7

The manuscript is reproduced by permission
of the Houghton Library

Introduction

In 1928 William James's son, Henry James, gave to the Harvard College Library the version of *The American* that his uncle and namesake had prepared as printers' copy for the New York Edition of 1907. The following letter accompanied the gift:

December 27, 1928

Harvard College Library:

Dear Sirs –

I present to the Library the manuscript of Henry James's [1843–1916] revision of the original text of his novel 'The American', which he prepared for the so called definitive edition of his novels and tales. This is in bound form and provided with dust covers and is, so far as I am aware, the only surviving manuscript of the revisions which were made for the definitive edition.

The history of the volume is this: the manuscript passed through the hands of Mr. James B. Pinker, who was the author's literary agent. Mr. Pinker bound it up and kept it and I heard of its existence after his death. I asked his son, Mr. Eric Pinker, whether he would consent to part with the manuscript, saying that I wished to acquire it to place in the Harvard Library. Mr. Pinker thereupon sent it to me as a gift: thus, the manuscript is here by virtue of Mr. Pinker's generosity as well as by my own act.

During my lifetime none of the pages of this volume of manuscript are to be reproduced. I make an exception to this stipulation in favor of any one holding a Harvard Faculty appointment with the rank of not less than Assistant Professor.

Yours truly,
Henry James

The revised text went in loose sheets from the author to Pinker and from Pinker to the Riverside Press in the summer of 1906. Pinker probably received it back in the same year and had it bound.

The date of its accession at Harvard was 26 December 1928, notwithstanding the date of Harry James's letter. It was initially housed in the Treasure Room of the Widener Library and given the shelfmark MS Am 157*. In 1942 it was transferred to the newly-opened Houghton Library, and in 1950 it was given its present shelfmark MS Am 1237 and placed at the head of the James Family Papers which the Library had recently acquired.

The American was first published in 1877. In the preparation of his working sheets Henry James used pages of two (or more) copies of the two-volume edition published in 1883 in London by Macmillan as volumes 6 and 7 of the Collective Edition (Edel and Laurence, *Bibliography*, no. A20). Each page of printed text was pasted more or less centrally onto the recto of a cream-colored sheet of paper measuring 257 by 205 mm., leaving wide margins all round. Although the present facsimile reproduces the revised pages on recto and verso of each leaf in order to make a more manageable volume, the versos of the original are uniformly blank and correspondingly it has twice as many folios. The revising that ensued (Edel has called *The American* 'the most rewritten of all the novels') was prodigious. When the alterations required by a passage were too great to be accommodated within the margins of the mounting sheets, James discarded the printed page in question and substituted typescript or, towards the end, autograph revisions on sheets of paper measuring 253 by 195 mm. In this way twenty-three printed pages have been removed and replaced by seventy-eight pages of typescript or handwriting. In one case, after page 205 of volume two (page 467 of the present facsimile), the author has simply expanded the text by seven pages. The revision is preceded by a title-page in James's hand.

Although the revision was carefully prepared for the printer by James, the text of the New York Edition as issued contains many variants from the version here presented. The corrected proofs which would presumably represent a further process of revision are not known to exist.

After the photography for this facsimile had been completed it was decided that the brittle acidic paper and sagging binding of the original required expert attention to arrest its deterioration and even prevent its possible total loss. Therefore the volume was entrusted to Douglas Cockerell and Son of Cambridge, England. It returned to Cambridge, Massachusetts, in July 1975 in greatly improved state. The report from Sydney M. Cockerell provides an excellent description of its physical condition:

Condition when received: Binding, buckram covered case, broken on joints, front board free, book sewn on four sawn-in cords, sewing broken, cords broken. The printed leaves stuck direct to larger cream paper leaves thus making very excessive swelling at the centre of the book causing a very severe sag at the edges of the leaves. The leaves guarded together, some sheets of typescript, a large number of corrections, some in red ink. Paper of poor quality, brittle at edges.

Paper tested for acidity, average reading pH 4.05. Book taken down, the leaves without red ink treated with a solution of barium hydroxide in methanol, the leaves with red ink inter-leaved with vapour phase sheets, reading after treatment pH 6.03. Damaged leaves repaired, frames of handmade paper cut for each leaf with a window to clear the printed text area, the paper heat-set to the leaves, handmade paper ends, linen joints, book resewn on four webbings, thread headbands, covered quarter brown morocco, marbled paper sides, vellum tips, gold lettering.

This curious volume constitutes the clearest possible record of the ripening of Henry James's artistry, and the world is lucky that it survives. Disputes about the relative merits of the early and late versions of *The American* can be expected to last as long as people are clever, critical, and energetic. And the pleasure that comes, for example, from seeing how the great 'poor Claire' passage which ends the 1907 edition came into being is a very particular pleasure. The publication of this facsimile would need no justification beyond that. There is however a further justification, and one with a certain special appeal to librarians: with an excellent facsimile widely available one can expect that reasonable demands to consult the original will greatly diminish. It can safely be said that there is little danger of the volume ever reverting to the condition so affectingly described by its restorer.

The Houghton Library Rodney G. Dennis

The American

by

Henry James.

THE AMERICAN.

CHAPTER I.

On a brilliant day in May, in the year 1868, a gentleman was reclining at his ease on the great circular divan which at that period occupied the centre of the Salon Carré, in the Museum of the Louvre. This commodious ottoman has since been removed, to the extreme regret of all weak-kneed lovers of the fine arts; but the gentleman in question had taken serene possession of its softest spot, and, with his head thrown back and his legs outstretched, was staring at Murillo's beautiful moon-borne Madonna in profound enjoyment of his posture. He had removed his hat, and flung down beside him a little red guide-book and an opera-glass. The day was warm; he was heated with walking, and he repeatedly passed his handkerchief over his forehead, with a somewhat wearied gesture. And yet he was evidently not a man to whom fatigue was familiar; long, lean, and muscular, he suggested the sort of vigour that is commonly known as "toughness." But his exertions on this particular day had been of an unwonted sort, and he had often performed great physical feats which left him less jaded than his tranquil stroll through the Louvre. He had looked out all the pictures to which an asterisk was affixed in those formidable pages of fine print in his Bädeker; his attention had been strained and his eyes dazzled, and he had sat down with an æsthetic headache. He had looked, moreover, not only at all the pictures, but at all the copies that were going forward around them in the hands of those innumerable young women in irreproachable toilets who devote themselves, in France, to the propagation of masterpieces; and if the truth must be told, he had often admired the copy much more than the original. His physiognomy would have sufficiently indicated that he was a shrewd and capable fellow, and in truth he had often sat up all night over a bristling bundle of accounts, and heard the cock crow without a yawn. But Raphael and Titian and Rubens were a new kind of arithmetic, and they inspired our friend, for the first time in his life, with a vague self-mistrust.

An observer with anything of an eye for national types would have had no difficulty in determining the local origin of this undeveloped connoisseur, and indeed such an observer might have felt a certain humorous relish of the almost ideal completeness with which he filled out the national mould. The gentleman on the divan was [illegible] He appeared to possess that kind of health and strength which, when found in perfection, are the most impressive—the physical capital which the owner does nothing to "keep up." If he was a muscular Christian it was quite without knowing it. If it was necessary to walk to a remote spot he walked, but he had never known himself to "exercise." He had no theory with regard to cold bathing or the use of Indian clubs; he was neither an oarsman, a rifleman, nor a fencer—he had never had time for these amusements—and he was quite unaware that the saddle is recommended for certain forms of indigestion. He was by inclination a temperate man; but he had supped the night before

long aprons, on high stools,

reproduction

person

him

local

referring this candid connoisseur to the scene of his origin,

made an ironic point of

the superlative American; to which affirmation of character he was partly helped by the general easy magnificence of his manhood.

doctrine.

his visit to the Louvre at the Café Anglais—some one had told him it was an experience not to be omitted—and he had slept none the less the sleep of the just. His usual attitude and carriage were of a rather relaxed and lounging kind, but when, under a special inspiration, he straightened himself, he looked like a grenadier on parade. He never smoked. He had been assured—such things are said—that cigars were excellent for the health, and he was quite capable of believing it; but he knew as little about tobacco as about homœopathy. He had a very well-formed head, with a shapely, symmetrical balance of the frontal and the occipital development, and a good deal of straight, rather dry brown hair. His complexion was brown, and his nose had a bold well-marked arch. His eye was of a clear, cold gray, and, save for a rather abundant moustache, he was clean-shaved. He had the flat jaw and sinewy neck which are frequent in the American type; but the traces of national origin are a matter of expression even more than of feature, and it was in this respect that our friend's countenance was supremely eloquent. The discriminating observer we have been supposing might, however, perfectly have measured its expressiveness, and yet have been at a loss to describe it. It had that typical vagueness which is not vacuity, that blankness which is not simplicity, that look of being committed to nothing in particular, of standing in an attitude of general hospitality to the chances of life, of being very much at one's own disposal, so characteristic of many American faces. It was our friend's eye that chiefly told his story; an eye in which innocence and experience were singularly blended. It was full of contradictory suggestions; and though it was by no means the glowing orb of a hero of romance, you could find in it almost anything you looked for. Frigid and yet friendly, frank yet cautious, shrewd yet credulous, positive yet sceptical, confident yet shy, extremely intelligent and extremely good-humoured, there

- spoke, as to cheek and chin, of the joy of the matutinal steel ⊙
- had
- the arch of
- the
- betrayal of native conditions is
- for names and terms to fix it ⊙
- the eye, in this case,
- had a liberal looseness,
- tasted tobacco ⊙
- are
- would no more have thought of "taking" one than of taking a dose of medicine ⊙
- and
- droop of his
- the firm, dry
- traveller's
- a posture
- inspired
- the
- the unacquainted and the Expert

was something vaguely defiant in its concessions, and something profoundly reassuring in its reserve. The cut of this gentleman's moustache, with the two premature wrinkles in the cheek above it, and the fashion of his garments, in which an exposed shirt-front and a cerulean cravat played perhaps an obtrusive part, completed the conditions of his identity. We have approached him, perhaps, at a not especially favourable moment; he is by no means sitting for his portrait. But listless as he lounges there, rather baffled on the æsthetic question, and guilty of the damning fault (as we have lately discovered it to be) of confounding the merit of the artist with that of his work (for he admires the squinting Madonna of the young lady with the boyish coiffure, because he thinks the young lady herself uncommonly taking), he is a sufficiently promising acquaintance. Decision, salubrity, jocosity, prosperity, seem to hover within his call; he is evidently a practical man, but the idea, in his case, has undefined and mysterious boundaries, which invite the imagination to bestir itself on his behalf.

- with yet partly folded wings
- blue satin necktie of too light a shade
- hair that somehow also advertises "art"
- of business
- working-out of her scheme
- vivid
- elements
- term appears to confess, for his particular benefit, to
- Call, in her view, for
- far-straying glance, which tripped up, occasionally, as it were, on the tall arrested gentleman.
- her attention addressed to her admirer from time to time for reciprocity, one of its blankest though not of its briefest, missions
- that
- a time
- invoking her intelligence
- and, putting on his hat as if for emphasis of an austere intention,
- presence

As the little copyist proceeded with her work she cast every now and then a responsive glance toward her admirer. The cultivation of the fine arts appeared to necessitate, to her mind, a great deal of by-play, a great standing off with folded arms and head dropping from side to side, stroking of a dimpled chin with a dimpled hand, sighing and frowning and patting of the foot, fumbling in disordered tresses for wandering hair-pins. These performances were accompanied by a restless glance, which lingered longer than elsewhere upon the gentleman we have described. At last he rose abruptly, put on his hat, and approached the young lady. He placed himself before her picture and looked at it for some moments, during which she pretended to be quite unconscious of his inspection. Then, addressing her with the single word which constituted the strength of his French vocabulary, and holding up one finger in a manner which appeared to him to illuminate his meaning, "*Combien?*" he abruptly demanded.

The artist stared a moment, gave a little pout, shrugged her shoulders, put down her palette and brushes and stood rubbing her hands.

"How much?" said our friend, in English. "*Combien?*"

"Monsieur wishes to buy it?" asked the young lady in French.

"Very pretty, splendide. *Combien?*" repeated the American.

"It pleases Monsieur, my little picture? It's a very beautiful subject," said the young lady.

"The Madonna, yes; I am not a Catholic, but I want to buy it. *Combien?* Write it here." And he took a pencil from his pocket, and showed her the fly-leaf of his guide-book. She stood looking at him and scratching her chin with the pencil. "Is it not for sale?" he asked. And as she still stood reflecting, and looking at him with an eye which, in spite of her desire to treat this avidity of patronage as a very old story, betrayed an almost touching incredulity, he was afraid he had offended her. She was simply trying to look indifferent, and wondering how far she might go. "I haven't made a mistake—*pas insulté*, no?" her interlocutor continued. "Don't you understand a little English?"

The young lady's aptitude for playing a part at short notice was remarkable. She fixed him with her conscious, perceptive eye, and asked him if he spoke no French. Then, "*Donnez!*" she said briefly, and took the open guide-book. In the upper corner of the fly-leaf she traced a number, in a minute and extremely neat hand. Then she handed back the book, and took up her palette again.

Our friend read the number: "2000 francs." He said nothing for a time, but stood looking at the picture, while the copyist began actively to dabble with her paint. "For a copy, isn't that a good deal?" he asked at last. "*Pas beaucoup?*"

The young lady raised her eyes from her palette, scanned him from head to foot, and alighted with admirable sagacity upon exactly the right answer. "Yes, it's a good deal. But my copy has remarkable qualities; it is worth nothing less."

The gentleman in whom we are interested understood no French, but I have said he was intelligent, and here is a good chance to prove it. He apprehended, by a natural instinct, the meaning of the young woman's phrase, and it gratified him to think that she was so honest. Beauty, talent, virtue; she combined everything! "But you must finish it," he said. "*Finish*, you know," and he pointed to the unpainted hand of the figure.

"Oh, it shall be finished in perfection—in the perfection of perfections!" cried Mademoiselle; and to confirm her promise, she deposited a rosy blotch in the middle of the Madonna's cheek.

But the American frowned. "Ah, too red, too red!" he rejoined. "Her complexion," pointing to the Murillo, "is more delicate."

"Delicate? Oh, it shall be delicate, Monsieur; delicate as Sèvres *biscuit*. I am going to tone that down; I know all the secrets of my art. And where will you allow us to send it to you? Your address?"

"My address? Oh yes!" And the gentleman drew a card from his pocket-book and wrote something upon it. Then hesitating a moment he said: "If I don't like it when it is finished, you know, I shall not be obliged to take it."

The young lady seemed as good a guesser as himself. "Oh, I am very sure that Monsieur is not capricious," she said, with a roguish smile.

"Capricious?" And at this Monsieur began to laugh.

Said

She

is extremely soigné. That is its value."

rectitude

promise you it shall have a surface!

full of point

"Oh no, I'm not capricious. I am very faithful. I am very constant. *Comprenez?*"

"Monsieur is constant; I understand perfectly. It's a rare virtue. To recompense you, you shall have your picture on the first possible day; next week—as soon as it is dry. I will take the card of Monsieur." And she took it and read his name: "Christopher Newman." Then she tried to repeat it aloud, and laughed at her bad accent. "Your English names are so droll!"

"Droll?" said Mr. Newman, laughing too. "Did you ever hear of Christopher Columbus?"

"*Bien sûr!* He invented America; a very great man. And is he your patron?"

"My patron?"

"Your patron saint, in the calendar."

"Oh, exactly; my parents named me for him."

"Monsieur is American then?"

"Don't you see it?" Monsieur inquired.

"And you mean to carry my little picture away over there?" and she explained her phrase with a gesture.

"Oh, I mean to buy a great many pictures—*beaucoup*, *beaucoup*," said Christopher Newman.

"The honour is not less for me," the young lady answered, "for I am sure Monsieur has a great deal of taste."

"But you must give me your card," Newman said; "your card, you know."

The young lady looked severe for an instant, and then said: "My father will wait upon you."

But this time Mr. Newman's powers of divination were at fault. "Your card, your address," he simply repeated.

"My address?" said Mademoiselle. Then, with a little shrug: "Happily for you, you are an American! It is the first time I ever gave my card to a gentleman." And, taking from her pocket a rather greasy porte-monnaie, she extracted from it a small glazed visiting card, and presented the latter to her patron. It was neatly inscribed in pencil, with a great many flourishes "Mlle. Noémie Nioche." But Mr. Newman, unlike his companion, read the name with perfect gravity; all French names to him were equally droll.

"And precisely here is my father, who has come to escort me home," said Mademoiselle Noémie. "He speaks English. He will arrange with you." And she turned to welcome a little old gentleman who came shuffling up, peering over his spectacles at Newman.

M. Nioche wore a glossy wig, of an unnatural colour, which overhung his little meek, white, vacant face, and left it hardly more expressive than the unfeatured block upon which these articles are displayed in the barber's window. He was an exquisite image of shabby gentility. His little ill-made coat, desperately brushed, his darned gloves, his highly-polished boots, his rusty, shapely hat, told the story of a person who had "had losses," and who clung to the spirit of nice habits though the letter had been hopelessly effaced. Among other things M. Nioche had lost courage. Adversity had not only ruined him, it had frightened him, and he was evidently going through his remnant of life on tiptoe, for fear of waking up the hostile fates. If this strange gentleman was saying anything improper to his daughter, M. Nioche would entreat him huskily, as a particular favour, to forbear; but he would admit at the same time that he was very presumptuous to ask for particular favours.

"Monsieur has bought my picture," said Mademoiselle Noémie. "When it is finished you will carry it to him in a cab."

"In a cab!" cried M. Nioche; and he stared, in a bewildered way, as if he had seen the sun rising at midnight.

"Are you the young lady's father?" said Newman. "I think she said you speak English."

"Speak English—yes," said the old man, slowly rubbing his hands. "I will bring it in a cab."

"Say something, then," cried his daughter. "Thank him a little—not too much."

"A little, my daughter, a little," said M. Nioche, perplexed. "How much?"

"Two thousand!" said Mademoiselle Noémie. "Don't make a fuss, or he will take back his word."

"Two thousand!" cried the old man; and he began to fumble for his snuff-box. He looked at Newman, from head to foot; at his daughter, and then at the picture. "Take care you don't spoil it!" he cried, almost sublimely.

"We must go home," said Mademoiselle Noémie. "This is a good day's work. Take care how you carry it!" And she began to put up her utensils.

"How can I thank you?" said M. Nioche. "My English does not suffice."

"I wish I spoke French as well," said Newman, good-naturedly. "Your daughter is very clever."

"Oh sir!" and M. Nioche looked over his spectacles with tearful eyes, and nodded several times with a world of sadness. "She has had an education—*très-supérieure!* Nothing was spared. Lessons in pastel at ten francs the lesson, lessons in oil at twelve francs. I didn't look at the francs then. She's an artiste, eh?"

"Do I understand you to say that you have had reverses?" asked Newman.

"Reverses? Oh sir, misfortunes—terrible!"

"Unsuccessful in business, eh?"

"Very unsuccessful, sir."

"Oh, never fear; you'll get on your legs again," said Newman, cheerily.

The old man drooped his head on one side, and looked at him with an expression of pain, as if this were an unfeeling jest.

"What does he say?" demanded Mademoiselle Noémie.

M. Nioche took a pinch of snuff. "He says I will make my fortune again."

"Perhaps he will help you. And what else?"

"He says thou art very clever." *[margin: hast a great deal of head "]*

"It is very possible. You believe it yourself, my father?"

"Believe it, my daughter? With this evidence!" And the old man turned afresh, with a staring, wondering homage, to the audacious daub on the easel.

"Ask him, then, if he would not like to learn French."

"To learn French?"

"To take lessons."

"To take lessons, my daughter? From thee?"

"From you!"

"From me, my child? How should I give lessons?"

"*Pas de raisons!* Ask him immediately!" said Mademoiselle Noémie, with soft brevity.

M. Nioche stood aghast, but under his daughter's eye he collected his wits, and, doing his best to assume an agreeable smile, he executed her commands. "Would it please you to receive instruction in our beautiful language?" he inquired, with an appealing quaver.

"To study French?" asked Newman, staring.

M. Nioche pressed his finger-tips together and slowly raised his shoulders. "A little conversation!"

"Conversation—that's it!" murmured Mademoiselle Noémie, who had caught the word. "The conversation of the best society."

"Our French conversation is famous, you know," M. Nioche ventured to continue. "It's a great talent." *[margin: rather]* *[margin: the genius of our nation]*

"But isn't it awfully difficult?" asked Newman, very simply.

"Not to a man of *esprit* like Monsieur, an admirer of beauty in every form!" and M. Nioche cast a significant glance at his daughter's Madonna.

"I can't fancy myself chattering French!" said Newman, with a laugh. "And yet, I suppose that the more a man knows the better." *[margin: reeling off fluent]* *[margin: Newman]* *[margin: protested]* *[margin: The better he can get round ⊙]*

"Monsieur expresses that very happily. *Hélas, oui!*"

[margin: things, the more names of things, a man knows the better he can get round "]

"I suppose it would help me a great deal, knocking about Paris, to know the language."

"Ah, there are so many things Monsieur must want to say: difficult things."

"Everything I want to say is difficult. But you give lessons?"

Poor M. Nioche was embarrassed; he smiled more appealingly. "I am not a regular professor," he admitted. "I can't nevertheless tell him that I'm a professor," he said to his daughter.

"Tell him it's a very exceptional chance," answered Mademoiselle Noémie; "an *homme du monde*—one gentleman conversing with another. Remember what you are—what you have been."

"A teacher of languages in neither case! Much more formerly and much less to-day! And if he asks the price of the lessons?"

"He won't ask it," said Mademoiselle Noémie.

"What he pleases, I may say?"

"Never! That's bad style."

"If he asks, then?"

Mademoiselle Noémie had put on her bonnet and was tying the ribbons. She smoothed them out, with her soft little chin thrust forward. "Ten francs," she said quickly.

"Oh, my daughter! I shall never dare."

"Don't dare, then! He won't ask till the end of the lessons, and then I will make out the bill."

M. Nioche turned to the confiding foreigner again, and stood rubbing his hands, with an air of seeming to plead guilty which was not intense only because it was habitually so striking. It never occurred to Newman to ask him for a guarantee of his skill in imparting instruction; he supposed, of course, M. Nioche knew his own language, and his appealing forlornness was quite the perfection of what the American, for vague reasons, had always associated with all elderly foreigners of the lesson-giving class. Newman had never reflected upon philological processes. His chief impression with regard to ~~ascertaining~~ those mysterious correlatives of his familiar English vocables which were current in this extraordinary city of Paris was, that it ~~was~~ simply a matter of ~~a good deal of unwonted and rather ridiculous muscular effort on his own part.~~ "How did you learn English?" he asked of the old man.

"~~When I was young,~~ before my miseries. ~~Oh,~~ I was wide awake, then. My father was a great *commerçant;* he placed me for a year in a counting-house in England. Some of it stuck to me; but I have forgotten!"

"How much French can I learn in a month?"

"What does he say?" asked Mademoiselle Noémie; ~~M. Nioche explained.~~

"~~He~~ will speak like an angel!" ~~said his daughter.~~

But the native integrity which had been vainly exerted to secure M. Nioche's commercial prosperity flickered up again. "*Dame*, Monsieur!" he answered. "All I can teach you!" And then, recovering himself at a sign from his daughter; "I will wait upon you at your hotel."

"Oh yes, I should like to ~~learn French,~~" Newman went on, ~~with democratic confidingness.~~ "Hang me if I should ever have thought of it! ~~I took for granted it was impossible. But if you learned my language, why shouldn't I learn yours?" and~~ His frank, friendly laugh drew the sting from the jest. "Only, if we are going to converse, you know, you must think of something cheerful to converse about."

"You are very good, sir; I am overcome!" ~~said~~ M. Nioche ~~throwing out~~ his hands. "But you have cheerfulness and happiness for two!"

"Oh no," said Newman, more seriously. "You must be bright and lively; that's part of the bargain."

M. Nioche bowed, with his hand on his heart. "Very well, sir; ~~you have already made me lively."~~

"Come and bring me my picture, then; I will pay you

would be

so much

Oh, I could do things when I was young—

giving his friends the benefit of any vagueness.

threw up

I do feel that you've brightened me."

any mastery of

calling sharply into play latent but dormant muscles and sinews.

much

about

and then when her father had explained: "He

converse with elegance,"

I seemed to feel it too far off. But you've brought it quite near, and if you could catch on at all to our speech, why shouldn't I catch on to yours?"

And

for it, and we will talk about that. That will be a cheerful subject!"

Mademoiselle Noémie had collected her accessories, and she gave the precious Madonna in charge to her father, who retreated backwards out of sight, holding it at arm's-length and reiterating his obeisances. The young lady gathered her shawl about her like a perfect Parisienne, and it was with the smile of a Parisienne that she took leave of her patron.

CHAPTER II.

This personage

He wandered back to the divan and seated himself on the other side, in view of the great canvas on which Paul Veronese has depicted the marriage feast of Cana. Weary as he was he found the picture entertaining; it had an illusion for him; it satisfied his conception, which was ambitious, of what a splendid banquet should be. In the left-hand corner of the picture is a young woman with yellow tresses confined in a golden head-dress; she is bending forward and listening, with the smile of a charming woman at a dinner-party, to her neighbour. Newman detected her in the crowd, admired her, and perceived that she too had her votive copyist—a young man with his hair standing on end. *whose genius, like that of Samson, might have been in his bristling hair Suddenly he became conscious of the germ of the mania of the "collector;" he had taken the first step; why should he not go on? It was only twenty minutes before that he had bought the first picture of his life, and now he was already thinking of art-patronage as a fascinating pursuit. His reflections quickened his good-humour, and he was on the point of approaching the young man with another "*Combien?*" Two or three facts in this relation are noticeable, although the logical chain which connects them may seem imperfect. He knew Mademoiselle

Nioche had asked too much; he bore her no grudge for doing so, and he was determined to pay the young man exactly the proper sum. At this moment, however, his attention was attracted by a gentleman who had come from another part of the room, and whose manner was that of a stranger to the gallery, although he was equipped with neither guide-book nor opera-glass. He carried a white sun-umbrella, lined with blue silk, and he strolled in front of the Paul Veronese, vaguely looking at it, but much too near to see anything but the grain of the canvas. Opposite [illegible] Christopher Newman he paused and turned, and then our friend, who had been observing him, had a chance to verify a suspicion aroused by an imperfect view of his face. The result of this larger scrutiny was that he presently sprang to his feet, strode across the room, and, with an outstretched hand, arrested the gentleman with the blue-lined umbrella. The latter stared, but put out his hand at a venture. He was corpulent and rosy; and though his countenance, which was ornamented with a beautiful flaxen beard, carefully divided in the middle and brushed outward at the sides, was not remarkable for intensity of expression, he looked like a person who would willingly shake hands with any one. I know not what Newman thought of his face, but he found a want of response in his grasp.

"Oh, come, come," he said, laughing; "don't say, now, you don't know me—if I have *not* got a white parasol!"

The sound of his voice quickened the other's memory, his face expanded to its fullest capacity, and he also broke into a laugh. "Why, Newman—I'll be blowed! Where in the world—I declare! Who would have thought? You know you have changed."

"You haven't," said Newman.

"Not for the better, no doubt. When did you get here?"

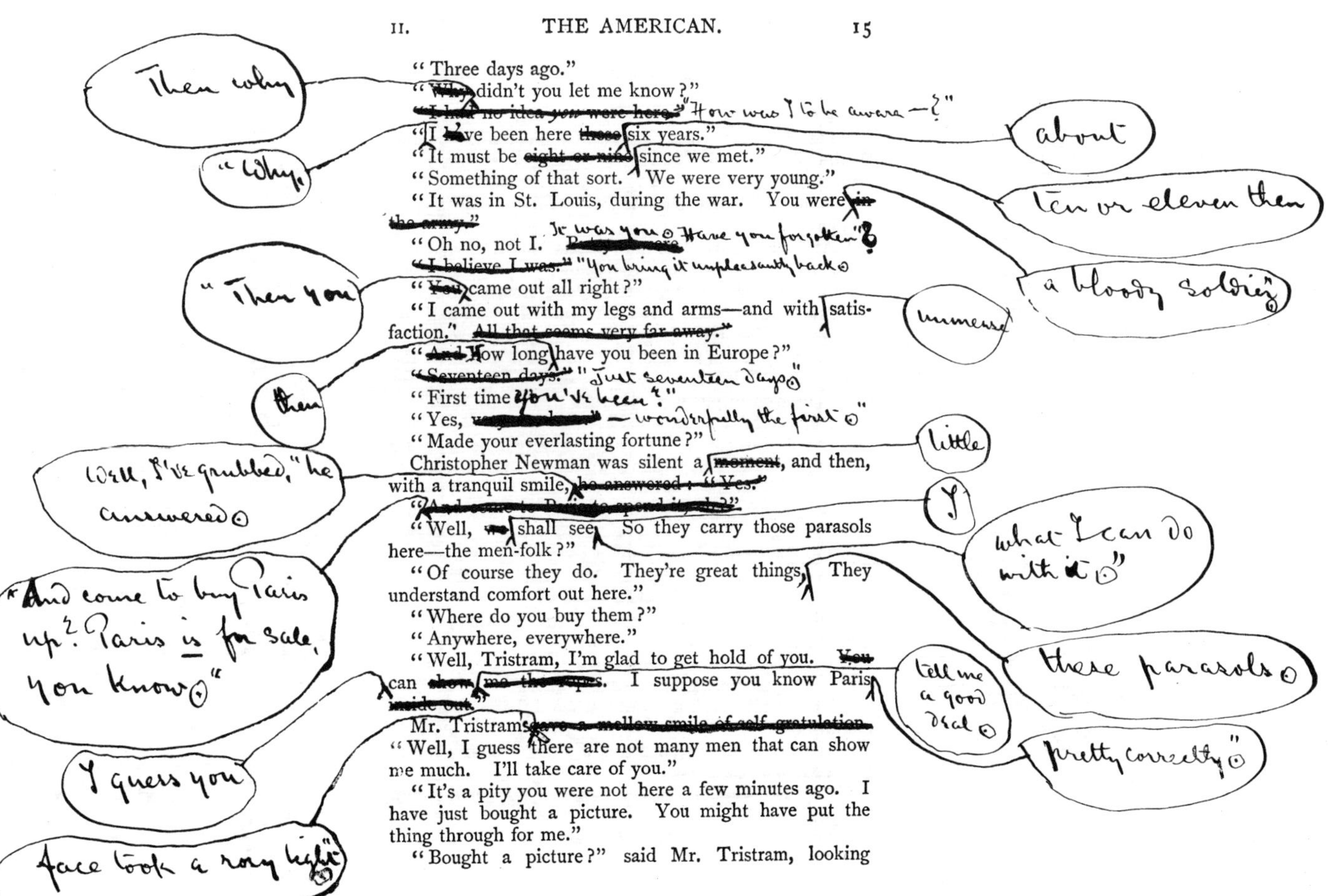

"Three days ago."

"Why didn't you let me know?"

"I had no idea you were here."

"I have been here three years."

"It must be eight or nine since we met."

"Something of that sort. We were very young."

"It was in St. Louis, during the war. You were in the army."

"Oh no, not I. [illegible]"

"I believe I was."

"You came out all right?"

"I came out with my legs and arms—and with satisfaction. All that seems very far away."

"And how long have you been in Europe?"

"Seventeen days."

"First time?"

"Yes, [illegible]"

"Made your everlasting fortune?"

Christopher Newman was silent a moment, and then, with a tranquil smile, he answered: "Yes."

"And come to Paris to spend it, eh?"

"Well, we shall see. So they carry those parasols here—the men-folk?"

"Of course they do. They're great things. They understand comfort out here."

"Where do you buy them?"

"Anywhere, everywhere."

"Well, Tristram, I'm glad to get hold of you. You can show me the ropes. I suppose you know Paris inside out."

Mr. Tristram gave a mellow smile of self-gratulation.

"Well, I guess there are not many men that can show me much. I'll take care of you."

"It's a pity you were not here a few minutes ago. I have just bought a picture. You might have put the thing through for me."

"Bought a picture?" said Mr. Tristram, looking

vaguely round at the walls. "Why, do they sell them?"

"I mean a copy."

"Oh, I see. These," said Mr. Tristram, nodding at the Titians and Vandykes, "these, I suppose, are originals?"

"I hope so," cried Newman. "I don't want a copy of a copy."

"Ah," said Mr. Tristram, ~~mysteriously~~, "you can never tell. They imitate, you know, so deucedly well. It's like the jewellers, with their false stones. Go into the Palais Royal, there; you see 'Imitation' on half the windows. The law obliges them to stick it on, you know; but you can't tell the things apart. To tell the truth," Mr. Tristram continued, ~~with a wry face~~, "I don't do much in pictures. I leave that to my wife."

"Ah, you have got a wife?"

"Didn't I mention it? She's a very nice woman; you must know her. She's up there in the Avenue d'Iéna."

"So you are regularly fixed—house and children and all?"

"Yes; a tip-top house, and a couple of ~~youngsters~~."

"Well," ~~said~~ Christopher Newman, stretching his arms a little, ~~with a sigh, "I envy you."~~

"Oh no, ~~you~~ don't," answered Mr. Tristram, giving him a little poke with his parasol.

"I beg your pardon; ~~I do!~~ you do."

"Well, ~~you won't~~ then, when—when——"

"You don't certainly mean when I have seen your establishment?"

"When you have seen Paris, my boy. You want to be ~~your own master here.~~"

"Oh, ~~I have been my own master~~ all my life, and I'm tired of it."

"Well, try ~~Paris~~. How old ~~are you?~~"

"Thirty ~~six~~-eight."

Sagaciously
— and his grimace seemed a turn of the screw of discrimination —
So very
They're one of the things
charming cubs."
Sighed
"You affect me with a queer feeling that I suppose to be envy."
I shan't
in light marching order here."
I've enjoyed that blessing, or that curse,
it on the basis of Paris; that makes a new thing of it.
may you be?"

"*C'est le bel âge*, as they say here."

"What does that mean?"

"It means that a man shouldn't send away his plate till he has eaten his fill."

"All that? I have just made arrangements to take French lessons."

"Oh, you don't want any lessons. You'll pick it up. I never took any."

"I suppose you speak French as well as English?"

"Better!" said Mr. Tristram, roundly. "It's a splendid language. You can say all sorts of bright things in it."

"But I suppose," said Christopher Newman, with an earnest desire for information, "that you must be bright to begin with."

"Not a bit; that's just the beauty of it."

The two friends, as they exchanged these remarks, had remained standing where they met, and leaning against the rail which protected the pictures. Mr. Tristram at last declared that he was overcome with fatigue, and should be happy to sit down. Newman recommended in the highest terms the great divan on which he had been lounging, and they prepared to seat themselves. "This is a great place; isn't it?" said Newman, with ardour.

"Great place, great place. Finest thing in the world." And then, suddenly, Mr. Tristram hesitated and looked about him. "I suppose they won't let you smoke here?"

Newman stared. "Smoke? I'm sure I don't know. You know the regulations better than I."

"I? I never was here before!"

"Never! in six years?"

"I believe my wife dragged me here once when we first came to Paris, but I never found my way back."

'But you say you know Paris so well!"

"I don't call this Paris!" cried Mr. Tristram, with

assurance. "Come; let's go over to the Palais Royal and have a smoke."

"I don't smoke," said Newman.

~~And Mr. Tristram~~ led his companion away. They passed through the glorious halls of the Louvre, down the staircases, along the cool, dim galleries of sculpture, and out into the enormous court. Newman looked about him as he went, but he made no comments; and it was only when they at last emerged into the open air that he said to his friend, "It seems to me that in your place I should have come here once a week."

"Oh no, you wouldn't!" said Mr. Tristram. "You think so, but you wouldn't. You wouldn't have had time. You would always mean to go, but you never would go. There's better fun than that, here in Paris. Italy's the place to see pictures; wait till you get there. There you have to go; you can't do anything else. It's an awful country; you can't get a decent cigar. I don't know why I went ~~in there~~ to-day. I was strolling along, rather hard up for amusement. I sort of ~~noticed~~ the Louvre as I passed, and I thought I would go ~~in~~ and see what was going on. But if I hadn't found you there I should have felt rather sold. Hang it, I don't care for ~~pictures~~; I prefer the ~~reality~~!" And Mr. Tristram tossed off this happy formula with an assurance which the numerous class of persons suffering from an overdose of ~~culture~~ might have envied him.

The two gentlemen proceeded along the Rue de Rivoli and into the Palais Royal, where they seated themselves at one of the little tables stationed at the door of the café which projects into the great open quadrangle. The place was filled with people, the fountains were spouting, a band was playing, clusters of chairs were gathered beneath all the lime-trees, and buxom, white-capped nurses, seated along the benches, were offering to their infant charges the amplest facilities for nutrition. There was an easy, homely gaiety in the whole scene, and Christopher Newman felt that it was most characteristically Parisian.

"And now," began Mr. Tristram, when they had tasted the decoction which he had caused to be served to them, "now just give an account of yourself. What are your ideas, what are your plans, where have you come from, and where are you going? In the first place, where are you staying?"

"At the Grand Hotel," said Newman.

Mr. Tristram puckered his plump visage. "That won't do! You must change."

"Change?" demanded Newman. "Why, it's the finest hotel I ever was in."

"You don't want a 'fine' hotel; you want something small and quiet and elegant, where your bell is answered and your your person is recognised."

"They keep running to see if I have rung before I have touched the bell," said Newman, "and as for my person, they are always bowing and scraping to it."

"I suppose you are always tipping them. That's very bad style."

"Always? By no means. A man brought me something yesterday, and then stood loafing about in a beggarly manner. I offered him a chair, and asked him if he wouldn't sit down. Was that bad style?"

"Very!"

"But he bolted, instantly. At any rate the place amuses me. Hang your elegance, if it bores me. I sat in the court of the Grand Hotel last night until two o'clock in the morning, watching the coming and going, and the people knocking about."

"You're easily pleased. But you can do as you choose—a man in your shoes. You have made a pile of money, eh?"

"I have made enough."

"Happy the man who can say that! Enough for what?"

"Enough to rest a while, to forget the confounded thing, to look about me, to see the world, to have a good time, to improve my mind, and, if the fancy takes me, to marry a wife." Newman spoke slowly, with a certain dryness of accent, and with frequent pauses. This was his habitual mode of utterance, but it was especially marked in the words I have just quoted.

"Jupiter! There's a programme!" cried Mr. Tristram. "Certainly, all that takes money, especially the wife; unless indeed she gives it, as mine did. And what's the story? How have you done it?"

Newman had pushed his hat back from his forehead, folded his arms, and stretched his legs. He listened to the music, he looked about him at the bustling crowd, at the plashing fountains, at the nurses and the babies. "I have worked!" he answered at last.

Tristram looked at him for some moments, and allowed his placid eyes to measure his friend's generous longitude and rest upon his comfortably contemplative face. "What have you worked at?" he asked.

"Oh, at several things."

"I suppose you're a smart fellow, eh?"

Newman continued to look at the nurses and babies; they imparted to the scene a kind of primordial, pastoral simplicity. "Yes," he said at last, "I suppose I am." And then, in answer to his companion's inquiries, he related briefly his history since their last meeting. It was an intensely Western story, and it dealt with enterprises which it will be needless to introduce to the reader in detail. Newman had come out of the war with a brevet of brigadier-general, an honour which in this case—without invidious comparisons—had lighted upon shoulders amply competent to bear it. But though he could manage a fight when need was, Newman heartily disliked the business; his four years in the army had left

let up
But enough
Damned long grind
effect of dry detachment,
recorded
I've
worked, worked,
considered
allowing a new curiosity
the
the
more things than I care to remember"
real live man, hey?"
Guess
with intensity, a tale of the western world, and it showed, in that bright alien air, very much as fine dessicated, articulated "specimens", bleached, monstrous, probably unique, show in the high light of museums of natural history
elements, incidents, enterprises,
the deeps and the shallows, the ebb and the flow, of great financial tides
carry
had proved he could handle his men, and still more the enemy's, with effect,
he

him with an angry, bitter sense of the waste of precious things—life and time and money ~~and [illegible] ness" and the early freshness of purpose; and he had~~ addressed himself to the pursuits of peace with passionate zest and energy. He ~~was, of course,~~ as penniless when he plucked off his shoulder-straps as when he put them on, and the only capital at his disposal ~~was his dogged~~ resolution and his lively perception of ends and means. Exertion and action were as natural to him as respiration; a more completely healthy mortal had never trod the elastic soil of ~~the West~~. His experience, moreover, [illegible] as wide as his capacity; ~~when he was fourteen years old,~~ necessity had taken him by his slim young shoulders and pushed him into the street to earn that night's supper. He had not earned it, but he had earned the next night's, and afterwards, whenever he had had none, it was because he had gone without [illegible] to use the money for something else, a keener pleasure or a finer profit. He had turned his hand, with his brain in it, to many things; he had ~~been enterprising, in an eminent sense of the term; he had been adventurous and even reckless, and he had known bitter failure as well as brilliant success; but he was a~~ born experimentalist, ~~and~~ he had always found something to enjoy in the pressure of ~~necessity~~, even when it was as irritating as the haircloth shirt of the mediæval monk. At one time ~~failure~~ seemed inexorably his portion; ill-luck became his bed-fellow, and whatever he touched he turned ~~not to gold, but to ashes~~. His most vivid conception of a supernatural element in the world's affairs ~~had~~ come to him once when this pertinacity of misfortune was at its climax; there seemed to him something stronger in life than his [illegible]. But the mysterious something could only be [illegible], and he [illegible] accordingly ~~seized with an intense personal enmity~~ to this impertinent force. He had known what it was to have utterly exhausted his credit, to be unable to raise a dollar, and to find himself at nightfall in a strange city,

and ingenuity and opportunity; and he had

had been of course

had been his whetted, knife-edged

had

great States of his option

had been

in his fourteenth year

defied example and precedent and probability, had adventured almost to madness and escaped almost by miracle, drinking alike of the flat water, when not the rank poison, of failure, and of the strong wine of success

A

direct

fate

defeat had

Selfish

had

had

to ashes out of which no gleaming particle could be raked

personal, intimate will

a demon as personal as himself

found himself in fine working opposition

without a penny to mitigate its strangeness. It was under these circumstances that he made his entrance into San Francisco, the scene, subsequently, of his happiest strokes of fortune. If he did not, like Dr. Franklin in Philadelphia, march along the street munching a penny loaf, it was only because he had not the penny loaf necessary to the performance. In his darkest days he had had but one simple, practical impulse—the desire, as he would have phrased it, to see the thing through. He did so at last, buffeted his way into smooth waters, and made money largely. It must be admitted, rather nakedly, that Christopher Newman's sole aim in life had been to make money; what he had been placed in the world for was, to his own perception, simply to invest a fortune, the bigger the better, from defiant opportunity. This idea completely filled his horizon and satisfied his imagination. Upon the uses of money, upon what one might do with a life into which one had succeeded in injecting the golden stream, he had up to his thirty-fifth year very scantily reflected. Life had been for him an open game, and he had played for high stakes. He had won at last, and carried off his winnings; and now what was he to do with them? He was a man to whom, sooner or later, the question was sure to present itself, and the answer to it belongs to our story. A vague sense that more answers were possible than his philosophy had hitherto dreamt of had already taken possession of him, and it seemed softly and agreeably to deepen as he lounged in this brilliant corner of Paris with his friend.

"I must confess," he presently went on, "that here I don't feel at all smart. My remarkable talents seem of no use. I feel as simple as a little child, and a little child might take me by the hand and lead me about."

"Oh, I'll be your little child," said Tristram, jovially; "I'll take you by the hand. Trust yourself to me."

"I am a good worker," Newman continued, "but

most victorious engagements
conclude the affair. He had ended by concluding many, had at last
had begun and continued to make
out of the hard substance of life
only proposal
gouge
this eve of his fortieth
finally won and had
I don't here at all feel my value
It's as if I were as
as if
grand

I'm afraid I must, as a loafer, be wanting in grit ⊙

rather think I am a poor loafer. I have come abroad to amuse myself, but I doubt whether I know how."

"Oh, that's easily learned."

"Well, I may perhaps learn it, but I am afraid I shall never do it by rote. I have the best will in the world about it, but my genius doesn't lie in that direction. As a loafer I shall never be original, as I take it that you are."

"Yes," said Tristram, "I suppose I am original; like all those immoral pictures in the Louvre."

"Besides," Newman continued, "I don't want to work at pleasure, any more than I played at work. I want to take it easily. I feel deliciously lazy, and I should like to spend six months as I am now, sitting under a tree and listening to a band. There's only one thing; I want to hear some good first-class music."

"Music and First-class music and first-class pictures! Lord, what refined tastes! You are what my wife calls intellectual. I ain't, a bit. But we can find something better for you to do than to sit under a tree. To begin with, you must come to the club."

"What club?"

"The Occidental. You will see all the Americans there; all the best of them, at least. Of course you play poker?"

"Oh, I say," cried Newman, with energy, "you are not going to lock me up in a club and stick me down at a card-table! I haven't come all this way for that."

"What the deuce *have* you come for? You were glad enough to play poker in St. Louis, I recollect, when you cleaned me out."

"I have come to see Europe, to get the best out of it I can. I want to see all the great things, and do what the clever people do."

"The clever people? Much obliged. You set me down as a blockhead, then?"

Newman was sitting sidewise in his chair, with his

let myself, to let & everything, go ⊙

"First-class music and first-class

You've got

then

best

'best'

then

elbow on the back and his head leaning on his hand. Without moving he looked a while at his companion, with his dry, guarded, half-inscrutable, and yet altogether good-natured smile. "Introduce me to your wife!" he said at last.

Tristram bounced about in his chair. "Upon my word, I won't. She doesn't want any help to turn up her nose at me, nor do you either!"

"I don't turn up my nose at you, my dear fellow; nor at any one, or anything. I'm not proud, I assure you I'm not proud. That's why I am willing to take example by the clever people."

"Well, if I'm not the rose, as they say here, I have lived near it. I can show you some clever people, too. Do you know General Packard? Do you know C. P. Hatch? Do you know Miss Kitty Upjohn?"

"I shall be happy to make their acquaintance; I want to cultivate society."

Tristram seemed restless and suspicious; he eyed his friend askance, and then, "What are you up to, any way?" he demanded. "Are you going to write a book?"

Christopher Newman twisted one end of his moustache a while in silence, and at last he made answer. "One day, a couple of months ago, something very curious happened to me. I had come on to New York on some important business; it was rather a long story—a question of getting ahead of another party, in a certain particular way, in the stock-market. This other party had once played me a very mean trick. I owed him a grudge, I felt awfully savage at the time, and I vowed that when I got a chance, I would, figuratively speaking, put his nose out of joint. There was a matter of some sixty thousand dollars at stake. If I put it out of his way, it was a blow the fellow would feel, and he really deserved no quarter. I jumped into a hack and went about my business, and it was in this hack—this immortal, historical hack—that the curious thing I speak

I'll do nothing of the sort.

here."

rare minds

he finally

heavy

too long, and too low, a story to tell you now

in

on a big transaction, and on information that was all my own.

off on me one of the clever meannesses the feeling of which works in a man like strong poison. I owed him a good one, the best one he was ever to have got in his life, and as his chance here—for he was after it, but on the wrong tip—would have been a remarkably sweet thing, a matter of half a million, I saw my way to show him the weight of my hand. The good it was going to do me, you see, to feel it come down on him!

of occurred. It was a hack like any other, only a trifle dirtier, with a greasy line along the top of the drab cushions, as if it had been used for a great many Irish funerals. It is possible I took a nap; I had been travelling all night, and though I was excited with my errand, I felt the want of sleep. At all events I woke up suddenly, from a sleep or from a kind of a reverie, with the most extraordinary feeling in the world—a mortal disgust for the thing I was going to do. It came upon me like *that!*"—and he snapped his fingers—"as abruptly as an old wound that begins to ache. I couldn't tell the meaning of it; I only felt that I loathed the whole business and wanted to wash my hands of it. The idea of losing that sixty thousand dollars, of letting it utterly slide and scuttle and never hearing of it again, seemed the sweetest thing in the world. And all this took place quite independently of my will, and I sat watching it as if it were a play at the theatre. I could feel it going on inside of me. You may depend upon it that there are things going on inside of us that we understand mighty little about."

"Jupiter! you make my flesh creep!" cried Tristram. "And while you sat in your hack, watching the play, as you call it, the other man marched in and bagged your sixty thousand dollars?"

"I have not the least idea. I hope so, poor devil! but I never found out. We pulled up in front of the place I was going to in Wall Street, but I sat still in the carriage, and at last the driver scrambled down off his seat to see whether his carriage had not turned into a hearse. I couldn't have got out, any more than if I *had* been a corpse. What was the matter with me? Momentary idiocy, you'll say. What I wanted to get out of was Wall Street. I told the man to drive down to the Brooklyn ferry and to cross over. When we were over I told him to drive me out into the country. As I had told him originally to drive for dear life down town, I suppose he thought me insane. Perhaps I was, but in that case I am insane still. I spent the morning looking at the first green leaves on Long Island. I was sick of business; I wanted to throw it all up and break off short; I had money enough, or if I hadn't I ought to have. I seemed to feel a new man inside my old skin, and I longed for a new world. When you want a thing so very badly you had better treat yourself to it. I didn't understand the matter, not in the least; but I gave the old horse the bridle and let him find his way. As soon as I could get out of the game I sailed for Europe. That is how I come to be sitting here."

"You ought to have bought up that hack," said Tristram; "it isn't a safe vehicle to have about. And you have really sold out, then; you have retired from business?"

"I have made over my hand to a friend; when I feel disposed, I can take up the hand again. I daresay that a twelvemonth hence the operation will be reversed. The pendulum will swing back again. I shall be sitting in the gondola or on a dromedary, and all of a sudden I shall want to clear out. But for the present I am perfectly free. I have even bargained that I am to receive no business letters."

"Oh, it's a real *caprice de prince*," said Tristram. "I back out; a poor devil like me can't help you to spend such very magnificent leisure as that. You should get introduced to the crowned heads."

Newman looked at him a moment, and then, with his easy smile, "How does one do it?" he asked.

"Come, I like that!" cried Tristram. "It shows you are in earnest."

"Of course I am in earnest. Didn't I say I wanted the best? I know the best can't be had for mere money, but I rather think money will do a good deal. In addition, I am willing to take a good deal of trouble."

"You are not bashful, eh?"

I had lost my wits on the way.
had
I had been so hot that it seemed as if I should never be cool enough again. As for the damned money, I have enough, already, not to miss it — you see how that spoils my beauty.
my sacrifice of them has become, in another way, my biggest stroke of business.
under
at all events
my case
You probably had better have it and see.
harness
"Well, I'm not at present transacting any, on any terms. There'll be plenty to be done again if I don't hold out, but I shall hold out as long as possible.
however,
repeated, in the opposite sense, and the
all
arranged
uncanny
considered
candours
wound up and sold out then? you've formally
too shrinking, hey?"

"I haven't the least idea. I want the biggest kind of entertainment a man can get. People, places, art, nature, everything! I want to see the tallest mountains, and the bluest lakes, and the finest pictures, and the handsomest churches, and the most celebrated men, and the most beautiful women."

"Settle down in Paris, then. There are no mountains that I know of, and the only lake is in the Bois de Boulogne, and not particularly blue. But there is everything else: plenty of pictures and churches, no end of celebrated men, and several beautiful women."

"But I can't settle down in Paris at this season, just as summer is coming on."

"Oh, for the summer go up to Trouville."

"What is Trouville?"

"The French Newport. Half the Americans go."

"Is it anywhere near the Alps?"

"About as near as Newport is to the Rocky Mountains."

"Oh, I want to see Mont Blanc," said Newman, "and Amsterdam, and the Rhine, and a lot of places. Venice in particular. I have great ideas about Venice."

"Ah," said Mr. Tristram, rising, "I see I shall have to introduce you to my wife. She'll have grand ideas for you!"

CHAPTER III.

HE performed that ceremony on the following day, when, by appointment, Christopher Newman went to dine with him. Mr. and Mrs. Tristram lived behind one of those chalk-coloured façades which decorate with their pompous sameness the broad avenues manufactured by Baron Haussmann in the neighbourhood of the Arc de Triomphe. Their apartment was rich in the modern conveniences,

and Tristram lost no time in calling his visitor's attention to their principal household treasures, the gas-lamps and the furnace-holes. "Whenever you feel homesick," he said, "you must come here. We'll stick you down before a register, under a good big burner, and——"

"And you ll soon get over your homesickness," said Mrs. Tristram.

Her husband stared; often had a tone ; he could t tell for his life The truth is that circumstances had done much to cultivate in Mrs. Tristram Her taste on many points differed from that of her husband; and though she made frequent concessions it must be confessed that her They were founded upon vague project

It should be added, without delay, to anticipate misconception, that , She had a very plain face, and she was entirely without illusions as to her appearance. She had taken its measure to a hair's-breadth, she knew the worst and the best, she had accepted herself. It had not been, indeed, without a struggle. As a she had spent hours with her back to her mirror, crying her eyes out; and later she had, from desperation and bravado, adopted the habit of proclaiming herself the most ill-favoured of women, in order that she might—as in common politeness was inevitable—be contradicted and reassured. It was since she had come to live in Europe that she had begun to take the matter philo-

frequent
thick-scattered
right
this lady
to the dull small fact that he had married her,
that defied any convenient test;
for whom her irony might be intended
reserves were not always muffled in pink gauze
the
the need for any little intellectual luxury she could pick up by the way
if she was thus saving herself up it was yet not to cover the expense of any foreseen outlay of that finest part of her substance that was known to her tacitly as her power of passion
of her some day affirming herself in her totality; to which end she was in advance getting herself together, building herself high, inquiring, in short, into her dimensions
mere mortified maiden

sophically. Her observation, acutely exercised here, had suggested to her that a woman's [illegible] She encountered so many women who pleased without beauty, that she began to feel that she had discovered her ~~mission~~. She had once heard an enthusiastic musician, out of patience with a gifted bungler, declare that a fine voice is really an obstacle to singing properly; and it occurred to her that it might perhaps be equally true that a beautiful face is an obstacle to the acquisition of charming manners. Mrs. Tristram, then, undertook to ~~be exquisitely agreeable~~, and she brought to the task ~~a really touching devotion~~. How well she would have succeeded I am unable to say; unfortunately she broke off in the middle. Her own excuse was the want of encouragement in her immediate circle. But ~~I am inclined to think that she had~~ not a real genius for the ~~matter, or~~ she would have pursued ~~the charming art~~ for itself. The poor lady was ~~very~~ incomplete. She fell back upon the harmonies of ~~the toilet~~, which she thoroughly understood, and contented herself with ~~dressing in perfection~~. She lived in Paris, which she pretended to detest, because it was only in Paris that one could find things to exactly suit one's complexion. Besides, out of Paris it was always more or less of a trouble to get ten-button gloves. When she railed at this serviceable city, and you asked her where she would prefer to reside, she returned some very unexpected answer. She would say in Copenhagen, or in Barcelona; having, while making the tour of Europe, spent a couple of days at each of these places. On the whole, with her poetic furbelows, and her misshapen, intelligent little face, she was, when ~~you knew her, a decidedly interesting woman~~. She was naturally ~~shy~~, and if she had been born a beauty, she would [illegible] extremely reserved sometimes with her friends, and strangely expansive with strangers.

Handwritten revisions:

Social service resides not in what she is but in what she appears, and that in the labyrinth of appearances she may always make others lose their clue if she only keeps her own.

had

refuge.

persuade by grace

no small ingenuity.

she had presumably

Charming art, or

it

after all

Dress,

playing in its lock that key to every appearance.

known, a figure to place, in the great gallery of the wistful, somewhere apart.

timid

(content with it) probably have taken no risks. At present she was both reckless and diffident;

She despised her husband; despised him too much, for she had been perfectly at liberty not to marry him. She had been in love with a clever man, who had slighted her, and she had married a fool, in the hope that the thankless wit, reflecting on it, would conclude that she had no appreciation of merit, and that he had flattered himself in supposing that she cared for his own. Restless, discontented, visionary, without personal ambitions, but with a certain avidity of imagination, she was, as I have said before, eminently incomplete. She was full—both for good and for ill—of beginnings that came to nothing; but she had nevertheless, morally, a spark of the sacred fire.

Newman was fond, under all circumstances, of the society of women; and now that he was out of his native element, and deprived of his habitual interests, he turned to it for compensation. He took a great fancy to Mrs. Tristram; she frankly repaid it, and after their first meeting he passed a great many hours in her drawing-room. After two or three talks they were fast friends. Newman's manner with women was peculiar, and it required some ingenuity on a lady's part to discover that he admired her. He had no gallantry, in the usual sense of the term; no compliments, no graces, no speeches. Very fond of what is called chaffing in his dealings with men, he never found himself on a sofa beside a member of the softer sex without feeling extremely serious. He was not shy, and, so far as awkwardness proceeds from a struggle with shyness, he was not awkward; grave, attentive, submissive, often silent, he was simply swimming in a sort of rapture of respect. This emotion was not at all theoretic, it was not even in a high degree sentimental; he had thought very little about the "position" of women, and he was not familiar, either sympathetically or otherwise, with the image of a President in petticoats. His attitude was simply the flower of his general good-nature, and a part of his instinctive and genuinely democratic assumption of every one's right to lead an easy life. If a shaggy pauper had a right to bed and board and wages and a vote, women, of course, who were weaker than paupers, and whose physical tissue was in itself an appeal, should be maintained, sentimentally, at the public expense. Newman was willing to be taxed for this purpose, largely, in proportion to his means. Moreover, many of the common traditions with regard to women were with him fresh personal impressions. He had never read ~~[illegible]~~ {a page of printed romance}. ~~He had been struck with their acuteness, their subtlety, their tact, their felicity of judgment. They seemed to him exquisitely organised. If it is true that one must always have in one's work here below a religion, or at least an ideal of some sort, Newman found his metaphysical inspiration in a vague acceptance of final responsibility to some illumined feminine brow.~~

He spent a great deal of time in listening to advice from Mrs. Tristram; advice, it must be added, for which he had never asked. He would have been incapable of asking for it, ~~for~~ {inasmuch} he had no perception of difficulties, and consequently no curiosity about remedies. The complex Parisian world about him seemed a very simple affair; it was an immense, ~~amusing~~ {surprising} spectacle, but it neither inflamed his imagination nor irritated his curiosity. He kept his hands in his pockets, looked on good-humouredly, desired to miss nothing important, observed a great many things narrowly, and never reverted to himself. Mrs. Tristram's "advice" was a part of the show, and a more entertaining element, in ~~her abundant gossip, than the others~~ {her free criticism, than any other}. He enjoyed her talking about himself; it seemed a part of her beautiful ingenuity; but he never made an application of anything she said, or remembered it when he was away from her. For herself, she appropriated him; he was the most interesting thing she had had to think about in many a month. She wished to do something with him—she hardly knew what. There was so he was beyond everything a child of nature, but she repeated it so often that it could have been but a term of endearment.

imagination

rapacity,

had somehow found means to be degenerate without the iridescence of decay.

Very

a sociability affirmed, on its anecdotic side, too much at the expense of those possible partakers who were not there to guard their interest in it. He was patient at poker; he was infallible upon the names and the other attributes of all the cocottes; his criticism of cookery, his comparative view of the great "years" of champagne, enjoyed the authority of the last word. And then he was

much of him; he was so rich and robust, so easy, friendly, well-disposed, that he kept her ~~fancy~~ constantly on the alert. For the present, the only thing she could do was to like him. She told him ~~that he was "thoroughly Western," but in this compliment the adverb was tinged with insincerity.~~ She led him about with her, introduced him to fifty people, ~~and~~ took extreme satisfaction in her conquest. Newman accepted every proposal, shook hands universally and promiscuously, and seemed equally unfamiliar with trepidation or with elation. Tom Tristram complained of his wife's ~~avidity, and~~ declared that he could never have a clear five minutes with his friend. If he had known how things were going to turn out, he never would have brought him to the Avenue d'Iéna. The two men, formerly, had not been intimate, but Newman remembered his earlier impression of his host, and did Mrs. Tristram, who had by no means taken him into her confidence, but whose secret he presently discovered, the justice to admit that her husband ~~was a rather degenerate mortal. At twenty-five he had been a good fellow, and in this respect he was unchanged; but of a man of his age one expected something more.~~ People said he was sociable, but this was as much a matter of course as for a dipped sponge to expand; and it was ~~not a high order of sociability. He was a great gossip and tattler, and to produce a laugh would hardly have spared the reputation of his aged mother. Newman had a kindness for old memories, but he found it impossible not to perceive that Tristram was nowadays a very light weight. His only aspirations~~ [illegible] idle, spiritless, sensual, snobbish. He irritated our friend by the tone of his allusions to their native country, and Newman was at a loss to understand why the United States were not good enough for Mr. Tristram. He had never been a very conscious patriot, but it vexed him to see them treated as little better than a vulgar smell in his friend's nostrils, and he finally broke out and swore that they were the greatest country in the world, that they could put all Europe into their breeches' pockets, and that an American who spoke ill of them ought to be carried home in irons and compelled to live in Boston. (This, for Newman, was putting it very vindictively.) Tristram was a comfortable man to snub; he bore no malice, and he continued to insist on Newman's finishing his evenings at the Occidental Club.

Christopher Newman dined several times in the Avenue d'Iéna, and his host always proposed an early adjournment to this institution. Mrs. Tristram protested, and declared that her husband exhausted his ingenuity in trying to displease her.

"Oh no, I never try, my love," he answered. "I know you loathe me quite enough when I take my chance."

Newman hated to see a husband and wife on these terms, and he was sure one or other of them must be very unhappy. He knew it was not Tristram. Mrs. Tristram had a balcony before her windows, upon which, during the June evenings, she was fond of sitting, and Newman used frankly to say that he preferred the balcony to the club. It had a fringe of perfumed plants in tubs, and enabled you to look up the broad street and see the Arch of Triumph vaguely massing its heroic sculptures in the summer starlight. Sometimes Newman kept his promise of following Mr. Tristram, in half an hour, to the Occidental, and sometimes he forgot it. His hostess asked him a great many questions about himself, but on this subject he was an indifferent talker. He was not what is called "subjective," though when he felt that her interest was sincere he made an almost heroic attempt

wherein such a country, as a whole, could fall short of Mr. Tristram's measure.
systematic
the United States
ran them down
spoke up for them quite as if it had been Fourth of July, proclaiming that any
which
But their visitor
yet he
he
he made a real effort to meet it

34 THE AMERICAN. III.

to be. He told her ~~a great~~ many things he had done, and regaled her with ~~anecdotes of Western life; she was from Philadelphia~~, and, with her eight years in Paris, talked of herself as a languid Oriental. But some other person was always the hero of the tale, by no means always to his advantage; and Newman's own ~~emotions~~ were but scantily chronicled. She had an especial wish to know whether he had ever been in love—seriously, passionately—and, failing to gather any satisfaction from his allusions, she at last ~~directly inquired~~. He hesitated a while, ~~and at last he~~ said: "No!" She declared that she was delighted to hear it, as it confirmed her private conviction that he was a man of no feeling.

"~~Really?~~" he asked, very gravely. "~~Do you think so?~~ How do you recognise a man of feeling?"

"I can't make out," said Mrs. Tristram, "whether you are very simple or very deep."

"I'm very deep. That's a fact."

"I believe that if I were to tell you with a certain air that ~~you have no feeling~~, you would implicitly believe me."

"A certain air?" said Newman. "~~Try it~~ and see."

"You would believe me, but you would not care," said Mrs. Tristram.

"You have got it all wrong. I should care immensely, but I shouldn't believe you. The fact is, I have never had time to feel things. I have had to *do* them, to make myself felt."

"I can imagine that you may have done that tremendously, ~~sometimes~~."

"Yes, there's no mistake about that."

"When you are in ~~a fury~~ it can't be pleasant."

~~"I am never in a fury."~~

~~"Angry, then, or displeased."~~

~~"I am never angry, and it is~~ so long since I have been displeased that I have quite forgotten it."

"I don't believe," ~~said Mrs. Tristram,~~ "that you are never angry. A man ought to be angry sometimes, and

pictures of the at "nature" as the child of which he figured for her; she herself was from Philadelphia

through

spirit

the states of

closely pressed him.

but he presently

real

"Is that so?"

real

"But how

You're as cold as a fish

"Oh,

"Well, try your air

So very beautifully.

had

one of your furies

indeed

"Ah, I don't have to get into a fury to do it."

sometimes

"Well, a man of any sense doesn't lay his plans to be angry," said Newman, "and it's as a fact

She returned

"I don't, nevertheless, see you always as you are now. You've something behind, beneath. You get harder, or you get softer. You're more displeased — or you're more pleased.

you are neither good enough nor bad enough always to keep your temper."

"I lose it perhaps once in five years."

"The time is coming round, then," said his hostess. "Before I have known you six months I shall see you in a ~~fine fury~~ magnificent rage."

"Do you mean to put me into one?"

"I should not be sorry. You take things too coolly. It exasperates me. And then you are too happy. You have what must be the most agreeable thing in the world—the consciousness of having bought your pleasure beforehand, and paid for it. You have not a day of reckoning staring you in the face. Your reckonings are over."

"Well, I suppose I am happy," said Newman, meditatively.

"You have been odiously successful."

"Successful in copper," said Newman, "~~only so-so in railroads, and a hopeless fizzle in oil.~~"

"It is very disagreeable to know how Americans have ~~made~~ their money. ~~Now you have~~ the world before you. You have only to enjoy."

"Oh, I suppose I am ~~very well off~~," said Newman. "Only I am tired of having it thrown up at me. Besides, there are several drawbacks. ~~I am not intellectual.~~"

"One doesn't expect it of you," Mrs. Tristram answered. Then in a moment: "Besides, you [illegible]"

"Well, I mean to have a good time, ~~whether or no~~," said Newman. ~~"I am not cultivated, I am not even educated; I know nothing about history, [illegible] foreign tongues, [illegible] other learned [illegible] But I [illegible] feel [illegible] and I shall undertake to kn[illegible] about Europe by the [illegible]~~ I feel something under my ribs here," he added in a moment, "that I can't explain—a sort of ~~mighty hankering~~, a desire to stretch out and haul in."

"Bravo!" said Mrs. Tristram, "that is very fine. You are the great Western Barbarian, stepping forth in

but very mixed in other mining ventures. And I've had to take quite a back seat on oil.

come by

his companion sighed. "Now, at all events, you've

all right,"

I don't come up to my standard of culture."

"I find I take notice as I go, and I guess I shan't have missed much by the time I've done.

Do come up. You are up!"

wherever I am;

strong yearning,

his innocence and might, gazing a while at this poor effete Old World, and then swooping down on it."

"Oh, come," said Newman. "I am not a barbarian, by a good deal. I am very much the reverse. I have seen barbarians; I know what they are."

"I don't mean that you are a Comanche chief, or that you wear a blanket and feathers. There are different shades."

"I am a highly civilized man," said Newman. "I stick to that. If you don't believe it, I should like to prove it to you."

Mrs. Tristram was silent a while. "I should like to make you prove it," she said at last. "I should like to put you in a difficult place."

"Pray do," said Newman.

"That has a little conceited sound!" his companion rejoined.

"Oh," said Newman, "I have a very good opinion of myself."

"I wish I could put it to the test. Give me time, and I will." And Mrs. Tristram remained silent for some time afterwards, as if she was trying to keep her pledge. It did not appear that evening that she succeeded; but as he was rising to take his leave, she passed suddenly, as she was very apt to do, from the tone of unsparing persiflage to that of almost tremulous sympathy. "Speaking seriously," she said, "I believe in you, Mr. Newman. You flatter my patriotism."

"Your patriotism?" Christopher demanded.

"Even so. It would take too long to explain, and you probably would not understand. Besides, you might take it—really, you might take it for a declaration. But it has nothing to do with you personally; it's what you represent. Fortunately you don't know all that, or your conceit would increase insufferably."

Newman stood staring and wondering what under the sun he represented."

what this great quantity this might be;

corrupt old world,

an honest

either,

a great fall-off from him ⊙

honest

have the instincts—have them deeply—if I haven't the forms, of a high old civilization", Newman went on ⊙

"Vous ne doutez de rien!"

he insisted,

latent

latent—?"

The question is of what you almost unconsciously

"Deep within me the Eagle shrieks, and I've known my heart at times to bristle with more feathers than my head ⊙

And then as Newman

"Forgive all my meddlesome chatter, and forget my advice. It is very silly in me to undertake to tell you what to do. When you are embarrassed, do as you think best, and you will do very well. When you are in a difficulty, judge for yourself."

"I shall remember everything you have told me," said Newman. "There are so many forms and ceremonies over here."

"Forms and ceremonies are what I mean, of course."

"Ah, but I want to observe them," said Newman. "Haven't I as good a right as another? They don't scare me, and you needn't give me leave to violate them. I won't take it."

"That is not what I mean. I mean, observe them in your own way. Settle nice questions for yourself. Cut the knot or untie it, as you choose."

"Oh, I am sure I shall never fumble over it," said Newman.

The next time that he dined in the Avenue d'Iéna was a Sunday, a day on which Mr. Tristram left the cards unshuffled, so that there was a trio in the evening on the balcony. The talk was of many things, and at last Mrs. Tristram suddenly observed to Christopher Newman that it was high time he should take a wife.

"Listen to her; she has the audacity!" said Tristram, who on Sunday evenings was always rather acrimonious.

"I don't suppose you have made up your mind not to marry?" Mrs. Tristram continued.

"Heaven forbid!" cried Newman. "I am sternly resolved on it."

"It's very easy," said Tristram; "fatally easy!"

"Well, then, I suppose you do not mean to wait till you are fifty."

"On the contrary, I am in a great hurry."

"One would never suppose it. Do you expect a lady to come and propose to you?"

Don't want not to take account of them,

Delicate

if there's ever a big knot," he returned — "and they all seem knots of ribbon over here — I shall simply pull it off and wear it!"

his wife went on,

Guess

twists and turns over here,

ignore them ⊙ I want to know all about them ⊙

that you're to deal with

toupet!"

a little peevish

quite viciously bent on it"

mistake,"

and when it's made it's made ⊙

an almost indecent

"No; I am willing to propose. I think a great deal about it."

"Tell me some of your thoughts."

"Well," said Newman, slowly, "I want to marry very well."

"Marry a woman of sixty, then," said Tristram.

"'Well' in what sense?"

"In every sense. I shall be hard to please."

"You must remember that, as the French proverb says, the most beautiful girl in the world can give but what she has."

"Since you ask me," said Newman, "I will say frankly that I want extremely to marry. It is time, to begin with; before I know it I shall be forty. And then I'm lonely, and helpless and dull. But if I marry now, so long as I didn't do it in hot haste when I was twenty, I must do it with my eyes open. I want to do the thing in handsome style. I not only want to make no mistakes, but I want to make a great hit. I want to take my pick. My wife must be a magnificent woman."

"Oh, I've thought an immense deal about it."

"Perhaps you think too much. The best thing is simply to fall in love."

"When I find the woman who pleases me I shall love her enough. My wife shall be very comfortable."

"You are superb. There's a chance for the magnificent women."

"You are not fair," Newman rejoined. "You draw a fellow out and put him off his guard, and then you laugh at him."

"I assure you," said Mrs. Tristram, "that I am very serious. To prove it, I will make you a proposal. Should you like me, as they say here, to marry you?"

"To hunt up a wife for me?"

"She is already found. I will bring you together."

"Oh, come," said Tristram, "we don't keep a

put the case before her myself.

about as well as you can."

suit.

"Let me be frank about it —

and I wasn't made really for solitude. There are things for which I want help.

set about it rather grandly.

pure pearl. I've

as satisfied as I shall."

satisfies

rise to the occasion

really superb," said Mrs. Tristram.

pure pearls!"

on

jibe

matrimonial bureau. He'will think you want your commission."

"Present me to a woman who comes up to my notion," said Newman, "and I'will marry her to-morrow."

"You have a strange tone about it, and I don't quite understand you. I didn't suppose you would be so cold-blooded and calculating."

Newman was silent a while. "Well," he said, at last, "I want a great woman. I stick to that. That's one thing I *can* treat myself to, and if it is to be had I mean to have it. What else have I toiled and struggled for all these years? I'have succeeded, and now what am I to do with my success? To make it perfect, as I see it, there must be a beautiful woman perched on the pile, like a statue on a monument. She must be as good as she's beautiful, and as clever as she's good. I can give my wife a good deal, so I am not afraid to ask a good deal myself. She shall have everything a woman can desire; I shall not even object to her being too good for me; she may be cleverer and wiser than I can understand, and I shall only be the better pleased. I want to possess, in a word, the best article in the market."

"Why didn't you tell a fellow all this at the outset?" Tristram demanded. "I'have been trying so to make you fond of *me!*"

"This is very interesting," said Mrs. Tristram. "I like to see a man know his own mind."

"I'have known mine for a long time," Newman went on. "I made up my mind tolerably early in life that a beautiful wife was the thing best worth having, here below. It's the greatest victory over circumstances. When I say beautiful, I mean beautiful in mind and in manners, as well as in person. It's a thing every man has an equal right to; he may get it if he can. He doesn't have to be born with certain faculties on purpose; he needs only to be a man. Then he needs only to use his will, and such wits as he has, and to try."

Some shining

crowning some high

many things,

certain others

some rare creature all one's own is the best kind of property

rare I mean rare all through — grown as a rarity and recognized as one.

get it.

— well, whatever he *is*.

to go in".

"It strikes me" said Mrs. Tristram "that your marriage is to be rather a matter of ~~vanity.~~ heartless pomp."

"Well, it's certain," ~~said~~ Newman returned, "that if people notice my wife and admire her, I shall ~~be mightily tickled.~~ count it a part of my success."

"After this," cried Mrs. Tristram, "call any man a modest ~~man~~ man."

"But none of them will admire her so much as I."

~~"I see you have a taste for splendour."~~ "You really have the imagination of greatness."

Newman hesitated a little; and then, "I ~~honestly believe I have?"~~ want the best thing going," he said.

"And I suppose you've already looked about you a good deal."

~~"A good deal,~~ "More or less, according to opportunity."

"And you've seen nothing that ~~satisfied~~ has tempted you?"

"No," said Newman, half reluctantly, "I'm bound to say in honesty that I've seen nothing that ~~really satisfied me."~~ has come up to my idea."

"You remind me of the heroes of the French romantic poets, Rolla and Fortunio and all those other insatiable gentlemen for whom nothing in this world was handsome enough. But I see you're in earnest, and I should like to help you," Mrs. Tristram wound up.

"Who the deuce is it, darling, that you are going to ~~put~~ palm off upon him?" ~~Tristram cried.~~ her husband asked. "We know a good many pretty girls, thank ~~Heaven,~~ goodness, but ~~magnificent women are not so common."~~ nobody to be mentioned in that light."

"Have you any objections to a foreigner?" ~~his wife~~ Mrs. Tristram continued, addressing ~~Newman,~~ their friend, who had tilted back his chair, and, with his feet on a bar of the balcony railing and his hands in his pockets, ~~was~~ sat looking at the stars.

"No Irish need apply," said Tristram.

Newman meditated a while. "~~As~~ Just as a foreigner, no," he ~~said~~ answered at last. "I've no prejudices."

"My dear fellow, you've no suspicions!" cried Tristram. "You don't know what terrible customers these foreign women are; especially ~~the magnificent~~ those grown, as you call it, for the use of millionaires."

How should you like Circassian, with a dagger in her ?"

Newman administered a vigorous slap to his knee. "I'd marry a if she pleased me."

"We had better confine ourselves to Europe," said Mrs. Tristram. "The only thing is, then, that the person

"She's going to offer you an unappreciated governess!" Tristram groaned.

I won't deny that, other things being equal, I should one of my own countrywomen. We should speak the same language, and that would be a comfort. But I'm not afraid of Besides, I rather like the idea of taking in Europe too. It enlarges the field of selection. When you choose from a greater number you can bring your choice to a finer point."

"Sardanapalus!" Tristram

Newman's hostess. "I happen to number among my friends the loveliest woman in the world. Neither more nor less. I don't say a very charming person or a very estimable woman or a very great beauty; I say simply the loveliest woman in the world."

cried Tristram, "you've kept very quiet about her. Were you afraid of me?"

"You've seen her," said his wife, "but you've no perception of such as Claire's."

"Ah, her name is Claire? I give it up."

"Does your friend wish to marry?" asked Newman.

"Not in the least. It's for you to make her change her mind. It be easy; she has had one husband, and he gave her a low opinion of the species."

"Oh, she's a widow, then?"

"Are you already afraid? She was married at eighteen, by her parents, in the French fashion, to the to die a couple of years afterwards, and she's now twenty-"

Handwritten revisions:

an expensive

baggy trousers

Patagonian

"Of course!"

herself should square with your standard?"

like

best," Newman pursued.

any foreigner who's the best thing in her own country.

"Well, you've come to the right market,"

sighed

brought out after a pause.

that

quality

won't

a man with advantages of fortune, but objectionable, detestable, on other grounds, and many years too old.

"I'm bound to say then,"

Discretion

He had, however,

Jr.

=seven."

"So she is French?"

"French by her father, English by her mother. She is really more English than French, and she speaks English as well as you or I—or rather much better. She belongs to the very top of the basket, as they say here. Her family, on each side, is of fabulous antiquity; her mother is the daughter of an English Catholic earl. Her father is dead, and since her widowhood she has lived with her mother and a married brother. There is another brother, younger, who I believe is wild. They have an old hôtel in the Rue de l'Université, but their fortune is small, and they make a common household, for economy's sake. When I was a girl I was put into a convent here for my education, while my father made the tour of Europe. It was a silly thing to do with me, but it had the advantage that it made me acquainted with Claire de Bellegarde. She was younger than I, but we became fast friends. I took a tremendous fancy to her, and she returned my passion as far as she could. They kept such a tight rein on her that she could do very little, and when I left the convent she had to give me up. I was not of her *monde*; I am not now, either, but we sometimes meet. They are terrible people—her *monde*; all mounted upon stilts a mile high, and with pedigrees long in proportion. It is the skim of the milk of the old *noblesse*. Do you know what a Legitimist is, or an Ultramontane? Go into Madame de Cintré's drawing-room some afternoon, at five o'clock, and you will see the best-preserved specimens. I say go, but no one is admitted who can't show his fifty quarterings."

"And this is the lady you propose to me to marry?" asked Newman. "A lady I can't even approach?"

"But you said just now that you recognised no obstacles."

Newman looked at Mrs. Tristram a while, stroking his moustache. "Is she a beauty?" he demanded.

"No."

Handwritten revisions: as they say here, / peer / rather amusing but quite impossible / for economy's sake, / of less than fifteen / fatuous / yet / adoration so / Did you ever hear of such a prehistoric monster as a / – to intimacy – / good cause in the form of a family tree." / Very great / reasons against you." / She hung fire a little. "No."

"Oh, then it's no use——!"

"She is not a beauty, but she is beautiful; two very different things. A beauty has no faults in her face; the face of a beautiful woman may have faults that only deepen its charm."

"I remember Madame de Cintré, now," said Tristram. "She is as plain as a pikestaff. A man wouldn't look at her twice."

"In saying that he would not look at her twice, my husband sufficiently describes her," Mrs. Tristram rejoined.

"Is she good; is she clever?" Newman asked.

"She is perfect! I won't say more than that. When you are praising a person to another who is to know her, it is bad policy to go into details. I won't exaggerate. I simply recommend her. Among all women I have known she stands alone; she is of a different clay."

"I should like to see her," said Newman simply.

"I will try to manage it. The only way will be to invite her to dinner. I have never invited her before, and I don't know that she will come. Her old feudal countess of a mother rules the family with an iron hand, and allows her to have no friends but of her own choosing, and to visit only in a certain sacred circle. But I can at least ask her."

At this moment Mrs. Tristram was interrupted; a servant stepped out upon the balcony and announced that there were visitors in the drawing-room. When Newman's hostess had gone in to receive her friends Tom Tristram approached his guest.

"Don't put your foot into *this*, my boy," he said, puffing the last whiffs of his cigar "There's nothing in it!"

Newman looked askance at him, inquisitive. "You tell another story, eh?"

"I say simply that Madame de Cintré is a great white doll of a woman, who cultivates quiet haughtiness."

Very great

Very, very

quite

a copy in a copy-book, all round o's and uprights a little slanting. She just slants toward us

of your large appetite would swallow her down without tasting her

telling how little use he has for her,

the

I'm not sure she'll be able to

invite

she

and that she

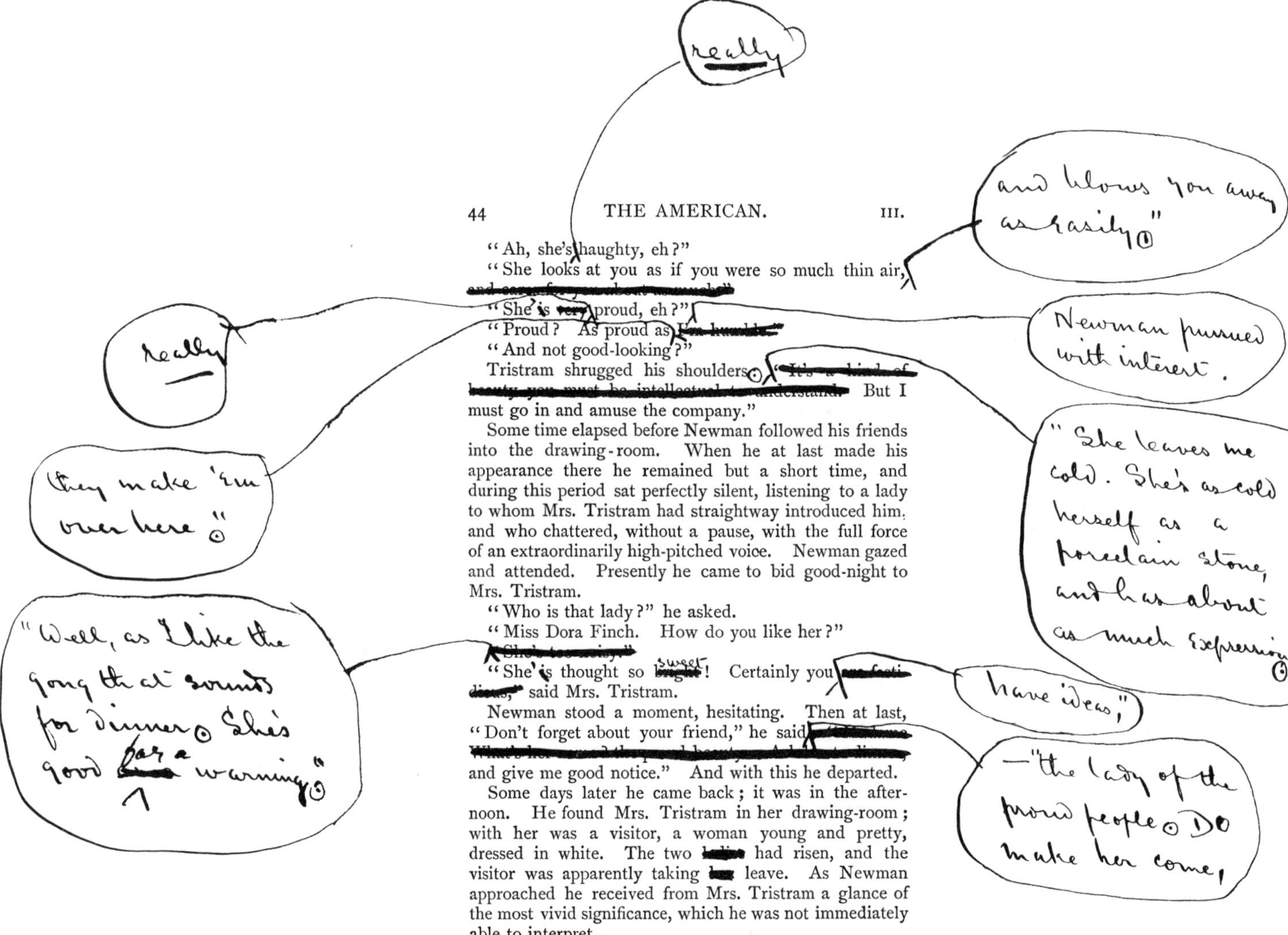

44 THE AMERICAN. III.

"Ah, she's haughty, eh?"

"She looks at you as if you were so much thin air," ~~and cared for you about as much.~~"

"She is very proud, eh?"

"Proud? As proud as"

"And not good-looking?"

Tristram shrugged his shoulders. ~~"It's a kind of beauty you must be intellectual to understand.~~ But I must go in and amuse the company."

Some time elapsed before Newman followed his friends into the drawing-room. When he at last made his appearance there he remained but a short time, and during this period sat perfectly silent, listening to a lady to whom Mrs. Tristram had straightway introduced him, and who chattered, without a pause, with the full force of an extraordinarily high-pitched voice. Newman gazed and attended. Presently he came to bid good-night to Mrs. Tristram.

"Who is that lady?" he asked.

"Miss Dora Finch. How do you like her?"

"She is thought so bright! sweet! Certainly you" ~~are fastidious,~~" said Mrs. Tristram.

Newman stood a moment, hesitating. Then at last, "Don't forget about your friend," he said ~~"What's her name? the proud beauty——Ask her to dine~~ and give me good notice." And with this he departed.

Some days later he came back; it was in the afternoon. He found Mrs. Tristram in her drawing-room; with her was a visitor, a woman young and pretty, dressed in white. The two ladies had risen, and the visitor was apparently taking her leave. As Newman approached he received from Mrs. Tristram a glance of the most vivid significance, which he was not immediately able to interpret.

"This is a good friend of ours," she said, turning to her companion. "Mr. Christopher Newman. I have spoken of you to him, and he has an extreme desire to make your acquaintance. If you had consented to come and dine, I should have offered him an opportunity."

The stranger turned her face toward Newman with a smile. He was not embarrassed, for his unconscious sangfroid was boundless; but as he became aware that this was the proud and beautiful Madame de Cintré, the loveliest woman in the world, the promised perfection, the proposed ideal, he made an instinctive movement to gather his wits together. Through the slight preoccupation that it produced he had a sense of a long, fair face, and of two eyes that were both brilliant and mild.

"I should have been most happy," said Madame de Cintré. "Unfortunately, as I have been telling Mrs. Tristram, I go on Monday to the country."

Newman had made a solemn bow. "I am very sorry," he said.

"Paris is getting too warm," Madame de Cintré added, taking her friend's hand again in farewell.

Mrs. Trisrtam seemed to have formed a sudden and somewhat venturesome resolution, and she smiled more intensely, as women do when they take such resolutions. "I want Mr. Newman to know you," she said, dropping her head on one side and looking at Madame de Cintré's bonnet-ribbons.

Christopher Newman stood gravely silent, while his native penetration admonished him. Mrs. Tristram was determined to force her friend to address him a word of encouragement which should be more than one of the common formulas of politeness; and if she was prompted by charity, it was by the charity that begins at home. Madame de Cintré was her dearest Claire, and her especial admiration; but Madame de Cintré had found it impossible to dine with her, and Madame de Cintré should for once be forced gently to render tribute to Mrs. Tristram.

"It would give me great pleasure," she said, looking at Mrs. Tristram.

"That's a great deal," cried the latter, "for Madame de Cintré to say!"

"I am very much obliged to you," said Newman. "Mrs. Tristram can speak better for me than I can speak for myself."

Madame de Cintré looked at him again with the same soft brightness. "Are you to be long in Paris?" She asked.

"We shall keep him," said Mrs. Tristram.

"But you are keeping *me!*" And Madame de Cintré shook her friend's hand.

"A moment longer," said Mrs. Tristram.

Madame de Cintré looked at Newman again; this time without her smile. Her eyes lingered a moment. "Will you come and see me?" she asked.

Mrs. Tristram kissed her. Newman expressed his thanks, and she took her leave. Her hostess went with her to the door, and left Newman alone a moment. Presently she returned, rubbing her hands. "It was a fortunate chance," she said. She had come to decline my invitation. You triumphed on the spot, making her ask you, at the end of three minutes, to her house."

"It was you who triumphed," said Newman. "You must not be too hard upon her."

Mrs. Tristram stared. "What do you mean?"

"She did not strike me as so proud. I should say she was shy."

"You are very discriminating. And what do you think of her face?"

"It's handsome!" said Newman.

"I should think it was! Of course you will go and see her."

"To-morrow!" cried Newman.

"No, not to-morrow; the next day. That will be Sunday; she leaves Paris on Monday. If you don't see her, it will at least be a beginning." And she gave him Madame de Cintré's address.

He walked across the Seine, late in the summer afternoon, and made his way through those gray and silent streets of the Faubourg St. Germain, whose houses present to the outer world a face as impassive and as suggestive of the concentration of privacy within as the blank walls of Eastern seraglios. Newman thought it a queer way for rich people to live; his ideal of grandeur was a splendid façade, diffusing its brilliancy outward too, irradiating hospitality. The house to which he had been directed had a dark, dusty, painted portal, which swung open in answer to his ring. It admitted him into a wide, gravelled court, surrounded on three sides with closed windows, and with a doorway facing the street, approached by three steps and surmounted by a tin canopy. The place was all in the shade; it answered to Newman's conception of a convent. The portress could not tell him whether Madame de Cintré was visible; he would please to apply at the further door. He crossed the court; a gentleman was sitting, bareheaded, on the steps of the portico, playing with a beautiful pointer. He rose as Newman approached, and, as he laid his hand upon the bell, said, with a smile, in English, that he was afraid Newman would be kept waiting; the servants were scattered; he himself had been ringing; he didn't know what the deuce was in them. He was a young man; his English was excellent, and his smile was very frank. Newman pronounced the name of Madame de Cintré.

"I think," said the young man, "that my sister is visible. Come in, and if you will give me your card I will carry it to her myself."

Newman had been accompanied on his present errand by a slight sentiment, I will not say of defiance—a readiness for aggression or defence, as they might prove needful—but of reflective good-humoured suspicion. He took from his pocket, while he stood on the portico, a card, upon which, under his name, he had written the words "San Francisco," and while he presented it he looked warily at his interlocutor. His glance was singularly reassuring; he liked the young man's face; it strongly resembled that of Madame de Cintré. He was evidently her brother. The young man, on his side, had made a rapid inspection of Newman's person. He had taken the card and was about to enter the house with it when another figure appeared on the threshold—an older man, of a fine presence, wearing evening dress. He looked hard at Newman, and Newman looked at him. "Madame de Cintré," the younger man repeated, as an introduction of the visitor. The other took the card from his hand, read it in a rapid glance, looked again at Newman from head to foot, hesitated a moment, and then said, gravely but urbanely, "Madame de Cintré is not at home."

The younger man made a gesture, and then turning to Newman, "I am very sorry, sir," he said.

Newman gave him a friendly nod, to show that he bore him no malice, and retraced his steps. At the porter's lodge he stopped; the two men were still standing on the portico.

"Who is the gentleman with the dog?" he asked of the old woman who reappeared. He had begun to learn French.

"That is Monsieur le Comte."

"And the other?"

"That is Monsieur le Marquis."

"A marquis?" said Christopher in English, which the old woman fortunately did not understand. "Oh, then, he's not the butler!"

CHAPTER IV.

EARLY one morning, before Christopher Newman was dressed, a little old man was ushered into his apartment, followed by a youth in a blouse, bearing a picture in a brilliant frame. Newman, among the distractions of Paris, had forgotten M. Nioche and his accomplished daughter; but this was an effective reminder.

"I am afraid you had given me up, sir," said the old man, after many apologies and salutations. "We have made you wait so many days. You accused us, perhaps, of inconstancy, of bad faith. But behold me at last! And behold also the pretty 'Madonna.' Place it on a chair, my friend, in a good light, so that Monsieur may admire it." And M. Nioche, addressing his companion, helped him to dispose the work of art.

It had been endued with a layer of varnish an inch thick, and its frame, of an elaborate pattern, was at least a foot wide. It glittered and twinkled in the morning light, and looked, to Newman's eyes, wonderfully splendid and precious. It seemed to him a very happy purchase, and he felt rich in the possession of it. He stood looking at it complacently, while he proceeded with his toilet, and M. Nioche, who had dismissed his own attendant, hovered near, smiling and rubbing his hands.

"It has wonderful *finesse*," he murmured, caressingly. "And here and there are marvellous touches; you probably perceive them, sir. It attracted great attention on the Boulevard as we came along. And then a gradation of tones! That's what it is to know how to paint. I don't say it because I am her father, sir; but as one man of taste addressing another I cannot help observing that you have there an exquisite work. It is hard to produce such things and to have to part with them. If our means only allowed us the luxury of

keeping it! I really may say, sir"—and M. Nioche gave a little feebly insinuating laugh—"I really may say that I envy you. You see," he added in a moment, "we have taken the liberty of offering you a frame. It increases by a trifle the value of the work, and it will save you the annoyance—so great for a person of your delicacy—of going about to bargain at the shops."

The language spoken by M. Nioche was a singular compound, which I shrink from the attempt to reproduce in its integrity. He had apparently once possessed a certain knowledge of English, and his accent was oddly tinged with the Cockneyism of the British metropolis. But his learning had grown rusty with disuse, and his vocabulary was defective and capricious. He had repaired it with large patches of French, with words anglicised by a process of his own, and with native idioms literally translated. The result, in the form in which he in all humility presented it, would be scarcely comprehensible to the reader, so that I have ventured to trim and sift it. Newman only half understood it, but it amused him, and the old man's decent forlornness appealed to his democratic instincts. The assumption of a fatality in misery always irritated his strong good-nature—it was almost the only thing that did so; and he felt the impulse to wipe it out, as it were, with the sponge of his own prosperity. The pupil of Mademoiselle Noémie, however, had apparently on this occasion been vigorously indoctrinated, and he showed a certain tremulous eagerness to cultivate unexpected opportunities.

"How much do I owe you, then, with the frame?" asked Newman.

"It will make in all three thousand francs," said the old man, smiling agreeably, but folding his hands in instinctive suppliance.

"Can you give me a receipt?"

"I have brought one," said M. Nioche. "I took the liberty of drawing it up in case Monsieur should happen to desire to discharge his debt." And he drew a paper from his pocket-book and presented it to his patron. The document was written in a minute, fantastic hand, and couched in the choicest language.

Newman laid down the money, and M. Nioche dropped the napoleons one by one, solemnly and lovingly, into an old leathern purse.

"And how is your young lady?" asked Newman. "She made a great impression on me."

"An impression? Monsieur is very good. Monsieur admires her appearance?"

"She is very pretty, certainly."

"Alas, yes, she is very pretty!"

"And what's the harm in her being pretty?"

M. Nioche fixed his eyes upon a spot on the carpet and shook his head. Then looking up at Newman with a gaze that seemed to brighten and expand, "Monsieur knows what Paris is. She is dangerous to beauty, when beauty hasn't the sou."

"Ah, but that's not the case with your daughter. She is rich now."

"Very true; we are rich for six months. But if my daughter were a plain girl I should sleep better, all the same."

"You're afraid of the young men?"

"The young and the old!"

"She ought to get a husband."

"Ah, Monsieur, one doesn't get a husband for nothing. Her husband must take her as she is; I can't give her a sou. But the young men don't see with that eye."

"Oh," said Newman, "her talent is in itself a dowry."

"Ah, sir, it needs first to be converted into specie!" and M. Nioche slapped his purse tenderly before he stowed it away. "The operation doesn't take place every day."

"Well, your young men are very shabby," said New-

Newman said,

man, "that's all I can say. They ought to pay for your daughter, and not ask money themselves."

"Those are very noble ideas, Monsieur; but what will you have? They are not the ideas of this country. We want to know what we are about when we marry."

"How big a portion does your daughter want?" M. Nioche stared, as if he wondered what was coming next; but he promptly recovered himself, at a venture, and replied that he knew a very nice young man, employed by an insurance company, who would content himself with fifteen thousand francs.

run on

"Let your daughter paint half a dozen pictures for me, and she shall have her dowry."

run on

you can offer him his figure."

his figure?

"Half a dozen pictures—her dowry! Monsieur is not speaking inconsiderately?"

"If she will make me six or eight copies in the Louvre as pretty as that 'Madonna,' I will pay her the same price," said Newman.

Poor M. Nioche was speechless a moment, with amazement and gratitude, and then he seized Newman's hand, pressed it between his own ten fingers, and gazed at him with watery eyes. "As pretty as that? They shall be a thousand times prettier—they shall be magnificent, sublime. Ah, if I only knew how to paint myself, sir, so that I might lend a hand! What can I do to thank you? *Voyons!*" and he pressed his forehead while he tried to think of something.

perfect little loves.

"Oh, you have thanked me enough," said Newman.

"Ah, here it is, sir!" cried M. Nioche. "To express my gratitude, I will charge you nothing for the lessons in French conversation."

"The lessons? I had quite forgotten them. Listening to your English," added Newman, laughing, "is almost a lesson in French."

really quite a

"Ah, I don't profess to teach English, certainly," said M. Nioche. "But for my own admirable tongue I am still at your service."

"Since you are here, then," said Newman, "we will begin. This is a very good hour, I am going to have my coffee; come every morning at half-past nine and have yours with me."

"Monsieur offers me my coffee also?" cried M. Nioche. "Truly, my *beaux jours* are coming back."

"Come," said Newman, "let us begin. The coffee is almighty hot. How do you say that in French?"

Every day, then, for the following three weeks, the minutely respectable figure of M. Nioche made its appearance, with a series of little inquiring and apologetic obeisances, among the aromatic fumes of Newman's morning beverage. I don't know how much French our friend learned; but, as he himself said, if the attempt did him no good, it could at any rate do him no harm. And it amused him; it gratified that irregularly sociable side of his nature which had always expressed itself in a relish for ungrammatical conversation, and which often, even in his busy and preoccupied days, had made him sit on rail fences in young Western towns, in the twilight, in gossip hardly less than fraternal with humorous loafers and obscure fortune-seekers. He had notions, wherever he went, about talking with the natives; he had been assured, and his judgment approved the advice, that in travelling abroad it was an excellent thing to look into the life of the country. M. Nioche was very much of a native, and though his life might not be particularly worth looking into, he was a palpable and smoothly-rounded unit in that picturesque Parisian civilization which offered our hero so much easy entertainment and propounded so many curious problems to his inquiring and practical mind. Newman was fond of statistics; he liked to know how things were done; it gratified him to learn what taxes were paid, what profits were gathered, what commercial habits prevailed, how the battle of life was fought. M. Nioche, as a reduced capitalist, was familiar with these considerations, and he formulated his information, which he was proud to be able to impart, in the neatest possible terms and with a pinch of snuff between finger and thumb. As a Frenchman—quite apart from Newman's napoleons—M. Nioche loved conversation, and even in his decay his urbanity had not grown rusty. As a Frenchman, too, he could give a clear account of things, and—still as a Frenchman—when his knowledge was at fault he could supply its lapses with the most convenient and ingenious hypotheses. The little shrunken financier was intensely delighted to have questions asked him, and he scraped together information, by frugal processes, and took notes, in his little greasy pocket-book, of incidents which might interest his munificent friend. He read old almanacs at the book-stalls on the quays, and he began to frequent another café where more newspapers were taken and his post-prandial demi-tasse cost him a penny extra, and where he used to con the tattered sheets for curious anecdotes, freaks of nature, and strange coincidences. He would relate with solemnity the next morning that a child of five years of age had lately died at Bordeaux, whose brain had been found to weigh sixty ounces—the brain of a Napoleon or a Washington! or that Madame P——, *charcutière* in the Rue de Clichy, had found in the wadding of an old petticoat the sum of three hundred and sixty francs, which she had lost five years before. He pronounced his words with great distinctness and sonority, and Newman assured him that his way of dealing with the French tongue was very superior to the bewildering chatter that he heard in other mouths. Upon this M. Nioche's accent became more finely trenchant than ever; he offered to read extracts from Lamartine, and he protested that, although he did endeavour according to his feeble lights to cultivate refinement of diction, Monsieur, if he wanted the real thing, should go to the Théâtre Français.

Newman took an interest in French thriftiness, and conceived a lively admiration for Parisian economies.

Small

bourgeois

Café, Rom:

Demi-tasse

pomp and circumstance

more flute-like than ever;

the wondrous

His own economic genius was so entirely for operations on a larger scale, and, to move at his ease, he needed so imperatively the sense of great risks and great prizes, that he found an ungrudging entertainment in the spectacle of fortunes made by the aggregation of copper coins, and in the minute subdivision of labour and profit. He questioned M. Nioche about his own manner of life, and felt a friendly mixture of compassion and respect [illegible] The worthy man told him how, at one period, he and his daughter had supported existence, comfortably, upon the sum of fifteen sous *per diem;* recently, having succeeded in hauling ashore the last floating fragments of the wreck of his fortune, his budget had been a trifle more ample. But they still had to count their sous very narrowly, and M. Nioche intimated with a sigh that Mademoiselle Noémie did not bring to this task that zealous co-operation which might have been desired.

"But what will you have?" he asked, philosophically. "One is young, one is pretty, one needs new dresses and fresh gloves; one can't wear shabby gowns among the splendours of the Louvre."

"But your daughter earns enough to pay for her own clothes," said Newman.

M. Nioche looked at him with weak, uncertain eyes. He would have liked to be able to say that his daughter's talents were appreciated, and that her crooked little daubs commanded a market; but it seemed a scandal to abuse the credulity of this free-handed stranger, who, without a suspicion or a question, had admitted him to equal social rights. He compromised, and declared that while it was obvious that Mademoiselle Noémie's reproductions of the old masters had only to be seen to be coveted, the prices which, in consideration of their altogether peculiar degree of finish, she felt obliged to ask for them, had kept purchasers at a respectful distance. "Poor little one!" said M. Nioche, with a sigh; "it is almost a pity that her work is so perfect! It would be in her interest to paint less well."

"But if Mademoiselle Noémie has this devotion to her art," Newman once observed, "why should you have those fears for her that you spoke of the other day?"

M. Nioche meditated; there was an inconsistency in his position; it made him chronically uncomfortable. Though he had no desire to destroy the goose with the golden eggs—Newman's benevolent confidence—he felt a tremendous impulse to speak out all his trouble. "Ah, she's an artist, my dear sir, most assuredly," he declared. "But to tell you the truth, she is also a *franche coquette*. I am sorry to say," he added in a moment, shaking his head with a world of harmless bitterness, "that she comes honestly by it. Her mother was one before her!"

"You were not happy with your wife?" Newman asked.

M. Nioche gave half a dozen little backwards jerks of his head. "She was my purgatory, Monsieur!"

"She deceived you?"

"Under my nose, year after year. I was too stupid, and the temptation was too great. But I found her out at last. I have only been once in my life a man to be afraid of; I know it very well: it was in that hour! Nevertheless I don't like to think of it. I loved her—I can't tell you how much. She was a bad woman."

"She is not living?"

"She has gone to her account."

"Her influence on your daughter, then," said Newman, encouragingly, "is not to be feared."

"She cared no more for her daughter than for the sole of her shoe! But Noémie has no need of influence. She is sufficient to herself. She is stronger than I."

"She doesn't obey you, eh?"

"She can't obey, Monsieur, since I don't command. What would be the use? It would only irritate her and drive her to some *coup de tête*. She is very clever, like

Spark of the flame",

particularly

weary need

has a spark of that flame,

accepted melancholy

has also more than a mere spark of another. She's a franche coquette, if there ever was one.

of that complexion."

it was to come to her as straight as a letter in the post."

heavy cross

— if I must say so —

wind in the chimney

why not

more use for bad examples than for good.

her mother; she would waste no time about it. As a child—when I was happy, or supposed I was—she studied drawing and painting with first-class professors, and they assured me she had talent. I was delighted to believe it, and when I went into society I used to carry her pictures with me in a portfolio and hand them round to the company. I remember, once, a lady thought I was offering them for sale, and I took it very ill. We don't know what we may come to! Then came my dark days, and my explosion with Madame Nioche. Noémie had no more twenty-franc lessons; but in the course of time, when she grew older, and it became highly expedient that she should do something that would help to keep us alive, she bethought herself of her palette and brushes. Some of our friends in the *quartier* pronounced the idea fantastic: they recommended her to try bonnet-making, to get a situation in a shop, or—if she was more ambitious—to advertise for a place of *dame de compagnie.* She did advertise, and an old lady wrote her a letter and bade her come and see her. The old lady liked her, and offered her her living and six hundred francs a year; but Noémie discovered that she passed her life in her armchair and had only two visitors, her confessor and her nephew: the confessor very strict, and the nephew a man of fifty, with a broken nose and a government clerkship of two thousand francs. She threw her old lady over, bought a paint-box, a canvas, and a new dress, and went and set up her easel in the Louvre. There, in one place and another, she has passed the last two years; I can't say it has made us millionaires. But Noémie tells me that Rome was not built in a day, that she is making great progress, that I must leave her to her own devices. The fact is, without prejudice to her genius, that she has no idea of burying herself alive. She likes to see the world, and to be seen. She says, herself, that she can't work in the dark. With her appearance that is very natural. Only, I can't help worrying and trembling and

poor

the gift.

little water-colours

'gift',

of the world.

Her appearance itself holds up the lamp for others.

wondering what may happen to her there all alone, day after day, amid all that coming and going of strangers. I can't be always at her side. I go with her in the morning, and I come to fetch her away, but she won't have me near her in the interval; she says I make her nervous. As if it didn't make me nervous to wander about all day without her. Ah, if anything were to happen to her!" cried M. Nioche, clenching his two fists and jerking back his head again, portentously.

"Oh, I guess nothing will happen," said Newman.

"I believe I should shoot her!" said the old man, solemnly.

"Oh, we'll marry her," said Newman, "since that's how you manage it; and I will go and see her to-morrow at the Louvre and pick out the pictures she is to copy for me."

M. Nioche had brought Newman a message from his daughter, in acceptance of his magnificent commission, the young lady declaring herself his most devoted servant, promising her most zealous endeavour, and regretting that the proprieties forbade her coming to thank him in person. The morning after the conversation just narrated Newman reverted to his intention of meeting Mademoiselle Noémie at the Louvre. M. Nioche appeared preoccupied, and left his budget of anecdotes unopened; he took a great deal of snuff, and sent certain oblique, appealing glances toward his stalwart pupil. At last, when he was taking his leave, he stood a moment, after he had polished his hat with his calico pocket-handkerchief, with his small, pale eyes fixed strangely upon Newman.

"What is the matter?" our hero demanded.

"Excuse the solicitude of a father's heart!" said M. Nioche. "You inspire me with boundless confidence, but I can't help giving you a warning. After all, you are a man, you are young and at liberty. Let me beseech you, then, to respect the innocence of Mademoiselle Nioche!"

Newman had wondered what was coming, and at this he broke into a laugh. He was on the point of declaring that his own innocence struck him as the more exposed, but he contented himself with promising to treat the young girl with nothing less than veneration. He found her waiting for him, seated upon the great divan in the Salon Carré. She was not in her working-day costume, but wore her bonnet and gloves, and carried her parasol, in honour of the occasion. These articles had been selected with unerring taste, and a fresher, prettier image of youthful alertness and blooming discretion was not to be conceived. She made Newman a most respectful curtsy, and expressed her gratitude for his liberality in a wonderfully graceful little speech. It annoyed him to have a charming young girl stand there thanking him, and it made him feel uncomfortable to think that this perfect young lady, with her excellent manners and her finished intonation, was literally in his pay. He assured her, in such French as he could muster, that the thing was not worth mentioning, and that he considered her services a great favour.

"Whenever you please, then," said Mademoiselle Noémie, "we will pass the review."

They walked slowly round the room, then passed into the others and strolled about for half an hour. Mademoiselle Noémie evidently relished her situation, and had no desire to bring her public interview with her striking-looking patron to a close. Newman perceived that prosperity agreed with her. The little thin-lipped, peremptory air with which she had addressed her father on the occasion of their former meeting had given place to the most lingering and caressing tones.

"What sort of pictures do you desire?" she asked. "Sacred, or profane?"

"Oh, a few of each," said Newman. "But I want something bright and gay."

"Something gay? There is nothing very gay in this

e

the neatest of little speeches ⊙

regarded

as a particular

to a close

a patron of such striking type ⊙

have you in mind?"

prettiest, easiest prattle ⊙

solemn old Louvre. But we will see what we can find. You speak French to-day like a charm. My father has done wonders."

"Oh, I'm a bad subject," said Newman. "I am too old to learn a language."

"Too old? *Quelle folie!*" cried Mademoiselle Noémie, with a clear, shrill laugh. "You are a very young man. And how do you like my father?"

"He is a very nice old gentleman. He never laughs at my blunders."

"He is very *comme il faut*, my papa," said Mademoiselle Noémie, "and as honest as the day. Oh, an exceptional probity! You could trust him with millions."

"Do you always obey him?" asked Newman.

"Obey him?"

"Do you do what he bids you?"

The young girl stopped and looked at him; she had a spot of colour in either cheek, and in her expressive French eye, which projected too much for perfect beauty, there was a slight gleam of audacity. "Why do you ask me that?" she demanded.

"Because I want to know."

"You think me a bad girl?" And she gave a strange smile.

Newman looked at her a moment; he saw that she was pretty, but he was not in the least dazzled. He remembered poor M. Nioche's solicitude for her "innocence," and he laughed out again as his eyes met hers. Her face was the oddest mixture of youth and maturity, and beneath her candid brow her searching little smile seemed to contain a world of ambiguous intentions. She was pretty enough, certainly, to make her father nervous; but, as regards her innocence, Newman felt ready on the spot to affirm that she had never parted with it. She had simply never had any; she had been looking at the world since she was ten years old, and he would have been a wise man who could tell her any secrets. In her

thankless

beau jeune homme.

a sharp spark of freedom.

little

clear, charming forehead

let it go.

to lose;

wonderful world about her

long mornings at the Louvre she had not only studied Madonnas and St. Johns; she had kept an eye upon all the variously-embodied human nature around her, and she had formed her conclusions. In a certain sense, it seemed to Newman, M. Nioche might be at rest; his daughter might do something very audacious, but she would never do anything foolish. Newman, with his long-drawn, leisurely smile, and his even, unhurried utterance, was always, mentally, taking his time; and he asked himself, now, what she was looking at him in that way for. He had an idea that she would like him to confess that he did think her a bad girl.

"Oh no," he said at last; "it would be very bad manners in me to judge you that way. I don't know you."

"But my father has complained to you," said Mademoiselle Noémie.

"He says you are a coquette."

"He shouldn't go about saying such things to gentlemen! But you don't believe it?"

"No," said Newman, gravely, "I don't believe it."

She looked at him again, gave a shrug and a smile, and then pointed to a small Italian picture, a Marriage of St. Catherine. "How should you like that?" she asked.

"It doesn't please me," said Newman. "The young lady in the yellow dress is not pretty."

"Ah, you are a great connoisseur," murmured Mademoiselle Noémie.

"In pictures? Oh no; I know very little about them."

"In pretty women, then?"

"In that I am hardly better."

"What do you say to that, then?" the young girl asked, indicating a superb Italian portrait of a lady. "I will do it for you on a smaller scale."

"On a smaller scale? Why not as large as the original?"

in which the scene no less abounded,

assert her liberty in some unmistakeable way,

publish her imprudence.

impolite

in any such

wretch.

free spirit."

he meant any harm by it."

"Well,"

enough."

I'm only picking up the rudiments of knowledge.

may be coming on, but I've ground to make up."

this

Mademoiselle Noémie glanced at the glowing splendour of the Venetian masterpiece and gave a little toss of her head. "I don't like that woman. She looks stupid."

"I do like her," said Newman. "Decidedly, I must have her, as large as life. And just as stupid as she is there."

The young girl fixed her eyes on him again, and with her mocking smile, "It certainly ought to be easy for me to make her look stupid!" she said.

"What do you mean?" asked Newman, puzzled.

She gave another little shrug. "Seriously, then, you want that portrait—the golden hair, the purple satin, the pearl necklace, the two magnificent arms?"

"Everything—just as it is."

"Would nothing else do, instead?"

"Oh, I want some other things, but I want that too."

Mademoiselle Noémie turned away a moment, walked to the other side of the hall, and stood there, looking vaguely about her. At last she came back. "It must be charming to be able to order pictures at such a rate. Venetian portraits, as large as life! You go at it *en prince*. And you are going to travel about Europe that way?"

"Yes, I intend to travel," said Newman.

"Ordering, buying, spending money?"

"Of course I shall spend some money."

"You are very happy to have it. And you are perfectly free?"

"How do you mean, free?"

"You have nothing to bother you—no family, no wife, no *fiancée*?"

"Yes, I am tolerably free."

"You are very happy," said Mademoiselle Noémie, gravely.

"*Je le veux bien!*" said Newman, proving that he had learned more French than he admitted.

"Well, she makes an impression on me,"

shiningly

stands

vaguely asked

a certain amount of

embêter

father, no

very

"And how long shall you stay in Paris?" the young girl went on.

"Only a few days more."

"Why do you go away?"

"It is getting hot, and I must go to Switzerland."

"To Switzerland? That's a fine country. I would give my new parasol to see it! Lakes and mountains, romantic valleys and icy peaks! Oh, I congratulate you. Meanwhile, I shall sit here through all the hot summer, daubing at your pictures."

"Oh, take your time about it," said Newman. "Do them at your convenience."

They walked farther and looked at a dozen other things. Newman pointed out what pleased him, and Mademoiselle Noémie generally criticised it, and proposed something else. Then suddenly she diverged and began to talk about some personal matter.

"What made you speak to me the other day in the Salon Carré?" she abruptly asked.

"I admired your picture."

"But you hesitated a long time."

"Oh, I do nothing rashly," said Newman.

"Yes, I saw you watching me. But I never supposed you were going to speak to me. I never dreamed I should be walking about here with you to-day. It's very curious."

"It is very natural," observed Newman.

"Oh, I beg your pardon: not to me. Coquette as you think me, I have never walked about in public with a gentleman before. What was my father thinking of when he consented to our interview?"

"He was repenting of his unjust accusations," replied Newman.

Mademoiselle Noémie remained silent; at last she dropped into a seat. "Well, then, for those five it is fixed," she said. "Five copies as brilliant and beautiful as I can make them. We have one more to choose.

the clothes on my back

Ranz des Vaches!

Deep green

Ah,

into the intimate.

remarkable

Sufficiently

'Free spirit' — in other words horrid creature —

Shouldn't you like one of those great Rubenses—the marriage of Marie de Médicis? Just look at it and see how handsome it is."

"Oh yes; I should like that," said Newman. "Finish off with that."

"Finish off with that—good!" And she laughed. She sat a moment, looking at him, and then she suddenly rose and stood before him, with her hands hanging and clasped in front of her. "I don't understand you," she said with a smile. "I don't understand how a man can be so ignorant."

"Oh, I am ignorant, certainly," said Newman, putting his hands into his pockets.

"It's ridiculous! I don't know how to paint."

"You don't know how?"

"I paint like a cat; I can't draw a straight line. I never sold a picture until you bought that thing the other day." And as she offered this surprising information she continued to smile.

Newman burst into a laugh. "Why do you tell me this?" he asked.

"Because it irritates me to see a clever man blunder so. My pictures are grotesque."

"And the one I possess——"

"That one is rather worse than usual."

"Well," said Newman, "I like it all the same!"

She looked at him askance. "That is a very pretty thing to say," she answered; "but it is my duty to warn you before you go farther. This order of yours is impossible, you know. What do you take me for? It is work for ten men. You pick out the six most difficult pictures in the Louvre, and you expect me to go to work as if I were sitting down to hem a dozen pocket-handkerchiefs. I wanted to see how far you would go."

Newman looked at the young girl in some perplexity. In spite of the ridiculous blunder of which he stood convicted, he was very far from being a simpleton, and he had a lively suspicion that Mademoiselle Noémie's sudden frankness was not essentially more honest than her leaving him in error would have been. She was playing a game; she was not simply taking pity on his ... What was it she expected to what? The stakes were high and the risk was great; the prize, therefore, must have been commensurate. But even granting that the prize might be great, Newman could not resist a movement of admiration for his companion's intrepidity. She was throwing away with one hand, whatever she might intend to do with the other, a very ... sum of money.

"Are you joking," he said, "or are you serious?"

"Oh, serious!" cried Mademoiselle Noémie, but with her extraordinary smile.

"I know very little about pictures, or how they are painted. If you can't do all that, of course you can't. Do what you can, then."

"It will be very bad," said Mademoiselle Noémie.

"Oh," said Newman, laughing, "if you are determined it shall be bad, of course it will. But why do you go on painting badly?"

"I can do nothing else; I have no real talent."

"You are deceiving your father, then."

The young girl hesitated a moment. "He knows very well!"

"No," Newman declared; "I am sure he believes in you."

"He is afraid of me. I go on painting badly, as you say, because ... I like being here; it is a place to come to every day; it is better than sitting in a little dark damp room, on a court, or selling buttons and whalebones over a counter."

"Of course it is much more amusing," said Newman. "But for a poor girl isn't it rather an expensive amusement?"

"Oh, I am very wrong, there is no doubt about that,"

said Mademoiselle Noémie. "But rather than earn my living as some girls do—toiling with a needle, in little black holes, out of the world—I would throw myself into the Seine."

"There is no need of that," Newman answered; "your father ~~told you my~~ offer?"

"The reason—?"

"He wants you to marry, and I told him I would give you a chance to earn your *dot*."

"He told me all about it, and you see the account I make of it! Why should you take such an interest in my marriage?"

"My interest was in your father. I hold to my ~~offer;~~ Do what you can, and I will buy what you paint."

She stood ~~for~~ some time, ~~meditating, with~~ her eyes on the ground. At last, looking up, "What sort of a husband can you get for twelve thousand francs?" she asked.

"Your father tells me he knows some very good young men."

"Grocers and butchers and little *maîtres de cafés!* I ~~will not~~ marry at all if I can't marry ~~well.~~"

"I would advise you not to be too fastidious," said Newman. "That's all the advice I can give you."

"I am ~~very much~~ vexed at what I have said!" cried ~~the young girl~~. "It has done me no good. But I couldn't help it."

"What good did you expect it to do you?"

"I couldn't help it, simply."

Newman looked at her a moment. "Well, your ~~pictures~~ may be ~~bad,~~" he said, "but you are too ~~clever~~ ~~for me, nevertheless.~~ I don't understand you. Good-bye!" And he put out his hand.

She made no response, ~~and~~ offered him no farewell. She turned away and seated herself sidewise on a bench, leaning her head on the back of her hand, which clasped the rail in front of the pictures. Newman stood

must have mentioned to you the reason of my

engagement.

in thought,

won't

more nobly than that."

his companion.

painting

a friend,"

honest for me, all the same.

She

near her another moment,

moment and then turned on his heel and retreated. He had understood her better than he confessed; this singular scene was a practical commentary upon her father's statement that she was a frank coquette.

V

CHAPTER V.

WHEN Newman related to Mrs. Tristram his fruitless visit to Madame de Cintré, she urged him not to be discouraged, but to carry out his plan of "seeing Europe" during the summer, and return to Paris in the autumn and settle down comfortably for the winter. "Madame de Cintré will keep," she said; "she is not a woman who will marry from one day to another." Newman made no distinct affirmation that he would come back to Paris; he even talked about Rome and the Nile, and abstained from professing any especial interest in Madame de Cintré's continued widowhood. This circumstance was at variance with his habitual frankness and may perhaps be regarded as characteristic of the incipient stage of that passion which is more particularly known as the mysterious one. The truth is that the expression of a pair of eyes, that were at once brilliant and mild, had become very familiar to his memory, and he would not easily have resigned himself to the prospect of never looking into them again. He communicated to Mrs. Tristram a number of other facts, of greater or less importance, as you choose; but on this particular point he kept his own counsel. He took a kindly leave of M. Nioche, having assured him that, so far as he was concerned, the blue-cloaked Madonna herself might have been present at his interview with Mademoiselle Noémie; and left the old man nursing his breast-pocket, in an ecstasy which the acutest misfortune might have been

Description of her as a free spirit (1)

he had told

the story of

for

"Claire

- after which he might

then

change her condition

Crudity

he kept in ice for you," she reasoned;

both intense and

romantic

sharpest paternal discomposure

defied to dissipate. Newman then started on his travels with all his usual appearance of slow-strolling leisure, and all his essential directness and intensity of aim. No man seemed less in a hurry, and yet no man achieved more in brief periods. He had certain practical instincts which served him excellently in his trade of tourist. He found his way in foreign cities by divination, his memory was excellent when once his attention had been at all cordially given, and he emerged from dialogues in foreign tongues, of which he had, formally, not understood a word, in full possession of the particular fact he had desired to ascertain. His appetite for facts was capacious, and although many of those which he noted would have seemed wofully dry and colourless to the ordinary sentimental traveller, a careful inspection of the list would have shown that he had a soft spot in his imagination. In the charming city of Brussels—his first stopping-place after leaving Paris—he asked a great many questions about the street cars, and took extreme satisfaction in the reappearance of this familiar symbol of American civilisation; but he was also greatly struck with the beautiful Gothic tower of the Hôtel de Ville, and wondered whether it would not be possible to "get up" something like it in San Francisco. He stood for half an hour in the crowded square before this edifice, in imminent danger from carriage-wheels, listening to a toothless old cicerone mumble in broken English the touching history of Counts Egmont and Horn; and he wrote the names of these gentlemen—for reasons best known to himself—on the back of an old letter.

At the outset, on his leaving Paris, his curiosity had not been intense; passive entertainment, in the Champs Élysées and at the theatres, seemed about as much as he need expect of himself, and although, as he had said to Tristram, he wanted to see the mysterious, satisfying *best*, he had not the Grand Tour in the least on his conscience, and was not given to cross-questioning the amusement of the hour. He believed that Europe was made for him, and not he for Europe. He had said that he wanted to improve his mind, but he would have felt a certain embarrassment, a certain shame even—a false shame possibly—if he had caught himself looking intellectually into the mirror. Neither in this nor in any other respect had Newman a high sense of responsibility; it was his prime conviction that a man's life should be easy, and that he should be able to resolve privilege into a matter of course. The world, to his sense, was a great bazaar, where one might stroll about and purchase handsome things; but he was no more conscious, individually, of social pressure than he admitted the existence of such a thing as an obligatory purchase. He had not only a dislike, but a sort of moral mistrust, of uncomfortable thoughts, and it was both uncomfortable and slightly contemptible to feel obliged to square oneself with a standard. One's standard was the ideal of one's own good-humoured prosperity, the prosperity which enabled one to give as well as take. To expand, without bothering about it—without shiftless timidity on one side, or loquacious eagerness on the other—to the full compass of what he would have called a "pleasant" experience, was ~~Newman's most definite programme of life.~~ He had always hated to hurry to catch railroad-trains, and yet he had always caught them; and just so an undue solicitude for "culture" seemed a sort of silly dawdling at the station, a proceeding properly confined to women, foreigners, and other unpractical persons. All this admitted, ~~Newman~~ enjoyed his journey, when once he had fairly entered the current, as profoundly as the most zealous *dilettante*. One's theories, after all, matter little; it is ~~one's humour~~ that is the great thing. Our friend was intelligent, and he could not help that. He lounged through Belgium and Holland and the Rhineland, through Switzerland and Northern Italy, planning about nothing, ~~but~~ seeing ~~everything~~. The

his nearest approach to a formulation of the future.

he

the state of one's nerves and one's digestion

healthily

and

all things.

guides and *valets de place* found him an excellent subject. He was always approachable, for he was much addicted to standing about in the vestibules and porticoes of inns, and he availed himself little of the opportunities for impressive seclusion which are so liberally offered in Europe to gentlemen who travel with long purses. When an excursion, a church, a gallery, a ruin was proposed to him, the first thing Newman usually did, after surveying his postulant in silence, from head to foot, was to sit down at a little table and order something to drink. The cicerone, during this process, usually retreated to a respectful distance; otherwise I am not sure that Newman would not have bidden him sit down and have a glass also, and tell him as an honest fellow whether his church or his gallery was really worth a man's trouble. At last he rose and stretched his long legs, beckoned to the man of monuments, looked at his watch, and fixed his eye on his adversary. "What is it?" he asked. "How far?" And whatever the answer was, although he seemed to hesitate, he never declined. He stepped into an open cab, made his conductor sit beside him to answer questions, bade the driver go fast (he had a particular aversion to slow driving), and rolled, in all probability through a dusty suburb, to the goal of his pilgrimage. If the goal was a disappointment, if the church was meagre, or the ruin a heap of rubbish, Newman never protested or berated his cicerone; he looked with an impartial eye upon great monuments and small, made the guide recite his lesson, listened to it religiously, asked if there was nothing else to be seen in the neighbourhood, and drove back again at a rattling pace. It is to be feared that his perception of the difference between good architecture and bad was not acute, and that he might sometimes have been seen gazing with culpable serenity at inferior productions. Ugly churches were a part of his pastime in Europe as well as beautiful ones, and his tour was altogether a pastime. But
to a
Sit down and
adviser;
were
the florid and the refined had not reached the stage of confidence,

there is sometimes nothing like the imagination of those people who have none, and Newman, now and then, in an unguided stroll in a foreign city, before some lonely, sad-towered church, or some angular image of one who had rendered civic service in an unknown past, had felt a singular ~~inward tremor.~~ It was not an excitement ~~or~~ a perplexity; ~~it was a placid, fathomless sense of diversion.~~

He encountered by chance in Holland a young American, with whom, for a time, he ~~formed a sort of~~ traveller's partnership. They were men of ~~a very different cast,~~ but each, in his way, ~~was so good a fellow that, for a few weeks at least, it seemed something of a pleasure to share the chances of the road. Newman's~~ comrade, whose name was Babcock, was a young Unitarian minister; a small, spare, neatly-attired man, with a strikingly candid physiognomy. He was a native of Dorchester, Massachusetts, and had spiritual charge of a small congregation in another suburb of the New England Metropolis. His digestion was weak, and he lived chiefly on Graham bread and hominy—a regimen to which he was so much attached that his tour seemed to him destined to be blighted when, on landing on the Continent, he found that these delicacies did not flourish under the *table d'hôte* system. In Paris he had purchased a bag of hominy at an establishment which called itself an American Agency, and at which the New York illustrated papers were also to be procured, and he had carried it about with him, and shown extreme serenity and fortitude in the somewhat delicate position of having his hominy prepared for him, and served ~~at anomalous hours~~ at the hotels he successively visited. Newman had once spent a morning, in the course of business, at Mr. Babcock's birthplace, and, for reasons too recondite to unfold, his visit there always assumed in his mind a jocular cast. To carry out his joke, which certainly seems poor so long as it is not explained, he used often to address his companion as "Dorchester." Fellow-travellers ~~may~~

Deep commotion.

it involved an extraordinary sense of recreation.

not

fell into a formal

greatly different complexion

So true to his type that each might seem to have something of value to contribute to the association. Newman's

on odd occasions

soon grow intimate; but it is highly improbable that at home these extremely ~~dissimilar~~ characters would have found any very convenient points of contact. They ~~were, indeed, as different~~ as possible. Newman, who never reflected on such matters, accepted the situation with great equanimity, but Babcock used to meditate over it privately; used often, indeed, to retire to his room early in the evening for the express purpose of considering it conscientiously and impartially. He was not sure that it was a good thing for him to ~~associate with~~ our hero, whose way of taking life was so little his own. Newman was an excellent, generous fellow; Mr. Babcock sometimes said to himself that he was ~~a noble fellow~~, and, certainly, it was impossible not to ~~like him~~. But would it not be desirable to try to ~~exert an influence~~ upon him, to try to quicken his moral life and ~~sharpen his sense of duty?~~ He liked everything, he accepted everything, he found amusement in everything; he was not discriminating, he had not a high tone. The young man from Dorchester accused Newman of a fault which he considered very grave, and which he did his best to avoid: what he would have called a want of "moral reaction." Poor Mr. Babcock was extremely fond of pictures and churches, and carried Mrs. Jameson's works about in his trunk; he delighted in æsthetic analysis, and received peculiar impressions from everything he saw. But nevertheless in his secret soul he detested Europe, and he felt an irritating need to protest against Newman's gross intellectual hospitality. Mr. Babcock's moral *malaise*, I am afraid, lay deeper than where any definition of mine can reach it. He mistrusted the "European" temperament, he suffered from the "European" climate, he hated the "European" dinner hour; "European" life seemed to him unscrupulous and impure. And yet he had ~~an exquisite sense of beauty; and as beauty~~ was often inextricably associated with the above displeasing conditions, as he wished, above all, to be just and dispassionate, and as

divergent

had

by constitution, as little in common

have given himself up so unreservedly to

truly noble,

find one's self drawn to him?

produce an effect

raise his sense of responsibility to a higher plane?

what he called an intimate need of the true beautiful in life, and as this element he was, furthermore, extremely ~~devoted to "culture,"~~ he could not bring himself to decide that Europe was utterly ~~bad~~. But he thought it ~~was~~ very ~~bad indeed~~, and his quarrel with Newman was ~~that this unregulated epicure had a sadly insufficient perception of the bad~~. Babcock himself really knew as little ~~about the bad~~ in any quarter of the world, as a nursing infant; his most vivid realisation of ~~evil~~ had been the discovery that one of his college classmates, who was studying architecture in Paris, had a love affair with a young woman who ~~did not expect him to marry her~~. Babcock had ~~related~~ this ~~incident~~ to Newman, and our hero had applied an epithet ~~of an unflattering sort~~ to the ~~young~~ girl. The next day his companion asked him whether he was very sure he had used exactly the right word to characterise the young architect's mistress. Newman ~~stared and laughed~~. "There are a great many words to express that idea," he said; "you can take your choice!"

"Oh, I mean," said Babcock, "was she possibly not to be considered in a different light? Don't you think she ~~really expected him to marry her~~?"

"I'm sure I don't know," ~~said~~ Newman. "Very likely she ~~did~~; I ~~have~~ no doubt she ~~is a grand woman~~." ~~And he began to laugh again.~~

"I didn't mean that either," said Babcock; "I was only afraid that I might have seemed yesterday not to remember—not to consider; well, I think I will write to Percival about it."

And he had written to Percival (who had answered him in a really impudent fashion), and he had reflected that ~~it was, somehow, raw and reckless in Newman to assume in that off-hand manner that the young woman in Paris might be "grand."~~ The brevity of ~~Newman's~~ judgments very often shocked and discomposed him. He had a way of damning people without further appeal, or ~~of pronouncing them capital company~~ ~~in the face of uncomfortable symptoms~~, which seemed unworthy of a man

Handwritten revisions:

rotten.

went on putting his finger on the inner principle of the highest art,

stale

over some of the dishes, insidious forms of evil, that this promiscuous feeder at the feast could swallow with no wry face.

about the forms of evil,

the most frequent form

didn't at all count on his marrying her.

described

situation

wondered and seemed amused.

marked by a rough justice

really had believed in his higher nature?"

had;

replied

Newman ought not to be encouraged, after all, to read a cheap idealism into flagrant cases of immorality.

levity and

his comrade's

judged it by her own." He was willing to meet his friend on any view of her.

"I'm not sure that she has a high nature.

else of appearing positively taken by their ominous exotic colour,

yearned toward him

phrases and

phrases and principles

were thus strenuously

it a proof of real value on Babcock's part to have

rough passes and smooth

by the edge and on the bosom of

recklessly

own

several spurious

but almost tragic eyes

whose conscience had been properly cultivated. And yet poor Babcock ~~liked him,~~ and remembered that even if he was sometimes perplexing and painful, this was not a reason for giving him up. Goethe recommended seeing human nature in the most various forms, and Mr. Babcock thought Goethe perfectly splendid. He often tried, in odd half-hours of conversation, to infuse into Newman a little of his own spiritual starch, but Newman's personal texture was too loose to admit of stiffening. His mind could no more hold principles than a sieve can hold water. He admired principles extremely, and thought ~~Babcock a mighty fine little fellow for having~~ so many. He accepted all that ~~his high-strung companion~~ offered him, and put them away in what he supposed to be a very safe place; but poor Babcock never afterwards recognised his gifts among the articles that Newman had in daily use.

They travelled together through Germany and into Switzerland, where for three or four weeks they trudged over ~~passes~~ and lounged ~~upon~~ blue lakes. At last they crossed the Simplon and made their way to Venice. Mr. Babcock had become gloomy and even a trifle irritable; he seemed moody, absent, preoccupied; he got his plans into a tangle, and talked one moment of doing one thing and the next of doing another. Newman led his usual life, made acquaintances, took his ease in the galleries and churches, spent an unconscionable amount of time in strolling in the Piazza San Marco, bought ~~a great many bad~~ pictures, and for a fortnight enjoyed Venice grossly. One evening, coming back to his inn, he found Babcock waiting for him in the little garden beside it. The young man walked up to him, looking very dismal, thrust out his hand, and said with solemnity that he was afraid they must part. Newman expressed his surprise and regret, and asked why a parting had become necessary. "Don't be afraid I'm tired of you," he said.

"You are not tired of me?" demanded Babcock, fixing him with ~~his~~ clear ~~gray eye.~~

"Why the deuce should I be? You are a very plucky fellow. Besides, I don't grow tired of things."

"We don't understand each other," said the young minister.

"Don't I understand you?" cried Newman. "Why, I hoped I did. But what if I don't; where's the harm?"

"I don't understand *you*," said Babcock. And he sat down and rested his head on his hand, and looked up mournfully at his immeasurable friend.

"Oh Lord, I don't mind that!" cried Newman, with a laugh.

"But it's very distressing to me. It keeps me in a state of unrest. It irritates me: I can't settle anything. I don't think it's good for me."

"You worry too much; that's what's the matter with you," said Newman.

"Of course it must seem so to you. You think I take things too hard, and I think you take things too easily. We can never agree."

"But we have agreed very well all along."

"No, I haven't agreed," said Babcock, shaking his head. "I am very uncomfortable. I ought to have separated from you a month ago."

"Oh, horrors! I'll agree to anything!" cried Newman.

Mr. Babcock buried his head in both hands. At last, looking up, "I don't think you appreciate my position," he said. "I try to arrive at the truth about everything. And then you go too fast. For me, you are too passionate, too extravagant. I feel as if I ought to go over all this ground we have traversed again, by myself, alone. I am afraid I have made a great many mistakes."

"Oh, you needn't give so many reasons," said Newman. "You are simply tired of my company. You have a good right to be."

"No, no, I am not tired!" cried the pestered young divine. "It is very wrong to be tired."

Handwritten revisions in margins:

- break down so easily
- remarkably nice man
- "But why should you mind that if I don't?"
- "It's
- all questions
- them
- There are things of which you take too little account
- observed
- all your right
- his
- companion

"I give it up!" laughed Newman. "But of course it will never do to go on making mistakes. Go your way, by all means. I shall miss you; but you have seen I make friends very easily. You will be lonely yourself; but drop me a line when you feel like it, and I will wait for you anywhere."

"I think I will go back to Milan. I am afraid I didn't do justice to Luini."

"Poor Luini!" said Newman.

"I mean that I am afraid I overestimated him. I don't think that he is a painter of the first rank."

"Luini?" Newman exclaimed; "why, he's enchanting—he's magnificent! There is something in his genius that is like a beautiful woman. It gives one the same feeling."

Mr. Babcock frowned and winced. And it must be added that this was, for Newman, an unusually metaphysical flight; but in passing through Milan he had taken a great fancy to the painter. "There you are again!" said Mr. Babcock. "Yes, we had better separate." And on the morrow he retraced his steps and proceeded to tone down his impressions of the great Lombard artist.

A few days afterwards Newman received a note from his late companion which ran as follows:—

"MY DEAR MR. NEWMAN—I am afraid that my conduct at Venice, a week ago, seemed to you strange and ungrateful, and I wish to explain my position, which, as I said at the time, I do not think you appreciate. I had long had it on my mind to propose that we should part company, and this step was not really so abrupt as it seemed. In the first place, you know, I am travelling in Europe on funds supplied by my congregation, who kindly offered me a vacation and an opportunity to enrich my mind with the treasures of nature and art in the Old World. I feel, therefore, as if I ought to use my time to the very best advantage. I have a high sense of responsibility. You appear to care only for the pleasure of the hour, and you give yourself up to it with a violence which I confess I am not able to emulate. I feel as if I must arrive at some conclusion and fix my belief on certain points. Art and life seem to me intensely serious things, and in our travels in Europe we should especially remember the immense seriousness of Art. You seem to hold that if a thing amuses you for the moment, that is all you need ask for it; and your relish for mere amusement is also much higher than mine. You put, moreover, a kind of reckless confidence into your pleasures which at times, I confess, has seemed to me—shall I say it?—almost cynical. Your way, at any rate, is not my way, and it is unwise that we should attempt any longer to pull together. And yet, let me add, that I know there is a great deal to be said for your way; I have felt its attraction, in your society, very strongly. But for this I should have left you long ago. But I was so perplexed. I hope I have not done wrong. I feel as if I had a great deal of lost time to make up. I beg you take all this as I mean it, which, Heaven knows, is not invidiously. I have a great personal esteem for you, and hope that some day, when I have recovered my balance, we shall meet again. I hope you will continue to enjoy your travels; only *do* remember that Life and Art *are* extremely serious. Believe me your sincere friend and well-wisher,

"BENJAMIN BABCOCK.

"P.S.—I am greatly perplexed by Luini."

This letter produced in Newman's mind a singular mixture of exhilaration and awe. At first, Mr. Babcock's tender conscience seemed to him a capital farce, and his travelling back to Milan only to get into a deeper muddle appeared, as the reward of his pedantry, exquisitely and ludicrously just. Then Newman reflected that these are mighty mysteries; that possibly he himself was indeed that baleful and barely mentionable thing, ~~a cynic,~~ ["almost cynical,"] and that his manner of considering the treasures of art and the privileges of life was probably ~~very base and immoral.~~ [coarse even to immorality.] Newman had a great contempt for immorality, and that evening, for a good half-hour, as he sat watching the star-sheen on the warm Adriatic, he felt rebuked and depressed. He was at a loss [to decide] how to answer Babcock's letter. His good-nature checked his ~~resenting the young minister's lofty admonitions,~~ [snubbing his late companion's earnestness,] and his tough, inelastic sense of humour forbade his taking ~~them~~ [it] seriously. He wrote no answer at all, but a day or two afterwards he found in a curiosity shop a grotesque little statuette in ivory, of the sixteenth century, which he sent off to Babcock, without a commentary. It represented a gaunt, ascetic-looking monk, in a tattered gown and cowl, kneeling with clasped hands and pulling a portentously long face. It was a wonderfully delicate piece of carving, and in a moment, through one of the rents of his gown, you espied a fat capon hung round the monk's waist. In Newman's intention what did the figure symbolise? Did it mean that he was going to try to be as "high-toned" as the monk looked at first, but that he feared he should succeed no better than ~~the friar,~~ [this personage,] on a closer inspection, proved to have done? It is not supposable that he intended a satire upon Babcock's own asceticism, for this would have been a truly cynical stroke. He made his late companion, at any rate, a ~~very~~ valuable little present.

Newman, on leaving Venice, went through the Tyrol to Vienna, and then returned westward, through Southern Germany. The autumn found him at Baden-Baden, where he spent several weeks. The place was charming, and he was in no hurry to depart; besides, he was looking about him and deciding what to do for the winter. His summer had been very full, and as he sat under the great trees beside the miniature river that trickles past the Baden flower-beds, he slowly rummaged it over. He had seen and done a great deal, enjoyed and observed a great deal; he felt older, and yet he felt younger too. He remembered Mr. Babcock and his desire to form conclusions, and he remembered also that he had profited very little by his friend's exhortation to cultivate the same respectable habit. Could he not scrape together a few conclusions? Baden-Baden was the prettiest place he had seen yet, and orchestral music in the evening, under the stars, was decidedly a great institution. This was one of his conclusions! But he went on to reflect that he had done very wisely to pull up stakes and come abroad; this seeing of the world was a very interesting thing. He had learned a great deal; he couldn't say just what, but he had it there under his hat-band. He had done what he wanted; he had seen the great things, and he had given his mind a chance to "improve," if it would. He cheerfully believed that it had improved. Yes, this seeing of the world was very pleasant, and he would willingly do a little more of it. Thirty-six years old as he was, he had a handsome stretch of life before him yet, and he need not begin to count his weeks. Where should he take the world next? I have said he remembered the eyes of the lady whom he had found standing in Mrs. Tristram's drawing-room; four months had elapsed, and he had not forgotten them yet. He had looked—he had made a point of looking—into a great many other eyes in the interval, but the only ones he thought of now were Madame de Cintré's. If he wanted to see more of the world, should he find it in Madame de Cintré's eyes? He would certainly find something there, call it this world or the next. Throughout these rather formless meditations he sometimes thought of his past life and the long array of years (they had begun so early) during which he had had nothing in his head but enterprise. They seemed far away now, for his present attitude was more than a holiday, it was almost a rupture. He had told Tristram that the pendulum was swinging back,

these waters of the free curiosity were very soothing,

Splash

in them.

Forty

on the point of being,

of interest

call it the interest of this world or of that of some other, some better, hypothetic one.

his possible "hand".

and it appeared that the backward swing had not yet ended. Still, which was over in the other quarter, wore to his mind a different aspect at different hours. In its train a thousand forgotten episodes came trooping back into his . Some of them he looked complacently enough in the face; from some he averted his head. They were old Some of them, as he felt decidedly proud of; he admired himself as if he had been looking at another man. And, in fact, many of the qualities that make a great deed were there; the decision, the resolution, the courage, the celerity, the clear eye, and the strong hand. Of certain other it would be going too far to say that he was ashamed of them, for Newman had never had a stomach for dirty work. He was blessed with a natural impulse to disfigure with a direct, unreasoning blow the of temptation. And, certainly, in no man could a want of have been less excusable. Newman knew the crooked from the straight at a glance, and the former had cost him, first and last, a great many moments of lively disgust. But none the less some of his memories seemed to wear at present a rather graceless and sordid mien, and it struck him that if he had never ~~done anything very ugly~~, he had never, on the other hand, ~~done anything particularly beautiful~~. He had spent his years in the unremitting effort to add thousands to thousands, and, now that he stood well outside of it, the business of money-getting

extremely dry and sterile~~. It is very well to money-getting after you have filled your pockets, and Newman, it may be said, should have begun somewhat earlier to moralise To it may be answered that he might have made another fortune, if he chose; and we ought to add that he was not exactly moralising. It had come back to him simply that what he had been looking at all the summer was a very rich

the possibility of hands,

mind ⊙

triumphs of nerve, even of bluff, mere cold memories of the heat of battle, the high competitive rage ⊙

they lived again,

performances

painted face

the stricter scruple

incurred any quite ineffaceable stain,

followed the line of beauty, as a sought direction, for a single line of its course ⊙

showed only in its uglinesses, vast and vague and dark, like a pirate ship with its lights turned inward ⊙

so

mere

that

think meanly of

with this superiority

men "live" in his old sense

and beautiful world, and that it had not all been made by ~~sharp railroad men and stockbrokers.~~

During his stay at Baden-Baden he received a letter from Mrs. Tristram, scolding him for the scanty tidings he had sent to his friends and begging to be definitely informed that he had not ~~concocted any horrid scheme for wintering in outlying regions, but was coming back sanely and promptly to the most comfortable city in

Newman's answer ran as follows :—

evil thought of not wintering within call of the Avenue d'Iéna

"I supposed you knew I was a miserable letter-writer, and didn't expect anything of me. I don't think I have written twenty letters of pure friendship in my whole life; in America I conducted my correspondence altogether by telegrams. This is a letter of pure friendship; you have got hold of a curiosity, and I hope you will value it. You want to know everything that has happened to me these three months. The best way to tell you, I think, would be to send you my half-dozen guide-books, with my pencil-marks in the margin. Wherever you find a scratch, or a cross, or a 'Beautiful!' or a 'So true!' or a 'Too thin!' you may know that I have had a sensation of some sort or other. That has been about my history ever since I left you. Belgium, Holland, Switzerland, Germany, Italy— I have been through the whole list, and I don't think I know much more about it. I know more about Madonnas and church steeples than I ever suspected.~~ I have seen some things, and shall perhaps talk them over this winter by your fireside. You see, my face is not altogether set against Paris. I have had all kinds of plans and visions, but your letter has blown most of them away. '*L'appétit vient en mangeant,*' says the French proverb, and I find that the more I see of the world the more I want to see. Now that I am in the shafts, why shouldn't I trot to the end of the course? Sometimes I

I've taken the whole list as the bare-backed rider takes the paper hoops at the circus, and I'm not even yet out of breath

I carry about six volumes of Ruskin in my trunk, and

Grand old

think of the far East, and keep rolling the names of Eastern cities under my tongue; Damascus and Bagdad, ~~Medina and Mecca~~. I spent a week last month in the company of a returned missionary, who told me I ought to be ashamed to be loafing about Europe when there ~~are such big things to be seen~~ out there. I do want ~~to explore~~, but I think I would rather ~~explore over~~ in the Rue de l'Université. Do you ever hear from that ~~pretty~~ lady? If you can get her to promise she will be at home the next time I call, I will go back to Paris straight. I am more than ever in the state of mind I told you about that evening; I want a [illegible]. I have kept an eye on all the ~~pretty girls~~ [illegible] this summer, but none of them [illegible] or [illegible] it. I should have enjoyed all this a thousand times more if I had had the lady just mentioned [illegible]. The nearest approach to her was a [illegible] from Boston, [illegible] very soon demanded a separation for incompatibility of temper. He told me I [illegible]. But shortly afterwards I met an Englishman, with whom I struck up an acquaintance which at first seemed to promise well—a very bright man, who writes in the London papers and knows Paris nearly as well as Tristram. We knocked about for a week together, but he very soon gave me up in disgust. [illegible] This was rather bewildering. Which of my two critics was I to believe? I didn't worry about it, and very soon made up my mind they were ~~both idiots~~. But there is one thing ~~in~~ which [illegible] to pretend I am wrong, that is, in being your faithful friend, C. N."

Trebizond and Samarcand.
more treats.
is such a treat to be had
take them
possible candidates that have come up
handsome tall
companion for life, and still want her to be a star of the first magnitude.
has filled the bill,
anything like
under my arm
who, however,
Cultivated young man
He pronounced me a painful "prig" — he talked to me as if I had come from Boston.
from me
hadn't it in me ever to become high-toned, and really made me half believe him. But
as to
really equally shallow.
I defy any one ever

NEWMAN gave up Damascus and Bagdad and returned to Paris before the autumn was over. He established himself in some rooms selected for him by Tom Tristram, in accordance with the latter's estimate of what he called his social position. When Newman learned that his social position was to be taken into account, he professed himself utterly incompetent, and begged Tristram to relieve him of the care. "I didn't know I had a social position," he said, "and if I have, I haven't the smallest idea what it is. Isn't a social position knowing some two or three thousand people and inviting them to dinner? I know you and your wife and little old Mr. Nioche, who gave me French lessons last spring. Can I invite you to dinner to meet each other? If I can, you must come to-morrow."

"That is not very grateful to me," said Mrs. Tristram, "who introduced you last year to every creature I know."

"So you did; I had quite forgotten. But I thought you wanted me to forget," said Newman, with that tone of simple deliberateness which frequently marked his utterance, and which an observer would not have known whether to pronounce a somewhat mysteriously humorous affectation of ignorance or a modest aspiration to knowledge. "You told me you disliked them all."

"Ah, the way you remember what I say is at least very flattering. But in future," added Mrs. Tristram, "pray forget all the wicked things, and remember only the good ones. It will be easily done, and it will not fatigue your memory. But I forewarn you that if you trust my husband to pick out your rooms you are in for something hideous."

"Hideous, darling?" cried Tristram.

"To-day ~~I must say nothing wicked;~~ otherwise I should use stronger language."

"What do you think she would say, Newman?" asked Tristram. "If she really tried, now? She can ~~express displeasure,~~ volubly, in two or three languages; that's what it is to be intellectual. It gives her the start of me completely, for I can't swear, for the life of me, except in ~~English.~~ When I get mad I have to fall back on our dear old mother tongue. There's nothing like it, after all."

Newman declared that he knew nothing about tables and chairs, and that he would accept, in the way of a lodging, with his eyes shut, anything that Tristram should offer him. This was partly pure veracity on our hero's part, but it was also partly charity. He knew that to pry about and ~~look at rooms,~~ and make people open windows, and poke into sofas with his cane, and gossip with landladies, and ask who lived above and who below —he knew that this was of all pastimes the dearest to Tristram's heart, and he felt the more disposed to put it in his way as he was conscious that, as regards his obliging friend, he had suffered the warmth of ancient good fellowship somewhat to abate. Besides, he had no taste for upholstery; he had even no very exquisite sense of comfort or convenience. He had a relish for luxury and splendour, but it was satisfied by rather gross contrivances. He scarcely knew a hard chair from a soft one, and he possessed a talent for stretching his legs which quite dispensed with adventitious ~~facilities.~~ His idea of comfort was to inhabit very large rooms, have a great many of them, and be conscious of their possessing a number of patented mechanical devices—half of which he should never have occasion to use. The apartments should be light and brilliant and lofty; he had once said that he liked rooms in which you ~~wanted~~ to keep your hat on. For the rest, he was satisfied with the assurance of any respectable person that everything was

I utter nothing base;
polish one off, for a wretch,
truly
pure Anglo-Saxon
count casseroles
beds and
aids
best
should want
"up to the mark"

"handsome." Tristram accordingly secured for him an apartment to which this epithet might be lavishly applied. It was situated on the Boulevard Haussmann, on a first floor, and consisted of a series of rooms, gilded from floor to ceiling a foot thick, draped in various light shades of satin, and chiefly furnished with mirrors and clocks. Newman thought them magnificent, thanked Tristram heartily, immediately took possession, and had one of his trunks standing for three months in his drawing-room.

One day Mrs. Tristram told him that her beautiful friend, Madame de Cintré, had returned from the country; that she had met her three days before, coming out of the Church of St. Sulpice; she herself having journeyed to that distant quarter in quest of an obscure lace-mender, of whose skill she had heard high praise.

"And how were those eyes?" Newman asked.

"Those eyes were red with weeping, if you please!" said Mrs. Tristram. "She had been to confession."

"It doesn't tally with your account of her," said Newman, "that she should have sins to confess."

"They were not sins; they were sufferings."

"How do you know that?"

"She asked me to come and see her; I went this morning."

"And what does she suffer from?"

"I didn't ask her. With her, somehow, one is very discreet. But I guessed easily enough. She suffers from her wicked old mother and her Grand Turk of a brother. They persecute her. But I can almost forgive them, because, as I told you, she is a saint, and a persecution is all that she needs to bring out her saintliness and make her perfect."

"That's a comfortable theory for her. I hope you will never impart it to the old folks. Why does she let them bully her? Is she not her own mistress?"

"Legally, yes, I suppose; but morally, no. In France you must never say Nay to your mother, whatever she

habitation over the price of which the Prince of Morocco had been haggling ⊙

didn't haggle,

their tall handsome lady

intense mild

"They

— neither more nor less ⊙

and from the manner in which her elder brother, the technical head of the family, abets the Marquise ⊙

grim

press her hard, and they press her all the while ⊙

what I call her quality" ⊙

But why

persecute

as a married woman,

requires of you. She may be the most abominable old woman in the world, and make your life a purgatory; but after all, she is *ma mère*, and you have no right to judge her. You have simply to obey. The thing has a fine side to it. Madame de Cintré bows her head and folds her wings."

"Can't she at least make her brother leave off?"

"Her brother is the *chef de la famille*, as they say; he is the head of the clan. With those people the family is everything; you must act, not for your own pleasure, but for the advantage of the family."

"I wonder what *my* family would like me to do!" exclaimed Tristram.

"I wish you had one!" said his wife.

"But what do they want to get out of that poor lady?" Newman asked.

"Another marriage. They are not rich, and they want to bring more money into the family."

"There's your chance, my boy!" said Tristram.

"And Madame de Cintré objects," Newman continued.

"She has been sold once; she naturally objects to being sold again. It appears that the first time they made rather a poor bargain; M. de Cintré left a scanty property."

"And to whom do they want to marry her now?"

"I thought it best not to ask; but you may be sure it is to some horrid old nabob, or to some dissipated little duke."

"There's Mrs. Tristram, as large as life!" cried her husband. "Observe the richness of her imagination. She has not asked a single question—it's vulgar to ask questions—and yet she knows everything. She has the history of Madame de Cintré's marriage at her fingers' ends. She has seen the lovely Claire on her knees, with loosened tresses and streaming eyes, and the rest of them standing over her with spikes and goads and red-hot irons, ready to come down on her if she refuses the tipsy duke. The simple truth is that they have made a fuss about her milliner's bill or refused her an opera box."

Newman looked from Tristram to his wife with a certain mistrust in each direction. "Do you really mean," he asked of Mrs. Tristram, "that your friend is being ~~forced~~ into an ~~unhappy~~ marriage?"

"I think it extremely probable. Those people are very capable of that sort of thing."

"It is like something in a play," said Newman; "that dark old house over there looks as if wicked things had been done in it, and might be done again."

"They have a still darker old house in the country, Madame de Cintré tells me, and there, during the summer, this scheme must have been hatched."

"*Must* have been; mind that!" said Tristram.

"After all," suggested Newman, after a silence, "she may be in trouble about something else."

"If it is something else, then it is something worse," said Mrs. Tristram, with rich decision.

Newman ~~was~~ silent a while, ~~and~~ seemed lost in meditation. "Is it possible," he asked at last, "that they do that sort of thing over here? that helpless women are ~~bullied~~ into marrying men they hate?"

"Helpless women, all over the world, have a hard time of it," said Mrs. Tristram. "There is plenty of ~~bullying~~ everywhere."

"A great deal of that kind goes on in New York," said Tristram. "Girls are bullied or coaxed or bribed, or all three together, into marrying ~~nasty fellows~~. There is no end of that always going on in ~~the~~ Fifth Avenue, and other bad things besides. The Mysteries of ~~the~~ Fifth Avenue! Some one ought to show them up."

"I don't believe it!" said Newman, very gravely. "I don't ~~believe that, in America, girls are ever subjected to compulsion. I don't believe there have been a dozen cases of it since the country began.~~"

Coerced

She really shrinks from?"

thumb-screwed — sentimentally, socially —

can

the thumb-screw for them

of thing

for money, horrible cads.

see how, in America, such cases can ever have occurred; for the simple reason that the men themselves would be the first to make them impossible. The American man sometimes takes advantage — I've known him too. But he doesn't take advantage of women.

"Listen to the voice of the spread eagle!" cried Tristram.

"The spread eagle ought to use his wings," said Mrs. Tristram. "Fly to the rescue of Madame de Cintré!"

"To her rescue?" Newman echoed.

"Pounce down, seize her in your talons, and carry her off. Marry her yourself."

Newman, for some moments, answered nothing; but presently, "I should suppose she had heard enough of marrying," he said. "The kindest way to treat her would be to admire her, and yet never to speak of it. But that sort of thing is infamous," he added; "it makes me feel savage to hear of it."

He heard of it, however, more than once afterwards. Mrs. Tristram again saw Madame de Cintré, and again found her looking very sad. But on these occasions there had been no tears; her beautiful eyes were clear and still. "She is cold, calm, and hopeless," Mrs. Tristram declared, and she added that on her mentioning that her friend Mr. Newman was again in Paris, and was faithful in his desire to make Madame de Cintré's acquaintance, this lovely woman had found a smile in her despair, and declared that she was sorry to have missed his visit in the spring, and that she hoped he had not lost courage. "I told her something about you," said Mrs. Tristram.

"That's a comfort," said Newman placidly. "I like people to know about me."

A few days after this, one dusky autumn afternoon, he went again to the Rue de l'Université. The early evening had closed in as he applied for admittance at the stoutly-guarded Hôtel de Bellegarde. He was told that Madame de Cintré was at home; he crossed the court, entered the farther door, and was conducted through a vestibule, vast, dim, and cold, up a broad stone staircase with an ancient iron balustrade, to an apartment on the second floor. Announced and ushered in, he found himself in a sort of panelled boudoir, at one end of which a lady and gentleman were seated before the fire. The gentleman was smoking a cigarette; there was no light in the room save that of a couple of candles and the glow from the hearth. Both persons rose to welcome Newman, who, in the firelight, recognised Madame de Cintré. She gave him her hand with a smile which seemed in itself an illumination, and, pointing to her companion, said softly, "My brother." The gentleman offered Newman a frank, friendly greeting, and our hero then perceived him to be the young man who had spoken to him in the court of the hotel on his former visit and who had struck him as ~~a good fellow.~~ of an easy commerce.

"Mrs. Tristram has ~~spoken to me a great deal of you,~~ often mentioned you to us," said Madame de Cintré gently, as she resumed her former place.

Newman, noticing her "us," began, after he had seated himself, ~~began~~ to consider what, in truth, was his errand. He had an unusual, unexpected sense of having wandered into a strange corner of the world. He was not given, as a general thing, to anticipating danger, or forecasting disaster, and he had had no social tremors on this particular occasion. He was not ~~timid and he was not impudent. He felt too kindly toward himself to be the one, and too good-naturedly toward the rest of the world to be the other.~~ without presence of mind, though he had no formed habit of light loquacity. But his native shrewdness sometimes placed his ease of temper at its mercy; with every disposition to take things simply, it was obliged to perceive that some things were not so simple as others. He felt as one does in missing a step, in an ascent, where one expected to find it. This strange, pretty woman, sitting in fireside talk with her brother, in the gray depths of her inhospitable-looking house—what had he to say to her? She seemed enveloped in ~~a sort of fantastic privacy;~~ triple defences of privacy; on what grounds had he ~~pulled away the curtain?~~ presumed on his having effected a breach? For a moment he felt as if he had plunged into some medium as deep as the ocean, and as if he must exert himself to keep from sinking. Meanwhile he was looking at Madame de Cintré, and she was settling herself in her chair and drawing in her long dress and turning her face towards him. Their eyes met; a moment afterwards she looked away and motioned to her brother to put a log on the fire. But the moment, and the glance which traversed it, had been sufficient to relieve Newman of the first and the last fit of personal embarrassment he was ever to know. He performed the movement which was so frequent with him, and which was always a sort of symbol of his taking mental possession of a scene—he extended his legs. The impression Madame de Cintré had made upon him on their first meeting came back in an instant; it had been deeper than he knew. She was pleasing, she was interesting; he had opened a book, and the first lines held his attention.

She asked him several questions: how lately he had seen Mrs. Tristram, how long he had been in Paris, how long he expected to remain there, how he liked it. She spoke English without an accent, or rather with that distinctively British accent which, on his arrival in Europe, had struck Newman as an altogether foreign tongue, but which, in women, he had come to like extremely. Here and there Madame de Cintré's utterance had a faint shade of strangeness, but at the end of ten minutes Newman found himself waiting for these soft roughnesses. He enjoyed them, and he marvelled to see that gross thing, error, brought down to so fine a point.

"You have a beautiful country," said Madame de Cintré, presently.

"Oh, magnificent!" said Newman. "You ought to see it."

"I shall never see it," said Madame de Cintré, with a smile.

"Why not?" asked Newman.

"I don't travel; especially so far."

"But you go away sometimes; you are not always here?"

him as constituting a complete foreignness — a foreignness that

that absence of any one of the accents, long familiar to him, which on

slightly exceeded this measure,

he

marvelling to hear the possible slip become the charming glide.

come over and

of your own

go over and

She answered

shouldn't you?"

"We

don't always stay right here?"

"I go away in summer, a little way, to the country."

Newman wanted to ask her something more, something personal, he hardly knew what. "Don't you find it rather—rather quiet here?" he said; "so far from the street?" Rather "gloomy," he was going to say, but he reflected that that would be impolite.

"Yes, it is very quiet," said Madame de Cintré; "but we like that."

"Ah, you like that," repeated Newman, slowly.

"Besides, I have lived here all my life."

"Lived here all your life," said Newman, in the same way.

"I was born here, and my father was born here before me, and my grandfather, and my great-grandfathers. Were they not, Valentin?" and she appealed to her brother.

"Yes, it is a family habit to be born here!" the young man said, with a laugh, and rose and threw the remnant of his cigarette into the fire, and then remained leaning against the chimney-piece. An observer would have perceived that he wished to take a better look at Newman, whom he covertly examined, while he stood, stroking his moustache.

"Your house is tremendously old, then," said Newman.

"How old is it, brother?" asked Madame de Cintré.

The young man took the two candles from the mantel-shelf, lifted one high in each hand, and looked up toward the cornice of the room, above the chimney-piece. This latter feature of the apartment was of white marble, and in the familiar rococo style of the last century; but above it was a panelling of an earlier date, quaintly carved, painted white, and gilded here and there. The white had turned to yellow, and the gilding was tarnished. On the top the figures ranged themselves into a sort of shield, on which an armorial device was cut. Above it, in relief, was a date—1627. "There you have it," said questions of

the young man. "That is old or new, according to your point of view."

"Well, over here," said Newman, "one's point of view gets shifted round considerably." And he threw back his head and looked about the room. "Your house is of a very curious style of architecture," he said.

"Are you interested in architecture?" asked the young man at the chimney-piece.

"Well, I took the trouble, this summer," said Newman, "to examine—as well as I can calculate—some four hundred and seventy churches. Do you call that interested?"

"Perhaps you are interested in theology," said the young man.

"Not particularly. Are you a Roman Catholic, madam?" And he turned to Madame de Cintré.

"Yes, sir," she answered, gravely.

Newman was struck with the gravity of her tone; he threw back his head and began to look round the room again. "Had you never noticed that number up there?" he presently asked.

She hesitated a moment, and then, "In former years," she said.

Her brother had been watching Newman's movement. "Perhaps you would like to examine the house," he said.

Newman slowly brought down his eyes and looked at him; he had a vague impression that the young man at the chimney-piece ~~was inclined to irony~~. He was a handsome ~~fellow~~, his face wore a smile, his moustachios were curled up at the ends, and there was ~~a little dancing gleam in his eye~~. "Damn his French impudence!" Newman was on the point of saying to himself. "What the deuce is he grinning at?" He glanced at Madame de Cintré; she was sitting with her eyes fixed on the floor. She raised them, they met his, and she looked at her brother. Newman turned again to this young man and observed that he strikingly resembled his sister.

had his forms, and sought his own opportunities, of amusement

figure of a young man;

Something — more than the firelight — that played in his eyes

This was in his favour, and our hero's first impression of the Count Valentin, moreover, had been agreeable. His mistrust expired, and he said he would be very glad to see the house.

The young man gave a frank laugh, and laid his hand on one of the candlesticks. "Good, good!" he exclaimed. "Come, then."

But Madame de Cintré rose quickly and grasped his arm. "Ah, Valentin!" she said. "What do you mean to do?"

"To show Mr. Newman the house. It will be very amusing."

She kept her hand on his arm and turned to Newman with a smile. "Don't let him take you," she said; "you will not find it amusing. It is a musty old house, like any other."

"It is full of curious things," said the Count, resisting. "Besides, I want to do it; it is a rare chance."

"You are very wicked, brother," Madame de Cintré answered.

"Nothing venture, nothing have!" cried the young man. "Will you come?"

Madame de Cintré stepped toward Newman, gently clasping her hands and smiling softly. "Would you not prefer my society, here, by my fire, to stumbling about dark passages after my brother?"

"A hundred times!" said Newman. "We will see the house some other day."

The young man put down his candlestick with mock solemnity, and shaking his head, "Ah, you have defeated a great scheme, sir!" he said.

"A scheme? I don't understand," said Newman.

"You would have played your part in it all the better. Perhaps some day I shall have a chance to explain it."

"Be quiet, and ring for the tea," said Madame de Cintré.

The young man obeyed, and presently a servant

brought in the tea, placed the tray on a small table, and departed. Madame de Cintré, from her place, busied herself with making it. She had but just begun when the door was thrown open and a lady rushed in, making a loud rustling sound. She stared at Newman, gave a little nod and a "Monsieur!" and then quickly approached Madame de Cintré and presented her forehead to be kissed. Madame de Cintré saluted her, and continued to make tea. The newcomer was young and pretty, it seemed to Newman; she wore her bonnet and cloak, and a train of royal proportions. She began to talk rapidly in French. "Oh, give me some tea, my beautiful one, for the love of God! I'm exhausted, mangled, massacred." Newman found himself quite unable to follow her; she spoke much less distinctly than M. Nioche.

"That is my sister-in-law," said the Count Valentin, leaning towards him.

"She is very pretty," said Newman.

"Exquisite," answered the young man, and this time, again, Newman suspected him of irony.

His sister-in-law came round to the other side of the fire with her cup of tea in her hand, holding it out at arm's-length, so that she might not spill it on her dress, and uttering little cries of alarm. She placed the cup on the mantel-shelf and began to unpin her veil and pull off her gloves, looking meanwhile at Newman.

"Is there anything I can do for you, my dear lady?" the Count Valentin asked, in a sort of mock-caressing tone.

"Present Monsieur," said his sister-in-law. The young man answered, "Mr. Newman!"

"I can't curtsy to you, Monsieur, or I shall spill my tea," said the lady. "So Claire receives strangers, like that?" she added in a low voice, in French, to her brother-in-law.

"Apparently!" he answered, with a smile. Newman

stood a moment, and then he approached Madame de Cintré. She looked up at him as if she were thinking of something to say. But she seemed to think of nothing; so she simply smiled. He sat down near her and she handed him a cup of tea. For a few moments they talked about that, and meanwhile he ~~looked at her.~~ He remembered what Mrs. Tristram had told him of her "perfection," and of her having, in combination, all the brilliant things that he dreamed of finding. This made him ~~observe~~ her not only without mistrust, but without uneasy conjectures; the presumption, from the first moment he looked at her, had been in her favour. And yet, if she was beautiful, it was not a dazzling beauty. She was tall, and moulded in long lines; she had thick, fair hair, a wide forehead, and features with a sort of harmonious irregularity. Her clear gray eyes were strikingly expressive; they were both gentle and intelligent, and Newman liked them immensely; but they had not those depths of splendour—those many-coloured rays—which ~~illumine the brow of famous beauties.~~ Madame de Cintré was ~~rather thin, and she~~ looked younger than probably she was. In her whole person ~~there~~ was something ~~both youthful and subdued, slender and yet ample, tranquil yet shy; a mixture of immaturity and repose, of innocence and dignity.~~ What had Tristram meant, Newman wondered, by calling her proud? She was certainly not proud now, to him; or if she was, it was of no use, it was lost upon him; she must pile it up higher if she expected him to mind it. She was a ~~beautiful woman,~~ and it was very easy to get on with her. Was she a countess, a *marquise*, a kind of historical formation? Newman, who had rarely heard these words used, had never been at pains to attach any particular image to them; but they occurred to him now, and seemed charged with a sort of melodious meaning. They signified something fair and softly bright, that had easy motions and spoke very agreeably.

Kept taking her in.

consider

so

light up the fair façade of the conquering type.

of attenuated substance and

still young and still passive, still uncertain and still suspended, yet that made, in its dignity, a presence withal, and almost made, in its serenity, a confidence.

clear, noble person,

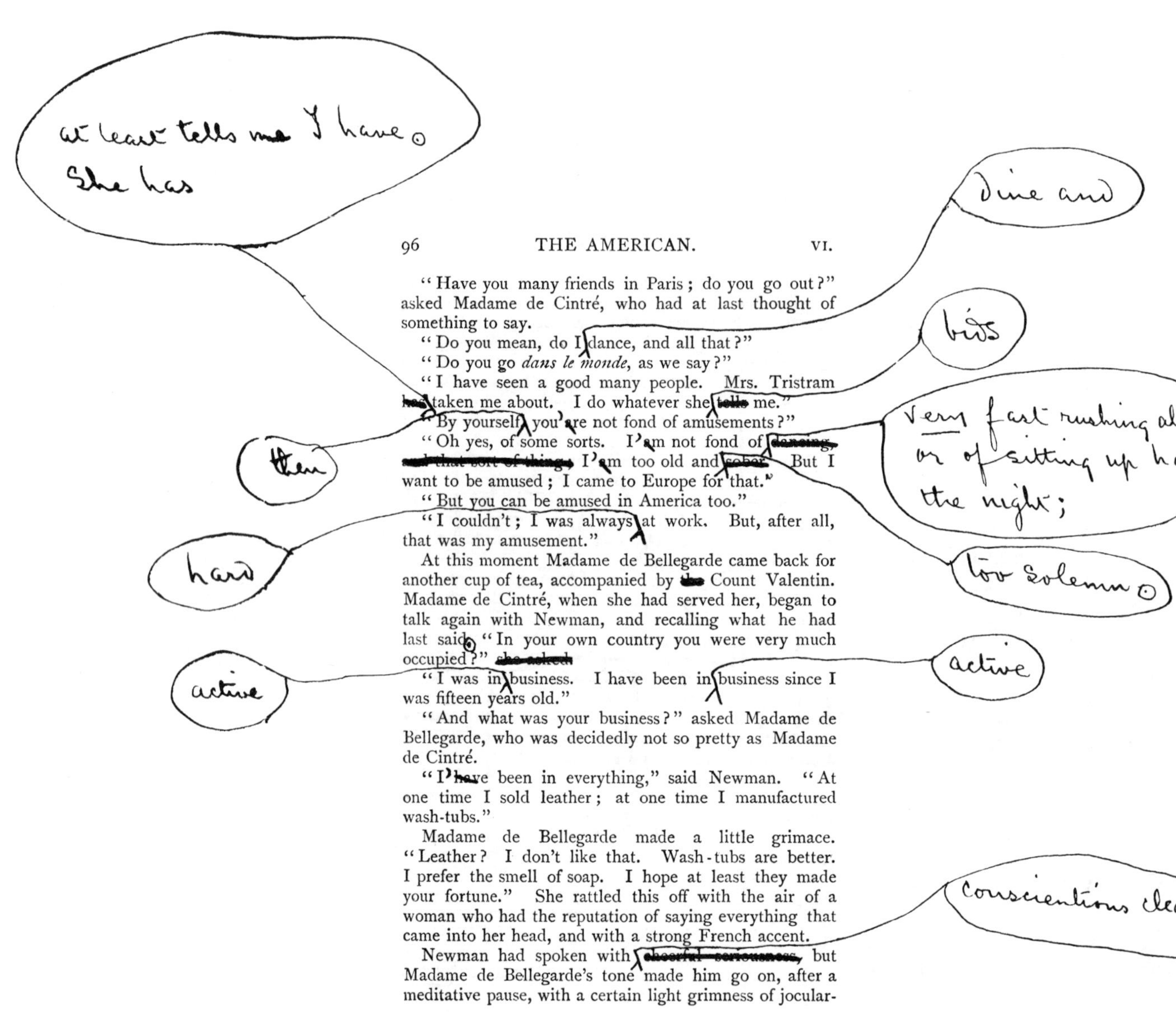

96 THE AMERICAN. VI.

"Have you many friends in Paris; do you go out?" asked Madame de Cintré, who had at last thought of something to say.

"Do you mean, do I dance, and all that?"

"Do you go *dans le monde*, as we say?"

"I have seen a good many people. Mrs. Tristram has taken me about. I do whatever she tells me."

"By yourself, you are not fond of amusements?"

"Oh yes, of some sorts. I am not fond of dancing, and that sort of thing; I am too old and sober. But I want to be amused; I came to Europe for that."

"But you can be amused in America too."

"I couldn't; I was always at work. But, after all, that was my amusement."

At this moment Madame de Bellegarde came back for another cup of tea, accompanied by the Count Valentin. Madame de Cintré, when she had served her, began to talk again with Newman, and recalling what he had last said, "In your own country you were very much occupied?" she asked.

"I was in business. I have been in business since I was fifteen years old."

"And what was your business?" asked Madame de Bellegarde, who was decidedly not so pretty as Madame de Cintré.

"I have been in everything," said Newman. "At one time I sold leather; at one time I manufactured wash-tubs."

Madame de Bellegarde made a little grimace. "Leather? I don't like that. Wash-tubs are better. I prefer the smell of soap. I hope at least they made your fortune." She rattled this off with the air of a woman who had the reputation of saying everything that came into her head, and with a strong French accent.

Newman had spoken with cheerful seriousness, but Madame de Bellegarde's tone made him go on, after a meditative pause, with a certain light grimness of jocularity. "No, I lost money on wash-tubs, but I came out pretty square on leather."

"I have made up my mind, after all," said Madame de Bellegarde, "that the great point is—how do you call it?—to come out square. I am on my knees to money; I don't deny it. If you have it, I ask no questions. For that I am a real democrat—like you, Monsieur. Madame de Cintré is very proud; but I find that one gets much more pleasure in this sad life if one doesn't look too closely."

"Just Heaven, dear madam, how you go at it," said the Count Valentin, lowering his voice.

"He's a man one can speak to, I suppose, since my sister receives him," the lady answered. "Besides, it's very true; those are my ideas."

"Ah, you call them ideas," murmured the young man.

"But Mrs. Tristram told me you had been in the army—in your war," said Madame de Cintré.

"Yes, but that is not business!" said Newman.

"Very true!" said M. de Bellegarde. "Otherwise perhaps I should not be penniless."

"Is it true," asked Newman in a moment, "that you are so proud? I had already heard it."

Madame de Cintré smiled. "Do you find me so?"

"Oh," said Newman, "I am no judge. If you are proud with me, you will have to tell me. Otherwise I shall not know it."

Madame de Cintré began to laugh. "That would be pride in a sad position!" she said.

"It would be partly," Newman went on, "because I shouldn't want to know it. I want you to treat me well."

Madame de Cintré, whose laugh had ceased, looked at him with her head half averted, as if she feared what he was going to say. and he continued, the next thing:

- and my worship is as public as you like ⊙
- radical
- make too many difficulties ⊙
- "Goodness gracious, chère madame,
- was not business — in the paying sense ,
- "You know" ⊙
- gave way to amusement ⊙
- on this
- My belle-sœur
- rush in!" groaned
- Even so poor a soldier as I would not be sans le sou ⊙
- You're all so alarmingly proud ?
- "Shan't be aware ⊙
- be aware, you know ⊙
- mirth had dropped,

"Mrs. Tristram told you the literal truth; he went on, I want very much to know you. I didn't come here simply to call to-day; I came in the hope that you might ask me to come again."

"Oh, pray come often," said Madame de Cintré.

"But will you be at home?" Newman insisted. Even to himself he seemed a trifle "pushing," but he was, in truth, a trifle excited.

"I hope so!" said Madame de Cintré.

Newman got up. "Well, we shall see," he said, smoothing his hat with his coat-cuff.

"Brother," said Madame de Cintré, "invite Mr. Newman to come again."

The Count Valentin looked at our hero from head to foot with his peculiar smile, in which impudence and urbanity seemed perplexingly commingled. "Are you a brave man?" he asked, eyeing him askance.

"Well, I hope so," said Newman.

"I rather suspect so. In that case, come again."

"Ah, what an invitation!" murmured Madame de Cintré, with something painful in her smile.

"Oh, I want Mr. Newman to come—particularly," said the young man. "It will give me great pleasure. I shall be desolate if I miss one of his visits. But I maintain he must be brave. A stout heart, sir," and he offered Newman his hand.

"I shall not come to see you; I shall come to see Madame de Cintré," said Newman.

"You will need, all the more courage."

"Ah, Valentin!" Madame de Cintré, appealingly.

"Decidedly," cried Madame de Bellegarde, "I'm the only person here capable of saying something polite! Come to see me; you will need no courage."

Newman gave a laugh which was not altogether an assent, and took his leave. Madame de Cintré did not take up her sister's challenge to be gracious, but she looked with a certain troubled air at the retreating guest.

Do
again,"
quavered.
"It depends on when you come!"
I guess I won't leave you much loop-hole".
And he smoothed
"Mon frère
irony
facial play,
try me,"
"Ah then, there you are!
of high courage.
"Dear me,
Exactly for that, all your arms".
her brother.
"Ah, de grâce!" sighed
and a firm front." And
at all, monsieur".
then, shaking hands all round, marched away.

VII

ONE evening, very late, about a week after this visit to Madame de Cintré, Newman's servant brought him a card; it was that of young M. de Bellegarde. When, a few moments later, he went to receive his visitor, he found him standing in the middle of his great gilded parlour and eyeing it from cornice to carpet. M. de Bellegarde's face, it seemed to Newman, expressed a sense of lively entertainment. "What the devil is he laughing at now?" our hero asked himself. But he put the question without acrimony, for he felt that Madame de Cintré's brother was a good fellow, and he had a presentiment that on this basis of good fellowship they were destined to understand each other. Only, if there was anything to laugh at, he wished to have a glimpse of it too.

"To begin with," said the young man, as he extended his hand, "have I come too late?"

"Too late for what?" asked Newman.

"To smoke a cigar with you."

"You would have to come early to do that," said Newman. "I don't smoke."

"Ah, you are a strong man!"

"But I keep cigars," Newman added. "Sit down."

"Surely, I may not smoke here," said M. de Bellegarde.

"What is the matter? Is the room too small?"

"It is too large. It is like smoking in a ball-room or a church."

"That is what you were laughing at just now?" Newman asked; "the size of my room?"

"It is not size only," replied M. de Bellegarde, "but splendour, and harmony, and beauty of detail. It was the smile of admiration."

five days
episode,
which proved to be
the greatest of his gilded saloons
him
not less than usual a sense of the comedy of things.
free nature,
food for mirth
the natural and the free
know how to
Sympathy and of

"ridiculous?""

"Ridiculous,"

Of course

have my little
entertainments a
success ⊙

began

gave him a long

Newman looked at him a moment, and then, "So it *is* very ~~ugly?"~~ he inquired.

"~~Ugly,~~ my dear sir? It is ~~magnificent.~~"

"That is the same thing, ~~I suppose,~~" said Newman. "Make yourself comfortable. Your coming to see me, I take it, is an act of friendship. You were not obliged to. Therefore, if anything around here amuses you, it will be all in a pleasant way. Laugh as loud as you please; I like to ~~see my visitors cheerful.~~ Only, I must make this request: that you explain the joke to me as soon as you can speak. I don't want to lose anything myself."

M. de Bellegarde ~~stared, with a~~ look of unresentful perplexity. He laid his hand on Newman's sleeve and seemed on the point of saying something, but he suddenly checked himself, leaned back in his chair, and puffed at his cigar. At last, however, breaking silence, "Certainly," he ~~said,~~ "my coming to see you is an act of friendship. Nevertheless, I was in a measure obliged to do so. My sister asked me to come, and a request from my sister is, for me, a law. I was near you, and I observed lights in what I supposed were your rooms. It was not a ceremonious hour for making a call, but I was not sorry to do something that would show I was not performing a mere ceremony."

"Well, here I am as large as life," said Newman, extending his legs.

Vivid ease

Superlative

a candour which
I find getting
the better of me,
you have interested
me without having
done me the honour,
I think, in the
least to try — by
having acted so
consistently in your
own interest: that,
I mean, of your
enlightened curiosity."⊙

"I don't know what you mean," the young man went on, "by giving me unlimited leave to laugh. Certainly I am a great laugher, and it is better to laugh too much than too little. But it is not in order that we may laugh together—or separately—that I have, I may say, sought your acquaintance. To speak with ~~almost impudent frankness, you interest me!"~~ All this was uttered by M. de Bellegarde with the ~~modulated smoothness~~ of the man of the world, and, in spite of his excellent English, of the Frenchman; but Newman, at the same time that he sat noting its ~~harmonious~~ flow, perceived that it was not mere mechanical urbanity. Decidedly, there was something in his visitor that he liked. M. de Bellegarde was a foreigner to his finger-tips, and if Newman had met him ~~on a Western prairie~~ he would have felt it proper to address him with a "How-d'ye-do, Mosseer?" ~~But~~ there was something in his physiognomy which seemed to ~~cast a sort of aerial bridge~~ over the impassable gulf produced by difference of race. He was ~~below the middle height,~~ and robust and agile in figure. Valentin de Bellegarde, Newman afterwards learned, had a mortal dread of ~~the~~ robustness ~~overtaking~~ the agility; he was afraid of growing stout; he was ~~too short,~~ as he said, to afford ~~a belly.~~ He rode and fenced and practised gymnastics with unremitting zeal, and if you greeted him with a "How ~~well~~ you are looking!" he started and turned pale. In your ~~well~~ he read a grosser monosyllable. He had a round head, high above the ears, a crop of hair at once dense and silky, a broad, low forehead, a short nose, of the ironical and inquiring rather than of the dogmatic or sensitive cast, and a moustache as delicate as that of a page in a romance. He resembled his sister not in feature, but in the ~~expression of his clear bright eye,~~ completely void of introspection, and in the ~~way he smiled.~~ The great point in his face was that it was intensely alive—frankly, ardently, gallantly alive. The look of it was like a bell, of which the handle might have been in the young man's soul: at a touch of the handle it rang with a loud silver sound. There was something in his ~~quick, light brown eye~~ which assured you that he was not economizing his consciousness. He was not living in a corner of it to spare the furniture of the rest. He was squarely encamped in the centre, and ~~he~~ was keeping open house. When he ~~smiled,~~ it was like the movement of a person who in emptying a cup turns it upside down: he gave you ~~the last drop of his jollity.~~ He inspired Newman with

- but in bare Arizona
- suspend a bold bridge of gilt wire
- but middling high
- to too short a story
- fresh
- fresh
- expansion of his fair eyes,
- as they were in his case
- quick expression
- flared into gaiety
- all the strength of the fine liquor
- Yet
- not subordinating the
- an important digression
- purity, or at least the quality, of his smile

something of the same kindness that our hero used to feel in his earlier years for those of his companions who could perform strange and clever tricks—make their joints crack in queer places or whistle at the back of their mouths.

"My sister told me," M. de Bellegarde continued, "that I ought to come and remove the impression that I had taken such great pains to produce upon you; the impression that I Did it strike you that I behaved very oddly the other day?"

"Rather so," said Newman.

"So my sister tells me." And M. de Bellegarde watched his host for a moment through his smoke-wreaths. "If that is the case, I think we had better let it stand. on the contrary, I wanted to produce a favourable impression. But if, after all, I made a fool of myself, it was the intention of Providence. I should injure myself by protesting too much, for I should seem to set up a claim for which, in the sequel of our acquaintance, I could by no means justify. Set me down as a with intervals of

"Oh, I guess you know what you are about," said Newman.

"When I am sane, I am very sane; that I admit," M. de Bellegarde answered. "But I didn't come here to talk about myself. I should like to ask you a few questions. You allow me?"

"Give me a specimen," said Newman.

"You live here all alone?"

"Absolutely. With whom should I live?"

"For the moment," said M. de Bellegarde, with a smile, "I am asking questions, not answering them. You have come to Paris for your pleasure?"

Newman was silent a while. Then, at last, "Every one asks me that!" he said with his "It sounds

was labouring under some temporary disorder

"I had never seen any one like you in real life," said Newman

I had no idea of putting you off by my eccentricity;

consistency

extraordinary energy"

shocking trifler

over

quite foolish — as if I were to get my pleasure, somehow, under a writ of extradition!"

almost pathetic plainness

"But at any rate ~~you had~~ a reason."

"Oh, ~~I came~~ for my pleasure!" said Newman. "Though ~~it is foolish, it is true!~~"

"And you're enjoying ~~it~~?"

~~Like any other good American, Newman thought it as well not to trouble to the foreigner. "Oh, so so," he answered.~~

M. de Bellegarde puffed his cigar again in silence. "For myself," he said at last, "I am entirely at your service. Anything I can do for you I shall be very happy to do. Call upon me at your convenience. Is there any one you desire to know—anything you wish to see? It is a pity you should not enjoy Paris."

"Oh, I do enjoy it!" said Newman, good-naturedly. "I'm much obliged to you."

"Honestly speaking," M. de Bellegarde went on, "there is something absurd to me in hearing myself make you these offers. They represent a great deal of good-will, but they represent little else. You are a successful man, and I am a ~~failure~~, and it's a turning of the tables to talk as if I could lend you a hand."

"In what way are you a failure?" asked Newman.

"Oh, I'm not a ~~tragical~~ failure [illegible] the young man ~~with a laugh~~. "I have not fallen from a height, and my fiasco has made no noise. You, evidently, ~~are a success~~. You have made a fortune, you have built up an edifice, you are a financial, commercial power, you can travel about the world until you have found a soft spot, and lie down in it with the consciousness of having earned your rest. Is not that true? Well, imagine the exact reverse of all that, and you have me. I have done nothing [illegible]"

"Why not?"

"It's a long story. Some day I will tell you. Meanwhile, I'm right, eh? You are a success? You have made ~~a fortune?~~ It's none of my business, but, in short, you are rich?"

Handwritten revisions:

- call it
- you've
- for being here"
- what you find?"
- it represents me as trying to reclaim a hopeless absentee, it describes well enough the logic of my conduct.
- Well, I'm keeping my head."
- fully
- fully
- raté—by which we mean a failure—
- to wring your heart,"
- returned
- at any rate, stand for accomplished facts.
- and I can never do anything."
- horrid
- beastly
- ore money than was ver made before by ne so young?

"That's another thing ~~that~~ it sounds foolish to say," said Newman. ~~[illegible]~~

~~[illegible] affirm," laughed M. de Bellegarde, "[illegible] your formula strikes me as an improvement. As a general thing, I confess, I don't like successful people, and I find clever men who have made great fortunes very offensive. They tread on my toes; they make me uncomfortable. [illegible] as soon as I saw you, I said to myself, 'Ah, there is a man with whom I shall get on. He has the good nature of success and none of the morgue; he has not our confoundedly irritable French vanity.' In short, I took a fancy to you.~~ We are very different, ~~[illegible]~~ I don't believe there is a subject on which we think or feel alike. But I rather think we shall get on, for there is such a thing, you know, as being too different to quarrel."

"Oh, I never quarrel," said Newman.

~~"Never? Sometimes it's a duty—or at least it's a pleasure. Oh, I [illegible] in my day!" and M. de Bellegarde's [illegible] smile assumed, at the memory of these incidents, an almost voluptuous intensity.~~

With the preamble embodied in ~~his share of the foregoing fragment of dialogue,~~ he paid our hero a long visit; as the two men sat with their heels on Newman's glowing hearth, they heard the small hours of the morning striking larger from a far-off belfry. Valentin de Bellegarde was, by his own confession, at all times a great chatterer, and on this occasion ~~he was evidently in a particularly loquacious mood.~~ It was a tradition of his race that people of its blood always conferred a favour by their ~~smiles,~~ and as his ~~enthusiasms were~~ as rare as his ~~civility was constant,~~ he had a double reason for not suspecting that his friendship could ever be importunate. Moreover, the flower of an ancient stem as he was, tradition (since I have used the word) had in his temperament nothing of ~~disagreeable rigidity.~~ It was

And do you think that's all I am?"

"No, I think you're original—that's why I'm here.

you and I, as products, I'm sure;

judge

"You mean you just shoot? Well, I notify you that till I'm shot," his visitor declared, "I shall have had a greater sense of safety with you than I have perhaps ever known in any relation of my life. And as a sense of danger is clearly a thing impossible to you, we shall therefore be all right."

rather shortly.

these remarks,

the habit of promptness of word and tone was upon him almost as a fever.

attentions

real confidence was

Surface was bright

outward rigour.

muffled in sociability and urbanity, as an old dowager in her laces and strings of pearls. Valentin was what is called in France a *gentilhomme*, of the purest source, and his rule of life, so far as it was definite, was to play the part of a *gentilhomme*. This, it seemed to him, was enough to occupy comfortably a young man of ordinary good parts. But all that he was he was by instinct and not by theory, and the amiability of his character was so great that certain of the aristocratic virtues, which in some aspects seem rather brittle and trenchant, acquired in his application of them an extreme geniality. In his younger years he had been suspected of low tastes, and his mother had greatly feared he would make a slip in the mud of the highway and bespatter the family shield. He had been treated, therefore, to more than his share of schooling and drilling, but his instructors had not succeeded in mounting him upon stilts. They could not spoil his safe spontaneity, and he remained the least cautious and the most lucky of young nobles. He had been tied with so short a rope in his youth that he had now a mortal grudge against family discipline. He had been known to say, within the limits of the family, that, light-headed as he was, the honour of the name was safer in his hands than in those of some of its other members, and that if a day ever came to try it, they should see. His talk was an odd mixture of almost boyish garrulity and of the reserve and discretion of the man of the world, and he seemed to Newman, as afterwards young members of the Latin races often seemed to him, now amusingly juvenile and now appallingly mature. In America, Newman reflected, lads of twenty-five and thirty have old heads and young hearts, or at least young morals; here they have young heads and very aged hearts, morals the most grizzled and wrinkled.

"What I envy you is your liberty," observed M. de Bellegarde, "your wide range, your freedom to come and go, your not having a lot of people, who take them-

"Isn't it then

your

selves awfully seriously, expecting something of you. I live," he added, with a sigh, "beneath the eyes of my admirable mother."

asked.

"It is your own fault; what is to hinder you ranging?" said Newman.

question

"There is a delightful simplicity in that remark! Everything is to hinder me. To begin with, I have not a penny."

in life

it.

"I had not a penny when I began to range."

"Ah, but your poverty was your capital. Being an American, it was impossible you should remain what you were born, and being born poor—do I understand it?—it was therefore inevitable that you should become rich. You were in a position that makes one's mouth water; you looked round you and saw a world full of things you had only to step up to and take hold of. When I was twenty, I look around me and saw a world with everything ticketed 'Hands off!' and the deuce of it was that the ticket seemed meant only for me. I couldn't go into business, I couldn't make money, because I was a Bellegarde. I couldn't go into politics, because I was a Bellegarde—the Bellegardes don't recognise the Bonapartes. I couldn't go into literature, because I was a dunce. I couldn't marry a rich girl, because no Bellegarde had ever married a *roturière*, and it was not proper that I should begin. We shall have to come to it yet. Marriageable heiresses, *de notre bord*, are not to be had for nothing; it must be name for name, and fortune for fortune. The only thing I could do was to go and fight for the Pope. That I did, punctiliously, and received an apostolic flesh-wound at Castelfidardo. It did neither the Holy Father nor me any good, that I could see. Rome was doubtless a very amusing place in the days of Caligula, but it has sadly fallen off since. I passed three years in the Castle of St. Angelo, and then came back to secular life."

however — you'll see.

make.

Heliogabalus,

was immured for three years, like some of the choicest scoundrels in history,

I

"So you have no profession—you do nothing?" said Newman.

"I do nothing! I am supposed to amuse myself, and, to tell the truth, I have amused myself. One can, if one knows how. But you can't keep it up for ever. I am good for another five years, perhaps, but I foresee that after that I shall lose my appetite. Then what shall I do? I think I shall turn monk. Seriously, I think I shall tie a rope round my waist and go into a monastery. It was an old custom, and the old customs were very good. People understood life quite as well as we do. They kept the pot boiling till it cracked, and then they put it on the shelf altogether."

"Are you very religious?" asked Newman, in a tone which gave the inquiry a grotesque effect.

M. de Bellegarde evidently appreciated the comical element in the question, but he looked at Newman a moment with extreme soberness. "I am a very good Catholic. I respect the Church. I adore the blessed Virgin. I fear the Devil."

"Well, then," said Newman, "you are very well fixed. You have got pleasure in the present and religion in the future; what do you complain of?"

"It's a part of one's pleasure to complain. There is something in your own circumstances that irritates me. You are the first man I have ever envied. It's singular, but so it is. I have known many men who, besides any factitious advantages that I may possess, had money and brains into the bargain; but somehow they have never disturbed my good humour. But you have got something that I should have liked to have. It is not money, it is not even brains—though no doubt yours are excellent. It is not your six feet of height, though I should have rather liked to be a couple of inches taller. It's a sort of air you have of being thoroughly at home in the world. When I was a boy, my father told me that it was by such an air as that that people recognised a Bellegarde.

you've no active interest? —
absolutely
absolutely
to pass the time,
three or four years more
at the bottom,
Spring a leak and sink. I shan't float any more; I shall go straight to the bottom.
"Do you attend church regularly?"
this
quaint
Due Decorum.
Cherish the Faith.
Father of Lies."
found myself envying.
inward peace.
impertubably — being indestructibly (that's the thing!) —
Superfluous

108 THE AMERICAN. VII.

He called my attention to it. He didn't advise me to cultivate it; he said that as we grew up it always came of itself. I supposed it had come to me, because I think I have always had the feeling. My place in life was made for me, and it seemed easy to occupy it. But you who, as I understand it, have made your own place, you who, as you told us the other day, have manufactured wash-tubs, you strike me, somehow, as a man who stands at his ease, who looks at things from a height. I fancy you going about the world like a man travelling on a railroad in which he owns a large amount of stock. You make me feel as if I had missed something. What is it?"

"It is the proud consciousness of honest toil—of having manufactured a few wash-tubs," said Newman, at once jocose and serious.

"Oh no; I have seen men who had done even more, men who had made not only wash-tubs, but soap—strong-smelling yellow soap, in great bars; and they never made me the least uncomfortable."

"Then it's the privilege of being an American citizen," said Newman. "That sets a man up."

"Possibly," rejoined M. de Bellegarde. "But I am forced to say that I have seen a great many American citizens who didn't seem at all set up or in the least like large stockholders. I never envied them. I rather think the thing is an accomplishment of your own."

"Oh, come," said Newman, "you will make me proud!"

"No, I shall not. You have nothing to do with pride, or with humility—that is a part of this easy manner of yours. People are proud only when they have something to lose, and humble when they have something to gain."

"I don't know what I have to lose," said Newman, "but I certainly have something to gain."

"What is it?" asked his visitor.

His visitor looked at him hard. "What sort of situation?"

in a fashion of your own,

made and sold articles of vulgar household use—

seem to see

gone beyond washtubs,

produced something yourself that somebody has been willing to pay you for—since that's the definite measure. Since you speak of my washtubs—which were lovely—isn't it just they and their loveliness that make up my good conscience?"

mountains of

they've left me perfectly cold."

right

some diabolical secret

persuade me against my humility."

humility any more than with swagger: that's just the essence of your confounded coolness.

Swagger

may

can quite see a situation in which I should have

show their delicacy only

Newman hesitated. "I will tell you when I know you better."

During the next three weeks several times, and without formally swearing an eternal friendship, To Newman Bellegarde was the Frenchman, the Frenchman of tradition and romance, so far as our hero was acquainted with these mystic Gallant, expansive, amusing, more pleased himself with the effect he produced than those (even when they were pleased) for whom he produced it; a master of all the distinctively social virtues and a votary of all agreeable sensations; a devotee of something mysterious and sacred to which he occasionally alluded in terms more ecstatic even than those in which he spoke of the last pretty woman, and which was simply the beautiful though somewhat superannuated image of he was irresistibly entertaining and enlivening, and he formed a character to which Newman was as capable of doing justice when he had once been placed in contact with it, as he was unlikely, in musing upon the possible of our human mentally to have foreshadowed it.

Valentin de Bellegarde lived in the basement of an old

("Oh, you'll soon know me by heart!" the young man sighed as he departed.

they met again

fell, for their course of life, instinctively into step together.

typical, ideal

fields.

quite duly

the

personal Honour:

combinations

mixture,

No two parties to an alliance could have come to it from a wider separation, but it was what each brought out of the queer dim distance that formed the odd attraction for the other.

queer dim distance

house in the Rue d'Anjou St. Honoré, and his small apartments lay between the court of the house and an old garden which spread itself behind it—one of those large, sunless, humid gardens into which you look unexpectingly in Paris from back windows, wondering how among the grudging habitations they find their space. When Newman returned Bellegarde's visit, he hinted that *his* lodging was at least as much a laughing matter as his own. But its oddities were of a different cast from those of our hero's gilded saloons on the Boulevard Haussmann: the place was low, dusky, contracted, and crowded with curious bric-à-brac. Bellegarde, penniless patrician ~~as he was~~, was an insatiable collector, and his walls were covered with rusty arms and ancient panels and platters, his doorways draped in faded tapestries, his floors muffled in the skins of beasts. Here and there was one of those uncomfortable tributes to elegance in which the upholsterer's art, in France, is so prolific; a curtained recess with a sheet of looking-glass ~~in which, among the shadows, you could see nothing;~~ a divan on which, for its festoons and furbelows, you could ~~not sit;~~ a fireplace draped, flounced, ~~and~~ frilled to the complete exclusion of fire. The young man's possessions were in picturesque disorder, and his apartment ~~was~~ pervaded by the odour of cigars, mingled ~~with perfumes more inscrutable.~~ Newman thought it a damp, gloomy place to live in, and was puzzled by the ~~obstructive and fragmentary character~~ of the furniture.

Bellegarde, ~~according to the custom~~ of his country, ~~talked very generously about himself~~, and unveiled the ~~mysteries of his private history with an unsparing hand.~~ Inevitably, he had a vast deal to say about women, and he used frequently to indulge in sentimental and ironical apostrophes to these authors of his joys and woes. "Oh, the women, the women, and the things they have made me do!" he would exclaim with a ~~lustrous eye~~. "*C'est égal*, of all the follies and stupidities I have committed

though he might be,

as dark as a haunted pool;

no more sit than on a dowager's lap;

romantic incoherence

like most men,

hid none of his lights under a bushel and made little of a secret of the more interesting passages of his personal history

wealth of reference

by the same analogy;

for inhalation with other dim ghosts of past presences

for them I would not have missed one!" On this subject Newman maintained an habitual reserve; to expatiate largely upon it had always seemed to him a proceeding vaguely analogous to the cooing of pigeons and the chatterings of monkeys, and even inconsistent with a fully-developed human character. But Bellegarde's confidences greatly amused him, and rarely displeased him, for the generous young Frenchman was not a cynic. "I really think," he had once said, "that I am not more depraved than most of my contemporaries. They are tolerably depraved, my contemporaries!" He said wonderfully pretty things about his female friends, and, numerous and various as they had been, declared that, on the whole, there was more good in them than harm. "But you are not to take that as advice," he added. "As an authority I am very untrustworthy. I'm prejudiced in their favour; I'm an idealist!" Newman listened to him with his impartial smile, and was glad, for his own sake, that he had fine feelings; but he mentally repudiated the idea of a Frenchman having discovered any merit in the amiable sex which he himself did not suspect. M. de Bellegarde, however, did not confine his conversation to the autobiographical channel; he questioned our hero largely as to the events of his own life, and Newman told him some better stories than any that Bellegarde carried in his budget. He narrated his career, in fact, from the beginning, through all its variations, and whenever his companion's credulity, or his habits of gentility, appeared to protest, it amused him to heighten the colour of the episode. Newman had sat with Western humorists in knots, round cast-iron stoves, and seen "tall" stories grow taller without toppling over, and his own imagination had learned the trick of piling up consistent wonders. Bellegarde's regular attitude at last became that of laughing self-defence; to maintain his reputation as an all-knowing Frenchman, he doubted of everything, wholesale. The result of this was that Newman found

There isn't one

make it shine in the direct light of one's own experience

compliment

garden of his past friends appeared to have bloomed with rare flowers, amid which memory was as light as a summer breeze.

must be misleading

a sentimental — in other words a donkey!

an uncommitted

Frenchman's

He

building straight and high

Bellegarde, however, was not merely anecdotic and indiscreet; he welcomed every light on our hero's own life, and so far as his revelations might startle and waylay Newman could cap them as from the long habit of capping.

mark the difference of his type from that of the occasionally witless, he cultivated the wit of never being caught in credulity it impossible to convince him of certain time-honoured verities.

"But the details don't matter," said M. de Bellegarde. "You have evidently had some surprising adventures; you have seen some strange sides of life, you have revolved to and fro over a whole continent as I walk up and down the Boulevard. You are a man of the world with a vengeance! You have spent some deadly dull hours, and you have done some extremely disagreeable things: you have shovelled sand, as a boy, for supper, and you have eaten roast dog in a gold-digger's camp. You have stood casting up figures for ten hours at a time, and you have sat through Methodist sermons for the sake of looking at a pretty girl in another pew. All that is rather stiff, as we say. But at any rate you have done something and you are something; you have used your will and you have made your fortune. You have not stupefied yourself with debauchery, and you have not mortgaged your fortune to social conveniences. You take things easily, and you have fewer prejudices even than I, who pretend to have none, but who in reality have three or four. Happy man, you are strong and you are free. But what the deuce," demanded the young man in conclusion, "do you propose to do with such advantages? Really to use them you need a better world than this. There is nothing worth your while here."

"Oh, I think there is something," said Newman.

"What is it?"

"Well," murmured Newman, "I will tell you some other time!"

In this way our hero delayed from day to day broaching a subject which he had very much at heart. Meanwhile, however, he was growing practically familiar with it; in other words, he had called again, three times, on Madame de Cintré. On only two of these occasions had he found her at home, and on each of them she had other visitors. Her visitors were numerous and extremely loquacious, and they exacted much of their hostess's attention. She found time, however, to bestow a little of it on Newman, in an occasional vague smile, the very vagueness of which pleased him, allowing him as it did to fill it out mentally, both at the time and afterwards, with such meanings as most pleased him. He sat by without speaking, looking at the entrances and exits, the greetings and chatterings, of Madame de Cintré's visitors. He felt as if he were at the play, and as if his own speaking would be an interruption; sometimes he wished he had a book to follow the dialogue; he half expected to see a woman in a white cap and pink ribbons come and offer him one for two francs. Some of the ladies looked at him very hard—or very soft, as you please; others seemed profoundly unconscious of his presence. The men only looked at Madame de Cintré. This was inevitable; for whether one called her beautiful or not, she entirely occupied and filled one's vision, just as an agreeable sound fills one's ear. Newman had but twenty distinct words with her, but he carried away an impression to which solemn promises could not have given a higher value. She was part of the play that he was seeing acted, quite as much as her companions; but how she filled the stage, and how much better she did it! Whether she rose or seated herself; whether she went with her departing friends to the door and lifted up the heavy curtain as they passed out, and stood an instant looking after them and giving them the last nod; or whether she leaned back in her chair with her arms crossed and her eyes resting, listening and smiling; she gave Newman the feeling that he should like to have her always before him, moving slowly to and fro along the whole scale of expressive hospitality. If it might be to him, it would be well; if it might be for him, it would be still better! She was so tall and yet so light, so active and yet so still, so elegant and yet so simple, so frank and yet so mysterious! It was the mystery—it

It was this unknown quantity that figured for him as a mystery; it

as yet unguessed even by herself and that it was kept for him to bring out.

he might feel

was what she was off the stage, as it were, that interested Newman most of all. He could not have told you what warrant he had for talking about mysteries; if it had been his habit to express himself in poetic figures he might have said that in observing Madame de Cintré he seemed to see the vague circle which sometimes accompanies the partly-filled disc of the moon. It was not that she was reserved; on the contrary, she was as frank as flowing water. But he was sure she had qualities which she herself did not suspect.

He had abstained for several reasons from saying some of these things to Bellegarde. One reason was that before proceeding to any act he was always circumspect, conjectural, contemplative; he had little eagerness, as became a man who felt that whenever he really began to move he walked with long steps. And then it simply pleased him, not to speak; it occupied him; it excited him. But one day Bellegarde had been dining with him at a restaurant, and they had sat long over their dinner. On rising from it, Bellegarde proposed that, to help them through the rest of the evening, they should go and see Madame Dandelard. Madame Dandelard was a little Italian lady who had married a Frenchman who proved to be a rake and a brute and the torment of her life. Her husband had spent all her money, and then, lacking the means of obtaining more expensive pleasures, had taken, in his dullest hours, to beating her. She had a blue spot somewhere which she showed to several persons, including Bellegarde. She had obtained a separation from her husband, collected the scraps of her fortune (they were very meagre), and come to live in Paris, where she was staying at a *hôtel garni*. She was always looking for an apartment, and visiting inquiringly those of other people. She was very pretty, very childlike, and she made very extraordinary remarks. Bellegarde had made her acquaintance, and the source of his interest in her was, according to his own declaration, a curiosity as to what

---

of

effaced, and still less that she was "sly"; distinct as the big figure on a banknote and of as straightforward a profession.

him

her

her brother.

Valentin – as Newman conveniently sounded the name –

further means for alien

and

him, not to give his case as he would have said free, naturally away.

the young man

to

On the Boulevard, and their sociability such that

for alien joys.

Valentin

an anxious

enjoyed

with a hundred earnest questions,

more intimate hours,

an

which

legal

the said Valentin

would become of her. "She is poor, she is pretty, and she is silly," he said; "it seems to me she can go only one way. It's a pity, but it can't be helped. I give her six months. She has nothing to fear from me, but I am watching the process. I am curious to see just how things will go. Yes, I know what you are going to say; this horrible Paris hardens one's heart. But it quickens one's wits, and it ends by teaching one a refinement of observation. To see this little woman's little drama play itself out, now, is for me an intellectual pleasure."

"If she is going to throw herself away," Newman had said, "you ought to stop her."

"Stop her? How stop her?"

"Talk to her; give her some good advice."

Bellegarde laughed. "Heaven deliver us both! Imagine the situation! Go and advise her yourself."

It was after this that Newman had gone with Bellegarde to see Madame Dandelard. When they came away Bellegarde reproached his companion. "Where was your famous advice? I didn't hear a word of it."

"Oh, I give it up," said Newman, simply.

"Then you are as bad as I!" said Bellegarde.

"No, because I don't take an 'intellectual pleasure' in her prospective adventures. I don't in the least want to see her going down hill. I had rather look the other way. But why," he asked, in a moment, "don't you get your sister to go and see her?"

Bellegarde stared. "Go and see Madame Dandelard—my sister?"

"She might talk to her to very good purpose."

Bellegarde shook his head with sudden gravity. "My sister can't see that sort of person. Madame Dandelard is nothing at all; they would never meet."

"I should think," said Newman, "that your sister might see whom she pleased." And he privately resolved that, after he knew her a little better, he would ask Madame de Cintré to go and talk to the foolish little Italian lady.

After his dinner with Bellegarde, on the occasion I have mentioned, he demurred to his companion's proposal that they should go again and listen to Madame Dandelard describe her sorrows and her bruises. "I have something better in mind, [illegible] come home with me and finish the evening before my fire."

Bellegarde always welcomed the prospect of a long stretch of conversation, and before long the two men sat watching the great blaze which scattered its scintillations over the high adornments of Newman's ballroom.

CHAPTER VIII.

"Tell me something about your sister," Newman began, abruptly.

Bellegarde turned and gave him a quick look. "Now that I think of it, you have never yet asked me a question about her."

"I know that very well."

"If it is because you don't trust me, you are very right," said Bellegarde. "I can't talk of her rationally. I admire her too much."

"Talk of her as you can," rejoined Newman. "Let yourself go."

"Well, we are very good friends; [illegible] such a brother and sister as have not been seen since Orestes and Electra. You have seen her [illegible] light, imposing, and gentle, half a *grande dame* and half an angel; a mixture of pride and humility, of the eagle and the dove. She looks like a statue which had failed as stone, resigned itself to its grave defects, and come to life as flesh and blood, to wear white capes and long trains. All I can say is that she really possesses every merit that ~~her face, her glance, her smile, the tone of her voice,~~ lead you to expect; ~~it is saying a great deal.~~ As a general thing, when a woman ~~seems very charming,~~ [blacked out] But in proportion as ~~Claire seems charming~~ you may fold your arms and let yourself float with the current; you are safe. She is so ~~good~~! I have never seen a woman half so ~~perfect or so complete~~. ~~She has everything;~~ that is all I can say about her. There!" ~~Bellegarde~~ concluded: "I told you I should ~~rhapsodise~~."

Newman ~~was silent a while, as if he were turning over his companion's words. "She is very good, eh?" he repeated at last.~~

"~~Divinely~~ good!"

"~~Kind, charitable, gentle, generous?~~"

"~~Generosity itself; kindness double-distilled!~~"

"~~Is she clever?~~"

"~~She is the most intelligent woman I know.~~ Try her, ~~some day,~~ with something ~~difficult~~, and you will see."

"~~Is she~~ fond of admiration?"

"~~Parbleu!" cried Bellegarde;~~ "what woman is not?"

"~~Ah, when they are too fond of admiration~~ they commit all kinds of follies to get it."

"I did not say she was too fond!" ~~Bellegarde~~ exclaimed. "Heaven forbid I should say anything so idiotic. She is not *too* anything. If I were to say she was ugly, I should not mean she was too ugly. She is fond of pleasing, and if you are pleased she is ~~grateful~~. If you are not pleased she lets it pass and thinks the worse neither of you nor of herself. I imagine, though, she hopes the saints in heaven are, for I am sure she is incapable of trying to please by any means of which they would disapprove."

~~"Is she grave or gay?" asked Newman.~~

~~"She is both, not alternately, for she is always the~~

the face she has, the eyes she has, the smile she has, the tone of voice she has, the way she has

and isn't it saying quite enough?

soft

you take Claire for right

how much

bore you."

"She'd have invented goodness if it didn't exist."

you think so yourself

Valentin

"Pardieu!" cried Valentin. "Should be no sister of mine if she weren't."

leaves it so.

honest and so gentille.

You'll only never imagine a person as right as she is.

charming. She has every blessed thing a man wants, and more, that

seems from different as right as that, she's altogether wrong — you've only to look out.

Valentin

"Well, then they're too fond of it," Newman heard himself hypocritically temporize.

"Oh, how can I try her?" sighed Newman with a lapse. But he picked himself up. "Is she

uttered no assurance that he was not bored; he only said after a little: "She's remarkably good, eh?"

"It seems to me," Newman remarked, "that you'd have invented her — ! But it's all right," he added — "I'd have invented you! Is she clever?" he then asked.

same. There is gravity in her gaiety, and gaiety in her gravity. But there is no reason why she should be particularly gay."

"Is she unhappy?"

"I won't say that, for unhappiness is according as one takes things, and Claire takes them according to some receipt communicated to her by the Blessed Virgin in a vision. To be unhappy is to be disagreeable, which, for her, is out of the question. So she has arranged her circumstances so as to be happy in them."

"She is a philosopher," said Newman.

"No, she is simply a very nice woman."

"Her circumstances, at any rate, have been disagreeable?"

Bellegarde hesitated a moment—a thing he very rarely did. "Oh, my dear fellow, if I go into the history of my family I shall give you more than you bargain for."

"No, on the contrary, I bargain for that," said Newman.

"We shall have to appoint a special séance, then, beginning early. Suffice it for the present that Claire has not slept on roses. She made, at eighteen, a marriage that was expected to be brilliant, but that turned out like a lamp that goes out; all smoke and bad smell. M. de Cintré was sixty years old, and an odious old gentleman. He lived, however, but a short time, and after his death his family pounced upon his money, brought a lawsuit against his widow, and pushed things very hard. Their case was a good one, for M. de Cintré, who had been trustee for some of his relatives, appeared to have been guilty of some very irregular practices. In the course of the suit some revelations were made as to his private history which my sister found so displeasing that she ceased to defend herself and washed her hands of the property. This required some pluck, for she was between two fires, her husband's family opposing her and her own family forcing her. My mother and my brother wished

"Is she happy then?" Newman presently pursued.

"Oh, oh, oh! That's much to ask."

"Do you mean for me—?"

"I mean for her. What should she be happy about?"

Newman wondered. "Then she has troubles?"

"My dear man, she has what we all have—even you strange to say. She has a history."

"That's just what I want to hear," said Newman.

Valentin hesitated—an embarrassment rare with him. "Then we shall have to appoint a special séance with music, refreshments and a turn outside between the acts.

my sister's situation has been far from folichonne.

fifty-five years old and pas du tout aimable.

turned all to

three or four years,

denouncing.

all her interests.

strength of conviction,

little to her taste

her to cleave to what they regarded as her rights. But she resisted firmly, and at last bought her freedom—obtained my mother's assent to dropping the suit at the price of a promise."

"What was the promise?"

"To do anything else for the next ten years, that was asked of her—anything, that is, but marry."

"She had disliked her husband very much?"

"No one knows how much!"

"The marriage had been made in your horrible French way," Newman continued, made by the two families, without her having any voice?"

"It was a chapter for a novel. She saw M. de Cintré for the first time a month before the wedding, after everything, to the minutest detail, had been arranged. She turned white when she looked at him, and white she remained till her wedding-day. The evening before the ceremony she swooned away, and she spent the whole night in sobs. My mother sat holding her two hands, and my brother walked up and down the room. I declared it was revolting, and told my sister publicly that if she would refuse downright, I would stand by her. I was told to go about my business, and she became Comtesse de Cintré."

"Your brother," said Newman, reflectively, "must be a very nice young man."

"He is very nice, though he is not young. He is upwards of fifty; fifteen years my senior. He has been a father to my sister and me. He is a very remarkable man; he has the best manners in France. He is extremely clever; indeed he is very learned. He is writing a history of The Princesses of France who never Married." This was said by Bellegarde with extreme gravity, looking straight at Newman, and with an eye that betokened no mental reservation; or that at least almost betokened none.

Newman perhaps discovered there what little there

her compromising

whatever,

might be asked of her—

first act for a melodrama.

and

—"by

—I shall never forget her face—

her nerves completely gave way;

really hold out

now

very

against all comers.

sent

type apart;

Valentin

in a tone

full of accomplishments.

our friend

Unmarried Princesses of the Maison de France."

"(Then you want some one to come right in and break it up?"

"Hein?" said Valentin.

"Oh which Newman, after an instant, put the matter another way. "Well, I'm glad I'm free not to like him!"

could struggle along without

was, for he presently said: "You ~~don't like~~ your brother."

"I beg your pardon," ~~said Bellegarde, ceremoniously; "well-bred people always love their brothers."~~

~~"Well, I don't love him, then!" Newman answered.~~

"Wait till you know him!" ~~rejoined Bellegarde,~~ and this time he smiled.

"Is your mother also ~~very remarkable?"~~ ~~Newman~~ asked after a pause.

"For my mother," ~~said Bellegarde,~~ now with intense gravity, "I have the highest admiration. She is a very extraordinary woman. You cannot approach her without perceiving it."

"She is the daughter, I believe, of an English nobleman."

"Of ~~the Earl of St. Dunstan's.~~"

~~"Is the Earl of St. Dunstan's a very old family?"~~

"~~So so; the~~ sixteenth century. It is on my father's side that we go back—back, back, back. The family antiquaries themselves lose breath. At last they stop, panting and fanning themselves, somewhere in the ninth century, under Charlemagne. That is where we begin."

"There is no mistake about it?" ~~said~~ Newman.

"I'm sure I hope not. We have been mistaken at least for several centuries."

"And you have always married into ~~old families?~~"

"As a rule; though in so long a stretch of time there have been some exceptions. Three or four Bellegardes, in the seventeenth and eighteenth centuries, took wives out of the *bourgeoisie*—~~married~~ lawyers' daughters."

"A lawyer's daughter; ~~that's very bad, is it?" asked Newman.~~

the young man said,

"And was he very grand?"

"Not as grand as we. They date only from the

pairing with

more convenient?

"A condescension. But

the young man still as gravely pro-tested "A house like ours is inevitably our."

Valentin returned)

demanded

Lord St. Dunstan's

what do you call them? "ancient houses?"

that's a comedown? Newman went on

"~~Horrible~~! one of us, in the Middle Ages, did better: he married a beggar-maid, like King Cophetua. That was really ~~better~~; it was like ~~marrying~~ a bird or a monkey; one didn't have to think about her family at all. Our women have always done well; they have never even gone into the *petite noblesse.* There is, I believe, not a case on record of a misalliance among the ~~women~~."

Newman turned this over a while, and then at last ~~he said~~: "You offered, the first time you came to see me, to render me any service you could. I told you ~~that some time~~ I would mention something you might do. Do you remember?"

"Remember? I ~~have~~ been counting the hours."

"Very well; here's your chance. Do what you can to make your sister think well of me."

~~Bellegarde stared, with a smile.~~ "Why, I'm sure she thinks as well of you as possible. already."

"An opinion founded on seeing me three or four times. That is putting me off with very little. I want something more. I ~~have~~ been thinking of it a good deal, and at last I have decided to tell you. I should like very much to marry Madame de Cintré."

~~Bellegarde~~ had been looking at him with quickened expectancy and with the smile with which he had greeted ~~Newman's~~ allusion to ~~his~~ promised request. At this last announcement he ~~continued to gaze; but his smile went through~~ two or three curious phases. It felt, apparently, ~~a momentary~~ impulse to ~~broaden~~; but this it immediately checked. Then it remained for some instants taking counsel with ~~itself~~, at the end of which it decreed a retreat. It slowly effaced itself and left a ~~look of seriousness~~ modified by the desire not to be rude. Extreme surprise had come into ~~the Count Valentin's~~ face; but he had reflected that it would be uncivil to leave it there. And yet what the deuce was he to do with it? He got up, in his agitation, and stood before the chimney-piece, still looking at ~~Newman~~. He was a longer time thinking what to say than one would have expected.

"If you can't render me the service I ask," said Newman, "~~say it out~~!"

"Let me hear it again, distinctly," ~~said Bellegarde~~.

ces dames

some time

The young man had a strange bright stare

his

the

Valentin

kept his eyes on him but this revision went through

let itself go further

sobriety

the service you ask

the danger of hilarity

Don't be afraid to tell me ~~I~~ — I'll be hanged if I could — for I'll get on without you!

at his host

M. de Bellegarde

"It's very important, you know, I shall plead your cause with my sister because you want—you want to marry her? That's it, eh?"

"Oh, I don't say plead my cause, exactly; I shall try and do that myself. But say a good word for me, now and then—let her know that you think well of me."

At this Bellegarde gave a little light laugh.

"What I want chiefly, after all," Newman went on, "is just to let you know what I have in mind. I suppose that is what you expect, isn't it? I want to do what is customary over here. If there is anything particular to be done, let me know, and I will do it. I wouldn't for the world approach Madame de Cintré without all the proper forms. If I ought to go and tell your mother, why, I will go and tell her. I will go and tell your brother, even. I will go and tell any one you please. As I don't know any one else. I begin by telling you. But that, if it is a social obligation, is a pleasure as well."

"Yes, I see—I see," said Bellegarde, lightly stroking his chin. "You have a very right feeling about it, but I'm glad you have begun with me." He paused, hesitated, and then turned away and walked slowly the length of the room. Newman got up and stood leaning against the mantel-shelf, with his hands in his pockets, watching Bellegarde's promenade. The young Frenchman came back and stopped in front of him. "I give it up," he said; "I will not pretend I am not surprised. I am—hugely! *Ouf!* It's a relief."

"That sort of news is always a surprise," said Newman. "No matter what you have done, people are never prepared. But if you are so surprised, I hope at least you are pleased."

"Come!" said Bellegarde. "I am going to be tremendously frank. I don't know whether I am pleased or horrified."

"If you are pleased, I shall be glad," said Newman, "and I shall be encouraged. If you are horrified, I

This was visibly, for the young man, a droll simplification. "... I shall have first, my dear fellow, to know myself!" But Newman pursued unheeding. "What I want chiefly, after all,

Valentin went on. "I'm to

at least what you take me for."

make you aware of

all expect making you formally aware

always to do over here what's customary.

I'll make it right.

save by schedule

Valentin

the young man broke out

let you have it. I don't know

impressed I hope at least you're impressed favourably

speaking

I'd go in to her on all-fours if that's what's required. all-fours

— well impressed.

his friend's evolution. This personage

speak to your mother first. Why, I'll speak to your brother, I'll speak to the porter in his lodge, to any one you like ...

Whether it lays me flat or makes me soar." "Well, if it corners you too much," said Newman, "I'm afraid you've got to stay there; for I assure you I mean, myself, to fight it out in the open." "My dear man, Samson was in the open when he pulled down the temple, but there wasn't much left of any one else." To which Valentin added:

shall be sorry, but I shall not be discouraged. You must make the best of it."

"That is quite right; that is your only possible attitude. You are perfectly serious?"

"Am I a Frenchman, that I should not be?" asked Newman. "But why is it, by the by, that you should be horrified?"

Bellegarde raised his hand to the back of his head and rubbed his hair quickly up and down, thrusting out the tip of his tongue as he did so. "Why, you are not noble, for instance," he said.

"The devil I am not!" exclaimed Newman.

"Oh," said Bellegarde, a little more seriously, "I did not know you had a title."

"A title? What do you mean by a title?" asked Newman. "A count, a duke, a marquis? I don't know anything about that, I don't know who is and who is not. But I say I am noble. I don't exactly know what you mean by it, but it's a fine word and a fine idea; I put in a claim to it."

"But what have you to show, my dear fellow; what proofs?"

"Anything you please! But you don't suppose I am going to undertake to prove that I am noble? It is for you to prove the contrary."

"That's easily done. You have manufactured wash-tubs."

Newman stared a moment. "Therefore I am not noble? I don't see it. Tell me something I have *not* done — something I cannot do."

"You cannot marry a woman like Madame de Cintré for the asking."

"I believe you mean," said Newman, slowly, "that I am not good enough."

"Brutally speaking — yes!"

Bellegarde had hesitated a moment, and while he hesitated Newman's attentive glance had grown somewhat

Newman asked.

a futile

M. de Bellegarde

— come to talk — that you are prostrated?

exclaimed

were noble.

his friend

"Well, for instance, you're not as we call it, if I'm not mistaken, 'born.'"

"Ah, that's your little local matter." Valentin just hesitated. "But aren't we all — that my admirable sister — particular — our little local matters?"

Newman met his eyes with a long hard look — exhaling at last however a sigh. "Is it a question of too mean that I must claim to be noble? What sort of swagger is that? — pretensions that is to effectively existing — Only it isn't your own ground, the very highest, to make it seems to me for you to make to them; it's for you honestly to invalidate them — in other words, the burden of disproof."

Valentin's fine smile suffered a further strain. "Haven't you manufactured and placed in the market certain washtubs?"

"With great temporary success. But it isn't a question of my achievements — it's a question of my failures. You might catch me."

continue from 123.

said our friend, "one or two are there of those. Only then, you know," he added, "I should have the right to ask you about yours."

"Oh, ours have partaken of our general brilliancy. They haven't at any rate prevented the great thing."

"And what do you call the great thing?"

"Well," Valentin smiled, "our being interesting."

Newman considered. "To yourselves?"

"To the world. That has been our value — that we've had the world's attention. We've felt to be worth it."

"Oh," said Newman, "if it's but a question of what you're worth —!" He hung fire an instant, and then: "Should you like to know what I am?" he demanded.

He held his companion by his pause, and his words prolonged a little the situation.

~~sage.~~ In ~~answer to~~ recognition of these last words ~~he~~ Newman for a moment said nothing. He ~~simply blushed a little.~~ only coloured as with a flush of hope. Then he raised his eyes to the ceiling and stood looking at one of the rosy cherubs ~~that were~~ painted ~~u~~pon it. "Of course I don't expect to marry any woman for the asking," he ~~said at last;~~ observed; "I expect first to make myself acceptable to her. She must like me, to begin with. But ~~that I am not good enough to make a trial is rather a surprise."~~ what I feel is I have, she must, from the moment she knows me as I want."

~~Bellegarde wore a look of mingled perplexity, sympathy, and amusement. "You should not hesitate, then, to go up to-morrow and ask a duchess to marry you!"~~

~~"Not if I thought she would suit me. But I am very fastidious; she might not at all."~~

~~Bellegarde's amusement began to prevail. "And you should be surprised if she refused you?"~~

~~Newman hesitated a moment. "It sounds conceited to say Yes, but, nevertheless, I think I should. For I should make a very handsome offer."~~

~~"What would it be?"~~

~~"Everything she wishes. If I get hold of a woman that comes up to my standard, I shall think nothing too good for her. I have been a long time looking, and I find such women are rare. To combine the qualities I require seems to be difficult, but when the difficulty is vanquished it deserves a reward. My wife shall have a good position, and I am not afraid to say that I shall be a good husband."~~

~~"And these qualities that you require — what are they?"~~

~~"Goodness, beauty, intelligence, a fine education, personal elegance — everything, in a word, that makes a splendid woman."~~

~~"And noble birth, evidently," said Bellegarde.~~

~~"Oh, throw that in, by all means, if it's there. The better!"~~

~~"And my sister seems to you to have all these things?"~~

"As the prince of husbands?"

"Well, yes — call it the prince, as you speak of such people."

"I believe," said Valentin after a moment, "that you'd be as good a prince as another."

"I should be as good a husband."

"And that — what you want me to tell my sister?"

"That's what I want you to tell her."

"No, thanks," Valentin then replied. "It's none of my business. It's enough for me that you're worth, delightfully, my acquaintance and my wonder."

~~"She is exactly what I have been looking for. She is my dream realised."~~

~~"And you would make her a very good husband?"~~

~~"That is what I wanted you to tell her."~~

~~Bellegarde~~ laid his hand on his companion's arm, ~~a moment~~, looked at him, ~~with his head on one side~~, from head to foot, and then, with a loud laugh, and shaking the other hand in the air, turned away. He walked again the length of the room, and again he came back and stationed himself in front of Newman. "All this is very interesting—it is very curious. In what I said just now I was speaking, not for myself, but for my traditions, my superstitions. For myself, really, your ~~proposal tickles me~~. It startled me at first, but the more I think of it the more I see in it. It's no use attempting to explain anything; you ~~won't understand me~~. After all, I don't see why you need; it's no great loss."

"Oh, if there is anything more to explain, try it! I ~~want to proceed with my eyes open. I will do my best to understand~~."

"No," said ~~Bellegarde, "it's disagreeable to me; I~~ give ~~it~~ up. ~~I liked~~ you the first time I saw you, and I ~~will~~ abide by that. It would be quite odious for me to come talking to you as if I could patronise you. I have told you before that I envy you; *vous m'imposez*, as we say. I didn't know you much ~~until within~~ five minutes. So we will let things go, and I will say nothing to you that, if our positions ~~were~~ reversed, you would not say to me."

I ~~do not~~ know whether, in renouncing the mysterious opportunity to which he alluded, ~~Bellegarde felt that he was doing~~ something very generous. If so, he was not rewarded; his generosity was not appreciated. Newman quite failed to recognise the ~~young Frenchman's~~ power to ~~wound his feelings~~, and he had now no sense of ~~escaping~~ coming off easily. ~~He did not thank his companion even with a glance. "My eyes are open, though," he said, "so far as that you have practically told me that~~

Handwritten revisions:

- The young man
- critically
- idea
- stirs me up
- me with
- I guess I've had to understand some queerer things than any you're likely to tell
- Valentin. "We'll do without
- wouldn't, I think, follow me
- with
- them; we'll let them go
- till
- not
- I took you for somebody—God knows whom or what—
- till these last
- Valentin himself felt
- He had not at his command the gratitude of a glance, and he was in truth occupied with a particular fear which he presently expressed
- disconcert or to wound him
- do

126

"Do you think," Newman presently asked, "that she may be, by chance, determined not to marry at all?"

"Oh, I quite think it! But that's not necessarily too much against you; such a determination never yet spoiled a right opportunity."

"But suppose I don't seem a right one. I'm afraid it will be hard," Newman said with a gravity that appeared to signify at the same time a sort of lucid respect for the fact.

"I don't think it will be easy. In a general way I don't see why a widow should ever marry again. She has gained has gained the benefits of matrimony—freedom and consideration—and she has got rid of the drawbacks. Why should she put her head into the noose again? Her usual motive is ambition; if a man can offer her a great position, make her a princess or an ambassadress, she may think the compensation sufficient."

"And—in that way—is Madame de Cintré ambitious?"

"Who knows?" said Bellegarde, with a profound shrug. "I don't pretend to say all that she is or all that she is not. I think she might be touched by the prospect of becoming the wife of a great man. But in a certain way, I believe, whatever she does will be the *improbable*. Don't be too confident, but don't absolutely doubt. Your best chance for success will be precisely in being, to her mind, unusual, unexpected, original. Don't try to be any one else; be simply yourself, out and out. Something or other can't fail to come of it; I am very curious to see what."

"I am much obliged to you for your advice," said Newman. "And," he added, with a smile, "I am glad, for your sake, I am going to be so amusing."

"It will be more than amusing," said Bellegarde; "it will be inspiring. I look at it from my point of view, and you from yours. After all, anything for a change! And only yesterday I was yawning so as to dislocate my jaw, and declaring that there was nothing new under the sun! If it isn't new to see you come into the family as a suitor, I am very much mistaken. Let me say that, my dear fellow; I won't call it anything else, bad or good; I will simply call it *new*." And overcome with a sense of the novelty thus foreshadowed, Valentin de Bellegarde threw himself into a deep arm chair before the fire, and with a fixed intense smile seemed to read a vision of it in the flame of the logs. After a while he looked up. "Go ahead, my boy; you have my good wishes," he said. "But it

back

she isn't.

slightly depressing detachment.

that:

as hard as ever you can, and harder perhaps indeed (if you understand) than you've ever been.

I'm

curiosity," Newman said—"if I may take it as your advice. I'm glad, for your sake at least, that I'm likely to prove

Bellegarde who had been staring at the fire a minute, looked up. "It's really a pity you don't understand me that you don't know just what I am doing."

"Oh," said Newman, laughing, "don't do anything wrong. Leave me to myself rather, or defy me out and out. I wouldn't lay any load on your conscience."

Bellegarde sprang up again; he was evidently excited; there was even more than usual spark in his eye. "You never will understand—you never will know," he said; "and if you succeed, and I turn out to have helped you, you will never be grateful, not as I shall deserve you should be. You will be an excellent fellow always, but you will not be grateful. But it doesn't matter, for I shall get my own fun out of it." And he broke into an extravagant laugh. "You look puzzled," he added; "you look almost frightened."

"It *is* a pity," said Newman, "that I don't understand you. I shall lose some very good jokes."

"I told you, you remember, that we were very strange people," Bellegarde went on. "I give you warning again. We are! My mother is strange, my brother is strange, and I verily believe that I am stranger than either. You will even find my sister a little strange. Old trees have crooked branches, old houses have queer cracks, old races have odd secrets. Remember that we are eight hundred years old!"

"Very good," said Newman; "that's the sort of thing I came to Europe for. You come into my programme."

"*Touchez-là*, then," said Bellegarde, putting out his hand. "It's a bargain; I accept you, I espouse your cause. It's because I like you, in a great measure; but that is not the only reason." And he stood holding Newman's hand and looking at him askance.

"What is the other one?"

"I am in the Opposition. I dislike some one else."

"Your brother?" asked Newman, in his unmodulated voice.

Bellegarde laid his finger upon his lips with a whis-

fully
laughed
out to try it.
His friend
quite inflamed.
'll never
know;
worried
alarmed.
pursued.
wholly catch on.
sport.
We're fit for a museum or a Balzac novel.
Roman letters
You're made for me to work in.
"To your
"Well, I'm
returned,
I have a position aversion.

pered *hush!* "Old races have strange secrets!" he said. "Put yourself into motion; come and see my sister, and be assured of my sympathy!" And on this he took his leave.

Newman dropped into a chair before his fire, and sat a long time staring into the blaze.

CHAPTER IX.

HE went to see Madame de Cintré the next day, and was informed by the servant that she was at home. He passed as usual up the large cold staircase, and through a spacious vestibule above, where the walls seemed all composed of small door-panels, touched with long-faded gilding; whence he was ushered into the sitting-room in which he had already been received. It was empty, and the servant told him that Madame la Comtesse would presently appear. He had time, while he waited, to wonder whether Bellegarde had seen his sister since the evening before and whether in this case he had spoken to her of their talk. In this case Madame de Cintré's receiving him was an encouragement. He felt a certain trepidation as he reflected that she might come in with the knowledge of his supreme admiration and of the project he had built upon it in her eyes; but the feeling was not disagreeable. Her face could wear no look that would make it less beautiful, and he was sure beforehand that, however she might take the proposal he had in reserve, she would not take it in scorn or in irony. He had a feeling that if she could only read the bottom of his heart, and measure the extent of his good-will toward her, she would be entirely kind.

She came in at last, after so long an interval that he wondered whether she had been hesitating. She smiled

~~with her usual frankness, and held out her hand; she looked at him straight with her soft and luminous~~ eyes, ~~and said,~~ without a tremor in her voice, that she was glad to see him, and that she hoped he was well. He found in her what he had found before—that faint perfume of a personal shyness worn away by contact with the world, but the more perceptible the more closely ~~you~~ approached ~~her~~. This lingering diffidence ~~seemed to give~~ a peculiar value to what was definite and assured in her manner; ~~it made it seem like an~~ accomplishment, a beautiful talent, something that one might compare to an exquisite touch in a pianist. It was, in fact, Madame de Cintré's "authority," as they say of artists, that especially impressed and fascinated Newman; he always came back to the feeling that when he should ~~complete himself by taking a wife,~~ that was the way he should like his wife to ~~interpret him~~ to the world. The only trouble, indeed, was that when the instrument was so perfect it seemed to interpose too much between ~~you and the genius that used it. Madame de Cintré gave Newman~~ the sense of an elaborate education, of her having passed through mysterious ceremonies and processes of culture in her youth, of her having been fashioned and made flexible to certain exalted social needs. All this, as I have ~~affirmed,~~ made her seem rare and precious—a very expensive article, as he would have said, and one which a man with an ambition to have everything about him of the best would find it highly agreeable to possess. ~~But~~ looking at the matter with an eye to private felicity, ~~Newman wondered~~ where, in so exquisite a compound, nature and art showed their dividing line. Where did the special intention separate from the habit of good manners? Where did urbanity end and sincerity begin? ~~Newman asked himself~~ these questions even while he stood ready to accept the admired object in all its complexity; he felt ~~that~~ he could do so in profound security, ~~and examine~~ its mechanism afterwards, at leisure.

at him, as usual, without constraint, and her great mild eyes, while she held out her hand, seemed to shine at him straight. She then remarkably observed

She was

gave

making it an acquired

have rounded out his "success" by the right big marriage

the audience and the composer. She gave him, the charming woman,

noted,

Yet

express the size of it

He asked himself

examining

indeed

and

He indulged in

"I am very glad to find you alone," he said. "You know I have never had such good luck before."

"But you have seemed before very well contented with your luck," said Madame de Cintré. "You have sat and watched my visitors with an air of quiet amusement. What have you thought of them?"

"Oh, I have thought the ladies were very elegant and very graceful, and wonderfully quick at repartee. But what I have chiefly thought has been that they only help me to admire you." This was not gallantry on Newman's part—an art in which he was quite unversed. It was simply the instinct of the practical man, who had quite made up his mind what he wanted, and was now beginning to take active steps to obtain it.

Madame de Cintré started slightly, and raised her eyebrows; she had evidently not expected so fervid a compliment. "Oh, in that case," she said, with a laugh, "your finding me alone is not good luck for me. I hope some one will come in quickly."

"I hope not," said Newman. "I have something particular to say to you. Have you seen your brother?"

"Yes, I saw him an hour ago."

"Did he tell you that he had seen me last night?"

"He said so."

"And did he tell you what we had talked about?"

Madame de Cintré hesitated a moment. As Newman asked these questions she had grown a little pale, as if she regarded what was coming as necessary, but not as agreeable. "Did you give him a message to me?" she asked.

"It was not exactly a message—I asked him to render me a service."

"The service was to sing your praises, was it not?" And she accompanied this question with a little smile, as if to make it easier to herself.

"Yes, that is what it really amounts to," said Newman. "Did he sing my praises?"

"He spoke very well of you. But when I know that it was by your special request of course I must take his eulogy with a grain of salt."

"Oh, that makes no difference," said Newman. "Your brother would not have spoken well of me unless he believed what he was saying. He is too honest for that."

"Are you very deep?" said Madame de Cintré. "Are you trying to please me by praising my brother? I confess it is a good way."

"For me any way that succeeds will be good. I will praise your brother all day, if that will help me. He is a noble little fellow. He has made me feel, in promising to do what he can to help me, that I can depend upon him."

"Don't make too much of that," said Madame de Cintré. "He can help you very little."

"Of course I must work my way myself. I know that very well; I only want a chance to. In consenting to see me, after what he told you, you almost seem to be giving me a chance."

"I am seeing you," said Madame de Cintré slowly and gravely, "because I promised my brother I would."

"Ah,

I just loved him you know, and I regard him as perfectly straight

head then!"

wonderfully

of Course

a great diplomatist?" she answered

cried

the woman he addressed, and on

adopted; yet

"Blessings on your brother's head!" cried Newman. "What I told him last evening was this: that I admired you more than any woman I had ever seen, and that I should like immensely to make you my wife." He uttered these words with great directness and firmness, and without any sense of confusion. He was full of his idea, he had completely mastered it, and he seemed to look down on Madame de Cintré, with all her gathered elegance, from the height of his bracing good conscience. It is probable that this particular tone and manner were the very best he could have hit upon. Yet the light, just visibly forced smile with which his companion had listened to him died away, and she sat looking at him with her lips parted and her face as solemn as a tragic mask. There was evidently ~~something very painful to her in the scene to which he was subjecting her, and yet~~ her impatience of it found no angry voice. Newman wondered ~~whether he was~~ hurting her; he could not imagine why the liberal devotion he meant to express should be disagreeable. He got up and stood before her, leaning one hand on the chimney-piece. "I know I have seen you very little to say this, ~~[illegible]~~ little that it may make what I say seem disrespectful. ~~That is~~ my misfortune; I could have said it the first time I saw you. Really, I had seen you before; I had seen you in imagination; you seemed almost an old friend. So what I say is ~~not mere gallantry and compliments and nonsense—I can't talk that way, I don't know how~~, and I wouldn't to you if I could. ~~It's~~ as serious as such words can be. I feel as if I knew you and knew ~~what a beautiful admirable woman you are.~~ I shall know better, perhaps, some day, but I have a general notion now. You are just the woman I have been looking for, except that you are far more perfect. I won't make any protestations and vows, but you can trust me. It is very soon, I know, to say all this; it is almost offensive. But why not gain time if one can? And if you want time to reflect—of course you do—the sooner you begin the better for me. I don't know what you think of me; but there is no great mystery about me; you see what I am. Your brother told me that my antecedents and occupations ~~were~~ against me; that your family ~~stands somehow on a higher level than I do. That is an idea which, of course, I don't understand and don't accept. But you don't~~ care anything about that. I can assure you that ~~I'm a very solid fellow,~~ and that if I give my mind to it I can arrange things so that in a very few years I shall not need to waste time in explaining who I am and what I am. You will decide for yourself ~~whether~~ you like me or not. ~~What there is you see before you.~~ I honestly believe I have

an inconvenience amounting to pain for her in this extravagant issue;

, however,

if he were

But that's

how fine and rare and true you are.

You can at least believe is not mere grand talk in the air, a big thing in compliments. I can't talk for any effect but one I want very much.

ill be

has a ~~[illegible]~~ social standing so high that I can't be taken as coming up to it. Well, I don't know about 'coming up'—I don't think you can very well ~~[illegible]~~ keep me down anywhere. You can't make a man feel low unless you can make him feel ~~[illegible]~~ base; and if you may fit yourself into any class you may see your way to, you can't fit him when he won't go. But I don't believe you

if

there's enough of me to last.

What I say's

nor anything at all difficult to tell about me for her to understand.

nor

grandeur

grandeur

can't

— has filled some places

no hidden vices or nasty tricks. I am kind, kind, kind! Everything that a man can give a woman I will give you. I have a large fortune, a very large fortune; some day, if you will allow me, I will go into details. If you want brilliancy, everything in the way of brilliancy that money can give you, you shall have. And as regards anything you may give up, don't take for granted too much that its place cannot be filled. Leave that to me; I'll take care of you; I shall know what you need. Energy and ingenuity can arrange everything. I'm a strong man! There, I have said what I had on my heart. It was better to get it off. I am very sorry if it's disagreeable to you; but think how much better it is that things should be clear. Don't answer me now, if you don't wish it. Think about it; think about it as slowly as you please. Of course I haven't said, I can't say, half I mean, especially about my admiration for you. But take a favourable view of me; it will only be just."

During this speech, the longest that Newman had ever made, Madame de Cintré kept her gaze fixed upon him, and it expanded at the last into a sort of fascinated stare. When he ceased speaking she lowered her eyes and sat for some moments looking down and straight before her. Then she slowly rose to her feet, and a pair of exceptionally keen eyes would have perceived that she was trembling a little in the movement. She still looked extremely serious. "I am very much obliged to you for your offer," she said. "It seems very strange, but I am glad you spoke without waiting any longer. It is better the subject should be dismissed. I appreciate all you say; you do me great honour. But I have decided not to marry."

I wouldn't talk if I didn't believe it & know how & I want you to feel I'm strong, because if you do that will be enough

only a little at a time, if you want

with the very innocence of pleading desire

personal plea of any kind, that he had ever uttered in his life, she

it worries you, but the air's clear. Don't you see? You already — a mistake or had better not have met at all; and I can't think that Madame de Cintré can you?" Newman asked

made out in her an extraordinary fine tremor

"Oh, don't say that!" cried Newman, in a tone absolutely naïf from its pleading and caressing cadence. She had turned away, and it made her stop a moment with her back to him. "Think better of that. You are too young, too beautiful, too much made to be happy and to make others happy. If you are afraid of losing your freedom, I can assure you that this freedom here, this life you now lead, is a dreary bondage to what I will offer you. You shall do things that I don't think you have ever thought of. I will take you to live anywhere in the wide world that you propose. Are you unhappy? You give me a feeling that you *are* unhappy. You have no right to be, or to be made so. Let me come in and put an end to it."

Madame de Cintré stood there a moment longer, looking away from him. If she was touched by the way he spoke, the thing was conceivable. His voice, always very mild and interrogative, gradually became as soft and as tenderly argumentative as if he had been talking to a much-loved child. He stood watching her, and she presently turned round again, but this time she did not look at him, and she spoke with a quietness in which there was a visible trace of effort.

"There are a great many reasons why I should not marry," she said, "more than I can explain to you. As for my happiness, I am very happy. Your offer seems strange to me, for more reasons also than I can say. Of course you have a perfect right to make it. But I cannot accept it—it is impossible. Please never speak of this matter again. If you cannot promise me this, I must ask you not to come back."

"Why is it impossible?" Newman demanded. "You may think it is, at first, without its really being so. I didn't expect you to be pleased at first, but I do believe that if you will think of it a good while, you may be satisfied."

"I don't know you," said Madame de Cintré. "Think how little I know you."

The young woman

again, but with her face not really meeting his own,

can't accept it — that's impossible

you may want

almost flatly soft (and interrogative for to pull an organ candidly and his too

of the matter

I'm perfectly content © Your proposal seems

she returned after a moment ©

(waited) but

ever

I'll

simply to put me off ©

I only ask You to let me "stay round" and by so doing

"Very little, of course, and therefore I don't ask for your ultimatum on the spot. I only ask you not to say no, and to let me hope. I will wait as long as you

~~three~~ Meanwhile you can see more of me and know me better, look at me ~~as a possible husband—as a candidate—~~and make up your mind."

Something was going on, rapidly, in ~~Madame de Cintré's thoughts~~; she was weighing a question there, beneath Newman's eyes, weighing it and deciding it. "From the moment I don't very respectfully beg you to leave the house and never return, ~~[illegible]~~ I listen to you, I seem to give you hope. I *have* listened to you—against my judgment. It is because ~~you are~~ eloquent. If I had been told this morning that I should consent to consider you as ~~a possible husband~~, I should have thought my informant a little crazy. I *am* listening to you, you see!" And she threw her ~~hands out~~ for a moment and let them drop with a gesture in which there was just ~~the slightest~~ expression of ~~appealing~~ weakness.

"Well, as far as saying goes, I have said everything," ~~said~~ Newman. "I believe in you, without restriction, and I think all the good of you that it is possible to think of a human creature. I firmly believe that in marrying me you will be *safe*. As I said just now," he went on with ~~a smile~~, "I have no bad ways. I can *do* so much for you. And if you are afraid that I am not what you have been accustomed to, not ~~refined and delicate and punctilious~~, you may easily carry that too far. ~~I *am* delicate! You shall see!~~"

Madame de Cintré walked some distance away, and paused before a great plant, an azalea, which was flourishing in a porcelain tub before her window. She plucked off one of the flowers and, twisting it in her fingers, retraced her steps. Then she sat down in silence, and her attitude seemed to be a consent that ~~Newman~~ should say more.

want

her spirit.

a person wishing to come so very near me,

an

replied,

his smile as of hard experience,

he

therefore

I am refined— I am delicate ⊙ Just you try me! "

in the light— well of my presumption, yes, but of other things too—

you see, your arms up surrendering

as refined and cultivated and even as delicate as your standard requires,

be liking it ⊙

already subject to that lie?—which must be awful, I admit, when it's only a, grind ⊙

"Why should you say it is impossible you should marry?" he continued. "The only thing that could make it really impossible would be your being ~~already married~~. Is it because you have been unhappy in marriage? That's all the more reason. Is it because your family exert a pressure upon you, interfere with you, annoy you? That's still another reason: you ought to be perfectly free, and marriage will make you so. I don't say anything against your family—understand that!" added Newman, with an eagerness which might have made a perspicacious observer smile. "Whatever way you feel ~~toward~~ them is the right way, and anything that you should wish me to do to make myself agreeable to them I'll do as well as I know how. ~~Depend upon that!~~"

~~Madame de Cintré~~ rose again and came ~~toward~~ to the ~~fireplace~~, near which ~~Newman was standing.~~ The expression of pain and embarrassment had passed out of her face, and it ~~was illuminated with something which, this time at least, Newman need not have been perplexed whether to attribute to habit or to intention, to art or to nature.~~ She had the air of a woman who had stepped across the frontier of friendship and, looks round her, ~~finds the region vast~~. A certain checked and controlled exaltation ~~seemed mingled with the usual level radiance of her glance.~~ "I will not refuse to see you again," ~~she said,~~ because much of what you've said has given me pleasure. But I will see you only on this condition: that you say nothing more in the same way for a long time."

"~~For how long?~~"

"~~For six months.~~ It must be a solemn promise."

"Very ~~well~~; I promise."

"Good-bye, then," she said, and ~~extended~~ her hand.

He held it a moment, as if ~~he were going~~ to say ~~something~~ more. But he only looked at her, then he took his departure.

That evening, on the Boulevard, he met Valentin de Bellegarde. After they had exchanged greetings ~~Newman~~ told him ~~that~~ he had seen ~~Madame de Cintré~~ a few hours before.

about

She

fire

a little bewildered to find the spaces larger than those marked in her customary chart.

They may put me through what they like—I guess I shall hold out."

he had hovered.

had submitted itself with a kind of grace in which there might have been indeed a kind of art.

"long

Good; | put out

he

his sister

— "long, long"

"What do you mean by 'long, long'—?"

played through the charm of her dignity.

"I won't

"Well, I mean six months.

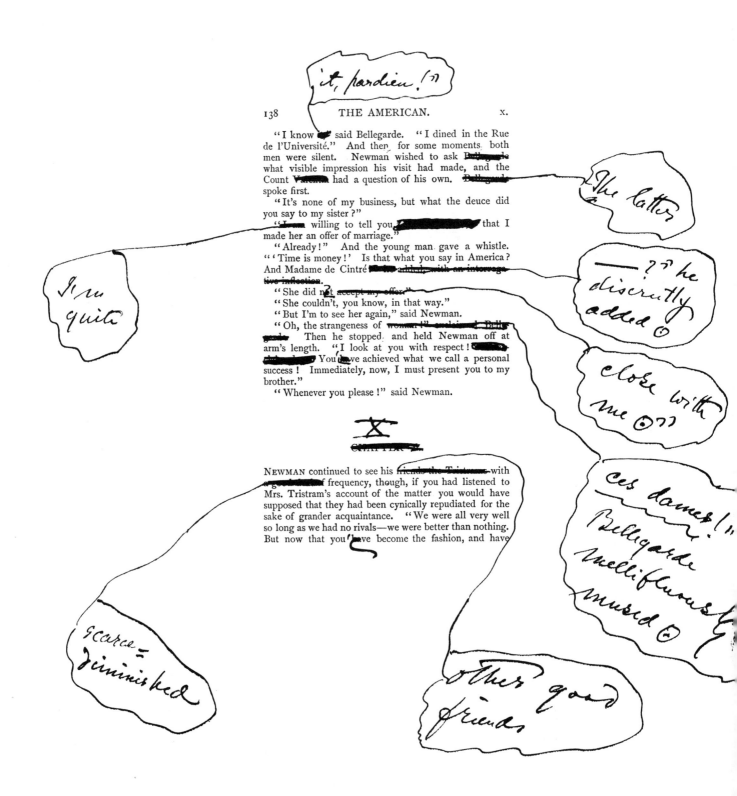

"I know," said Bellegarde. "I dined in the Rue de l'Université." And then for some moments both men were silent. Newman wished to ask what visible impression his visit had made, and the Count had a question of his own. spoke first.

"It's none of my business, but what the deuce did you say to my sister?"

" willing to tell you that I made her an offer of marriage."

"Already!" And the young man gave a whistle. "'Time is money!' Is that what you say in America? And Madame de Cintré

"She did not

"She couldn't, you know, in that way."

"But I'm to see her again," said Newman.

"Oh, the strangeness of Then he stopped and held Newman off at arm's length. "I look at you with respect! You've achieved what we call a personal success! Immediately, now, I must present you to my brother."

"Whenever you please!" said Newman.

ces dames!" Bellegarde mellifluously murid ⊙

X

~~CHAPTER

scarce-diminished

other good friends

NEWMAN continued to see his with frequency, though, if you had listened to Mrs. Tristram's account of the matter you would have supposed that they had been cynically repudiated for the sake of grander acquaintance. "We were all very well so long as we had no rivals—we were better than nothing. But now that you have become the fashion, and have your pick every day of three invitations to dinner, we are tossed into the corner. I am sure it is very good of you to come and see us once a month; I wonder you don't send us your cards in an envelope. When you do, pray have them with black edges; it will be for the death of my last illusion." It was in this incisive strain that Mrs. Tristram moralised over Newman's so-called neglect, which was in reality a most exemplary constancy. Of course she was joking, but there was always something ironical in her jokes, as there was always something jocular in her gravity.

"I know no better proof that I have treated you very well," Newman had said, "than the fact that you make so free with my character. Familiarity breeds contempt; I have made myself too cheap. If I had a little proper pride I would stay away a while, and when you asked me to dinner say I was going to the Princess Borealska's. But I have not any pride where my pleasure is concerned, and to keep you in the humour to see me—if you must see me only to call me bad names—I will agree to anything you choose; I will admit that I am the biggest snob in Paris." Newman, in fact, had declined an invitation personally given by the Princess Borealska, an inquiring Polish lady to whom he had been presented, on the ground that on that particular day he always dined at Mrs. Tristram's; and it was only a tenderly perverse theory of his hostess of the Avenue d'Iéna that he was faithless to his early friendships. She needed the theory to explain a certain moral irritation by which she was often visited; though, if this explanation was unsound, a deeper analyst than I must give the right one. Having launched our hero upon the current which was bearing him so rapidly along, she appeared but half pleased at its swiftness. She had succeeded too well; she had played her game too cleverly and she wished to mix up the cards. Newman had told her, in due season, that her friend was "satisfactory." The epithet was not romantic, but Mrs. Tristram had no difficulty in perceiving that, in essentials, the feeling which lay beneath it was. Indeed the mild expansive brevity with which it was uttered, and a certain look, at once appealing and inscrutable, that issued from Newman's half-closed eyes as he leaned his head against the back of his chair, seemed to her the most eloquent attestation of a mature sentiment that she had ever encountered. Newman was, according to the French phrase, only abounding in her own sense, but his temperate raptures exerted a singular effect upon that ardour which she herself had so freely manifested a few months before. She now seemed inclined to take a purely critical view of Madame de Cintré, and wished to have it understood that she did not in the least answer for her being a compendium of all the virtues. "No woman was ever so good as that woman seems," she said. "Remember what Shakespeare calls Desdemona: 'a supersubtle Venetian.' Madame de Cintré is a supersubtle Parisian. She is a charming woman, and she has five hundred merits; but you had better keep that in mind." Was Mrs. Tristram simply finding out that she was jealous of her dear friend on the other side of the Seine and that in undertaking to provide Newman with an ideal wife she had counted too much on her own disinterestedness? We may be permitted to doubt it. The inconsistent little lady of the Avenue d'Iéna had an insuperable need of changing her place, intellectually. She had a lively imagination, and she was capable at certain times, of imagining the direct reverse of her most cherished beliefs, with a vividness more intense than that of conviction. She got tired of thinking right; but there was no serious harm in it, as she got equally tired of thinking wrong. In the midst of her mysterious perversities she had admirable flashes of justice. One of these occurred when Newman related to her that he had made a formal proposal to Madame de Cintré. He repeated in a few words what he had

her friend's

He

n't

pretend to have gone into a final analysis or in other words of her honesty of her life, "No woman" she played with this idea "can be so good as that one seems"

Claire

special favourite

intellectual movement of critical, of ironic exercise

mentioned

at times of holding views, of entertaining beliefs, elaborately opposed to her most cherished opinions and convictions

offer of his hand

said, and in a great many what she had answered. Mrs. Tristram listened with extreme interest.

"But after all," said Newman, "there is nothing to congratulate me upon. It is not a triumph."

"I beg your pardon," said Mrs. Tristram; "it is a great triumph. It is a great triumph that she did not silence you at the first word, and request you never to speak to her again."

"I don't see that," observed Newman.

"Of course you don't; Heaven forbid you should! When I told you to go your own way and do what came into your head, I had no idea you would go over the ground so fast. I never dreamed you would offer yourself after five or six morning calls. As yet, what had you done to make her like you? You had simply sat—not very straight—and stared at her. But she does like you."

"That remains to be seen."

"No, that is proved. What will come of it remains to be seen. That you should propose to marry her, without more ado, could never have come into her head. You can form very little idea of what passed through her mind as you spoke; if she ever really marries you, the affair will be characterised by the usual justice of all human things towards women. You will think you take generous views of her; but you will never begin to know through what a strange sea of feeling she passed before she accepted you. As she stood there in front of you the other day she plunged into it. She said, 'Why not?' to something which, a few hours earlier, had been inconceivable. She turned about on a pivot of a thousand gathered prejudices and traditions as on a pivot, and looked where she had never looked hitherto. When I think of it—when I think of Claire de Cintré and all that she represents, there seems to me something very fine in it. When I recommended you to try your fortune with her I of course thought well of you, and in spite of your sins

he admitted,
It's dazzling triumph that she didn't
it's a
much of a
You'd
You'd propose
"She wouldn't have got much by
me near
it only remains to criticised.
She looked at ... a moment. "No one ... think gets as much ... anything as ... you ⊙
takes
marked
She'll have
make but a mouthful of her marrying you,
till that instant ⊙
base ingratitude

I think so still. But I confess I don't see quite what you are and what you have done, to make such a woman do this sort of thing for you."

"Oh, there is something very fine in it!" said Newman, with a laugh, repeating her words. He took an extreme satisfaction in hearing that there was something fine in it. He had not the least doubt of it himself, but he had already begun to value the world's admiration of Madame de Cintré as adding to the prospective glory of possession.

It was immediately after this conversation that Valentin de Bellegarde came to conduct his friend to the Rue de l'Université to present him to the other members of his family. "You are already introduced," he said, "and you have begun to be talked about. My sister has mentioned your successive visits to my mother, and it was an accident that my mother was present at none of them. I have spoken of you as an American of immense wealth, and the best fellow in the world, who is looking for something very superior in the way of a wife."

"Do you suppose," asked Newman, "that Madame de Cintré has related to your mother the last conversation I had with her?"

"I am very certain that she has not; she will keep her own counsel. Meanwhile you must make your way with the rest of the family. Thus much is known about you: you have made a great fortune in trade, you are a little eccentric, and you frankly admire our dear Claire. My sister-in-law, whom you remember seeing in Madame de Cintré's sitting-room, took, it appears, a fancy to you; she has described you as having *beaucoup de cachet*. My mother, therefore, is curious to see you."

"She expects to laugh at me, eh?" said Newman.

"She never laughs. If she does not like you, don't hope to purchase favour by being amusing. Take warning by me!"

This conversation took place in the evening, and half

— Newman laughed as he repeated

the person in question

this

passage

reported

you — that you're

that you're

charming

a frank outsider and an honest eccentric and that you furiously

Ital.

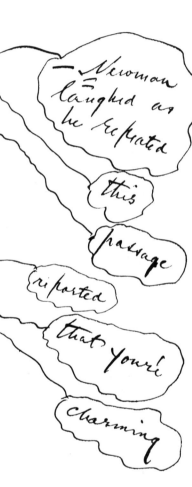

an hour later Valentin ushered his companion into an apartment of the house of the Rue de l'Université into which he had not yet penetrated, the salon of the dowager Marquise de Bellegarde. It was a vast high room, with elaborate and ponderous mouldings, painted a whitish gray, along the upper portion of the walls and the ceiling; with a great deal of faded and carefully-repaired tapestry in the doorways and chair-backs; a Turkey carpet in light colours, still soft and deep, in spite of great antiquity, on the floor; and portraits of each of Madame de Bellegarde's children, at the age of ten, suspended against an old screen of red silk. The ~~room was illumined~~, exactly enough for conversation, by half a dozen candles, placed in odd corners, at a great distance apart. In a deep armchair near the fire sat an old lady in black; at the other end of the room another person was seated at the piano, playing a very expressive waltz. In this latter person Newman recognised the young Marquise de Bellegarde.

Valentin presented his friend, and Newman ~~walked up~~ to the old lady by the fire ~~and shook hands with her.~~ He received a rapid impression of a white, delicate, aged face, with a high forehead, a small mouth, and a pair of cold blue eyes which had kept much of the freshness of youth. Madame de Bellegarde looked hard at him, and ~~returned his hand shake with~~ a sort of British positiveness which reminded him that she was the daughter of the Earl of St. Dunstan's. Her daughter-in-law stopped playing and gave him an agreeable smile. ~~Newman~~ sat down and looked about him while Valentin went and kissed the hand of the young Marquise.

"I ought to have seen you before," said Madame de Bellegarde. "You have paid several visits to my daughter."

"Oh yes," ~~said~~ Newman smiling; "Madame de Cintré and I are old friends by this time."

"You have gone fast," said Madame de Bellegarde.

with

with

dimness was diminished,

came sufficiently near

to take in that she could offer him no handshake, so that he knew he had the air of waiting a little like a customer in a shop, to see what she would offer.

refused what she did refuse with

He

liberally

very

"Not so fast as I should like," said Newman, bravely.

"Oh, you are very ambitious," answered the old lady.

"Yes, I confess I am," said Newman, smiling.

Madame de Bellegarde looked at him with her cold fine eyes, and he returned her gaze, reflecting that she was a possible adversary, and trying to take her measure. Their eyes remained in contact for some moments. Then Madame de Bellegarde looked away, and without smiling, "I am very ambitious too," she said.

Newman felt that taking her measure was not easy; she was a formidable, inscrutable little woman. She resembled her daughter, and yet she was utterly unlike her. The colouring in Madame de Cintré was the same, and the high delicacy of her brow and nose was hereditary. But her face was a larger and freer copy, and her mouth in especial a happy divergence from that conservative orifice, a little pair of lips at once plump and pinched, that looked, when closed, as if they could not open wider than to swallow a gooseberry or to emit an "Oh dear no!" which probably had been thought to give the finishing touch to the aristocratic prettiness of the Lady Emmeline Atheling as represented, forty years before, in several Books of Beauty. Madame de Cintré's face had, to Newman's eye, a range of expression as delightfully vast as the wind-streaked, cloud-flecked distance on a Western prairie. But her mother's white, intense, respectable countenance, with its formal gaze and its circumscribed smile, suggested a document signed and sealed; a thing of parchment, ink, and ruled lines. "She is a woman of conventions and proprieties," he said to himself as he looked at her; "her world is the world of things immutably decreed. But how she is at home in it, and what a paradise she finds it! She walks about in it as if it were a blooming park, a Garden of Eden; and when she sees 'This is genteel,' or 'This is improper,' written on a milestone she stops ecstatically, as if she were listening to a nightingale or smelling a rose." Madame de Bellegarde wore a little black velvet hood tied under her chin and she was wrapped in an old black cashmere shawl.

"You are an American?" she said presently. "I have seen several Americans."

"There are several in Paris," said Newman, jocosely.

"Oh, really? It was in England I saw these, or somewhere else; not in Paris. I think it must have been in the Pyrenees, many years ago. I am told your ladies are very pretty. One of these ladies was very pretty with a wonderful complexion. She presented me a note of introduction from some one—I forget whom—and she sent with it a note of her own. I kept her letter a long time afterwards, it was so strangely expressed. I used to know some of the phrases by heart. But I have forgotten them now, it is so many years ago. Since then I have seen no more Americans. I think my daughter-in-law has; she is a great gad-about, she sees every one."

At this the younger lady came rustling forward, pinching in a very slender waist and casting idly preoccupied glances over the front of her dress, which was apparently designed for a ball. She was, in a singular way, at once ugly and pretty; she had protuberant eyes and lips that were strangely red. She reminded Newman of his friend Mademoiselle Nioche; this was what that much-obstructed young lady would have liked to be. Valentin de Bellegarde walked behind her at a distance, hopping about to keep off the far-spreading train of her dress.

"You ought to show more of your shoulders behind," he said, very gravely. "You might as well wear a standing ruff as such a dress as that."

The young woman turned her back to the mirror over the chimney-piece and glanced behind her to verify Valentin's assertion. The mirror descended low, and yet it reflected nothing but a large unclad flesh-surface. The young Marquise put her hands behind her and gave a downward pull to the waist of her dress. "Like that, you mean?" she asked.

"That's a little better," said Bellegarde, in the same tone, "but it leaves a good deal to be desired."

"Oh, I never go to extremes," said his sister-in-law. And then, turning to Madame de Bellegarde: "What were you calling me just now, Madame?"

"I called you a gad-about," said the old lady. "But I might call you something else too."

"A gad-about? What an ugly word! What does it mean?"

"A very beautiful person," Newman ventured to say, seeing that it was in French.

"That's a pretty compliment but a bad translation," said the young Marquise. And then, looking at him a moment: "Do you dance?"

"Not a step."

"You are very wrong," she said, simply. And with another look at her back in the mirror she turned away.

"Do you like Paris?" asked the old lady, who was apparently wondering what was the proper way to talk to an American.

"Yes, rather," said Newman. And then he added, with a friendly intonation: "Don't you?"

"I can't say I know it. I know my house—I know my friends—I don't know Paris."

"Oh, you lose a great deal," said Newman, sympathetically.

Madame de Bellegarde stared; it was presumably the first time she had been condoled with on her losses.

"I am content with what I have," she said with dignity.

Newman's eyes, at this moment, were wandering round the room, which struck him as rather sad and shabby; passing from the high casements, with their small thickly-framed panes, to the sallow tints of two or three portraits in pastel, of the last century, which hung between them.

He ought obviously to have answered that the contentment of his hostess was quite natural—she had a great deal; but the idea did not occur to him during the pause of some moments which followed.

"Well, my dear mother," said Valentin, coming and leaning against the chimney-piece, "what do you think of my friend Newman? Is he not the excellent fellow I told you?"

"My acquaintance with Mr. Newman has not gone very far," said Madame de Bellegarde. "I can as yet only appreciate his great politeness."

"My mother is a great judge of these matters," said Valentin to Newman. "If you have satisfied her it is a triumph."

"I hope I shall satisfy you some day," said Newman, looking at the old lady. "I have done nothing yet."

"You must not listen to my son; he will bring you into trouble. He is a sad scatterbrain."

"Oh, I like him—I like him," said Newman, genially.

"He amuses you, eh?"

"Yes, perfectly."

"Do you hear that, Valentin?" said Madame de Bellegarde. "You amuse Mr. Newman."

"Perhaps we shall all come to that," Valentin exclaimed.

"You must see my other son," said Madame de Bellegarde. "He is much better than this one. But he will not amuse you."

"I don't know—I don't know!" murmured Valentin reflectively. "But we shall very soon see. Here comes *Monsieur mon frère*."

The door had just opened to give ingress to a gentleman who stepped forward, and whose face Newman remembered. He had been the author of our hero's discomfiture the first time he tried to present himself to Madame de Cintré. Valentin de Bellegarde went to

so much;

good friend? Isn't he the remarkably fine man I told you of?"

replied.

said

to

she declared.

"I think it must be that."

went on

Newman took it genially. "Oh, I've got to like him so that I can't do without him."

exist for the amusement of Mr. Newman."

thoughtfully objected.

that

of his calling.

meet his brother, looked at him a moment, and then, taking him by the arm, led him up to ~~Newman~~. "This ~~gentleman~~ is my excellent friend Mr. Newman," he said very blandly. "You must know him."

"I'm delighted to know Mr. Newman," said the Marquis, with ~~a low bow, but without offering his hand~~.

"He's the old woman at second-hand," Newman said to himself, ~~as he returned M. de Bellegarde's greeting~~. And this was the starting-point of a speculative theory, in his mind, that the late Marquis had been a very amiable foreigner, with an inclination to take life easily and a sense that it was difficult for the husband of the stilted little lady by the fire to do so. But if he had ~~taken~~ little comfort in his wife he had ~~taken~~ much in his two younger children, who were after his own heart, while Madame de Bellegarde had paired with her eldest-born.

"My brother has spoken to me of you," said M. de Bellegarde; "and as you are also acquainted with my sister, it was time we should meet." He turned to his mother and gallantly bent over her hand, touching it with his lips, and then he assumed an attitude before the chimney-piece. With his long lean face, his high-bridged nose, and his small opaque eyes, he ~~looked much like an Englishman~~. His whiskers were fair and glossy, and he had a large dimple, of unmistakable British origin, in the middle of his handsome chin. He was "distinguished" to the tips of his polished nails, and there was not a movement of his fine perpendicular person that was not noble and majestic. Newman had never yet been confronted with such an incarnation of ~~the art of taking oneself seriously~~; he felt ~~a sort of~~ impulse to step backward, as you ~~do~~ to get a view of ~~a great façade~~.

"Urbain," said young Madame de Bellegarde, who had apparently been waiting for her husband to take her to her ball, "I call your attention to the fact that I'm dressed."

[Handwritten marginal revisions: "This" ; "their guest" ; "if you can" ; "an unaccompanied salutation" ; "~~wondered how~~ with the sense of having his health drunk from an empty glass" ; "found" ; "found" ; "favoured, in the old phrase, the English strain in his blood" ; "~~preserved~~ the maintained attitude" ; "something high and unusual" ; "step"]

"That's a good idea, to show what you claim for it," Valentin commented.

"I'm at your orders, my dear friend," said M. de Bellegarde. "Only, you must allow me first the pleasure of a little conversation with Mr. Newman."

"Oh, if you're going to a party, don't let me keep you," ~~objected Newman~~. "I am very sure we shall meet again. Indeed if you'd like to ~~converse with~~ meet me I'll gladly name an hour." He was eager to make it known that he would readily answer all questions and satisfy all exactions.

M. de Bellegarde stood in a well-balanced position before the fire, caressing one of his fair whiskers with one of his white hands and looking at our friend half askance, with eyes from which a particular ray of observation made its way through a general meaningless smile. "It's very kind of you to make such an offer. If I'm not mistaken your occupations are such as to make your time precious. You're in—a—as we say, *dans les affaires*."

"In business, you mean? Oh no, I have thrown business overboard for the present. I'm 'loafing,' as *we* say. My time's quite my own."

"Ah, you're taking a holiday," rejoined M. de Bellegarde. "'Loafing.' Yes, I've heard that expression."

"Mr. Newman's a distinguished American," ~~said~~ Madame de Bellegarde regularly echoed.

"My brother's a great ethnologist," said Valentin.

"An ethnologist?" ~~said~~ Newman, "you collect negroes' skulls and that sort of thing?"

The Marquis looked hard at his brother and began to caress his other whisker. Then turning to ~~Newman~~ their new acquaintance, with sustained urbanity: "You're travelling for pure recreation?"

~~"Oh, I am knocking about to pick up one thing and another.~~ "Well, I'm visiting your country, sir," Newman replied with a certain conscious patience—a patience he felt he on his side too could push, should need be, to stiffness—"and I confess I'm having a good time in it. Of course I get a good deal of pleasure out of it."

"What more especially interests you?" ~~inquired~~ the Marquis benevolently pursued.

"Well," our friend continued, "the life of the people, for one thing, interests me. Your people are very taking. But economically, technically, as it were,

"~~Well, everything interests me," said Newman. "I am not particular.~~ Manufactures are what I care most about."

"~~That has~~ been your specialty?"

"I can't say I have had any specialty. My specialty has been to ~~make the largest possible fortune~~ in the shortest possible time." Newman made this last remark very deliberately; he wished to open the way, ~~if it were~~ necessary, to an authoritative statement of his means.

M. de Bellegarde laughed agreeably. "I hope ~~you have succeeded," he said.~~

"~~Yes, I have made a fortune in a reasonable time. I am not so old, you see.~~"

"~~Paris~~ is a very good place to spend a fortune. I wish you ~~great enjoyment~~ of yours." And M. de Bellegarde drew forth his gloves and began to put them on.

Newman for a few moments watched him sliding his ~~white~~ hands into the ~~white~~ kid, and as he did so his feelings took a singular turn. M. de Bellegarde's good wishes seemed to ~~descend out of the white expanse of his sublime serenity~~ with the soft, scattered movement of a shower of snow-flakes. Yet ~~Newman~~ was not irritated; he did not feel that he was being patronised; he was conscious of no especial impulse to introduce a discord into so noble a harmony. Only he felt himself suddenly in personal contact with the forces with which ~~his friend Valentin~~ had told him that he would have to contend, and he became sensible of their intensity. He wished to make some answering manifestation, to stretch himself out at his own length, to sound a note at the uttermost end of *his* scale. It must be added that if this impulse was ~~not~~ vicious ~~or~~ malicious, it was by no means ~~void of humorous expectancy. Newman was quite as ready to give play to that loosely adjusted smile of his, if his hosts should happen to be shocked, as he was far from deliberately planning to shock them.~~

~~"Paris is a very good place for idle people," he said,~~

"Those—a—articles have

You enjoy the sense of that success.

accumulate the largest convenient competency

should it be

"Well, Paris

"Oh, one has still at my age, the sense also of what's left to do. I'm not so very old," our hero candidly explained.

pearly

flutter down on him from the upper cold air with

all the advantages

neither

"Paris," he presently remarked, "is a very good place for people

fair, fat

unattended by the play in him of his occasional disposition to ironic adventure. He hated the idea of shocking people, he respected the liability to be shocked. But there were impressions that threw him back after all on his own measures of proportion.

Yet

he

his so valued ally

who take a great deal of stock, as we say, in their location, and want to be very much aware of it all the time; or it's

is a very good place if your family has been settled here for a long time and you have made acquaintances and got your relations round you; or if you've got a big house like this, and a wife and children and mother and sister, and everything ~~comfortable~~. I don't like that ~~way of~~ living all in rooms ~~next door to~~ each other. But ~~I am not an idler. I try to be, but I can't manage it;~~ it goes against the grain. My business habits are too deep-seated. Then I haven't any house to call my own, or anything in the way of a family. My sisters are five thousand miles away, my mother died when I was ~~a youngster~~, and I haven't ~~any wife; I wish I had!~~ So, you see, I ~~don't exactly know what to do with myself.~~ I'm not ~~fond of books~~, as you are, sir, and I get tired of dining out and going to the opera. I miss my business activity. You see I began to earn my living when I was almost a baby, and until a few months ago I've never had my hand off the plough. ~~Elegant leisure comes hard.~~"

This speech was followed by a profound silence of some moments on the part of Newman's entertainers. Valentin stood looking at him fixedly, with his hands in his pockets, and then he slowly, with a half-sidling motion, went out of the room. The Marquis continued to draw on his gloves and to smile benignantly. began to earn your living ~~when you were a mere baby?~~" said the Marquise.

~~"Hardly more—a small boy."~~

"You say you're not ~~fond of books," said~~ M. de Bellegarde, "but you must do yourself the justice to remember that your studies were interrupted early."

"That's very true; on my tenth birthday ~~I stopped going to school~~. I thought a grand way to keep it. ~~But I picked up some information afterwards," said Newman, reassuringly.~~

"You have some sisters?" asked Madame de Bellegarde.

"Yes, two splendid sisters. ~~Splendid women!~~"

way, that prevails in many of your districts, of people's

right there.

door to door with

I'm not, as I may put it, a natural, a real inspired loafer. I'm a poor imitation and

pretty small,

What a man has when a man has taken the right way to get her—if I express myself clearly; and I often miss that pleasantness very much.

I'm sometimes rather conscious of a void.

proficient in literature,

I miss the regular call on my attention.

my schooling stopped short.

resumed,

that

I wish you knew them!"

"Still, I have 'picked up' knowledge," Newman smiled.

proficient in literature?"

"You began to earn your living in the cradle?" said the old Marquise, who appeared to wish to encourage, a little grimly, yet not wholly without an effect of pleasantry, her guest's autobiographic strain.

"Well, madam, I'm not absolutely convinced I had a cradle!"

ces dames

"I hope that for ~~them~~ the hardships of life commenced less early."

"They married very early, if you call that a hardship, as girls do in our Western country. ~~One of them is married to~~ the owner of the largest india-rubber house in the West."

The husband of one of them is

"Ah, you make houses also of india-rubber?" inquired the Marquise.

"You can stretch them as your family increases," said young Madame de Bellegarde, who was muffling herself in a long white shawl.

Newman indulged in a burst of hilarity, and explained that the house in which his brother-in-law lived was a large wooden structure, but that he manufactured and sold india-rubber on a colossal scale.

"My children have some little india-rubber shoes which they put on when they go to play in the Tuileries in damp weather," said the young Marquise. "I wonder ~~whether~~ *if* your brother-in-law made them?"

"~~Very likely,~~" said Newman, ~~and if~~ he did, you may be very sure ~~that they are well made.~~" *you've got a good article"*

"I guess he did," Newman returned; "and if

"Well, you must not be discouraged," said M. de Bellegarde with vague urbanity.

"Oh, I don't mean to be. I ~~have~~ a project ~~which~~ gives me plenty to think about, and that's an occupation." And then Newman was silent a moment, hesitating, yet ~~thinking~~ rapidly; he wished ~~to make~~ his point, ~~and yet~~ to do so forced him to ~~speak out in a way that was disagreeable to him.~~ "Nevertheless," he continued, addressing himself to old Madame de Bellegarde, "I'll ~~will~~ tell you my ~~project~~; perhaps you can help me. I want ~~to choose a wife.~~"

too much

— really a grand one —

again to meas … get

which

though

debating

"It is a very good project, ~~but I am no matchmaker,~~" said the old lady.

Newman looked at her an instant, and then, ~~with perfect sincerity,~~ "I should have thought ~~you were,~~" he declared.

all.

Sincerely

with her odd mincing plainness ⊙

You a great hand,"

great idea;

still further from the form of not asking favours. He had to ask that of their attention?

not only to marry, but to marry remarkably well ⊙"

but I never made a match in my life,"

x. THE AMERICAN. 153

Madame de Bellegarde ~~appeared to think~~ him too sincere. She murmured something sharply in French and fixed her eyes on her son. At this moment the door of the room was thrown open, and with a rapid step Valentin reappeared.

"I ~~have~~ a message for you," he said to his sister-in-law. "Claire bids me ~~to request~~ you not to start for your ball. ~~She will~~ go with you."

"Claire will go with us!" cried the young Marquise. "*En voilà, du nouveau!*"

"She has changed her mind; she decided half an hour ago, and she ~~is~~ sticking the last diamond into her hair!" said Valentin.

"What has taken possession of my daughter?" ~~demanded~~ Madame de Bellegarde ~~sternly~~. "She has not been ~~into the world these three years~~. Does she take such a step at half an hour's notice and without consulting me?"

"She consulted me, dear mother, five minutes since," said Valentin, "and I told her that such a beautiful woman—she ~~is beautiful~~, you ~~will~~ see—had no right to bury herself alive."

"You should have referred Claire to her mother, my brother," said M. de Bellegarde in French. "This is ~~very strange~~."

"I refer her to the whole company!" ~~said~~ Valentin. "Here she comes!" ~~and~~ he went to the open door, met Madame de Cintré on the threshold, took her by the hand and led her into the room. She was dressed in white; but a ~~long blue~~ cloak, which hung almost to her feet, was fastened across her shoulders by a silver clasp. She had tossed it back, however, and her long white arms were uncovered. In her dense fair hair there glittered a dozen diamonds. She looked serious and, Newman thought, rather pale; but she glanced round her and, when she saw him, smiled and put out her hand. He thought her ~~tremendously handsome~~. He had a chance

might well have thought

ask

If you'll wait a minute she'll

asked with a coldness of amazement.

more beautiful than ever,

cloak in.

of dark blue,

on earth

this age where any candle was lighted.

not the way—!

—and

at this moment far and away the handsomest woman he had ever seen.

to look at her full in the face, for she stood ~~[illegible]~~ in the centre of the room, ~~hesitating, apparently, what~~ she should do, without meeting his eyes. Then she went up to her mother, who sat in ~~her~~ deep chair by the fire. ~~looking at Madame de Cintré almost fiercely. With~~ Her back turned to the others, Madame de Cintré held her cloak apart to show her dress.

"What do you think of me?" ~~[illegible]~~.

"I think ~~you are audacious," said the [illegible]~~ It was but three days ago, when I asked you, as a particular favour to myself, to go to the Duchesse de Lusignan's, that you told me you were going nowhere, and that one must be consistent. Is this your consistency? Why should you distinguish Madame Robineau? Who is it you wish to please to-night?"

"I wish to please myself, dear mother," said Madame de Cintré. And she bent over and kissed the old lady.

"I don't like surprises, my sister," said Urbain de Bellegarde; "especially when one is on the point of entering a drawing-room."

Newman at this juncture felt inspired to speak. "Oh, if you are going ~~into society with Madame de Cintré~~ you needn't be afraid of being noticed yourself!"

M. de Bellegarde turned to his sister with a ~~smile too intense to be easy.~~ "I hope you appreciate a compliment that is paid you at your brother's expense. ~~[illegible]~~." And offering Madame de Cintré his arm he led her rapidly out of the room. Valentin rendered the same service to young Madame de Bellegarde, who had apparently been reflecting on the fact that the ball-dress of her sister-in-law was much less brilliant than her own, and yet had failed to derive absolute comfort from the reflection. With a ~~farewell~~ smile she sought the complement of her consolation in the eyes of the American visitor, and perceiving in them ~~a certain mysterious brilliancy, it is not improbable that~~ ~~[illegible]~~ may have flattered herself she had found it.

a little
where she seemed to consider what
the
with an air of immeasurable detachment
You seem to have lost your head.
violent
anywhere with this lady
intense a little glare
Venez donc, madame."
leave-taking
an almost unnatural glitter, she not improbably

Newman, left alone with ~~old Madame de Bellegarde,~~ stood before her a few moments in silence. "Your daughter is very beautiful," he said at last.

"She is very ~~strange," said Madame de Bellegarde.~~

"I'm glad to hear it," ~~Newman rejoined, smiling.~~ "It makes me hope."

"Hope what?"

"That she'll consent some day, to marry me."

~~The old lady rose slowly to her feet.~~ "That really is your ~~project, then?~~"

"Yes; will you ~~favour it?~~"

~~"Favour it?"~~ Madame de Bellegarde looked at him ~~a moment and then shook her head. "No!" she said, softly.~~

"Will you ~~suffer it, then? Will you let it pass?~~"

"You don't know what you ask. I'm a very proud and meddlesome ~~old woman.~~"

"Well, I'm very rich," ~~said Newman.~~

~~Madame de Bellegarde~~ fixed her eyes on the floor, and Newman thought it probable she was weighing the reasons in favour of resenting ~~the brutality of this remark.~~ But at last looking up, ~~she said simply~~, "How rich?"

~~Newman expressed his income~~ in a round number which had the magnificent sound that large aggregations of dollars put on when they are translated into francs. He added ~~a few remarks of a financial character,~~ which completed a sufficiently striking presentment of his resources.

~~Madame de Bellegarde listened in silence.~~ "You're very frank," she ~~said~~ finally said. "I will be the same. I would rather ~~favour you, on the whole, than suffer you. It will be easier."~~

~~"I am thankful for any terms," said Newman. "But, for the present, you have suffered me long enough. Good night!" And he took his leave.~~

his hostess of the night so be called,

She slowly got up.

"great idea"?"

perverse," the old woman returned.

he smiled.

hard and shook her head. Then her so peculiarly pretty little mouth rounded itself to a "No!" which she seemed to blow at him as for a mortal chill.

give it my countenance?"

on the whole, get all the good of you there is — rather, I mean, than, as you call it, let you

You then just let me alone with my chance?"

He gave her at this the figure of his income — gave it

had let him enjoy her undisguised attention.

he returned with a world of desperate intention.

She

the enunciation of certain financial particulars to the mere brute quantity

she simply articulated.

his so calculated directness.

alone. I would rather," she coldly smiled, "take you in our way than in your way. I think it will be easier."

"I'm thankful for any terms," Newman quite radiantly answered. "It's enough for me to feel I'm taken. But it mustn't be for you" ... he at the same time rather grimly laughed, "in too big doses to begin with. Good night!" and he rapidly quitted her.

XI

~~CHAPTER XI.~~

Newman, on his return to Paris, had not resumed the study of French conversation with M. Nioche; he found that he had too many other uses for his time. M. Nioche, however, came to see him very promptly, having learned his whereabouts by a mysterious process to which his patron never obtained the key. The shrunken little capitalist repeated his visit more than once. He seemed oppressed by a humiliating sense of having been overpaid, and wished apparently to redeem his debt by the offer of grammatical and statistical information in small instalments. He wore the same decently melancholy aspect as a few months before; a few months more or less of brushing could make little difference in the antique lustre of his coat and hat. But the poor old man's spirit was a trifle more threadbare; it seemed to have received some hard rubs during the summer. Newman inquired with interest about Mademoiselle Noémie; and M. Nioche, at first, for answer, simply looked at him in lachrymose silence.

"Don't ask me, sir," he said at last. "I sit and watch her, but I can do nothing."

"Do you mean that she misconducts herself?"

"I don't know, I am sure. I can't follow her. I don't understand her. She has something in her head; I don't know what she is trying to do. She is too deep for me."

"Does she continue to go to the Louvre? Has she made any of those copies for me?"

"She goes to the Louvre, but I see nothing of the copies. She has something on her easel; I suppose it is one of the pictures you ordered. Such a magnificent order ought to give her fairy fingers. But she is not in earnest. I can't say anything to her; I am afraid of her.

He had not,

had been conscious of

That amiable man,

once; he

an

his spirit itself

it had clearly

ascertained

some art of curiosity too refined to be challenged. He exhaled

asked

press me on that subject, sir.

She gives you serious cause—?"

sir, what I mean!

Who can say what's in the head of a little person so independent—and so pleasing?

if you must know.

splendid commission

her poor papa."

Newman continued.

One evening, last summer, when I took her to walk in the Champs Élysées, she said some things to me that frightened me."

"What were they?"

"Excuse an unhappy father from telling you," said M. Nioche, unfolding his calico pocket-handkerchief.

Newman promised himself to pay Mademoiselle Noémie another visit at the Louvre. He was curious about the progress of his copies, but it must be added that he was still more curious about the progress of the young lady herself. He went one afternoon to the great museum, and wandered through several of the rooms in fruitless quest of her. He was bending his steps to the long hall of the Italian masters, when suddenly he found himself face to face with Valentin de Bellegarde. The young Frenchman [illegible] he was a godsend. He himself was in the worst of humours, [illegible] wanted some one to contradict.

"In a bad humour among all these beautiful things?" said Newman. "I thought you were so fond of pictures, especially the old black ones. There are two or three here that ought to keep you in spirits."

"Oh, to-day," answered Valentin, "I am not in a mood for pictures, and the more beautiful they are the less I like them. Their great staring eyes and fixed positions irritate me. I feel as if I were at some big dull party, in a room full of people I shouldn't wish to speak to. What should I care for their beauty? It's a bore, and, worse still, it's a reproach. I have a great [illegible] I feel vicious."

"If [illegible] the world [illegible]"

"That is one of my [illegible]. I came to meet my cousin—a dreadful English cousin, a member of my mother's family—who is in Paris for a week for her husband, and who wishes me to point out the 'principal beauties.' Imagine a woman who wears a green crape

"And what things?"

while he unfolded

but

and

eagerly greeted him assuring him [illegible]

personal

the copyist

without finding her; and then on his way

stopped

returned,

damnably

I've a tas d'ennuis

Worries

with

this grand sight works you up so why do you expose yourself?" Newman asked with his [illegible] quiet play of reason bonnet in December, and has straps sticking out of the ankles of her interminable boots! My mother begged I would do something to oblige them. I have undertaken to play *valet de place* this afternoon. They were to have met me here at two o'clock, and I have been waiting for them twenty minutes. Why doesn't she arrive? She has at least a pair of feet to carry her. I don't know whether to be furious at their playing me false, or delighted to have escaped them."

"I think in your place I would be furious," said Newman, "because they may arrive yet, and then your fury will still be of use to you. Whereas if you were delighted and they were afterwards to turn up, you might not know what to do with your delight."

"You give me excellent advice, and I already feel better. I will be furious; I will let them go to the deuce and I myself will go with you—unless by chance you too have a rendezvous.

"It is not exactly a rendezvous," said Newman. "But I have in fact come to see a person, not a picture."

"A woman, presumably?"

"A young lady."

"Well," said Valentin, "I hope for you with all my heart that she is not clothed in green tulle and that her feet are not too much out of focus."

"I don't know much about her feet, but she has very pretty hands."

Valentin gave a sigh. "And on that assurance I must part with you?"

"I am not certain of finding my young lady," said Newman, "and I am not quite prepared to lose your company on the chance. It does not strike me as particularly desirable to introduce you to her, and yet I should rather like to have your opinion of her."

"Is she pretty?"

"I guess you will think so."

Bellegarde passed his arm into that of his companion.

"Conduct me to her on the instant! I should be ashamed to make a pretty woman wait for my verdict."

Newman suffered himself to be gently propelled in the direction in which he had been walking, but his step was not rapid. He was turning something over in his mind. The two men passed into the long gallery of the Italian masters, and ~~Newman,~~ after having scanned for a moment its brilliant vista, turned aside into the smaller apartment devoted to the same school on the left. It contained very few persons, but at the farther end of it sat Mademoiselle Nioche, before her easel. She was not at work; her palette and brushes had been laid down beside her, her hands were folded in her lap, and she ~~was leaning~~ back in her chair ~~and looking~~ intently at two ladies on the other side of the hall, who, with their backs turned to her, had stopped before one of the pictures. These ladies were apparently persons of high fashion; they were dressed with great splendour, and their long silken trains and furbelows were spread over the polished floor. It was ~~at~~ their dresses Mademoiselle Noémie ~~was looking,~~ though what she was thinking of I am unable to say. I hazard the supposition ~~that she was saying to herself that to be able to drag such a train over a polished floor was a felicity worth any price~~. Her reflections, at any rate, were disturbed by the advent of ~~Newman and his companion. She glanced at them quickly, and then, coloring a little,~~ rose and stood before her easel.

"I came here on purpose to see you," ~~said Newman in his bad French, offering to shake hands~~. And then, like a good American, he introduced Valentin formally: "Allow me to make you acquainted with the Comte Valentin de Bellegarde."

Valentin made a bow which must have seemed to Mademoiselle Noémie quite in harmony with the impressiveness of his title, but the graceful brevity of her own response made no concession to underbred surprise. She turned to ~~Newman~~, putting up her hands to her hair and

our friend,

had leaned

to look

on

had fixed her eyes,

that to carry about such a mass of ponderable pleasure would surely be one of the highest uses of freedom.

of her mutely remarking

her unannounced visitors, whom, as she

she greeted with a precipitation of eye and lip that was like the glad clap of a pair of hands.

— ~~Seulement~~ — Seulement vous, exprès, exprès," Newman said in his fairest, squarest, distinctest French.

her generous patron,

smoothing its delicately-felt roughness. Then, rapidly, she turned the canvas that her easel over upon its face. "You have not forgotten me?"

"I shall never forget you, You may be sure of that."

"Oh," "there are a great many different ways of remembering a person." And she looked straight at Valentin de Bellegarde, who was looking at her as a gentleman may when a "verdict" is expected of him.

"Have you painted anything for me?" said Newman. "Have you been industrious?"

"No, I have done nothing." And, taking up her palette, she began to mix her colours at hazard.

"But your father tells me you have come here constantly."

"I have nowhere else to go! Here, all summer, I was cool, at least."

"Being here, then," said Newman, "you might have tried something?"

"I told you before," she answered, softly, "that I don't know how to paint."

"But you have something charming on your easel, now," said Valentin, "if you would only let me see it."

She spread out her two hands, with the fingers expanded, over the back of the canvas—those hands which Newman had called pretty and which, in spite of several paint-stains, Valentin could now admire. "My painting is not charming," she said.

"It is the only thing about you that is not, then, Mademoiselle," quoth Valentin, gallantly.

She took up her little canvas and silently passed it to him. He looked at it, and in a moment she said: "I am sure you are a judge."

"Yes," he answered, "I am."

"You know, then, that that is very bad."

"*Mon Dieu!*" said Valentin, shrugging his shoulders, "let us distinguish."

graced

she protested!

see a pretty picture?" Newman went on.

one could breathe

she sweetly answered

your attendance has been regular ⊙"

gaily objected,

little smudges of colour,

isn't of interest ⊙"

m

"Yes," he admitted; "I recognize merit ⊙"

"Only when it's there, I hope! I've given up = the ~~declared~~ trying to have it." bravely ~~faced~~

He ~~———— her,~~ with a smile over his demoralised little daub. "If one hasn't one sort

the young man gallantly returned ⊙

shamefaced study

One can always have another." She considered with downcast eyes—which, however, she presently raised. "You're talking of the sort of which you're a judge." Then, as to anticipate too obvious a rejoinder, she turned, for more urgent good manners, to Newman. "Where

"You know that I ought not to attempt to paint," the young girl continued.

"Frankly, then, Mademoiselle, I think you ought not."

She began to look at the dresses of the two splendid ladies again—a point on which, having risked one conjecture, I think I may risk another. While she was looking at the ladies she was seeing Valentin de Bellegarde. He, at all events, was seeing her. He put down the roughly-besmeared canvas and addressed a little click with his tongue, accompanied by an elevation of the eyebrows, to Newman.

"Where have you been all these months?" asked Mademoiselle Noémie of Newman. "You took those great journeys, you amused yourself well?"

"Oh yes," said Newman, "I amused myself well enough."

our hero returned—"always beaucoup, beaucoup!"

"I am very glad," said Mademoiselle Noémie, with extreme gentleness, and she began to dabble in her colours again. She was singularly pretty, with the look of serious sympathy that she threw into her face.

"Ah, so much the better." She spoke with charming unction, and, having taken back her canvas from Valentin, who meanwhile had looked at his friend with eyes of rich meaning.

"Tell me," she continued, "a little of all you've done."

Valentin took advantage of her downcast eyes to telegraph again to his companion. He renewed his mysterious physiognomical play, making at the same time a rapid tremulous movement in the air with his fingers. He was evidently finding Mademoiselle Noémie extremely interesting; the blue devils had departed, leaving the field clear.

"Tell me something about your travels," murmured the young girl.

"Oh, I went to Switzerland—to Geneva, and Zermatt, and Zürich, and all those places, you know; and down to Venice, and all through Germany, and down the Rhine, and into Holland and Belgium—the regular round. How do you say that in French—the regular round?" Newman asked of Valentin.

Mademoiselle Nioche fixed her eyes an instant on

Bellegarde, and then with a little smile, "I don't understand Monsieur [blacked out] when he says so much at once. Would you be so good as to translate?"

"I would rather talk to you out of my own head," Valentin declared.

"No," said Newman gravely, still in his bad French, "you must not talk to Mademoiselle Nioche, because you say discouraging things. You ought to tell her to work, to persevere."

"And we French, Mademoiselle," said Valentin, "are accused of being false flatterers!"

"I don't want any flattery, I want only the truth. But I know the truth."

"All I say is that I suspect there are some things that you can do better than paint," said Valentin.

"I know the truth—I know the truth," Mademoiselle Noémie repeated. And, dipping a brush into a clot of red paint, she drew a great horizontal daub across her unfinished picture.

"What is that?" asked Newman.

Without answering, she drew another long crimson daub, in a vertical direction, down the middle of her canvas, and so, in a moment, completed the rough indication of a cross. "It is the sign of the truth," she said at last.

The two men looked at each other, and Valentin indulged in another flash of physiognomical eloquence.

"You have spoiled your picture," said Newman.

"I know that very well. It was the only thing to do with it. I had sat looking at it all day without touching it. I had begun to hate it. It seemed to me something was going to happen."

"I like it better that way than as it was before," said Valentin. "Now it is more interesting. It tells a story. Is it for sale, Mademoiselle?"

"Everything I have is for sale," said Mademoiselle Noémie.

with all the candour of her appeal:

formal

Parisians, mademoiselle," the young man exclaimed, "are accused of paying hollow compliments!"

compliments—

wretched

the girl

"I utter no truth more wretched," Valentin returned, "than that there are probably many things you can do very well."

"Oh I can at least do this!"

if I didn't know it's by this time—!"

"What are you making that mark for?" Newman asked with his impartial interest.

m

little story now.

pure

the girl promptly replied.

my picture," said his friend.

as with vivid intelligence.

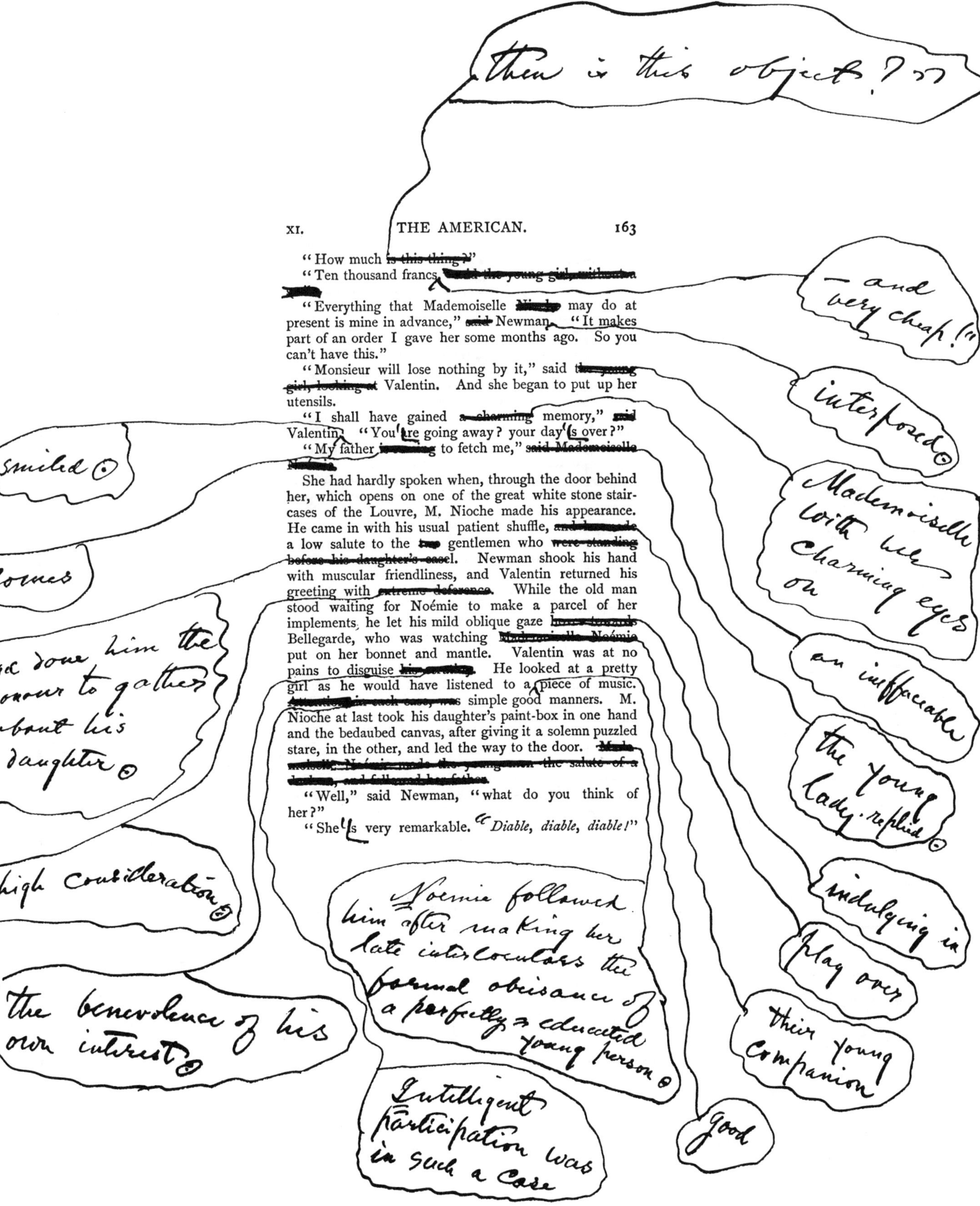

XI. THE AMERICAN. 163

"How much ~~is this thing?~~"

"Ten thousand francs, ~~said the young girl, without a smile.~~"

"Everything that Mademoiselle ~~Nioche~~ may do at present is mine in advance," ~~said~~ Newman. "It makes part of an order I gave her some months ago. So you can't have this."

"Monsieur will lose nothing by it," said ~~the young girl, looking at~~ Valentin. And she began to put up her utensils.

"I shall have gained ~~a charming~~ memory," ~~said~~ Valentin. "You are going away? your day is over?"

"My father ~~is coming~~ to fetch me," ~~said Mademoiselle Noémie.~~

She had hardly spoken when, through the door behind her, which opens on one of the great white stone staircases of the Louvre, M. Nioche made his appearance. He came in with his usual patient shuffle, ~~and he made~~ a low salute to the ~~two~~ gentlemen who ~~were standing before his daughter's easel~~. Newman shook his hand with muscular friendliness, and Valentin returned his greeting with ~~extreme deference~~. While the old man stood waiting for Noémie to make a parcel of her implements, he let his mild oblique gaze ~~hover towards~~ Bellegarde, who was watching ~~Mademoiselle Noémie~~ put on her bonnet and mantle. Valentin was at no pains to disguise ~~his scrutiny~~. He looked at a pretty girl as he would have listened to a piece of music. ~~Attention, in each case, was~~ simple good manners. M. Nioche at last took his daughter's paint-box in one hand and the bedaubed canvas, after giving it a solemn puzzled stare, in the other, and led the way to the door. ~~Mademoiselle Noémie made the young men the salute of a duchess, and followed her father.~~

"Well," said Newman, "what do you think of her?"

"She is very remarkable. *Diable, diable, diable!*"

then is this object?"
— and very cheap!"
interposed
smiled
Mademoiselle with her charming eyes on
comes
an ineffaceable
had done him the honour to gather about his daughter
the young lady replied
high consideration
indulging in
Noémie followed him after making her late interlocutors the formal obeisance of a perfectly educated young person
play over
the benevolence of his own interest
their young companion
Intelligent participation was in such a case
good

Valentin

164 THE AMERICAN. XI.

~~repeated M. de Bellegarde,~~ reflectively; "she is ~~very remarkable.~~"

"I am afraid she is a sad little ~~adventuress," said Newman.~~

"Not a little one—~~a great~~ one. She has the material." And Valentin began to walk ~~away~~ slowly, looking vaguely at the pictures on the walls, ~~with a thoughtful illumination in his eye~~. Nothing could have appealed to his imagination more than the possible ~~adventures~~ of a young lady ~~endowed with the material of Mademoiselle Nioche~~. "She is very interesting," he went on. "~~She is a beautiful type.~~"

"~~A beautiful type? What the deuce do you mean?" asked Newman.~~

"~~I mean from the artistic point of view. She is an artist—outside of her painting, which obviously is execrable.~~"

"~~But she is not beautiful. I don't even think her very pretty.~~"

"~~She is quite pretty enough for her purposes, and it is~~ a face and figure in which everything tells. If she were prettier she would be less intelligent, and her intelligence is half of her charm."

"In what way ~~[blotted] amused at his companion's immediate philosophisation of Mademoiselle Nioche~~ does her intelligence strike you as so remarkable?" asked Newman,

"She has taken the measure of life, and she has determined to *be* something—to succeed at any cost. Her painting, of course, is a mere trick to gain time. She is waiting for her chance; she wishes to launch herself, and to do it well. She knows her Paris. She is one of fifty thousand, so far as ~~the mere ambition goes; but I am very sure that in the way of resolution and capacity she is a rarity. And in one gift—perfect heartlessness—I will warrant she is unsurpassed. She has not as much heart as will go on the point of a needle. That is an~~

Handwritten revisions:

repeated;

the perfection of the type."

off,

trifler," Newman conscientiously remarked.

futility

rather an immense

through with such opened eyes,

so equipped for futility.

"'The' type? The type of what?"

"Yes, the type shines out in her."

at once puzzled, and impressed and vaguely scandalised by his friend's investment of such a subject with so much of the dignity of demonstration.

Newman wondered, but presently followed. "Surely her great originals will have had more beauty."

"Not always. She has enough to look as if she had more, and that's always plenty. It's

"Well, of soaring ambition! She's a very bad little copyist, but, endowed with the artistic sense in another line, I suspect her none the less of a strong feeling for her great originals."

as her impatiences and appetites go, but I'm sure she has an exceptional number of ideas."

Newman raised his strong eyebrows. "Are you also sure they are really good ones?"

"Ah, 'good, good'!" cried Valentin; "you people are too wonderful with your goodness. Good for what, please —? They'll be excellent, I warrant, for some things! They'll be much better than the hopeless game she has just given up. They'll be good enough to make her, I daresay, one of the celebrities of the future."

"Lord o' mercy, you have sized her up! But don't — I must really ask it of you — let her quite run away with you," Newman went on. "I shall owe it to her good old father not to have started her, you see. For he's a very nice man."

"Oh, oh, oh, her good old father!" Valentin incorrigibly mocked. And then as his companion looked grave: "He expects her to assure his future."

"I thought he rather expected me! And don't you judge him, as a friend of mine," Newman asked, " too cruelly? He's as poor as a rat, but very high-toned."

"Why, my dear man, I should adore his tone, and you're right to do the same: it's much better than mine, and he'll do you more good, as a companion, he'll protect your innocence better, than ever I shall. I don't mean," Valentin explained, "that he wouldn't much rather his daughter were a good girl, that she remained as 'nice' — as worthy, that is, say, of your particular use — as he may himself remain. But, all the same, he won't, if the worst comes to the worst — well, he won't do what Virginius did. He doesn't want her to be a failure — as why should he? — and if she isn't a failure it's plain she'll be a success. On the whole he has confidence."

"He has touching fears, sir — I admit he has betrayed them to me." Newman felt himself loyally concerned to defend a character that had struck him as pleasingly complete — though completeness was, after all, what Valentin also claimed for it.

The difference was in their view of that picturesque grace, and Newman would, to an appreciable degree, have sentimentally suffered from not being able to keep Monsieur Nioche before him as he had first seen him. He was, to an extent he never fully revealed, a collector of impressions as romantically concrete, the blest images and even when profane, as sanctified relics of one of the systematically devout, and he at bottom liked as little to hear anything he had picked up with the hand of the spirit pronounced unauthentic. "I don't quite remember what Virginius did," he presently pursued, "and I don't say for certain that my old friend would shoot. He doesn't affect me, no, as a shooting man. But I guess he wouldn't want to make very much out of anything."

"Then he'll be very different," Valentin laughed, "from any of the rest of his species! Why, my dear fellow, we all here in Paris want to make as much as possible out of everything. That's how we differ, I conceive, from the people of <u>your</u> country: the objects of your exploitation appear to be fewer, and above all of fewer kinds. I don't mind telling you," he declared in the same tone, "that I don't see the end of what I might be capable of making out of *this*."

"Of 'this' — ?"

"Of the relation of Monsieur Nioche to his daughter, and of the relation of his daughter to — well, to as many other persons as you like!"

"I shan't at all like *you* to be one of them," Newman still gravely returned. "I didn't ask you to come round with me just to set you after her."

The young man appeared for an instant embarrassed. "Do you object then to her having engaged my enlightened curiosity?"

Newman considered. "Well, no — since, from the moment I recognise she'll never deliver my goods, I don't quite see where I stand or how I can improve her."

"Oh, you certainly can't improve her!" Valentin gaily cried.

Newman looked at him a moment. "I should like then to improve *you*. I guess, at any rate, you had better leave her alone."

"Oh, oh, oh!" his companion exclaimed, at this, with an accent that made him pull up. "Do you mean, *mon cher*, that you warn me off?"

They had stopped a minute before, and he stood there staring. "Hanged if I don't believe you suppose I'm afraid of you!"

Valentin had given a cock to his moustache, and he stroked it an instant, meeting this exclamation with a glance of some obliquity and a smile just slightly strained. "Oh, I shouldn't put it that way: you don't even yet know me enough to fear me! Which gives you the advantage — for you've yourself attitudes that, I confess, make me tremble. I think you're afraid, at most," he continued, "of my bad example."

Newman had again — for he had had it before — a strange fine sense of something that he would have called, in relation to this brilliant friend, the waste of animadversion. It was somehow one with the accepted economic need of keeping him pleasantly in view. Even to argue with him was somehow to misuse a luxury, and to think of him as perverse was somehow to miss an occasion. No one had ever given him that impression, which he might have compared to the absolute pleasure, for the palate, of wine of the highest savour. One didn't put anything "into" such a vintage and there was a way of handling the very bottle. The grace in him was all precious, the growth of him all fortunate, the quantity of him all doubtless limited.

"I perhaps *might* have been a factor in that young lady's moral future," he presently said — "but I don't come in now. And evidently," he added, "you've no room for me in yours."

The young man gave a laugh, and the next moment, arm in arm, they had resumed their walk. "Oh, on the contrary," Valentin then replied; "since what I want, precisely, is to keep it spacious and capacious — at least on the scale, if you please, of my moral past; which indeed seems to me, when I look back on it, as boundless as the desert. It's a prospect that, at all events, such figures as you and your wonderful friends, my dear man, help to people. And I may say about *them*," he went on, "that I should like really — in the interest of the impression that I confess that the young lady makes on me — to propose to you a fair agreement."

On which, amusedly enough, Newman debated as they went. "That I shall shut my eyes to what you want to do?"

"Well, yes — say I may expect you'll shut them to me as soon as I shall find you've opened them to the grand manner in which your old gentleman *is* a man of the world. You'll be obliged, I'm convinced, to recognise it, and I only ask you to let me know, in all honesty, when you've done so."

"So that *you*, in all honesty — ?"

"Well, call it in all delicacy!" Valentin suggested.

Newman continued to wonder. "May have a free hand — ?"

"Without your being shocked," the young man gracefully said.

But it only made our friend rather quaintly groan. "I think it's your delicacies, all round, that shock me most!"

"Ah, don't say," Valentin pleaded, "that I'm at the worst a man of duty! See for yourself!" His English cousins had come into view, and he advanced gallantly to meet the lady in the green crape bonnet.

~~drifting about unpiloted, and evidently deemed that they had a grievance. Newman left him to their mercies, but with a boundless faith in his power to plead his cause.~~

XII

~~CHAPTER XII.~~

THREE days after his introduction to the family of Madame de Cintré, ~~Newman, coming in toward evening,~~ found upon his table the card of the Marquis de Bellegarde. On the following day he received a note informing him that ~~the Marquise de Bellegarde would be grateful for the honour~~ of his company at dinner.

He went, of course, though he had ~~to break another engagement to do it.~~ He was ushered into the room in which Madame de Bellegarde had received him before, and here he found his venerable hostess, surrounded by her entire family. The room was lighted only by the crackling fire, which illumined the very small pink slippers of a lady who, ~~seated in~~ a low chair, ~~was~~ stretch~~ing~~ out her toes ~~before~~ it. This lady was the younger Madame de Bellegarde. ~~Madame de Cintré~~ was seated at the other end of the room, holding a little girl against her knee, the child of her brother Urbain, to whom she was apparently relating a wonderful story. Valentin ~~was sitting~~ on a puff close to his sister-in-law, into whose ear he was certainly distilling the finest nonsense. The Marquis was stationed before the ~~fire with~~ his head erect and his hands behind him, in an attitude of formal expectancy.

~~Old Madame de Bellegarde~~ stood up to give Newman her greeting, and there was that in the way she did so which seemed to measure narrowly the ~~extent of her condescension.~~ "We ~~are~~ all alone, you see; we ~~have~~ asked no one else," she said austerely.

Handwritten additions:

- Coming in toward evening,
- he
- requested the pleasure
- this gentleman's mother
- from
- ed
- first to disengage himself from appeals that struck him as in comparison, the babble of vain things.
- perched
- had
- chimney,
- always less effectively present, somehow than perceptibly posted. Mme. de Cintré, not posted at all but oh so present,
- The old Marquise
- quantity of importance such a demonstration might appear to attach to him.
- 're
- 've

"I am very glad you didn't; this is much more sociable," said Newman. "Good evening, sir," and he offered his hand to the Marquis.

M. de Bellegarde was affable, but in spite of his dignity he was restless. He began to pace up and down the room; he looked out of the long windows, he took up books and laid them down again. Young Madame de Bellegarde gave Newman her hand without moving and without looking at him.

"You may think that is coldness," exclaimed Valentin, "but it is not, it is warmth. It shows she is treating you as an intimate. Now she detests me, and yet she is always looking at me."

"No wonder I detest you if I am always looking at you!" cried the lady. "If Mr. Newman does not like my way of shaking hands I will do it again."

But this charming privilege was lost upon our hero, who was already making his way across the room to Madame de Cintré. She looked at him as she shook hands, but she went on with the story she was telling her little niece. She had only two or three phrases to add, but they were apparently of great moment. She deepened her voice, smiling as she did so, and the little girl gazed at her with round eyes.

"But in the end the young prince married the beautiful Florabella, [struck through] and carried her off to live with him in the Land of the Pink Sky. There she was so happy that she forgot all her troubles, and went out to drive every day of her life in an ivory coach drawn by five hundred white mice. Poor Florabella," she explained to Newman, "had suffered terribly."

"She had had nothing to eat for six months," said little Blanche.

"Yes, but when the six months were over she had a plum-cake as big as that ottoman," said Madame de Cintré. "That quite set her up again."

"What a chequered career!" said Newman. "Are

yet

changed his place, fidgetted about,

explained;

as she accepted from him the customary form,

over

the last confidence, and you'll grow up to it.

for him

mentioned

strong constitution and what a

Newman's visitor

returned.

you very fond of children?" He was certain that she was, but he wished to make her say it.

"I like to talk with them; [illegible] we can talk with them so much more seriously than with grown persons. That is great nonsense that I have been telling Blanche, but it is a great deal more serious than most of what we say in society."

"I wish you would talk to me, then, as if I were Blanche's age," said Newman, laughing. "Were you happy at your ball the other night?"

"Ecstatically!"

"Now you are talking the nonsense that we talk in society," said Newman. "I don't believe that."

"It was my own fault if I was not happy. The ball was very pretty, and every one very amiable."

"It was on your conscience," said Newman, "that you had annoyed your mother and your brother."

Madame de Cintré looked at him a moment without answering. "That is true," she replied at last. "I had undertaken more than I could carry out. I have very little courage; I am not a heroine." She said this with a certain soft emphasis, but then changing her tone, "I could never have gone through the sufferings of the beautiful Florabella," she added, "not even for her prospective rewards."

Dinner was announced, and Newman betook himself to the side of old Madame de Bellegarde. The dining-room, at the end of a cold corridor, was vast and sombre; the dinner was simple and delicately excellent. Newman wondered whether Madame de Cintré had had something to do with ordering the repast, and greatly hoped she had. Once seated at table, with the various members of the ancient house of Bellegarde round him, he asked himself the meaning of his position. Was the old lady responding to his advances? Did the fact that he was a solitary guest augment his credit or diminish it? Were they ashamed to show him to other people, or did they

must be

has much more value

Extravagantly

ed.

he presently risked,

in

possibly

silence.

She

he could feel, to be very true, to be

and, with a fine applied power of remote projection, hoped this might have been

with him, and it touched him as if she had pressed into his hand, for reminder, some note she had scrawled or some ribbon or ring she had worn

if the daughter of the house

so rigidly closed a circle

X Remote projection,

wish to give him a sign of sudden adoption into their last reserve of favour? ~~Newman~~ was on his guard; he was watchful and conjectural, ~~and~~ yet at the same time he was vaguely indifferent. Whether they gave him a long rope or a short ~~one~~ he was there now, and Madame de Cintré was opposite ~~to~~ him. She had a tall candlestick on each side of her; she would sit there for the next hour, and that was enough. The dinner was extremely solemn and measured; he wondered ~~whether~~ this was always the state of things in "old families." Madame de Bellegarde held her head very high, and fixed her eyes, which looked peculiarly sharp in her little finely-wrinkled white face, very intently ~~upon~~ the table-service. The Marquis appeared to have decided that the fine arts offered a safe subject of conversation, as not leading to startling personal revelations. Every now and then, having learned from Newman that he had been through the museums of Europe, he uttered some polished aphorism upon the flesh-tints of Rubens and the good taste of Sansovino. ~~His~~ manners seemed to indicate a fine nervous dread that something disagreeable might happen if the atmosphere were not ~~purified by allusions of a thoroughly superior cast.~~ "What under the sun is the man afraid of?" Newman asked himself. "Does he think I'm going to offer to swap jack-knives with him?" It was useless to shut his eyes to the fact that the Marquis ~~was profoundly disagreeable to him.~~ He had never been a man of strong personal aversions; his nerves had not been at the mercy of the mystical qualities of his neighbours. But here was a man ~~towards~~ whom he was irresistibly in opposition; a man of forms and phrases and postures; a man full of possible impertinences and treacheries. M. de Bellegarde made him feel as if he were standing barefooted on a marble floor; and yet, to gain his desire, Newman felt perfectly able to stand. He ~~wondered~~ what Madame de Cintré thought of his being accepted, if ~~accepted it was.~~ There was

He

if

on

He struck his guest as pre-cautionary, as ~~and~~ apprehending his

kept clear of stray currents from windows open at hazard.

was as disagreeable to him as some queer, rare, possibly dangerous biped, perturbingly akin to humanity, in one of the cages of a "show."

asked himself

in respect to

it were acceptance that was thus conveyed to him.

no judging from her face, which expressed simply the desire to ~~[illegible]~~ in a manner which should require as little explicit recognition as possible. Young Madame de Bellegarde had always the same manner,; ~~she was always~~ preoccupied, distracted, listening to everything and hearing nothing, looking at her dress, her rings, her finger-nails, ~~seeming rather bored, and yet puzzling you to decide what was~~ her ideal of social diversion. Newman was enlightened on this point later. Even Valentin ~~did not quite seem~~ master of his wits; his vivacity was fitful and forced, ~~yet Newman observed that in the lapses of his talk he appeared excited. His eyes had an intenser spark than usual. The effect of all this was that Newman,~~ for the first time in his life, was not himself; ~~that~~ he measured his ~~movements~~ and counted his words; ~~and resolved that if the occasion demanded that he should appear to have swallowed a ramrod, he would meet the emergency.~~

After dinner M. de Bellegarde proposed to his guest that they should go into the smoking-room, and he led the way towards a small somewhat musty apartment, the walls of which were ornamented with old hangings of stamped leather and trophies of rusty arms. Newman refused a cigar, but he established himself upon one of the divans while the Marquis puffed his own weed before the fireplace and Valentin sat looking through the light fumes of a cigarette from one to the other.

"I can't keep quiet any longer," ~~said Valentin~~ at last. "I must tell you the news and congratulate you. My brother seems unable to come to the point; he revolves round his announcement like the priest round the altar. You are accepted as a candidate for the hand of our sister."

"Valentin, be a little proper!" murmured the Marquis, with a look of the most delicate irritation contracting the bridge of his high nose.

"There has been a family council," ~~the young man~~

Show kindness

You to pronounce on

and seeming ineffably bored she yet defied!

failed quite to seem

motions

but his friend felt his fine eyes shine through the lapses of the talk very much as the effect of Newman's himself being pinched very hard in the dark.

The sense

This personage,

his brother

the young man broke out

he had the sense of sitting in a boat that required inordinate balancing and that a wrong movement might cause to capsize.

continued; "my mother and Urbain have put their heads together, and even my testimony has not been altogether excluded. My mother and the Marquis sat at a table covered with green cloth; my sister-in-law and I were on a bench against the wall. It was like a committee at the Corps Législatif. We were called up, one after the other, to testify. We spoke of you very handsomely. Madame de Bellegarde said that if she had not been told who you were, she would have taken you for a duke—an American duke, the Duke of California. I said ~~that~~ I could warrant you grateful for the smallest favours—modest, humble, unassuming. I was sure ~~that~~ you would know your own place always, and never give us occasion to remind you of certain differences. ~~After all, you couldn't help it if you were not a duke.~~ There were none in your country; but if there had been, it was certain that, ~~smart and active as you are~~, you would have got the pick of the ~~titles~~. At this point I was ordered to sit down, but I think I made an impression in your favour."

M. de Bellegarde ~~looked at his brother with dangerous coldness, and gave a smile as thin as the edge of a knife.~~ Then he removed a spark of cigar-ash from the sleeve of his coat; he fixed his eyes for a while on the cornice of the room, and at last he inserted one of his white hands into the breast of his waistcoat. "I must apologise to you for ~~the deplorable levity of~~ [illegible] notify you that this is probably not the last time that his want of tact will cause you serious embarrassment."

"No, I confess I ~~h~~ave no tact," said Valentin. "Is your embarrassment really ~~painful~~, Newman? ~~The Marquis will~~ put you right again; ~~his own touch is deliciously delicate~~."

"~~Valentin, I am~~ sorry to say," the Marquis continued, "has never ~~possessed the tone, the manner, that belong to a young man in his position. It has been a great~~

You couldn't help it, after all, if you had not come in for a duke-dom.

honours.

with your energy and agility,

Valentin's inveterate bad taste, as well as

looked at his brother as Newman had seen unfortunates look at who have told before waiting auditors stories of no effect.

My brother, I'm

Urbain will

serious,

he'll know just how you feel."

had the real sense of his duties as his opportunities – of what one must after all call his position. It has been a great pain

affliction to his mother, who is very fond of the old traditions. But you must remember that he speaks for no one but himself."

"Oh, I don't mind him, sir," said Newman, good humouredly. "I know what he amount to."

"In the good old times," said Valentin, "marquises and counts used to have their appointed fools and jesters, to crack jokes for them. Nowadays we see a great strapping democrat keeping a count about him to play the fool. It's a good situation, but I certainly am very degenerate."

M. de Bellegarde fixed his eyes for some time on the floor. "My mother informed me," he said, presently, "of the announcement that you made to her the other evening."

"That I desired to marry your sister?" said Newman.

"That you wished to arrange a marriage," said the Marquis, slowly, "with my sister, the Comtesse de Cintré. The proposal was serious, and required, on my mother's part, a great deal of reflection. She naturally took me into her counsels, and I gave my most zealous attention to the subject. There was a great deal to be considered; more than you appear to imagine. We have viewed the question on all its faces, we have weighed one thing against another. Our conclusion has been that we favour your suit. My mother has desired me to inform you of our decision. She will have the honour of saying a few words to you on the subject herself. Meanwhile, by us, the heads of the family, you are accepted."

Newman got up and came nearer to the Marquis. "You will do nothing to hinder me, and all you can to help me, eh?"

"I will recommend my sister to accept you."

Newman passed his hand over his face, and pressed it for a moment upon his eyes. This promise had a great sound, and yet the pleasure he took in it was embittered by his having to stand there so and receive his passport

sir" – Newman was all good-humour.

the Valentines of this world

buffoons

resumed

want so much to

the young man said,

has let me know,

one of 'us' as Urbain would say,

gave my mother – you can perhaps even yourself imagine a great deal to think about.

desire to approach the Comtesse de Cintré with that idea, and ask of us therefore your facility for so doing.

engage to you to throw my weight into the scale of your success.

You have our sanction, as

personally will do all you can to back me up, eh?"

You thus of our favourable attitude.

see no reason to oppose your pretention – though of course the matter, the question of your success, rests mainly with yourself."

perhaps appear to conceive

the subject has had my most careful attention.

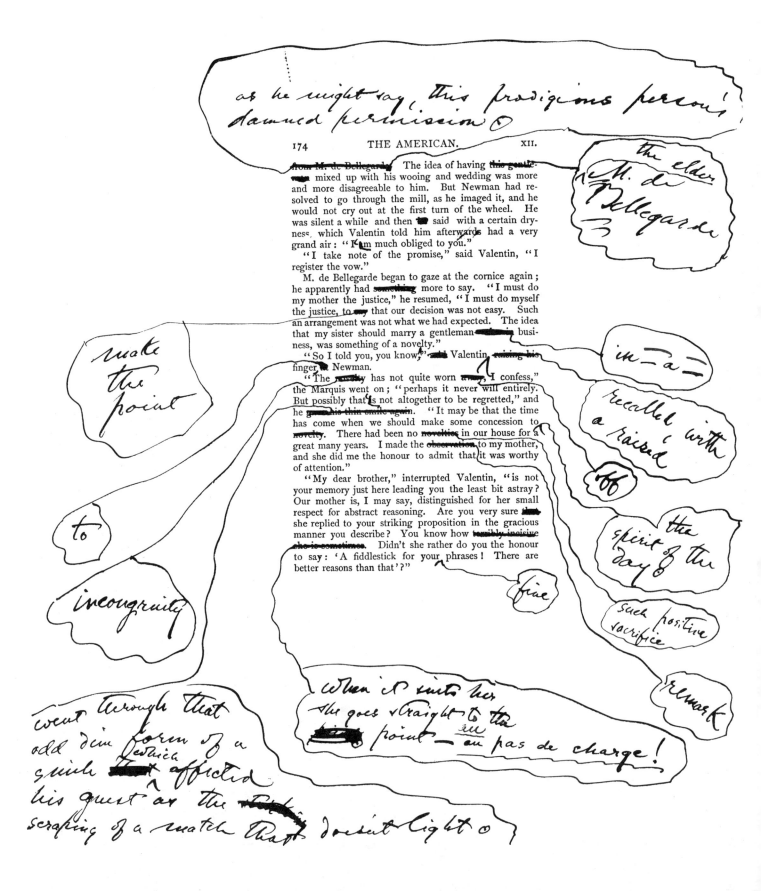

as he might say, this prodigious person's damned permission

~~from M. de Bellegarde.~~ The idea of having ~~this gentleman~~ mixed up with his wooing and wedding was more and more disagreeable to him. But Newman had resolved to go through the mill, as he imaged it, and he would not cry out at the first turn of the wheel. He was silent a while and then ~~he~~ said with a certain dryness, which Valentin told him afterwards had a very grand air: "I am much obliged to you."

"I take note of the promise," said Valentin, "I register the vow."

M. de Bellegarde began to gaze at the cornice again; he apparently had ~~something~~ more to say. "I must do my mother the justice," he resumed, "I must do myself the justice, to ~~say~~ that our decision was not easy. Such an arrangement was not what we had expected. The idea that my sister should marry a gentleman ~~engaged in~~ business, was something of a novelty."

"So I told you, you know," ~~said~~ Valentin, ~~raising his~~ finger ~~at~~ Newman.

"The ~~novelty~~ has not quite worn ~~away~~, I confess," the Marquis went on; "perhaps it never will entirely. But possibly that is not altogether to be regretted," and he ~~gave his thin smile again~~. "It may be that the time has come when we should make some concession to ~~novelty~~. There had been no ~~novelties~~ in our house for a great many years. I made the ~~observation~~ to my mother, and she did me the honour to admit that it was worthy of attention."

"My dear brother," interrupted Valentin, "is not your memory just here leading you the least bit astray? Our mother is, I may say, distinguished for her small respect for abstract reasoning. Are you very sure ~~that~~ she replied to your striking proposition in the gracious manner you describe? You know how ~~terribly incisive she is sometimes~~. Didn't she rather do you the honour to say: 'A fiddlestick for your phrases! There are better reasons than that'?"

the elder M. de Bellegarde

make the point

in — a —

recalled, with a raised

off

to

incongruity

the spirit of the day

fine

such positive sacrifice

remark

When it suits her she goes straight to the point — au pas de charge!

went through that odd dim form of a smile which affected his guest as the scraping of a match that doesn't light

"Other reasons were discussed," said the Marquis, without looking at Valentin, but with an audible tremor in his voice; "some of them possibly were better. We are conservative, Mr. Newman, but we are not also bigots. We judged the matter liberally. We have no doubt that everything will be comfortable."

Newman had stood listening to these remarks with his arms folded and his eyes fastened upon M. de Bellegarde. "Comfortable?" he said, with a sort of grim flatness of intonation. "Why shouldn't we be comfortable? If you are not, it will be your own fault; I have everything to make *me* so."

"My brother means that with the lapse of time you may get used to the change," and Valentin paused, to light another cigarette.

"What change?" asked Newman, in the same tone.

"Urbain," said Valentin, very gravely. "I am afraid that Mr. Newman does not quite realise the change. We ought to insist upon that."

"My brother goes too far," said M. de Bellegarde. "It is his fatal want of tact again. It is my mother's wish, and mine, that no such allusions should be made. Pray never make them yourself. We prefer to assume that the person accepted as the possible husband of my sister is one of ourselves, and that he should have no explanations to make. With a little discretion on both sides everything [illegible] will be easy. That is exactly what I wished to say—that we quite understand what we have undertaken, and that you may depend upon our adhering to our resolution."

Valentin shook his hands in the air and then buried his face in them. "I have less tact than I might have, no doubt; but oh, my brother, if you knew what you yourself are saying!" And he went off into a long laugh.

highly

a slightly more nasal pitch;

"Justified?" he echoed with his way of putting rather less than more sense into the words he repeated. Why shouldn't we be? I assure you I've ~~quite~~ no fear for myself.

we have never, I trust been stupidly narrow; we are judging this so interesting question on its merits only. We've no doubt we shall be fully justified."

difference? unimaginatively Newman asked.

He has no sense of what shouldn't be said.

I don't quite stir them myself.

not breaking down.

ought to

difference.

observed to Newman.

necessary

~~draught~~ tact

ful

Comparisons

M. de Bellegarde's face flushed a little, but he held his head higher, as if to repudiate this concession to vulgar perturbability. "I ~~am~~ sure you ~~understand me,~~" he said to Newman.

"Oh no, ~~I don't understand you at all~~," said Newman. "But you needn't mind that. I don't care. In fact, I ~~think I had better not understand you. I might not like it. Th~~at wouldn't suit me at all, you know. I ~~want to marry your sister~~, that's all; to do it as quickly as possible, and to ~~find fault with nothing~~. I don't care ~~how I do it. I am not marrying you, you know, sir. I~~ [illegible], and that is all I want."

"You had better ~~receive~~ the last word from my mother," said the Marquis.

"Very good; I'~~will~~ go and get it," ~~said~~ Newman ~~and he~~ prepared to return to the drawing-room.

M. de Bellegarde made a motion for him to pass first, and ~~when Newman had gone out he~~ shut himself into the room with Valentin. Newman had been a trifle bewildered by the ~~audacious irony of the younger brother, and he~~ had not needed its aid to ~~point the moral of M. de Bellegarde's transcendent patronage. He had wit enough to appreciate the force of that civility which consists in calling your attention to the impertinences it spares you.~~ But he had ~~felt warmly the delicate sympathy~~ [illegible] ~~himself~~ that underlay Valentin's ~~fraternal irreverence~~, and ~~he~~ was ~~most~~ unwilling ~~that his friend~~ should pay a tax ~~upon~~ it. He paused a moment in the corridor, after he had gone a few steps, expecting to hear the resonance of M. de Bellegarde's displeasure; but he detected only a perfect stillness. The stillness itself seemed a trifle portentous; he reflected, however, that he had no right to stand listening, and he made his way back to the salon. In his absence several persons had come in. They were scattered about the room in groups, two or three of them having passed into a small boudoir, next to the drawing-room, which had now been lighted and opened. Old Madame de Bellegarde was in her place by the fire, talking to a very old gentleman in a wig and a profuse white

quite know what I mean,

not quite—or perhaps not at all," Newman answered.

I want,

I want,

whether I know—or even, really, I think, what you say; for if I did there might be things I shouldn't like, and that

nevertheless receive

And

very obstinately, to marry your sister, and nobody other

do as little else beside.

Therefore how I do it—as regards the rest of you.

recognised all the bravery of Valentin's backing

felt the limits of the elder brother's. That was what he had heard of as patronage—a great historic and traditional force that he now personally encountered for the first time in his life. Didn't it consist in calling attention to the impertinences it spared you?

play of his friend's wit and free

I must take care, with so many of you in it, that it doesn't become practical polygamy. I've got my footing.

on his going so

neckcloth of the fashion of 1820. Madame de Cintré ~~was bending~~ a listening head to the historic confidences of an old lady who was presumably the wife of the old gentleman in the neckcloth, an old lady in a red satin dress and an ermine cape, ~~who wore across her~~ forehead ~~a band with a topaz set in it~~. Young Madame de Bellegarde, when ~~Newman~~ came in, left some people among whom she was sitting and took the place ~~that~~ she had occupied before dinner. Then she gave a little push to the puff that stood near her, and ~~by a glance at Newman~~ seemed to indicate that she had placed it in position for him. He went and took possession of it; the Marquis's wife amused and puzzled him.

"I know your secret," she said, in her bad but charming English; "you need make no mystery of it. You wish to marry my sister-in-law. *C'est un beau choix.* A man like you ought to marry a tall thin woman. You must know that I ~~have~~ spoken in your favour; you owe me a famous taper!"

"You ~~have~~ spoken to Madame de Cintré?" said Newman.

"Oh no, not that. You may think it strange, but my sister-in-law and I are not so intimate as that. ~~Newman spoke to~~ my husband and my mother-in-law. I said I was sure we could do what we chose with you."

"I am much obliged to you," ~~said Newman~~, laughing; "but you can't."

"I know that very well; I didn't believe a word of it. But I wanted you to come into the house; I thought we should be friends."

"I am very sure of it," said Newman.

"Don't be too sure. If you like ~~Madame de Cintré~~ so much, perhaps you ~~will not~~ like me. We are as different ~~as blue and~~ ~~pink~~. But you and I have something in common. I ~~have~~ come into this family by marriage; you want to come into it in the same way."

had bent

whose

was adorned with a topaz set in a velvet band

he

by a glance

in effect

well of me

I'm really on your side and in your interest

~~But~~ Taking my courage in my hand, I put in my word for you to

Newman

you'll find

won't

the Comtesse

— well as this fan and that poker

178 THE AMERICAN. XII.

"Oh no, I don't," interrupted Newman. "I only want to take Madame de Cintré out of it."

"Well, to cast your nets you have to go into the water. Our positions are alike; we shall be able to compare notes. What do you think of my husband? It's a strange question, isn't it? But I shall ask you some stranger ones yet."

"Perhaps a stranger one will be easier to answer," said Newman. "You might try me."

"Oh, you get off very well; the old Comte de la Rochefidèle, yonder, couldn't do it better. I told them that if we only gave you a chance you ~~would~~ be a perfect ~~[illegible]~~. I know something about men. Besides, you and I belong to the same camp. I am a ferocious ~~democrat~~. By birth I am *vieille roche;* a good little bit of the history of France is the history of my family. Oh, you never heard of us, of course! *Ce que c'est que la gloire!* We are much better than the Bellegardes, at any rate. But I don't care a pin for my pedigree; I want to belong to my time. ~~I'm a revolutionist, a radical, a child of the age.~~ I am sure I go beyond you. I like clever people, wherever they come from, and I take my amusement wherever I find it. I don't pout at the Empire; here all the world pouts at the Empire. Of course I have to mind what I say; but I expect to take my revenge with you." ~~Madame de Bellegarde~~ discoursed for some time longer in this sympathetic strain, with an eager abundance which seemed to indicate that her opportunities for revealing her esoteric philosophy were indeed rare. She hoped ~~that~~ Newman would never be afraid of her, however he might be with the others, for, really, she went very far indeed. "Strong people"—*les gens forts* —were in her opinion equal, all the world over. Newman listened to her with an attention at once beguiled and irritated. He wondered what the deuce she, too, was driving at, with her hope ~~that~~ he would not be afraid of her and her protestations of equality. In so far as he

want to come into it all

—not a wee mite!

I'm more modern than you, you know—because I've been through this and come out, very far out, which you haven't. Oh, you don't know what this. Vous allez bien voir.

So, being a reactionary—from the reaction—

The little lady

That's what you lack, you know—that you're not reactionary enough.

could understand her, she was wrong; a silly rattling woman was certainly not the equal of a sensible man, preoccupied with an ambitious passion. Madame de Bellegarde stopped suddenly, and looked at him sharply, shaking her fan. "I see you don't believe me; you are too much on your guard. You will not form an alliance, offensive or defensive? You are very wrong; I could help you."

Newman answered that he was very grateful, and that he would certainly ask for help; she should see. "But first of all," he said, "I must help myself." And he went to join Madame de Cintré.

"I have been telling Madame de la Rochefidèle that you are an American," she said as he came up. "It interests her greatly. Her father went over with the French troops to help you in your battles in the last century, and she has always, in consequence, wanted greatly to see an American. But she has never succeeded till to-night. You are the first—to her knowledge—that she has ever looked at."

Madame de la Rochefidèle had an aged cadaverous face, with a falling of the lower jaw which prevented her from bringing her lips together, and reduced her conversation to a series of impressive but inarticulate gutturals. She raised an antique eye-glass, elaborately mounted in chased silver, and looked at Newman from head to foot. Then she said something to which he listened deferentially, but which he completely failed to understand.

"Madame de la Rochefidèle says that she is convinced that she must have seen Americans without knowing it," Madame de Cintré explained. Newman thought it probable she had seen a great many things without knowing it; and the old lady, again addressing herself to utterance, declared—as interpreted by Madame de Cintré—that she wished she had known it.

At this moment the old gentleman who had been talking to the elder Madame de Bellegarde drew near, leading the

— he didn't admit her equality

never on a level with

you're

really

The young Marquise

won't

their hostess

that lady

~~Marquise~~ on his arm. His wife pointed out Newman to him, apparently explaining his remarkable origin. M. de la Rochefidèle, whose old age was rosy and ~~rotund~~, spoke very neatly and ~~clearly~~; almost as prettily, Newman thought, as M. Nioche. When he had been enlightened, he turned to Newman with an inimitable elderly grace.

"Monsieur is by no means the first American that I have seen," he said. "Almost the first person I ever saw—to notice him—was an American."

"Ah!" said Newman sympathetically.

"The great Dr. Franklin," said M. de la Rochefidèle. "Of course I was ~~very young~~. He was received very well in our *monde*."

"Not better than Mr. Newman," said Madame de Bellegarde. "I beg he will offer me his arm into the other room. I could have offered no higher privilege to Dr. Franklin."

Newman, complying with ~~Madame de Bellegarde's~~ request, perceived that her two sons had returned to the drawing-room. He scanned their faces an instant for traces of the scene that had followed his separation from them, but the Marquis ~~seemed neither more nor less frigidly grand than usual, and~~ ~~Valentin~~ was kissing ladies' hands ~~with at least his habitual air of self-abandonment to the act~~. Madame de Bellegarde gave a glance at her eldest son, and by the time she had crossed the threshold of her boudoir he was at her side. The room was now empty and offered a sufficient degree of privacy. The old lady disengaged herself from Newman's arm and rested her hand on ~~the arm of the Marquis~~; and in this position she stood a moment, ~~holding her head high and biting her small under lip~~. I am afraid the picture was lost upon Newman, but Madame de Bellegarde was, in fact, at this moment a striking image of the dignity which—even in the case of a little time-shrunken old lady—may reside in the habit of unquestioned authority and the absoluteness of a social theory favourable to yourself.

"My son has spoken to you as I desired, and you understand that we shall not interfere. The rest will lie with yourself."

"M. de Bellegarde told me several things I didn't understand," said Newman, "but I made out that. You will leave me an open field. I am much obliged."

"I wish to add a word that my son probably did not feel at liberty to say," the Marquise rejoined. "I must say it for my own peace of mind. We are stretching a point; we are doing you a great favour."

"Oh, your son said it very well; didn't you?" said Newman.

"Not so well as my mother," declared the Marquis.

"I can only repeat—I am much obliged."

"It is proper I should tell you," Madame de Bellegarde went on, "that I am very proud and that I hold my head very high. I may be wrong, but I am too old to change. At least I know it, and I don't pretend to anything else. Don't flatter yourself that my daughter is not proud. She is proud in her own way—a somewhat different way from mine. You will have to make your terms with that. Even Valentin is proud, if you touch the right spot—or the wrong one. Urbain is proud—that you see for yourself. Sometimes I think he is a little too proud; but I wouldn't change him. He is the best of my children; he cleaves to his old mother. But I have said enough to show you that we are all proud together. It is well that you should know the sort of people you have come among."

"Well," said Newman, "I can only say, that I am not proud; I shan't mind you! But you speak as if you intended to be very disagreeable."

"I shall not enjoy having my daughter marry you, and I shall not pretend to enjoy it. If you don't mind that, so much the better."

the person holding it.

'll

You have nothing to fear from our opposition.

let me stand on my merits. I'm

ed

pursued.

nevertheless

we've gone very far to meet you.

as if to relieve an insistent inward need,

declared.

to feel certain things as I do, but it's too late for me to change. At least I know it's so and I know also why.

"Well," Newman returned, "I don't know what I can do but make a note of it and try to profit by it."

hope I'm as little like you as may be. But though I don't think I'm easy to scare you spoke as if you quite intended to be as disagreeable as you know how."

if my

decides to

very much aware of ourselves and very absurd and rather impossible,

a very stiff old person and that I don't pretend not to be.

His hostess fixed him a moment.

× then

"If you stick to your own side of the contract we shall not quarrel; that is all I ask of you," said Newman. "Keep your hands off, and give me an open field. I am very much in earnest, and there is not the slightest danger of my getting discouraged or backing out. You will have me constantly before your eyes; if you don't like it, I am sorry for you. I will do for your daughter, if she will accept me, everything that a man can do for a woman. I am happy to tell you that, as a promise—a pledge. I consider that on your side you make me an equal pledge. You will not back out, eh?"

"I don't know what you mean by 'backing out,'" said the Marquise. "It suggests a movement of which I think no Bellegarde has ever been guilty."

"Our word is our word," said Urbain. "We have given it."

"Well," said Newman, "I am very glad you are so proud; it makes me believe you will keep it."

The Marquise was silent a moment, and then, suddenly, "I shall always be polite to you, Mr. Newman," she declared, "but, decidedly, I shall never like you."

"Don't be too sure," said Newman, laughing.

"I am so sure that I will ask you to take me back to my armchair without the least fear of having my sentiments modified by the service you render me." And Madame de Bellegarde took his arm, and returned to the salon and to her customary place.

M. de la Rochefidèle and his wife were preparing to take their leave, and Madame de Cintré's interview with the mumbling old lady was at an end. She stood looking about her, asking herself, apparently, to whom she should next speak, when Newman came up to her.

"Your mother has given me leave—very solemnly—to come here often," he said. "I mean to come often."

"I shall be glad to see you," she answered, simply. And then in a moment: "You probably think it very strange that there should be such a solemnity—as you say—about your coming."

"Well, yes; I do, rather."

"Do you remember what my brother Valentin said, the first time you came to see me—that we were a strange, strange family?"

"It was not the first time I came, but the second," ~~said~~ Newman.

"Very true. Valentin annoyed me at the time, but now I know you better. I may tell you he was right. If you come often, you will see!" And Madame de Cintré turned away.

~~Newman~~ watched her a while, talking with other people, and then ~~he~~ took his leave. He shook hands last with Valentin, ~~de Bellegarde,~~ who came out with him to the top of the staircase. "Well, you ~~have got your permit," said Valentin.~~ "I hope you liked the process."

"I like your sister more than ever. But don't worry your brother any more, for my sake," Newman ~~[illegible] I don't mind him. I am~~ afraid he came down on you in the smoking-room after I went out."

"When my brother comes down on me," said Valentin, "he falls hard. I have a ~~peculiar~~ way of receiving him. I must say," he continued, "that ~~they came up to the mark much~~ sooner than I expected. I don't understand it; they must have ~~had to turn the screw pretty tight~~. It's a tribute to your ~~[illegible]~~ solidity."

"Well, ~~it's the most precious one they have ever received," said Newman.~~

~~He~~ was turning away when Valentin stopped him, ~~looking at him with a brilliant softly-cynical glance.~~ "I should like to know whether, within a few days, you have seen your venerable friend M. Nioche."

"He was yesterday at my rooms," ~~Newman answered.~~

"What ~~did he~~ tell you?"

"Nothing particular."

[Manuscript revisions:]
amended ⊙
He
've taken out your passport," said that young man ⊙
and that you admire our red tape ⊙"
added ⊙ "There must be something the matter with him ⊙"
"There's a good deal!" said his friend with an odd laugh ⊙
more effectually
had he to
"Well I don't seem to mind him—I don't seem to mind anything!" Newman just a bit musingly acknowledged ⊙ I'm only
"You can cut them a daily slice of it and let them have it with their morning coffee?" But he was
"Well if my solidity's all they want!" Newman again rather pensively breathed ⊙
particular
put forward their clock!
They've fallen into line—for it has been a muster of all our forefathers too!—

"You didn't see the ~~muzzle of a pistol~~ sticking out of his pocket?"

"What are you driving at?" Newman demanded. "I thought he seemed rather cheerful, for him."

Valentin broke into a laugh. "I am delighted to hear ~~it! I win my bet.~~ ~~Mademoiselle Noémie~~ has ~~thrown her cap over the mills, as they say. She has left the paternal domicile. She is launched! And M. Nioche is~~ rather cheerful—*for him!* Don't brandish your tomahawk at that ~~rate. I have~~ not seen her nor communicated with her since that day at the Louvre. Andromeda has found another Perseus than I. My information is exact; on such matters it always is. I suppose that now you will raise your protest?"

~~"My protest be hanged!" murmured Newman, disgustedly.~~

~~But his tone found no echo in that in which Valentin, with his hand on the door, to return to his mother's apartment, exclaimed: "But I shall see her now! She is very remarkable—she is very remarkable!"~~

~~CHAPTER~~ XIII.

NEWMAN kept his promise, or his menace, of ~~going often to~~ the Rue de l'Université, and during the next six weeks he saw Madame de Cintré more times than he could have numbered. He flattered himself ~~that he was not~~ in love, but his biographer may be supposed to know better. He claimed, at least, none of the exemptions and emoluments of the ~~romantic passion. Love, he believed, made a fool of a man, and his present emotion was not folly but wisdom—wisdom sound, serene, well directed.~~ What he ~~felt~~ was an intense all-consuming tenderness, which had for its object an extraordinarily

[Manuscript revisions, in the author's hand:]

weapon of Virginius

"Hate" the young man went on; "I'm

he wound up "that I may now so elaborately cease to neglect her?"

"Oh, if this a matter of conscience with you—!" Newman resignedly growled. On which Valentin held him a moment with a wonderful smile. "How can't a young person be in whom I see such elements?"

of his high spirits—they make me so beautifully right and so innocently happy. For what they mean, you see, is that his charming child is placed, favourably, at last, for the real exercise of her talents, and that they are relieved, almost equally, from the awkwardness of a false position. And M. Nioche is

was conscious of

never had a control of his reason or a higher opinion of his judgement.

merely infatuated state. That state he

considered was consistent with asininity, and he had

presenting himself often in

he had not fallen, as the foolish phrase had it,

graceful and harmonious, yet at the same time insidiously agitating woman, who lived in a grand grey house on the left bank of the Seine. His theory of his relation to her was that he had become conscious of how beautifully she might, for the question of his future, come to his aid; but this left unexplained the fact that his confidence had somehow turned to a strange, muffled heart-ache. He was in truth infinitely anxious, and, when he questioned his anxiety, knew it was not all for himself. If she might come to his aid he might come to hers; and he had the imagination — more than he had ever had in his life about anything — of fantastic straits or splendid miseries in the midst of which, standing before her with wide arms out, he would have seen her let herself, even if still just desperately and blindly, make for his close embrace as for a refuge. He really wouldn't have minded if some harsh need for mere money had most driven her; the creak of that hinge would have been sweet to him had it meant the giving way of the door of separation. What he wanted was to _take_ her, and that her feeling herself taken should come back to him for their common relief. The full surrender, so long as she didn't make it, left the full assurance an unrest and a yearning — from which all his own refuge was in the fine ingenuity, the almost grim extravagance, of the prospective provision he was allowing to accumulate. She gave him the sense of "suiting" him so, exactly as she was, that his desire to interpose for her and close about her had something of the quality of that solicitude with which a fond mother might watch from the window even the restricted garden-play of a child recovering from an accident. But he was above all simply charmed, and the more for feeling wonderstruck, as the days went on, at the proved rightness of the instinct and of the calculation that had originally moved him. It was as if there took place for him, each day, such a revelation of the possible number of forms of the "personal" appeal as he could otherwise never have enjoyed, and as made him yet ask himself how, *how*, all unaided (save as Mrs. Tristram, subtle woman, had aided him!) he could have known. For he *had*, amazingly, known. And the impression must now thereby have been for him, he thought, very much that of the wistful critic or artist who studies "style" in some exquisite work or some quiet genius, and who sees it come and come, and never fail, like the truth of a perfect voice or the safety of a perfect temper. And just as such a student might say to himself "How could I have got on without this particular research?" so Newman could only say "Fancy this being to be had and — with my general need — my not having it!"

He made no violent love and, as he would have said, no obvious statements; he just attended regularly, as he would also have said, in the manner of the "interested party" present at some great liquidation where he must keep his eye on what concerns him. He never trespassed on ground she had made his regard, ruefully enough, as forbidden; but he had none the less a sustaining sense that she knew better from day to day all the good he thought of her. Though in general no great talker , and almost incapable, on any occasion, of pitching his voice for the gallery, he now had his advances as well as his retreats, and felt that he often succeeded in bringing her, as he might have called it, into the open. He determined early not to care if he should bore her, whether by speech or by silence — since he certainly meant she should so suffer, at need, before he had done; and he seemed at least to know that even if she actually suffered she liked him better, on the whole, with too few fears than with too many. Her visitors, coming in often while he sat there, found a tall, lean, slightly flushed and considerably silent man, with a lounging, permanent-looking seat, who laughed out sometimes when no one had meant to be droll, and remained grave in the presence of those calculated witticisms and those initiated gaieties for the appreciation of which he apparently lacked the proper culture and the right acquaintances. It had to be confessed that the number of the subjects upon which he was without ideas was only equalled by the number of the families to which he was not allied; and it might have been added more gravely still that as regards those subjects upon which he was without ideas he was also quite without professions. He had little of the small change of conversation, and rarely rose to reach down one of those ready-made forms and phrases that drape, whether fresh or frayed, the hooks and pegs of the general wardrobe of talk — that repository in which alone so many persons qualify for the ordeal of society, as supernumerary actors prepare, amid a like provision, for that of the footlights. He was able, on the other hand, at need, to make from where he sat one of the long arms that stretch quite out of the place — to the effect, as might mostly be felt, of coming back with some proposition as odd as a single shoe.

Bent, at any rate, on attendance, he had at his command treasures of attention, and never measured the possibilities of interest in a topic by his own power of contribution to it: he liked topics to grow at least big enough for him to walk round them and see. This made, for his advantage, to his being little acquainted with satiety either of sound or of sense; he was not himself more often bored than he was often alarmed, and there was no man with whom it would have been a greater mistake than to take his

intermissions always for absences, or his absences always for [holidays].
What it was that entertained or that occupied him during some of his speechless sessions I shall not, however, undertake fully to say. The Marquis[e] Urbain had once found occasion to declare to her that he reminded [her], in company, of a swimming-master she had once had, who would never himself go into the water, and who yet, at the baths, en costume de ville, managed to control and direct the floundering scene without so much as getting splashed. He had so made her angry, she professed, when he turned her awkwardness to ridicule. Newman affected her in [like] manner as keeping [so much] too dry: it was urgent for her that he should be splashed — otherwise what was he doing at the baths? — and she even hoped to get him into the water. We know in a general way that many things which were old stories to those about him had for him the sharp high note, [but] should probably find a complete list of his new impressions surprising enough. He related to Madame de [C]intré stories, sometimes not brief, from his own repertory; he was full of

reference to his own great country, over the greatness of which it seldom occurred to him that everyone mightn't, on occasion offered, at least intellectually yearn; and he explained to her, in talking of it, the working of a hundred institutions and the ingenuity of almost all arrangements. Judging by the sequel, judging even by the manner in which she suffered his good faith to lay an apparent spell upon her attitude, she was mildly — oh mildly and inscrutably! — beguiled; but one wouldn't have been sure beforehand of the shade of her submission. As regards any communication she herself made him he couldn't on the whole but guess she "wanted" to make it: this was in so far an amendment to the portrait Mrs. Tristram had drawn of her.

He had been right at first in feeling her a little — or more than a little — proudly shy; her shyness, in a woman whose circumstances and tranquil beauty afforded every facility for sublime self-possession was only a charm the more. For Newman it had lasted some time and had, even when it went, left something behind it that for a while performed the same office. Was this the uneasy secret of which Mrs. Tristram had had a glimpse, and of which, as of her friend's reserve, her high breeding and her profundity, she had given a sketch marked by outlines perhaps rather too emphatic? He supposed so, yet as a result to find himself wondering rather less what Madame de Cintré's secrets might consist of and rather more convinced that secrets would be in themselves hateful and inconvenient things, things as depressing and detestable as inferior securities, for such a woman to have to lug, as he inwardly put it, round with her. She was a creature for the sun and the air, for no sort of hereditary shade or equivocal gloom, and her natural line was neither imposed reserve nor mysterious melancholy, but positive life, the life of the great world — *his* great world, not the *grand monde* as there understood if he wasn't mistaken, which seemed squeezable into a couple of rooms of that inconvenient and ill-warmed house: all with nothing worse to brood about, when necessary, than the mystery, perhaps, of the happiness that would so queerly have come to her. To some perception of his view and his judgment, and of the patience with which he was prepared to insist on them, he fondly believed himself to be day by day bringing her round. She mightn't, she couldn't yet, no doubt, wholly fall in with them, but she saw, he made out, that he had built a bridge that would bear the very greatest weight she should throw on it, and it was for him often, all charmingly, as if she were admiring, from this side and that, the bold span of the arch and the high line of the parapet — as if indeed, on occasion, she stood straight there at the spring just watching him at his extremity, and with nothing, when the hour should strike, to prevent her crossing with a rush.

He often spent an evening, and when Madame de Cintré had so appointed — her motives and her method and her logic being meanwhile something of her own, though something thus beautifully between them, even if never named, and which he wouldn't for the world have asked her to name — he often passed a stiff succession of minutes at the somewhat chill fireside of Madame de Bellegarde; contenting himself there, for the most part, with looking across the room, through narrowed eyelids, at his mistress, who always made a point, before her family, of talking to someone else. Her mother on the other scene would sit by the fire conversing neatly and coldly with whomsoever approached her and yet detaching for his own especial benefit a glance that seemed to say: "See how completely I'm interested, how agreeably I'm occupied, how deeply I'm absorbed." He often wondered what those supposedly honoured by this intensity of participation thought of her at such moments, and he sometimes answered her look by looking at *them*; but no one, for all the fine community of taste, that air in the place as of bitter convictions dissolved in iced indifference and partaken of, for refreshment, with small rare old "family" spoons, appeared to meet him on any such particular question, any more intimately than on any other and all by direct default of ability; which would have made him again ask himself, but for his constant anxious ache, what he was doing in so deadly a hole at all. To ache very hard at one point, he found, was practically to be unconscious of punctures at any other. When he at all events made his bow to the old lady by the fire

~~ing round the room with her slowly-restless eye, the effect of which, when it lighted upon him, was to Newman's sense identical with that of a sudden spurt of damp ing. When he shook hands with her~~ he always asked her with a laugh whether she could "stand him" another evening, and she replied, without a laugh, that, thank God, she had always been able to do her duty. ~~Newman, talking once of the Marquise~~ to Mrs. Tristram, ~~said~~ that, after all, it was very easy to get on with her; it always was easy to get on with out-and-out rascals.

"And is it by that elegant term [illegible] that you designate the Marquise ~~de Bellegarde~~?"

"Well, [illegible] she is wicked, [illegible] old sinner."

"What ~~is her crime~~?" [illegible]

"I shouldn't wonder if she had ~~murdered~~ some one,—all from a sense of duty, of course."

"How can you be so dreadful?" ~~sighed~~ Mrs. Tristram.

"I am not dreadful. I am speaking of her favourably."

"Pray what will you say when you want to be severe?"

"I shall keep my severity for some one else,—~~for the~~ Marquis. There's a man I can't swallow, mix the drink as I will."

"And what has *he* done?"

"I can't quite make out, it is something ~~dreadfully bad, something mean and underhand, and~~ not redeemed ~~by audacity, as his mother's misdemeanours may have been.~~ If he has never committed murder he has at least turned his back and looked the other way while some one else was committing it."

In spite of this ~~invidious~~ hypothesis, ~~which must be taken for nothing more than an example of the capricious play of "American humour,"~~ Newman did his best to maintain an easy and friendly style of communication with M. de Bellegarde. So long as he was in personal contact with people he disliked extremely to have anything to forgive them, and ~~he~~ was capable of a good deal of unsuspected imaginative effort (for the sake of his own personal comfort) to assume for the time that they were good fellows. He did his best to treat the Marquis as [illegible]; he believed honestly, moreover, that he could not, in reason, be such a confounded fool as he seemed. Newman's familiarity was never importunate; his sense of human equality was not an aggressive taste or an æsthetic theory, but something as natural and organic as a physical appetite which had never been put on a scant allowance, and consequently was innocent of ungraceful eagerness. His tranquil unsuspectingness of the relativity of his own place in the social scale was probably irritating to M. de Bellegarde, who saw himself reflected in the mind of his potential brother-in-law in a crude and colourless form, unpleasantly dissimilar to the impressive image projected upon his own intellectual mirror. He never forgot himself for an instant, and replied to what he must have considered Newman's "advances" with mechanical politeness. Newman, who was constantly forgetting himself, and indulging in an unlimited amount of irresponsible inquiry and conjecture, now and then found himself confronted by the conscious ironical smile of his host. What the deuce M. de Bellegarde was smiling at he was at a loss to divine. M. de Bellegarde's smile may be supposed to have been, for himself, a compromise between a great many emotions. So long as he smiled he was polite, and it was proper he should be polite. A smile, moreover, committed him to nothing more than politeness, and left the degree of politeness agreeably vague. A smile, too, was neither dissent—which was too serious—nor agreement, which might have brought on terrible complications. And then a smile covered his own personal dignity, which in this critical situation he was resolved to keep immaculate; it was quite enough that the glory of his house should pass into eclipse. Between him and Newman, his whole manner seemed to declare, that there could be no interchange of opinion; he could but hold his breath so as not to inhale tha strong smell — since who liked such very strong smells? — of a democracy so gregarious as to be unable not to engender heat and perspiration.

Newman was far from being versed in "European" issues, as he liked to call them; but he was now on the very basis of aspiring to light, and it had more than once occurred to him that he might here both arrive at it and give this acquaintance the pleasure of his treating him as an oracle. Interrogated, however, as to what he thought of public affairs, M. de Bellegarde answered on each occasion, and quite indeed as if thanking him for the opportunity, that he thought as ill of them as possible, that they were going from bad to worse, though there was always at least the comfort of their being too dreadful to touch. This gave our friend, momentarily, almost an indulgence for a spirit so depressed; he pitied the man who had to look at him in such a fashion when he ventured to insist, particularly about their great shining France, "Why, don't you see anything anywhere?" — and he was brought by it to an attempt, possibly indiscreet, to call attention to some of the great features of the world's progress. This had presently led the Marquis to observe, once for all, that he entertained but a single political conviction — dearer to him, however, than all the others, put together, that other people might entertain: he believed, namely, in the divine right of Henry of Bourbon, Fifth of his name, to the throne of France. This had in truth, upon Newman, as many successive distinct effects as the speaker could conceivably have desired. It made him in the first place look at the latter very hard, harder than he had ever done before; which had the appearance somehow of affording M. de Bellegarde another of the occasions he personally appreciated. It was as if he had never yet shown how he could return such a look; whereby, producing that weapon of his armoury, he made the demonstration brilliant. Then he reduced his guest, further, just to staring, with a conscious, foolish failure of every resource, at one of the old portraits on the wall, out of which some dim light for him might in fact have presently glimmered. Lastly it determined on Newman's part a wise silence as to matters he didn't understand. He relapsed, to his own sense, into silence, very much as he would have laid down, on consulting it by mistake, some flat-looking back-number or some superseded time-table. It might do for the collection craze, but wouldn't do for use.

One afternoon, on his presenting himself, he was requested by the servant to be so good as to wait, a very few minutes, till Madame la Comtesse should be at liberty. He moved about the room a little, taking up a book here and there as with a vibration of tact in his long and strong fingers; he hovered, with a bent head, before flowers that he recognised as of a "lot" he himself must have sent; he raised his eyes to old framed prints and grouped miniatures and disposed photographs, ten times as many of which she should some day possess; and at last he heard the opening of a door to which his back was turned. On the threshhold stood an old woman whom he remembered to have met more than once in entering and leaving the house. She was tall and straight, and dressed in black, and she wore a cap which, if Newman had been initiated into such mysteries, would have sufficiently assured him she was not a Frenchwoman; a cap of

XIII. THE AMERICAN. 191

pure British composition. She had a pale, decent, depressed-looking face, and a clear, dull, English eye. She looked at Newman a moment, both intently and timidly, and then she dropped a short, straight, English curtsy.

"~~Madame de Cintré~~ begs you will kindly wait, [illegible] [illegible] She has just come in; she will soon have finished dressing."

"Oh, I will wait as long as she wants," said Newman. "Pray tell her not to hurry."

"Thank you, sir," said the woman softly; and then, instead of retiring with the message, ~~she~~ advanced into the room. She looked about her for a moment and presently ~~went to the~~ table and began to ~~arrange certain books and nick-nacks~~. Newman was struck with the high respectability of her appearance; he was afraid to address her as a servant. She busied herself for some moments with ~~putting the table in order and pulling the~~ curtains straight, while Newman ~~walked slowly to and fro~~. He perceived at last, from her reflection in the mirror, as he was passing, that her hands were idle and ~~that she was looking at him intently~~. She evidently wished to say something, and ~~Newman~~, perceiving it, helped her to begin.

"~~You~~ are English?" [illegible]

"~~Yes, sir, please~~," she answered, quickly and softly; "I was born in Wiltshire."

"And what do you think of Paris?"

"Oh, I don't think of Paris, sir," she said in the same tone. "It's so long ~~since I have~~ been here."

"Ah, you have been here very long?"

"~~It's~~ more than forty years, sir. I came over with Lady Emmeline."

"You mean with old Madame de Bellegarde?"

"Yes, sir. I came with her when she ~~was~~ married. I was my lady's own woman."

"And you have been with her ever since?"

The Countess

a

Mother attentively hovered○

he

"I guess you're English, aint you?"

"Oh dear, yes"

dispose again several small articles○

ordering various trifles with putting out cushions and pulling

her eyes fixed on him○

that seat

"I have been in the house ever since. My lady has taken a younger person. You see I am very old. I do nothing regular now. But I keep about."

"You look very strong and well," said Newman, observing the erectness of her figure, and a certain venerable rosiness in her cheek.

"Thank God I am not ill, sir; I hope I know my duty too well to go panting and coughing about the house. But I am an old woman, sir, and it is as an old woman that I venture to speak to you."

"Oh, speak out," said Newman, curiously. "You needn't be afraid of me."

"Yes, sir. I think you are kind. I have seen you before."

"On the stairs, you mean?"

"Yes, sir. When you have been coming to see the Countess. I have taken the liberty of noticing that you come often."

"Oh yes; I come very often," said Newman, laughing. "You need not have been very wide-awake to notice that."

"I have noticed it with pleasure, sir," said the ancient tirewoman, gravely. And she stood looking at Newman with a strange expression of face. The old instinct of deference and humility was there; the habit of decent self-effacement and knowledge of her "own place." But there mingled with it a certain mild audacity, born of the occasion and of a sense, probably, of Newman's unprecedented approachableness, and, beyond this, a vague indifference to the old proprieties; as if my lady's own woman had at last begun to reflect that, since my lady had taken another person, she had a slight reversionary property in herself.

"You take a great interest in the family?" said Newman.

"A deep interest, sir. Especially in the Countess."

kink

"Very good of you, sir"

his

he asked

Keep about remarkably

"I like," he genially added "to see you about"

he laughed

this interesting member of the family

our friends? →

She looked at him as if she liked that expression and had never ~~before~~ heard anything quite like it.

"I'm glad of that," said Newman. And ~~in a moment he added, smiling, "So do I!"~~

"So I supposed, sir. We can't help noticing these things and having our ideas; can we, sir?"

"You mean as a servant?" ~~said Newman.~~

"Ah, there it is, sir. I'm afraid that when I let my thoughts meddle with such matters I ~~am no longer a servant.~~ But I'm so devoted to the Countess; if she were my own child I couldn't love her more. That's how I come to be so bold, sir. They say you want to marry her."

Newman eyed his interlocutress, ~~and satisfied himself that she was not a gossip, but a zealot; she looked anxious, appealing, discreet. "It is quite true," he added.~~ I want to marry Madame de Cintré."

"And to take her away to America?"

"I'll take her wherever she wants to go."

"The farther away the better, sir!" exclaimed the old woman with sudden intensity. But she checked herself and, taking up a paper-weight in mosaic, began to polish it with her black apron. "I don't mean anything against the house or the family, sir. But I think a great change would do the poor Countess good. ~~It is very sad here."~~

~~"Yes, it's not very lively," said Newman.~~ "But Madame de Cintré ~~is gay herself."~~

"She ~~is everything~~ that is good. You will not be vexed to hear that she has been ~~gayer for a couple of~~ months past than she had been for many a day before."

Newman was delighted to gather this testimony to the prosperity of his suit, but he ~~repressed all violent marks of elation. "Has Madame de Cintré been in bad spirits before this?" he asked.~~

~~"Poor lady, she had good reason. M. de Cintré was no husband for a sweet young lady like that. And then, as I say, it has been a sad house. It is better, in my humble opinion, that she were out of it.~~ So, if you

Handwritten revisions:

an old

He smilingly followed it up ⊙ "You can't take more than I do!"

Rather a step out of my place ⊙

Her boldness failed her a moment but she brought it round with a turn ⊙

There's no great life here ⊙"

has everything in her heart

"Oh, life—!" he quite sarcastically sighed ⊙

more her natural self these two

he added "has great courage in her heart ⊙"

[illegible]ore than I ever wanted anything in my life ⊙

"It's perfectly true ⊙

and, as if something had suddenly begun to depend on it, made up his mind about her ⊙ Something at least passed between them with his exchange of distinct truths and at the end of a minute he felt almost like a lost child kindly taken by the hand. He gave the hand a responsive grasp ⊙ He looked quite up into the deep tried face ⊙

will excuse me for saying so, I hope she will marry again."

"I hope she will!" said Newman.

"But you must not lose courage, sir, if she doesn't make up her mind at once. That is what I wanted to beg of you, sir. Don't give it up, sir. You will not take it ill if I say it's a great risk for any lady at any time; all the more when she has got rid of one bad bargain. But if she can marry a good, kind, respectable gentleman, I think she had better make up her mind to it. They speak very well of you, sir, in the house, and, if you will allow me to say so, I like your face. You have a very different appearance from the late Count; he wasn't five feet high. And they say your fortune is beyond everything. There's no harm in that. So I beseech you to be patient, sir, and bide your time. If I don't say this to you, sir, perhaps no one will. Of course it is not for me to make any promises. I can answer for nothing. But I think your chance is not so bad, sir. I am nothing but a weary old woman in my quiet corner, but one woman understands another, and I think I make out the Countess. I received her in my arms when she came into the world, and her first wedding-day was the saddest of my life. She owes it to me to show me another and a brighter one. If you will hold firm, sir—and you look as if you would—I think we may see it."

"I am much obliged to you for your encouragement," said Newman, heartily. "One can't have too much. I mean to hold firm. And if Madame de Cintré marries me, you must come and live with her."

The old woman looked at him strangely, with her soft lifeless eyes. "It may seem a heartless thing to say, sir, when one has been forty years in a house, but I may tell you that I should like to leave this place."

"Why, it's just the time to say it," said Newman, fervently. "After forty years one wants a change."

"You are very kind, sir;" and this faithful servant dropped another curtsy and seemed disposed to retire. But she lingered a moment, and gave a timid joyless smile. Newman was disappointed, and his fingers stole half shyly, half irritably into his waistcoat-pocket. His informant noticed the movement. "Thank God I am not a Frenchwoman," she said. "If I were, I would tell you, with a brazen simper, old as I am, that if you please, Monsieur, my information is worth something. Let me tell you so in my own decent English way. It *is* worth something."

"How much, please?" said Newman.

"Simply this, a promise not to hint to the Countess that I have said these things."

"If that is all, you have it," said Newman.

"That is all, sir. Thank you, sir. Good-day, sir." And having once more slid down telescope-wise into her scanty petticoats, the old woman departed. At the same moment Madame de Cintré came in by an opposite door. She noticed the movement of the other *portière*. and asked Newman who had been entertaining him.

"The British female," said Newman. "An old lady in a black dress and a cap, who curtsies up and down, and expresses herself ever so well."

"An old lady who curtsies and expresses herself? Ah, you mean poor Mrs. Bread. I happen to know that you have made a conquest of her."

"Mrs. Cake, she ought to be called," said Newman. "She is very sweet. She is a delicious old woman."

Madame de Cintré looked at him a moment. "What can she have said to you? She is an excellent creature, but we think her rather dismal."

"I suppose," Newman answered, presently, "that I like her because she has lived near you so long. Since your birth, she told me."

"Yes," said Madame de Cintré simply, "she is very faithful; I can trust her."

- impatiently
- mercenary
- gone so far off
- "Oh, I promise all right"
- "I do believe you keep, sir!"
- His friend
- So much
- dim,
- ey
- person
- (by a single word)
- sir: your solemn
- "And when I promise — !"
- — in her most venerable form ⊙
- bobs
- bobs
- declared ⊙
- answered,
- absolutely
- Yes — such an age as that makes! She's very faithful" Madame de Cintré went on simply ⊙

"Why, respect's a big feeling. But I guess I do." "You guess? &c, &c

Newman had never made any reflection to this lady upon her mother and her brother Urbain; had given no hint of the impression they made upon him. But, as if she had guessed his thoughts, she seemed careful to avoid all occasion for making him speak of them. She never alluded to her mother's domestic decrees; she never quoted the opinions of the Marquis. They had talked, however, of Valentin, and she had made no secret of her extreme affection for her younger brother. Newman listened sometimes with a certain harmless jealousy; he would have liked to divert some of her tender allusions to his own credit. Once Madame de Cintré told him, with a little air of triumph, about something that Valentin had done which she thought very much to his honour. It was a service he had rendered to an old friend of the family; something more "serious" than Valentin was usually supposed capable of being. Newman said he was glad to hear of it, and then began to talk about something which lay upon his own heart. Madame de Cintré listened, but after a while she said: "I don't like the way you speak of my brother Valentin." Hereupon Newman, surprised, said that he had never spoken of him but kindly.

"It is too kindly," said Madame de Cintré. "It is a kindness that costs nothing; it is the kindness you show to a child. It is as if you didn't respect him."

"Respect him? Why, I think I do."

"You think? If you are not sure, it is no respect."

"Do you respect him?" said Newman. "If you do, I do."

"If one loves a person, that is a question one is not bound to answer," said Madame de Cintré.

"You should not have asked it of me, then. I am very fond of your brother."

"He amuses you. But you would not like to resemble him."

perfectly could guess his feeling and subtly spare his nerves, she had markedly avoided any

a vague, irrepressible pang; if he could only have caught in his own cup a few drops of that overflow

She once spoke to him with candid elation of

and useful

poor

he

His companion

guess

asked

then

But I guess I do.

respect's a big feeling.

It's as if you rather looked down on him.

he protested.

"Well, it's just the sort of kindness," she smiled; "the

save in kindness.

But

"I shouldn't like to resemble any one. It's hard enough work resembling oneself."

"What do you mean," ~~asked Madame de Cintré,~~ "by resembling oneself?"

"Why, doing what's expected of one. Doing one's duty."

"But that's ~~only~~ when one's very good."

"Well, a great many people are good ~~said Newman.~~ "Valentin ~~is quite~~ good enough for me."

~~Madame de Cintré was silent for a short time. "He is not good enough for me," she said at last.~~ "I wish he would do something."

"~~What can he do?" asked Newman.~~

"~~Nothing. Yet~~ he's very clever."

"~~It is a proof of cleverness," said Newman,~~ "to be happy without doing anything."

"I don't think Valentin's ~~happy, in reality~~ ... ~~clever~~, generous, brave—but what is there to show for it? To me there's something sad in his life, and sometimes I have a sort of foreboding about him. I don't know why, ~~but I fancy he will have some great trouble—perhaps an~~ unhappy end."

"Oh, leave him to me," ~~said Newman, jovially. "I will watch over him and keep harm away."~~

One evening at ~~in~~ Madame de Bellegarde's, ~~salon~~, the conversation had flagged most sensibly. The Marquis walked up and down in silence, like a sentinel at the door of some ~~smooth-fronted~~ citadel of the proprieties; his mother sat staring at the fire; ~~young Madame de Bellegarde~~ worked at an enormous band of tapestry. Usually there were three or four visitors, but on this occasion a violent storm sufficiently accounted for the absence of even the most ~~devoted habitués~~. In the long silences the howling of the wind and the beating of the rain were distinctly audible. Newman sat perfectly still, watching the clock, determined to stay till the stroke of eleven, ~~but~~ not a moment longer. Madame

She asked,

e,

at all events is

could

hard—or at any rate it's urgent—only enough—so long as they insist on being so," he laughed optimistically.

She was silent a little, and then, with inconsequence, "Well, I could wish him rather better!" she declared.

"Well,

Her companion considered; after which, candidly: "What in the world can Valentine do?"

"But I guess it is a proof of power," Newman went on,

assiduous,

his wife

and

menaced

however this might be,

had in that lady's own apartment

Newman cheerfully returned. "I guess I can keep him all right."

really so happy. He's intelligent,

"Ah but I don't think

but it seems to come to me that he may have some great trouble—perhaps a really de Cintré had turned her back to the circle, and had been standing for some time within the uplifted curtain of a window, with her forehead against the pane, gazing out into the deluged darkness. Suddenly she turned round toward her sister-in-law.

"For heaven's sake," she said with peculiar eagerness, "go to the piano and play something."

Madame de Bellegarde held up her tapestry and pointed to a little white flower. "Don't ask me to leave this. I am in the midst of a masterpiece. My flower is going to smell very sweet; I am putting in the smell with this gold-coloured silk. I am holding my breath; I can't leave off. Play something yourself."

"It is absurd for me to play when you are present," said Madame de Cintré. But the next moment she went to the piano and began to strike the keys with vehemence. She played for some time, rapidly and brilliantly; when she stopped, Newman went to the piano and asked her to begin again. She shook her head, and, on his insisting, she said: "I have not been playing for you; I have been playing for myself." She went back to the window again and looked out, and shortly afterwards left the room. When Newman took leave Urbain de Bellegarde accompanied him, as he always did, just three steps down the staircase. At the bottom stood a servant with his overcoat. He had just put it on when he saw Madame de Cintré coming towards him across the vestibule.

"[illegible] you be at home on Friday?" Newman asked.

She looked at him a moment before answering his question. "You don't like my mother and my brother," she said.

He hesitated a moment, and then he said softly, "No."

She laid her hand on the balustrade and prepared to ascend the stairs, fixing her eyes on the first step.

~~[blotted]~~ be at home on Friday," and she passed up ~~the wide dusky staircase~~.

On the Friday, as soon as he came in, she asked him to ~~please to tell her why he disliked~~ her family.

"~~Dislike your family?" he exclaimed.~~ That has a ~~horrid sound. I didn't say so, did I? I didn't mean it, if I did~~."

"I wish you would tell me what you think of them," ~~said Madame de Cintré~~.

"I don't think of any of them but you."

"That's because you dislike them. Speak the truth; you can't offend me."

"Well, ~~I don't exactly love your brother," said Newman.~~ "I remember now. But what's the use of ~~my saying so? I had forgotten it~~."

"You're too good-natured," ~~said~~ Madame de Cintré ~~gravely~~. Then, as if to avoid the appearance of inviting him to speak ill of ~~the Marquis~~, she turned away, motioning him to sit down.

But he remained standing before her, and said presently, "What's of much more importance is that they ~~don't like me~~."

"~~No, they don't," she said~~.

"And don't you think they're wrong?" Newman asked. "I don't ~~believe I am~~ a man to dislike."

"I suppose that a man who may be liked may also be disliked. ~~And~~ my brother—my mother," she added, "have ~~not~~ made you angry?"

"~~Yes, sometimes.~~"

"You've never shown it."

"So much the better."

"Yes, so much the better. They think they've treated you ~~very well~~."

"~~I have no doubt they might have handled me much more roughly," said Newman.~~ ~~[blotted]~~ ~~obliged to them~~. Honestly."

she brought out; and she passed up while he watched her.

be so good as to tell her why he had such an aversion to

Such an aversion? Did I call it that? Don't think I make too much of it. See how easily I work it.

said

gravely

I could live, at a pinch, without the Marquis," Newman confessed. "It comes to me now if you mention it.

she simply said.

too much.

But

our bringing it up? I don't think him."

They must have let me off pretty easily," Newman went on; "for see how little I feel damaged. And I think I show you everything.

her brother,"

they can scarcely stand me."

don't strike myself as

rather handsomely."

"Scarcely," she said with a mild, odd distinctness.

"Well, I can no doubt they could much have been worse.

"Oh yes, often."

never

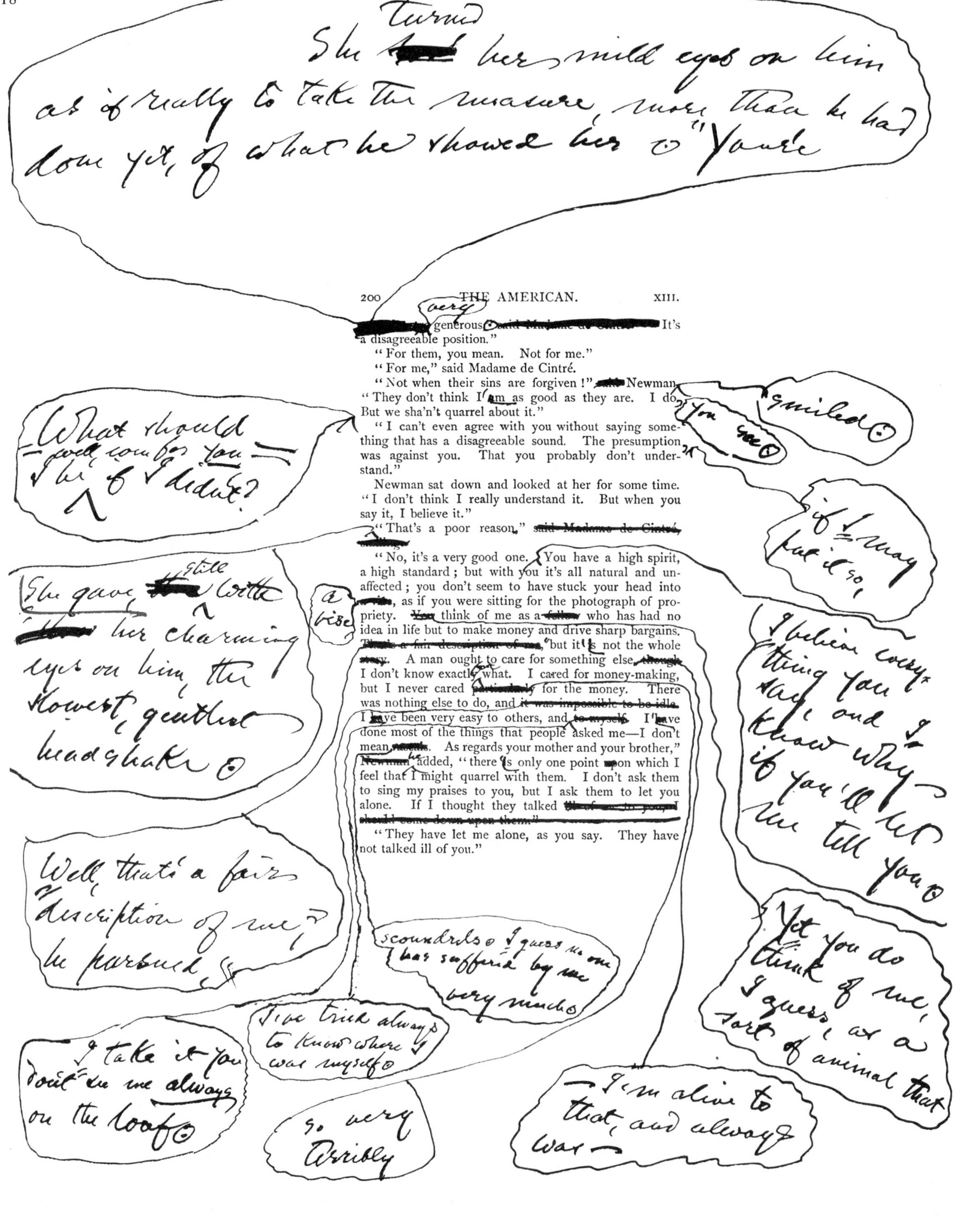

generous, said Madame de Cintré. It's a disagreeable position."

"For them, you mean. Not for me."

"For me," said Madame de Cintré.

"Not when their sins are forgiven!" said Newman. "They don't think I am as good as they are. I do. But we sha'n't quarrel about it."

"I can't even agree with you without saying something that has a disagreeable sound. The presumption was against you. That you probably don't understand."

Newman sat down and looked at her for some time. "I don't think I really understand it. But when you say it, I believe it."

"That's a poor reason," said Madame de Cintré,

"No, it's a very good one. You have a high spirit, a high standard; but with you it's all natural and unaffected; you don't seem to have stuck your head into a vise, as if you were sitting for the photograph of propriety. You think of me as a fellow who has had no idea in life but to make money and drive sharp bargains. That's a fair description of me, but it is not the whole story. A man ought to care for something else, though I don't know exactly what. I cared for money-making, but I never cared particularly for the money. There was nothing else to do, and it was impossible to be idle. I have been very easy to others, and to myself. I have done most of the things that people asked me—I don't mean rascals. As regards your mother and your brother," Newman added, "there is only one point upon which I feel that I might quarrel with them. I don't ask them to sing my praises to you, but I ask them to let you alone. If I thought they talked ill of me to you, I should come down upon them."

"They have let me alone, as you say. They have not talked ill of you."

- She turned her mild eyes on him as if really to take the measure, more than he had done yet, of what he showed her. "You're very
- You see
- smiled.
- What should I be of comfort to you if I didn't?
- if I may put it so,
- She gave still with her charming eyes on him the slowest, gentlest headshake.
- a vise
- I believe everything you say and I know why if you'll let me tell you.
- Yet you do think of me, I guess, as a sort of animal that
- Well, that's a fair description of me, he pursued,
- scoundrels. I guess no one has suffered by me very much.
- I've tried always to know where I was myself.
- I take it you don't see me always on the loaf.
- so very horribly
- I'm alive to that, and always was

(201

"In that case," cried Newman, "I declare they are only too good for this world!"

Madame de Cintré appeared to find something startling in his exclamation. She would, perhaps, have replied, but at this moment the door was thrown open, and Urbain de Bellegarde stepped across the threshold. He appeared surprised at finding Newman, but his surprise was but a momentary shadow across the surface of an unwonted jollity. Newman had never seen the Marquis so exhilarated; his pale unlighted countenance had a sort of thin transfiguration. He held open the door for some one else to enter, and presently appeared old Madame de Bellegarde, leaning on the arm of a gentleman whom Newman had not seen before. He had already risen, and Madame de Cintré rose, as she always did before her mother. The Marquis, who had greeted Newman almost genially, stood apart, slowly rubbing his hands. His mother came forward with her companion. She gave a majestic little nod at Newman, and then she released the strange gentleman, that he might make his bow to her daughter.

"My daughter," she said, "I have brought you an unknown relative, Lord Deepmere. Lord Deepmere is our cousin, but he has done only to-day what he ought to have done long ago—come to make our acquaintance."

Madame de Cintré smiled, and offered Lord Deepmere her hand. "It is very extraordinary," said this noble laggard, "but this is the first time that I have ever been in Paris for more than three or four weeks."

"And how long have you been here now?" asked Madame de Cintré.

"Oh, for the last two months," said Lord Deepmere.

These two remarks might have constituted an impertinence; but a glance at Lord Deepmere's face would have satisfied you, as it apparently satisfied Madame de Cintré, that they constituted only a naïveté. When his

against me to you at all badly I would come down on them. For I feel that then I really could."

They have let me alone, as you say. They haven't talked against you to me badly at all badly."

She gave him, with this, the exquisite pleasure of a sense that she liked to use and adopt, as it were, his words. "Well then I'm ready to cheer."

This brought something into her face that, as it was apparently relief, he didn't quite understand; and she might have spoken in the same sense if at the moment the door had not been thrown open and

followed by the old Marquise, supported

had not

him

was

He produced the effect of an old faded portrait that had suddenly undergone restoration.

saw for the first time. He was already on his feet,

connect

His other observations

The young man—he was still a young man—showed no hesitation.

in my life I've

he ingenuously remarked

she said.

dropped her soft but steady light on this visitor, who had advanced to take her hand.

nothing about him could be well explained save in the light of his simplicity. When their group was

[illegible] seated, Newman, who was out of the conversation, ~~occupied himself with observing the new comer. Observation, however, as regards Lord Deepmere's person, had no great range. He was a small meagre man, of some three and thirty years of age, with a bald head, a short nose, and no front teeth in the upper jaw; he had round, candid, blue eyes, and several pimples on his chin. He was evidently very shy, and he laughed a great deal, catching his breath with an odd startling sound, as the most convenient imitation of repose. His physiognomy denoted great simplicity, a certain amount of brutality, and a probable failure in the past to profit by rare educational advantages. He remarked that Paris was awfully jolly, but that~~ [illegible]. ~~He even preferred Dublin to London.~~ Had Madame de Cintré ever been to Dublin? They must all come over ~~there~~ some day, and he would show them some Irish sport. ~~He always went to Ireland for the fishing, and he came to Paris for the new Offenbach things. They always brought them out in Dublin, but he couldn't wait. He had been nine times to hear La Pomme de Paris.~~ Madame de Cintré, leaning back, with her arms folded, ~~looked at Lord Deepmere with a more visibly puzzled face than she usually showed to society. Madame de Bellegarde, on the other hand, wore a fixed smile.~~ The Marquis said that among light operas his favourite was the "Gazza Ladra." The Marquise then began a series of inquiries about the duke and the cardinal, the old ~~countess~~ duchess and Lady Barbara, after listening to which, and to Lord Deepmere's somewhat irreverent responses, for a quarter of an hour, Newman rose to take his leave. The Marquis went with him three steps into the hall.

"Is he Irish?" asked Newman, nodding in the direction of the visitor.

"His mother was the daughter of Lord Fincucane; [illegible] he has great Irish estates. Lady

His other advantages beyond his three and thirty years were a scant stature and an odd figure, a bald head, a short nose, round clear blue eyes, and a frank and natural smile which made the loss of a couple of front teeth by some misadventure constantly conspicuous. Perceptibly diffident, he laughed more than once as if in sign he were bold, catching his breath with a loud startling sound. He admitted that Paris was charming, but he was a wild bog-trotting Paddy, who preferred his Dublin even to his London and who would [illegible] caught him [illegible] save for his taste for light music. He came over for the new Offenbach things, for though they always brought them out in Dublin he couldn't wait.

He had been nine times to hear "La Pomme de Paris."

and her eyes, attached to him, might have been drifting away from him conveniently and resignedly on some deep slow current. Her mother on the other hand smiled as if in celebration of him, but without looking at him.

[illegible] inflicted on him [illegible] that unless he had the benefit of that he had the benefit of nothing.

Bridget, in the complete absence of male heirs, either direct or collateral—a most extraordinary circumstance—came in for ~~everything. But~~ Lord Deepmere's title is ~~English, and his English property is immense.~~ He's a charming young man."

Newman answered nothing, but he detained the Marquis as the latter was beginning gracefully to recede. "It's a good time for me to thank you, ~~he said,~~ for sticking so punctiliously to our bargain, for doing so much to help me ~~on~~ with your sister."

The Marquis stared. "Really, I've done nothing that I can boast of," ~~he said~~.

"Oh, don't be modest," Newman ~~answered, laughing~~. "I can't flatter myself ~~that~~ I'm doing so well simply by my own merit. ~~And thank your mother for me, too~~!" And, ~~he turned~~ away, ~~leaving~~ M. de Bellegarde looking after him.

no end of things."

takes his principal title, however, from his English property, which

Please tell your Mother too, won't you? how I feel it."

turning

he left

so well, that is, as I hope and pray—

END OF VOL. I.

blank copy

Printed by R. & R. Clark, *Edinburgh.*

THE AMERICAN.

XIV.

The next time Newman came to the Rue de l'Université he had the good fortune to find Madame de Cintré alone. He had come with a definite intention, and he lost no time in executing it. She wore, moreover, a look which he eagerly interpreted as expectancy. [illegible] [illegible] coming to see you for six months, now, [illegible] I have never spoken to you a second time of marriage. That was what you asked me; I obeyed. Could any man have done better?"

"You have acted with great delicacy," said Madame de Cintré.

"Well, I am going to change now. [illegible] [illegible] don't mean that I am going to be indelicate, but I am going to go back to where I began. I *am* back there. I have been all round the circle. Or rather, I have never been away from there. I have never ceased to want what I wanted then. Only now I am more sure of it, if possible; I am more sure of myself, and more sure of you. I know you better, though I don't know anything I didn't believe three months ago. You are everything, you are beyond everything, I can imagine or desire. You know me now, you *must* know me. I won't say that you have seen the best—but you have seen the worst. I hope you have been thinking all this while. You must have seen that I was only waiting; you can't suppose that I was changing. What will you say to me now? Say that everything is clear and reasonable and that I have been very patient and considerate, and deserve my reward. And then give me your hand. Madame de Cintré, do that. Do it."

"I knew you were only waiting," she said; "and I was very sure this day would come. I have thought about it a great deal. At first I was half afraid of it. But I am not afraid of it now." She paused a moment and then she added: "It's a relief."

She was sitting on a low chair and Newman was on an ottoman near her. He leaned a little and took her hand, which for an instant she let him keep. "That means that I have not waited for nothing," he said. She looked at him for a moment, and he saw her eyes fill with tears. "With me," he went on, "you will be as safe—as safe"—and even in his ardour he hesitated a moment for a comparison—"as safe," he said with a kind of simple solemnity, "as in your father's arms."

Still she looked at him and her tears increased. Then, abruptly, she buried her face on the cushioned arm of the sofa beside her chair and broke into noiseless sobs. "I am weak—I am weak," he heard her say.

"All the more reason why you should give yourself up to me," he answered. "Why are you troubled? There is nothing here that should trouble you. I offer you nothing but happiness. Is that so hard to believe?"

"To you everything seems so simple," she said, raising her head. "But things are not so. I like you extremely. I liked you six months ago, and now I am sure of it, as you say you are sure. But it is not easy, simply for that, to decide to marry you. There are a great many things to think about."

"There ought to be only one thing to think about—

that we love each other, And as she remained silent he quickly added: "Very good; if you can't accept that, don't tell me so."

"I should be very glad to think of nothing," she said at last; "not to think at all; only to shut both my eyes and give myself up. But I can't. I'm cold, I'm old, I'm a coward; I never supposed I should marry again, and it seems to me very strange I should ever have listened to you. When I used to think, as a girl, of what I should do if I were to marry freely by my own choice, I thought of a very different man from you."

"That's nothing against me," said Newman, with an immense smile; "your taste was not formed."

His smile made Madame de Cintré smile. "Have you formed it?" And then she said, in a different tone: "Where do you wish to live?"

"Anywhere in the wide world you like. We can easily settle that."

"I don't know why I ask you," she presently continued. "I care very little. I think if I were to marry you I could live almost anywhere. You have some false ideas about me; you think that I need a great many things—that I must have a brilliant worldly life. I am sure you are prepared to take a great deal of trouble to give me such things. But that is very arbitrary; I have done nothing to prove that." She paused again, looking at him, and her mingled sound and silence were so sweet to him that he had no wish to hurry her, any more than he would have had a wish to hurry a golden sunrise. "Your being so different, which at first seemed a difficulty, a trouble, began one day to seem to me a pleasure, a great pleasure. I was glad you were different. And yet if I had said so no one would have understood me; I don't mean simply to my family."

"They would have said I was a queer monster, eh?" said Newman.

"They would have said I could never be happy with

you—you were too different; and I would have said it was just *because* you were so different that I might be happy. But they would have given better reasons than I. My only reason——" and she paused again.

But this time, in the midst of his golden sunrise, ~~Newman~~ felt the impulse to grasp at a rosy cloud. "Your only reason is that you love me!" ~~he murmured, with an eloquent gesture, and for want of a better reason Madame de Cintré reconciled herself to this one.~~

~~Newman~~ came back the next day, and in the vestibule, as he entered the house, ~~he~~ encountered his friend Mrs. Bread. She was wandering about in honourable idleness, and when his eyes fell upon her ~~she delivered him one of her curtsies~~. Then turning to the servant who had admitted him, she said, with ~~the combined majesty of her native superiority and of a rugged English accent~~: "You may retire; I ~~will~~ have the honour of conducting Monsieur." In spite of this ~~combination~~, however, it appeared to Newman that her voice had a slight quaver, as if the tone of command were not habitual to it. The man gave her an impertinent stare, but he walked slowly away, and she led Newman upstairs. At half its course the staircase ~~gave a bend, forming a little platform. In the angle of the wood~~ stood an indifferent statue of an eighteenth-century nymph, simpering, ~~sallow and cracked~~. Here Mrs. Bread stopped and looked with shy kindness at her companion.

"I know the good news, sir," ~~she murmured~~.

"You ~~have~~ a good right to be first to know it," said Newman. "You ~~have~~ taken such a friendly interest." ~~Mrs. Bread~~ turned away and began to blow the dust off the ~~statue~~, as if this might ~~be mockery~~ you want to congratulate me," ~~said Newman~~ greatly obliged." And then he added: "You gave me much pleasure the other day."

She turned round, apparently reassured. "You ~~are~~

he

he almost groaned for deep insistence; and he laid his two hands on her with a persuasion that she rose to meet. He let her feel as he drew her close and bent his face to her the fullest force of his imposition; which she took from him with a silent surrender that he felt long enough to be complete.

less space

He

delivered to him straight one of her Wiltshire curtsies

a cognate respectability to which, evidently, a proper pronunciation of French had never had anything to add:

clean consciousness,

put forth two arms with an ample rest between. In a niche of this landing

with sallow elegance

connect

've

've

And then as she

image

he went on; "and I'm

but be free pleasantry, "I suppose

're

not to think that I have been told anything; I've only guessed. But when I looked at you as you came in I was sure I had guessed right."

"You're very sharp," said Newman. "I'm sure that in your quiet way you see everything."

"I'm not a fool, sir, thank God. I've guessed something else beside," said Mrs. Bread.

"What's that?"

"I needn't tell you that, sir; I don't think you would believe it. At any rate it wouldn't please you."

"Oh, tell me nothing but what will please me," laughed Newman. "That's the way you began."

"Well, sir, I suppose you won't be vexed to hear that the sooner everything's over the better."

"The sooner we're married, you mean? The better for me, certainly."

"The better for every one."

"The better for you, perhaps. You know you're coming to live with us," said Newman.

"I'm extremely obliged to you, sir, but it's not of myself I was thinking. I only wanted, if I might take the liberty, to recommend you to lose no time."

"Whom are you afraid of?"

Mrs. Bread looked up the staircase and then down, and then she looked at the undusted nymph, as if she possibly had sentient ears. "I'm afraid of every one," she said.

"What an uncomfortable state of mind!" said Newman. "Does 'every one' wish to prevent my marriage?"

"I'm afraid of already having said too much," Mrs. Bread replied. "I won't take it back, but I won't say any more." And she took her way up the staircase again and led him into Madame de Cintré's salon.

Newman indulged in a brief and silent imprecation when he found that Madame de Cintré was not alone. With her sat her mother, and in the middle of the room stood young Madame de Bellegarde in her bonnet and mantle. The old Marquise, who was leaning back in her chair with a hand clasping the knob of each arm, looked at him without moving. She seemed barely conscious of his greeting; she appeared to be musing intently. Newman said to himself that her daughter had been announcing her engagement, and that the old lady found the morsel hard to swallow. But Madame de Cintré, as she gave him her hand, gave him also a look by which she appeared to mean that he should understand something. Was it a warning or a request? Did she wish to enjoin speech or silence? He was puzzled, and young Madame de Bellegarde's pretty grin gave him no information.

"I have not told my mother," said Madame de Cintré abruptly, looking at him.

"Told me what?" demanded the Marquise. "You tell me too little; you should tell me everything."

"That is what I do," said Madame Urbain, with a little laugh.

"Let *me* tell your mother," said Newman.

The old lady stared at him again, and then turned to her daughter. "You are going to marry him?" she cried, softly.

"*Oui, ma mère,*" said Madame de Cintré.

"Your daughter has consented, to my great happiness," said Newman.

"And when was this arrangement made?" asked Madame de Bellegarde. "I seem to be picking up the news by chance!"

"My suspense came to an end yesterday," said Newman.

"And how long was mine to have lasted?" said the Marquise to her daughter. She spoke without irritation, with a sort of cold noble displeasure.

Madame de Cintré stood silent, with her eyes on the ground. "It is over now," she said.

"Where is my son — where is Urbain?" asked

the Marquise. "Send for your brother and ~~tell~~ ~~him~~."

Young Madame de Bellegarde laid her hand on the bell-rope. "He was to make some visits with me, and I was to go and knock—very softly, very softly—at the door of his study. But he can come to me!" She pulled the bell, and in a few moments Mrs. Bread appeared, with a face of calm inquiry.

"Send for your brother," ~~said~~ the old lady.

But Newman felt an irresistible impulse to speak, and to speak in a certain way. "~~Tell~~ the Marquis we want ~~him~~," he said to Mrs. Bread, who quietly retired.

Young Madame de Bellegarde ~~went to~~ her sister-in-law and embraced her. Then she turned ~~to~~ Newman, ~~with an intense smile~~. "She's ~~charming~~. I congratulate you."

"I ~~congratulate you, sir~~," said Madame de Bellegarde with extreme solemnity. "My daughter is an extraordinarily good woman. She may have faults, but I don't know them."

"My mother does not often make jokes," ~~said Madame de Cintré; "but~~ when she does they are terrible."

"She's ravishing, ~~the~~ Marquise Urbain resumed, looking at her sister-in-law, with her head on one side. "Yes, I congratulate you."

Madame de Cintré turned away, and, taking up a piece of tapestry, began to ply the needle. Some minutes of silence elapsed, which were interrupted by the arrival of M. de Bellegarde. He came in with ~~his~~ hat in ~~his~~ hand, gloved, and was followed by his brother Valentin, who appeared to have just entered the house. ~~M. de Bellegarde~~ looked round the circle and ~~greeted Newman with his usual finely-measured courtesy.~~ Valentin saluted his mother and his sisters, and, as he shook hands with ~~Newman, gave him a glance of acute interrogation~~.

"*Arrivez donc, Messieurs!*" cried young Madame de Bellegarde. "We have great news for you."

let him know.
went on Claire.
him immediately"
"Please tell
approached
intensely smiling:
"She is as charming as you like.
do the same, Mr. Newman,"
Madame de Cintré observed; "but
and
The Marquis
she's adorable,"
his friend, appeared to put him a sharp mute question.
administered to Newman his due little measure of recognition.

"Speak to your brother, my daughter," said the old ~~lady~~.

Madame de Cintré had been looking at her tapestry. ~~She~~ raised her eyes ~~to her brother~~. "I have accepted Mr. Newman."

"Your sister has consented," said Newman. "You see after all I knew what I was about."

"I ~~am~~ charmed!" ~~said~~ M. de Bellegarde with superior benignity.

"So am I," said Valentin to Newman. "The Marquis and I are charmed. I can't marry myself, but I can understand it. I can't stand on my head, but I can applaud a clever acrobat. My dear sister, I bless your union."

The Marquis stood looking for a while into the crown of his hat. "We have been prepared," he said at last, "but it is inevitable that in the face of the event one should experience a certain emotion." And he gave a ~~most unhilarious smile~~.

"I feel no emotion that I was not perfectly prepared for," ~~said~~ his mother, *upon this, remarked.*

"I can't say that for myself," said Newman, ~~smiling, but differently from~~ the Marquis. "I am happier than I expected to be. I suppose it's the sight of ~~your~~ *all your* happiness!"

"Don't exaggerate that," said Madame de Bellegarde, ~~getting up and laying~~ her hand upon her daughter's arm. "You can't expect an honest old woman to thank you for taking away her beautiful only daughter."

"You forget me, dear Madame," ~~said~~ the young Marquise, demurely *interposed.*

"Yes, she is ~~very beautiful," said Newman~~.

"And when is the wedding, pray?" asked young Madame de Bellegarde. "I must have a month to think over ~~my dress~~."

"~~That~~ must be discussed," said the Marquise.

Handwritten revisions in the margins:

- woman to Claire.
- but on this she
- Urbain."
- "Yes sir, your
- beg you to believe I'm
- I, my dear man,"
- nobly
- replied
- with this delightful gentleman.
- in others when the inducements to it are overwhelming
- when he brings down the house.
- the oddest smile his visitor had ever beheld.
- "Ah" — the time
- particularly
- the question of my falbalas."
- who felt in his face a different light from that of
- as she got up and laid
- very, very beautiful," Newman agreed while he covered Claire with his bright still protection.
- distinctly

"Oh, we will discuss it and let you know!" Newman exclaimed.

"I have no doubt we shall agree," said Urbain.

"If you don't agree with Madame de Cintré, you will be very unreasonable."

"Come, come, Urbain," said young Madame de Bellegarde; "I must go straight to my tailor's."

The old lady had been standing with her hand on her daughter's arm, looking at her fixedly. [struck out]

"Oh, I know that!" he answered. "I feel tremendously proud. I feel like crying it on the housetops—like stopping people in the street to tell them."

Madame de Bellegarde narrowed her lips. "Pray [struck out]

"The more people that know it, the better," Newman declared. "I haven't yet announced it here, but I telegraphed it this morning to America."

"Telegraphed it to America?" the old lady murmured.

"To New York, to St. Louis, and to San Francisco; those are the principal cities, you know. To-morrow I shall tell my friends here."

"Have you many?" asked Madame de Bellegarde in a tone of which I am afraid that Newman but partly measured the impertinence.

"Enough to bring me a great many hand-shakes and congratulations. To say nothing," he added, in a moment, "of those I shall receive from your friends."

"They will not use the telegraph," said the Marquise, taking her departure.

M. de Bellegarde, whose wife, her imagination having apparently taken flight to the tailor's, was fluttering her silken wings in emulation, shook hands with Newman, and said, with a more persuasive accent than the latter

Handwritten revisions: thoroughly; promptly; gaily declared.; make very little; his visitor went on.; and her eyes on her face. Madame de Cintré had got up; the seemed inevitably to wait. Her mother exhaled a long heavy breath. "No, I can't say I had been there of you. You're a very lucky gentleman," she added with rather a grand turn to their guest.; do nothing of the sort!"; roundly returned.; cabled; "Oh, is the; So; he perhaps; own; "'Cabled' it?" She spoke as if—what indeed well might be—she had never heard the expression.; as she took; very pertinently; "Our own won't had ever heard him use: "~~You may count upon me.~~" Then his wife led him away.

Valentin stood looking from his sister to ~~our hero~~. "I ~~[struck through]~~ hope you ~~ha~~ve both reflected seriously," ~~he said~~.

Madame de Cintré smiled. "We ~~ha~~ve neither your powers of reflection nor your depth of seriousness; but we ~~ha~~ve done our best."

"Well, I ~~ha~~ve a great regard for each of you," ~~Valentin~~ continued. "You ~~a~~re charming, ~~young people~~. But I ~~a~~m not satisfied, on the whole, that you belong to that small and superior class—that exquisite group—composed of persons who are worthy to remain unmarried. These are rare souls; they are the salt of the earth. But I don't mean to be invidious; the marrying people are often very nice."

"Valentin holds that women should marry, and that men should not," said Madame de Cintré. "I don't know how he arranges it."

"I arrange it by adoring you, my sister," ~~said Valentin~~ ardently. ~~[struck through]~~

"~~Adore~~ some one whom you can marry," ~~said Newman~~. "I ~~wi~~ll arrange that for you some day. I foresee ~~that~~ I ~~a~~m going to turn apostle."

Valentin was on the threshold; he looked back a moment, with a face that had turned grave. "I adore some one I can't marry!" ~~[struck through]~~ And he dropped the ~~[struck through]~~ and departed.

"They don't ~~[struck through] said Newman, standing alone before Madame de Cintré~~.

"No," she ~~said~~ after a moment; "they don't like it."

"Well, now, do you mind that?" ~~asked Newman~~.

"Yes!" she said, after another interval.

"~~That's a mistake~~?"

"~~I~~ can't help it. I should prefer that my mother were pleased."

"Why the ~~deuce," demanded Newman, "is she not~~ pleased? She gave you leave to marry me."

"I beg you to count on me for everything."

, on this,

his friend.

the young

very

innocent beautiful creatures.

answered.

But I relieve you both of my superfluous presence. Good-bye." Good-by my example," Newman laughed.

"You had better adore

he asked.

portière

It may be, but I

really

returned

the dickens then," he yearningly enquired, isn't she

"But isn't that a mistake?"

really like it, you know," Newman said as he stood there before his mistress.

"Very true; I don't understand it. And yet I do 'mind' it, as you say. You will call it superstitious."

"That will depend upon how much you let it bother you. Then I shall call it an awful bore."

"I will keep it to myself," said Madame de Cintré. "It shall not bother you." And they then talked of their marriage-day, and Madame de Cintré assented unreservedly to Newman's desire to have it fixed for an early date.

Newman's telegrams were answered with interest. Having despatched but three electric missives, he received no less than eight gratulatory bulletins in return. He put them into his pocket-book, and the next time he encountered old Madame de Bellegarde drew them forth and displayed them to her. This, it must be confessed, was a slightly malicious stroke; the reader must judge in what degree the offence was venial. Newman knew that the Marquise disliked his telegrams, though he could see no sufficient reason for it. Madame de Cintré, on the other hand, liked them, and, most of them being of a humorous cast, laughed at them immoderately, and inquired into the character of their authors. Newman, now that his prize was gained, felt a peculiar desire that his triumph should be manifest. He more than suspected that the Bellegardes were keeping quiet about it, and allowing it, in their select circle, but a limited resonance; and it pleased him to think that if he were to take the trouble, he might, as he phrased it, break all the windows. No man likes being repudiated, and yet Newman, if he was not flattered, was not exactly offended. He had not this good excuse for his somewhat aggressive impulse to promulgate his felicity; his sentiment was of another quality. He wanted for once to make the heads of the house of Bellegarde feel him; he knew not when he should have another chance. He had had for the past six months a sense of the old lady and her son looking straight over his head, and he was now resolved that they should toe a mark which he would give himself the satisfaction of drawing.

"It is like seeing a bottle emptied when the wine is poured too slowly," he said to Mrs. Tristram. "They make me want to joggle their elbows and force them to spill their wine."

To this Mrs. Tristram answered that he had better leave them alone and let them do things in their own way. "You must make allowances for them, [redacted] natural enough [redacted] they should hang fire a little. They thought they accepted you when you made your application; but they are not people of imagination, they could not project themselves into the future, and now they will have to begin again. But they *are* people of honour and they will do whatever is necessary."

Newman spent a few moments in narrow-eyed meditation.

"I am not hard on them," he presently said; "and to prove it I will invite them all to a festival."

"[redacted]"

"You have been laughing at my great gilded rooms all winter; I will show you [redacted] they are good for something. I will give a party. What is the grandest thing one can do here? I will hire all the great singers from the opera and all the first people from the Théâtre Française, and [redacted]"

"And whom will you invite?"

"You, first of all. And [redacted] the old [redacted] and her son. And then every one [redacted] friends whom I have met at [redacted] house or elsewhere, every one who has shown me the minimum of politeness, every duke of them [redacted]. And then all my friends, without exception—Miss Kitty Upjohn, Miss Dora Finch, General Packard, C. P. Hatch, and all the rest. And every one shall know what it is about [redacted] to celebrate my engagement to the Countess de Cintré. What do you think of the idea?"

—it's

"A festival—?"

I'll hold an entertainment—the biggest kind of show."

of their

their

[redacted] such as they are, every doddering old duchess, every great name in the place.

woman, damn her, and her son and her son's wife. And Valentine of course—for the fun of him.

[redacted] who shall sit through it all on a golden chair above their heads and look as beautiful—and perhaps, poor dear, as bored—as a saint in paradise.

"I think it is odious!" said Mrs. Tristram. And then in a moment: "I think it is delicious!"

The very next evening Newman repaired to Madame de Bellegarde's salon, where he found her surrounded by her children, and invited her to honour his poor dwelling by her presence on a certain evening a fortnight distant.

The Marquise stared a moment. "My dear sir," she cried, "what do you want to do to me?"

"To make you acquainted with a few people, and then to place you in a very easy chair and ask you to listen to Madame Frezzolini's singing."

"You mean to give a concert?"

"Something of that sort."

"And to have a crowd of people?"

"All my friends, and I hope some of yours and your daughter's. I want to celebrate my engagement."

It seemed to Newman that Madame de Bellegarde turned pale. She opened her fan, a fine old painted fan of the last century, and looked at the picture, which represented a *fête champêtre*—a lady with a guitar, singing, and a group of dancers round a garlanded Hermes.

"We go out so little," murmured the Marquis, "since my poor father's death."

"But *my* dear father is still alive, my friend," said his wife. "I am only waiting for my invitation to accept it;" and she glanced with amiable confidence at Newman. "It will be magnificent; I am very sure of that."

I am sorry to say, to the discredit of Newman's gallantry, that this lady's invitation was not then and there bestowed; he was giving all his attention to the old Marquise. She looked up at last smiling. "I can't think of letting you offer me a fête until I have offered you one. We want to present you to our friends; we will invite them all. We have it very much at heart. We must do things in order. Come to me about the 25th; I will let you know the exact day immediately. We shall not have any one so fine as Madame

own drawingroom

on earth

him she had turned perceptibly

singing to.

her elder son

poor

poor

her mother-in-law Madame de Bellegarde

with a prodigious extemporized grace

Frezzolini, but we shall have some very good people. After that you may talk of your own fête." The old lady spoke with a certain quick eagerness, smiling more agreeably as she went on.

It seemed to Newman a handsome proposal, and such proposals always touched the sources of his good-nature. He ~~said to Madame de Bellegarde~~ that he should be glad to come on the 25th or any other day, and that it mattered very little whether he met his friends at her house or at his own. ~~I have said that Newman was observant, but it must be admitted that~~ on this occasion he failed to ~~notice a certain delicate glance~~ which passed between Madame de Bellegarde and the Marquis, and which we may presume to have been a commentary upon the innocence displayed in that latter clause of his speech.

~~Valentin de Bellegarde~~ walked away with ~~Newman~~ that evening, and, when they had left the ~~[illegible]~~ behind them, ~~he~~ said reflectively: "My mother is very strong—very strong." Then in answer to an interrogative movement of Newman's ~~he continued~~: "She was driven to the wall, but you would never have thought it. Her fête of the 25th was an invention of the moment. She had no idea whatever of giving a fête, but, finding it the only issue from your proposal, she looked straight at the dose—excuse the expression—and bolted it, as you saw, without winking. ~~She is very strong~~."

"~~[illegible]~~ said Newman, divided between relish and compassion. "I don't care a straw for her fête; I'm ~~am~~ willing to take the will for the deed."

~~[illegible] said Valentin, with a little~~ inconsequent touch of family pride. "The thing will be done now, ~~and done handsomely.~~"

replied after a little discussion

We have noted him far observant, yet he

catch a thin sharp eyebeam, as cold as the flash of steel,

him

Count Valentin

the scene of so many recent anxieties well.

"No, no!" and Valentin showed an

— ah but uncommonly

She's really rather grand, you know."

"Well, I wonder!" said Newman, this time, divided, rather whimsically, quite appreciatingly, between the sense of his own force and the sense of hers.

and I daresay it will be quite ~~[illegible]~~ folichon!"

~~CHAPTER~~ XV.

VALENTIN ~~DE BELLEGARDE'S announcement~~ of the secession of Mademoiselle Nioche from her father's domicile, and his irreverent reflections upon the attitude of this anxious parent in so grave a catastrophe, received a practical commentary in the fact that M. Nioche was slow to seek another interview with his late pupil. It had cost Newman some disgust to be forced to assent to ~~Valentin's somewhat cynical interpretation~~ of the old man's philosophy, and, though circumstances seemed to indicate that he had not given himself up to a noble despair, ~~Newman~~ thought it ~~very~~ possible he might be suffering more keenly than ~~was apparent~~. M. Nioche had been in the habit of paying him a respectful little visit every two or three weeks, and his absence might be a proof quite as much of extreme depression as of a desire to conceal the success with which he had patched up his sorrow. Newman presently ~~learned~~ from Valentin several ~~details touching this new phase of Mademoiselle Noémie's career~~.

"I told you she was remarkable," this ~~unshrinking observer~~ declared, "and ~~the way she has managed this performance proves it~~. She has had other chances, but she was resolved to take none but the best. She did you the honour to think for a while that you might be such a chance. You were not; so she gathered up her patience and waited a while longer. At last her occasion ~~came along~~, and she made her move with her eyes wide open. I'm very sure she had no innocence to lose, but she had all her respectability. Dubious little damsel as you thought her, she had kept a firm hold of that; nothing could be proved against her, and she was determined not to let her reputation go till she had got her equivalent. About her equivalent she had high ideas. Apparently her ideal has been satisfied. It is fifty years old, bald-headed, and deaf, but it's very easy about money."

"And where in the world," asked Newman, "did you pick up this valuable information?"

"In conversation. Remember my frivolous habits. In conversation with a young woman engaged in the humble trade of glove-cleaner, who keeps a small shop in the Rue St. Roch. M. Nioche lives in the same house, up six pair of stairs, across the court, in and out of whose ill-swept doorway Miss Noémie has been flitting for the last five years. The little glove-cleaner was an old acquaintance; she used to be the friend of a friend of mine, who has married and dropped such friends. I often saw her in his society. As soon as I espied her behind her clear little window-pane, I recollected her. I had on a spotlessly fresh pair of gloves, but I went in and held up my hands, and said to her: 'Dear Mademoiselle, what will you ask me for cleaning these?' 'Dear Count,' she answered immediately, 'I will clean them for you for nothing.' She had instantly recognised me, and I had to hear her history for the last six years. But after that, I put her upon that of her neighbours. She knows and admires Noémie, and she told me what I have just repeated."

A month elapsed without M. Nioche reappearing, and Newman, who every morning read two or three suicides in the *Figaro*, began to suspect that, mortification proving stubborn, he had sought a balm for his wounded pride in the waters of the Seine. He had a note of M. Nioche's address in his pocket-book, and, finding himself one day in the *quartier*, he determined, in so far as he might, to clear up his doubts. He repaired to the house in the Rue St. Roch which bore the recorded number, and observed in a neighbouring basement, behind a dangling row of neatly inflated gloves, the attentive physiognomy of Bellegarde's informant—a sallow person in a dressing-gown—peering into the street as if she were

her requirements have been met. Well, they've been met in a form. The form's

given up friendship.

— the foolish friend of a foolish friend —

made her out

m

from ever so far back.

any reappearance of

for practice, the suicides of the day in a news-paper, about

the poor gentleman's

Valentin's

unmistakable face of

expecting that amiable nobleman to pass again. But it was not to her that Newman applied; he simply asked of the portress if M. Nioche were at home. The portress replied, as the portress invariably replies, that her lodger had gone out barely three minutes before; but then, through the little square hole of her lodge-window taking the measure of Newman's [illegible] and seeing them, by an unspecified process, refresh the dry places of servitude to occupants of fifth floors on courts, she added that M. Nioche would have had just time to reach the Café de la Patrie, round the second corner to the left, at which establishment he regularly spent his afternoons. Newman thanked her for the information, took the second turning to the left, and arrived at the Café de la Patrie. He felt a momentary hesitation to go in; was it not rather mean to "follow up" poor old Nioche at that rate? But there passed across his vision an image of a haggard little septuagenarian taking measured sips of a glass of sugar and water, and finding them quite impotent to sweeten his desolation. He opened the door and entered, perceiving nothing at first but a dense cloud of tobacco-smoke. Across this, however, in a corner, he presently descried the figure of M. Nioche, stirring the contents of a deep glass, with a lady seated in front of him. The lady's back was turned to Newman, but M. Nioche very soon perceived and recognised his visitor. Newman had gone toward him, and the old man rose slowly, gazing at him with a more blighted expression even than usual.

"If you are drinking hot punch," said Newman, "I suppose you are not dead. That's all right. Don't move."

M. Nioche stood staring, with a fallen jaw, not [illegible] to put out his hand. The lady who sat facing him turned round in her place and glanced upward with a spirited toss of her head, displaying the agreeable features of his daughter. She looked at Newman sharply, to see how he was looking at her, then—I don't know what she discovered—she said graciously: "How d'ye do, Monsieur? won't you come into our little corner?"

"Did you come—did you come after me?" asked M. Nioche very softly.

"I went to your house to see what had become of you. I thought you might be sick," said Newman.

"It is very good of you, as always," said the old man. "No, I am not well. Yes, I am *seek*."

"Ask Monsieur to sit down," said Mademoiselle Nioche. "Garçon, bring a chair."

"Will you do us the honour to *seat?*" said M. Nioche, timorously, and with a double foreignness of accent.

Newman said to himself that he had better see the thing out, and he took a chair at the end of the table, with Mademoiselle Nioche on his left and her father on the other side. "You will take something, of course," said Miss Noémie, who was sipping a [illegible]. Newman said that he believed not, and then she turned to her papa with a smile. "What an honour, eh? he has come only for us." M. Nioche drained his pungent glass at a long draught and looked out from eyes more lachrymose in consequence. "But you didn't come for me, eh?" Mademoiselle Noémie went on. "You didn't expect to find me here?"

Newman observed the change in her appearance. She was very elegant, and prettier than before; she looked a year or two older, and it was noticeable that, to the eye, she had only gained in respectability. She looked "lady-like." She was dressed in quiet colours, and she wore her expensively unobtrusive toilet with a grace that might have come from years of practice. Her present self-possession and *aplomb* struck Newman as really infernal, and he inclined to agree with Valentin de Bellegarde that the young lady was very remarkable. "No, to tell the truth, I didn't come for you," he said, "and

m

me, monsieur?

monsieur said mildly enough.

m

inquired

the brilliant girl

he guessed

parent

returned.

for, monsieur?

place

a brown madère. madère.

presence of mind, her perfect equilibrium, struck Newman as portentous,

gear

and that the

really

He

added an accent to the appearance of "propriety" only taken a longer step toward distinction.

I didn't expect to find you. I was told," he added in a moment, "that you had left your father."

"*Quelle horreur!*" ~~cried Mademoiselle Nioche, with a smile~~. "Does one leave one's father? You have the proof of the contrary."

"Yes, convincing proof," said Newman, ~~glancing at~~ M. Nioche. The old man caught his glance obliquely, with his faded deprecati[on] and then, lifting his empty glass, pretended to drink again.

"Who told you that?" Noémie demanded. "I know very well. It was M. de Bellegarde. Why don't you say yes? You're not polite."

~~"I am embarrassed," said Newman.~~

"I set you a better example. I know M. de Bellegarde told you. He knows a great deal about me—or he thinks he does. He has taken a great deal of trouble to find out, but half of it isn't true. In the first place I haven't left my father; I'm much too fond of him. Isn't it so, little father? M. de Bellegarde's a charming young man; it is impossible to ~~be cleverer~~. I know a good deal about him too; you can tell him that when you next see him."

"No," said Newman, with a sturdy grin; "I won't carry any messages for you."

"Just as you please," ~~said Mademoiselle Nioche~~. "I don't depend upon you, nor does M. de Bellegarde either. He's very much interested in me; he can be left to his own devices. He is a contrast to [you]."

"Oh, he's a great contrast to me, I've no doubt," said Newman. "But I don't exactly know how you mean it."

"I mean it in this way. First of all, he never offered to help me to a *dot* and a husband." And Mademoiselle Nioche ~~paused, smiling~~. "I won't say that's in his favour, for I do you justice. What led you, by the way, to make me such a ~~queer~~ offer? You didn't care for me."

happy

she cried with the brightest of all her smiles

with his ~~almost~~ embarrassed eyes on

and never so fond as now, when he has been gentil, mais gentil—!

Haven't you been gentil, mais gentil?

mieux causer

"Seen so shy and simple and stupid," Newman said with a certain fond good faith

expressively paused

monstrous

in

"You, monsieur," Noémie went on with a fine little flight of dignity

his young friend placidly returned

"Oh yes, I did," said Newman.

"How so?"

"It would have given me real pleasure to see you married to a respectable young fellow."

"With six thousand francs of income!" cried Mademoiselle Nioche. "Do you call that caring for me? I'm afraid you know little about women. You were not *galant;* you were not what you might have been."

Newman flushed, a trifle fiercely. "Come!" he exclaimed, "that's rather strong. I had no idea I had been so shabby."

Mademoiselle Nioche smiled as she took up her muff.

"It's something, at any rate, to have made you angry."

Her father had leaned both his elbows on the table, and his head, bent forward, was supported in his hands, the thin white fingers of which were pressed over his ears. In this position he was staring fixedly at the bottom of his empty glass, and Newman supposed he was not hearing. Mademoiselle Noémie buttoned her furred jacket and pushed back her chair, casting a glance charged with the consciousness of an expensive appearance first down over her flounces and then up at Newman.

"You had better have remained an honest girl," Newman said, quietly.

M. Nioche continued to stare at the bottom of his glass, and his daughter got up, still bravely smiling. "You mean that I look so much like one? That's more than most women do nowadays. Don't judge me yet a while," she added. "I mean to succeed; that's what I mean to do. I leave you; I don't mean to be seen in cafés, for one thing. I can't think what you want of my poor father; he's very comfortable now. It isn't his fault either. *Au revoir,* little father." And she tapped the old man on the head with her muff. Then she stopped a minute, looking at Newman. "Tell M. de Bellegarde, when he wants news of me, to come and get it from *me!*" And she turned and departed, the

"Well, how much?"

Noémie cried

"I say

She laughed out as she took up her muff — it was almost her only hint of vulgarity

stared

Noémie

his obstinate sense of his old friend's [raisonsvoiture] prompted him at last to remark

again at their visitor,

such places as this,

white-aproned waiter, with a bow, holding the door wide open for her.

M. Nioche sat motionless, and Newman hardly knew what to say to him. The old man looked dismally foolish. "So you determined not to shoot her, after all," Newman said presently.

M. Nioche, without moving, raised his eyes and ~~gave him a long peculiar look. It seemed to confess every-thing, and yet~~ ~~to ask for pity,~~ ~~to pretend, on the~~ ~~other hand,~~ to a rugged ability to do without it. It might have expressed the state of mind of an innocuous insect, flat in shape, ~~and~~ conscious of the impending pressure of a boot-sole, and reflecting that he was perhaps too flat to be crushed. M. Nioche's gaze was a profession of moral flatness. "You despise me terribly," he said, in the weakest possible voice.

"Oh no; ~~It's a good plan to take things easily."~~

"I made you too many fine speeches," M. Nioche added. "I meant them at the time."

"I am sure I am very glad you didn't shoot her," ~~said~~ Newman. "I was afraid you might have shot yourself. That is why I came to look you up." And he began to button his coat.

"Neither, You despise me, and I can't explain to you. I hoped I shouldn't see you again."

"Why, that's ~~rather shabby~~," said Newman. "You shouldn't drop your friends that way. Besides, the last time you came to see me I thought you ~~particularly jolly~~."

"Yes, I remember," ~~said M. Nioche, musingly,~~ was in a fever. I didn't know what I said, what I did. ~~It was delirium!~~

"Ah well, you are quieter now."

M. Nioche ~~was silent a moment~~. "As quiet as the grave," ~~he whispered, softly~~.

"Are you very unhappy?" ~~asked~~ Newman.

They didn't somehow presume to ask for pity, yet they doubtless pretended even less.

all let their confession quit dismally and abjectly come.

it's your own affair. And hanged if I understand your institutions anyway!"

went on.

hélas!

bethought himself.

more ingenuously asked.

pretty mean."

felt rather fine."

"I spoke, no doubt, wild words."

— M. Nioche musingly recalled it. "I must have been

he then struck off.

M. Nioche rubbed his forehead slowly and even pushed back his wig a little, looking askance at his empty glass. "Yes—yes. But that's an old story. I have always been unhappy. My daughter does what she will with me. I take what she gives me, good or bad. I have no spirit, and when you have no spirit you must keep quiet. I sha'n't trouble you any more."

"Well," said Newman, rather disgusted at the smooth operation of the old man's philosophy, "that's as you please."

M. Nioche seemed to have been prepared to be despised, but nevertheless he made a feeble movement of appeal from Newman's faint praise. "After all, she is she's my daughter, and I can still look after her. If she will do wrong, why she will. But there are many different paths, there are degrees. I can give her the benefit, give her the benefit"—and M. Nioche paused, staring vaguely at Newman, who began to suspect that his brain had softened—"the benefit of my experience," M. Nioche added.

"Your experience?" inquired Newman, both amused and amazed.

"My experience of business," said M. Nioche, gravely.

"Ah yes," said Newman, laughing, "that will be a great advantage to her!" And then he said good-bye, and offered the poor foolish old man his hand.

M. Nioche took it and leaned back against the wall, holding it a moment and looking up at him. "I suppose you think my wits are going. Very likely; I have always a pain in my head. That's why I can't explain, I can't tell you. And she's so strong, she makes me walk as she will, anywhere! But there's this—there's this." And he stopped, still staring up at Newman. His little white eyes expanded and glittered for a moment like those of a cat in the dark. "It's not as it seems. I haven't forgiven her. Never!"

pluck,

pluck

appealed feebly from his patron's

has her bad idea, why she has it, and she won't let go of it. And then now," he pointed out—"it's fine talking!

his mind of really going wobbly—

his visitor.

Oh, par exemple, no!

I make a face, but I take it.

You can't go about telling people.

she

place at her disposal

his friend

laughed,

present the case.

"That's right; don't

"It's horrible, it's terrible," said M. Nioche; "but do you want to know the truth? I hate her! I take what she gives me and I hate her more. To-day she brought me three hundred francs; they are here in my waistcoat-pocket. Now I hate her almost cruelly. No, I haven't forgiven her."

"Why did you accept the money?" Newman asked.

"If I hadn't I should have hated her still more. That's what misery is. No, I haven't forgiven her."

"Take care you don't hurt her!" said Newman, laughing again. And with this he took his leave. As he passed along the glazed side of the café, on reaching the street, he saw the old man motioning the waiter, with a melancholy gesture, to replenish his glass.

One day, a week after his visit to the Café de la Patrie, he called upon Valentin de Bellegarde and by good fortune found him at home. Newman spoke of his interview with M. Nioche and his daughter, and said he was afraid Valentin had judged the old man correctly. He had found the couple hobnobbing together in amity; the old gentleman's rigour was purely theoretic. Newman confessed that he was disappointed; he should have expected to see M. Nioche take high ground.

"High ground, my dear fellow," said Valentin, laughing; "there is no high ground for him to take. The only perceptible eminence in M. Nioche's horizon is Montmartre, which is not an edifying quarter. You can't go mountaineering in a flat country."

"He remarked, indeed," said Newman, "that he had not forgiven her. But she'll never find it out."

"We must do him the justice to suppose he doesn't

Nioche is like the great artists whose biographies we read, who at the beginning of their career have suffered opposition in the domestic circle. Their vocation has not been recognised by their families, but the world has done it justice. Mademoiselle Nioche has a vocation."

"Oh, come," said Newman impatiently. "You take the little baggage too seriously."

"I know I do; but when one has nothing to think about, one must think of little baggages. I suppose it is better to be serious about light things than not to be serious at all. This little baggage entertains me."

"Oh, she has discovered that. She knows you have been hunting her up and asking questions about her. She is very much tickled by it. That's rather annoying."

"Annoying, my dear fellow," laughed Valentin; "not the least!"

"Hanged if I should want to have a greedy little adventuress like that know I was giving myself such pains about her!" said Newman.

"A pretty woman is always worth one's pains," objected Valentin. "Mademoiselle Nioche is welcome to be tickled by my curiosity, and to know that I am tickled that she is tickled. She is not so much tickled, by the way."

"You had better go and tell her," Newman rejoined. "She gave me a message for you of some such drift."

"Bless your quiet imagination," said Valentin. "I have been to see her—three times in five days. She's a charming hostess; we talk of Shakespeare and the musical glasses. She's extremely clever, and a very curious type; not at all coarse or wanting to be coarse—determined not to be. She means to take very good care of herself. She's extremely perfect; she is as hard and clear-cut as some little figure of a sea-nymph on an antique intaglio, and I will warrant that she has not a grain more sentiment or heart than if she were scooped out of a big amethyst. You can't scratch her even with a diamond. Extremely pretty—really, when you know

Damn her vocation!"

Noémie

a cold-blooded crew!" Valentin sounded him a moment with curious eyes. "You must be very fond of beef and cabbage to have such a suspicion of peaches and plums." But Newman sturdily met his look. "I shouldn't think I'd have to tell you what fruit I gather!" The young man, at this, closed his eyes an instant and then, with a motion of his hand, shook his head; after which he gravely said: "I back you more than ever!"

"Let me then," his companion returned, "do what I suppose you'd call the fair thing by you. Miss Noémie desired me to tell you—but hanged if I know what!"

attack the noblest subjects of discussion.

low

true sensibility

as perfect as you please, and

really very clever and a rare and remarkable type;

Do you suppose I've been waiting for you? I've been to see her for myself her, she is wonderfully pretty—intelligent, determined, ambitious, unscrupulous, capable of ~~looking at~~ a man strangled without changing colour, she is, upon my honour, ~~extremely entertaining.”~~

~~“It's a fine list of attractions,” said Newman; “they would serve as a police detective's description of a favourite criminal. I should sum them up by another word than 'entertaining.'”~~

~~“Why, that is just the word to use. I don't say she is laudable or lovable. I don't want her as my wife or my sister. But she is a very curious and ingenious piece of machinery; I like to see it in operation.”~~

“~~Well, I have seen some very curious machines, too,” said Newman; “and once, in a needle factory, [illegible]~~ a gentleman from the city who had stepped too near ~~one of them,~~ picked up as ~~neatly~~ as if he had been ~~prodded by a fork,~~ swallowed down straight, and ground into small pieces.”

Re-entering his ~~domicile,~~ late in the evening, three days after Madame de Bellegarde had ~~made~~ her bargain with him ~~—the expression is sufficiently correct—touching~~ the entertainment at which she was to present him to the world, he found on his table a ~~card of goodly dimensions bearing an announcement that this lady~~ would be at home on the 27th of the month, at ten o'clock in the evening. He stuck it into the frame of his mirror and eyed it with some complacency; it seemed ~~an agreeable~~ emblem of triumph, ~~documentary evidence that his prize was gained.~~ Stretched out on a chair, he ~~was looking~~ at it lovingly, ~~when~~ Valentin ~~de Bellegarde~~ was shown into the ~~room. Valentin's~~ glance presently followed the direction of Newman's, and he perceived his mother's invitation.

“And what have they put into the corner? ~~[illegible]~~ Not the customary 'music,' 'dancing,' or '*tableaux vivants*'? They ought at least to put 'An American'”

seeing

remarkably agreeable. On

“Well,” said Newman, after reflection, “I once saw in a needle-factory,

a machine that struck him as curious

removed by a silver fork from a china plate,

clean

rooms,

of Americans?”

struck her bargain with him, as he might feel, over the

to him a document of importance and an

the place. The young man's

and

looked

and while he was so engaged

goodly card of announcement to the effect that she

"Oh, there are to be several of us," Newman said. "Mrs. Tristram told me to-day she had received a card and sent an acceptance."

"Ah then, with Mrs. Tristram and her husband you'll have support. My mother might have put on her card 'Three Americans in a Row' — which you can pronounce in either way you like, though I know the one I should suppose most American. I dare say at least you'll not lack amusement. You'll see a great many of the best people in France — I mean of the long pedigrees, and the beaux noms, and the great fidelities, and the rare stupidities, and the faces and figures that, after all, sometimes, I suppose, God did make. We've already shown you specimens in numbers — you know by which end to take them."

"Oh, they haven't hurt me yet," said Newman, "and I guess they would, by this time, if they were going to. I seem to want to like people, these days — seem regularly to like liking them, and almost any one will do. I feel so good that if I wasn't sure I'm going to be married I might think I'm going to die."

"Do you make," the young man inquired, "so much of a distinction?" But he dropped rather wearily into a chair and went on before his host could answer. "Happy man, only remember that there are poor devils whom the flaunted happiness of others sometimes irritates."

"Do you call a person a poor devil," demanded Newman, "who's as good as my brother-in-law?"

"Your brother-in-law?" his friend a trifle musingly echoed.

"Say then my brother," Newman kindly returned — "and leave the other description for yours."

It made Valentin after an instant rise to him. "You're really very charming. You have your own for it which must have been your way of making love. Well," he sighed with a dimmer smile than usual, "I don't wonder and I don't question! Only you *are*, I understand" — he immediately took himself up — "'Really and truly' in love?"

"Yes, sir!" said Newman after a pause.

"And do you hold that she is?"

"You had better ask her," Newman answered. "Not for me, but for yourself."

"I never ask anything for myself. Haven't you noticed that? Besides, she wouldn't tell me, and it's after all none of my business."

Newman hesitated, but "She doesn't know!" he the next thing brought out. "However, she will know."

"Ah then, you will — which I see you don't yet. But what you'll know will be what you want, for that's the way things turn out for you." And Valentin's grave fine eyes, as if under some impression oddly quickened, measured him again a moment up and down. "The way you cover the ground! However, being as you are a giant, you move naturally in seven-league boots." With which again he turned restlessly off.

Newman's attention, from before the fire,

followed him a little. "There's something the matter with you to-night: you're kind of perverse — you're almost kind of vicious. But wait till I'm through with my business — to which I wish to give just now my undivided attention — and then we'll talk. By which I mean I'll fix you somehow."

"Ah, there will be plenty of me for you, such as I am — for you always. Only when, then," the young man asked, "*is* the event?"

"About five weeks hence — on a day not quite yet settled."

Valentin accepted this answer with interest; in spite of which, however, "You feel very confident of the future?" he next attentively inquired.

"Confident," said Newman with that large accent from which semi-tones were more than ever absent. "I knew what I wanted exactly, and now I know what 'Ive got."

"You're sure then you're going to be happy?"

"Sure?" — Newman competently weighed it. "So foolish a question deserves a foolish answer. Yes — I'll be hanged if I ain't sure!"

Well, if Valentin was to pass for perverse it wouldn't be, he seemed to wish to show, for nothing. "You're not afraid of anything?"

"What should I be afraid of? You can'y hurt me unless you kill me by some violent means. That I should indeed regard as a tremendous sell. I want to live and I mean to live: I mean to have a good time. I can't die of sickness, because I'm naturally healthy, and the time for dying of old age won't come round yet awhile. I can't lose my wife, I shall take too good care of her. I can't lose my money, or much of it — I've fixed it so on purpose. So what have I to be afraid of?"

"You're not afraid it may be rather a mistake for such an infuriated modern to marry — well, such an old-fashioned product? a daughter, as one may say, of the Crusaders, almost of the Patriarchs."

Newman, who had been moving about as they talked, stopped before his visitor. "Does that mean you're worried for her?"

Valentin met his eyes. "I'm worried for everything."

"Ah, if that's all — !" And then: "Trust me — because I am modern and can compare, all round — to know where I stand!" With which, as from the impulse to celebrate his happy certitude by a bonfire, he turned to thow a couple of logs on the already blazing hearth. Valentin watched a few moments the quickened flame; after which, with his elbow supported on the chimney and his head on his hand, he gave an expressive sigh. "Got a headache?" Newman asked.

"*Je suis triste,*" said Valentin with Gallic simplicity.

Newman stared at the remark as if it had been scrawled on a slate by a schoolboy a weakling whom he wouldn't wish however too harshly to snub. "You've got a sentimental stomach-ache, eh? Have you caught it from the lady you told me the other night you adored and couldn't marry?"

"Did I really speak of her?" the young man asked as if a little struck. "I was afraid afterwards I had made some low allusion — for I don't as a general thing (and it's a rare scruple I have!) drag in *ces dames* before Claire. But I was feeling the bitterness of life, as who should say, when I spoke; and — yes, if you want to know — I've my mouth full of it still. Why did you ever introduce me to that girl?"

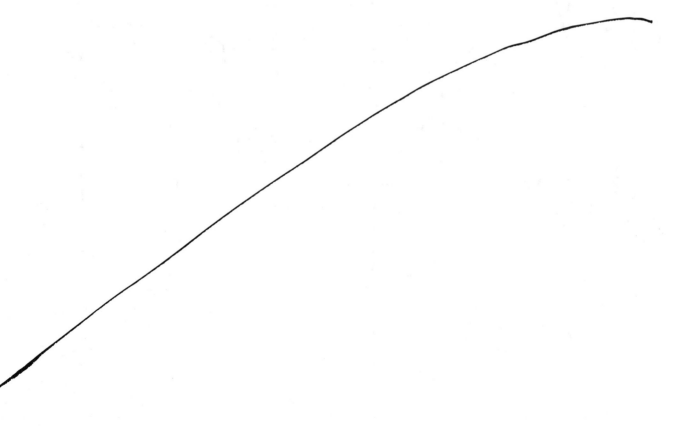

~~gloomy, still. Why did you ever introduce me to that girl?"~~

"Oh, it's Noémie, is it? Lord deliver us! You don't mean to say you are lovesick about her?"

"Lovesick, no; it's not a grand passion. But the cold-blooded little demon sticks in my thoughts; she has bitten me with those even little teeth of hers; I feel as if I might turn rabid and do something crazy in consequence. It's very low; it's disgustingly low. She's the most mercenary little jade in Europe. Yet she really affects my peace of mind; she's always running in my head. It's a striking contrast to your noble and virtuous attachment ~~—a vile contrast!~~ It's rather pitiful that it should be the best I'm able to do for myself at my present respectable age. I'm a nice young man, eh, *en somme?* You can't warrant my future, as you do your own."

"Drop ~~that girl short~~," said Newman; "don't go near her again, and your future will ~~do~~. Come over to America and I'll get you a place in a bank."

"It's easy to say drop her," ~~said~~ Valentin, ~~with a light laugh~~. "~~You can't drop a pretty woman like that. One must be polite, even with Noémie. Besides, I'll not have her suppose I'm afraid of her.~~"

"~~So, between politeness and vanity, you'll get deeper into the mud? Keep them both for something better.~~ Remember, ~~too, that~~ I didn't want to introduce you to her; you insisted. I had a sort of ~~uneasy~~ creepy feeling about ~~her~~ it even at the time."

"Oh, I ~~don't reproach you," said Valentin. "Heaven forbid! I wouldn't for the world have missed knowing her.~~ She's really extraordinary. The way she has already spread her wings is amazing. I don't know when a woman has amused me more. But ~~excuse~~ me," he added in an instant; "she doesn't amuse you, at second hand; ~~and the subject is an impure one~~. Let us talk of something else." Valentin introduced another

and a vile

the creature right here,"

be all right?

spoke

a certain gravity in his lucidity.

"You ~~must~~ might as well drop a pretty panther who has every one of her claws in your ~~his~~ flesh and who's in the act of biting your heart out."

Your interest appears to flag just where that of many men would wake up.

pardon

too," Newman went on, "that

"You've better things to keep up, it seems to me," than such acquaintances.

One has to keep up the acquaintance, if only to show one isn't afraid.

no more reproach you with misleading my innocence than I reproach myself with practising upon hers.

topic, but within five minutes ~~Newman observed that,~~ by a bold transition ~~he had reverted~~ to Mademoiselle Nioche, and was ~~giving pictures of her manners~~ and quoting specimens of her *mots*. These were very ~~witty~~, and, for a young woman who six months before had ~~been painting the most artless Madonnas, startlingly cynical~~. But at last, abruptly, he stopped, became thoughtful, and for some time afterwards said nothing. When he rose to go it was evident that his thoughts were still running ~~upon Mademoiselle Nioche~~. "Yes," she's a ~~frightful~~ little monster!" ~~he said~~.

~~CHAPTER~~ XVI.

THE next ten days were the happiest ~~that~~ Newman had ever known. He saw Madame de Cintré every day and never saw either ~~old Madame de Bellegarde~~ or the elder of his prospective brothers-in-law. ~~Madame de Cintré~~ at last seemed to think it becoming to apologise for their never being present. "They are much taken up," she said, "with doing the honours of Paris to Lord Deepmere." ~~There was a smile in her gravity~~ as she made this declaration, ~~and~~ it deepened as she added: "He is our seventh cousin, you know, and blood is thicker than water. And then, he is so interesting!" And with this ~~she laughed~~.

~~Newman~~ met young Madame de Bellegarde two or three times, always roaming about with graceful vagueness, as if in search of an unattainable ideal of amusement. She ~~always~~ reminded him of ~~a painted perfume bottle with a crack in it~~; but he ~~had grown to have a kindly feeling for her, based on the fact of her owing conjugal allegiance~~ to Urbain de Bellegarde. He pitied ~~M. de Bellegarde's wife, especially since~~ she was a silly.

Handwritten revisions:

- he had
- reverted
- throwing off sketches of her *intérieur*
- latter
- droll
- been copying sacred subjects,
- he wound up
- beautiful
- remarkably profane
- to be
- The woman of his choice
- on his rare young friend
- her mother
- Her gravity
- was almost prodigious, and it soon
- she strangely smiled
- that nobleman's wife the more also, that
- felt he owed indulgence to a lady who in her side owed submission
- some elegant painted phial cracked fragrantly and leaking;
- and
- He

thirstily-smiling little brunette with a suggestion of an unregulated heart. The small Marquise sometimes looked at him with an intensity too marked not to be innocent, for ~~coquetry is more finely shaded~~. She apparently wanted to ask him something or tell him something; he wondered what it ~~was~~. But he was shy of giving her an opportunity, because, if her communication bore upon the aridity of her matrimonial lot, he was at a loss to see how he could help her. He had a fancy, however, of her coming up to him some day and saying (after looking round behind her) with a little passionate hiss: "I know you detest my husband; let me have the pleasure of assuring you for once you're right. Pity a poor woman who is married to a clock-image in *papier-mâché!*" Possessing, ~~however~~, in default of a competent knowledge of the principles of etiquette, a very downright sense of the "meanness" of certain actions, it seemed to him to belong to his position to keep on his guard; he was not going to put it into the power of these people to say ~~that~~ in their house ~~he had done~~ anything ~~unpleasant~~. As it was, Madame de Bellegarde used to give him news of the dress she meant to wear at his wedding, and which had not yet, in her creative imagination, in spite of many interviews with the tailor, resolved itself into its composite totality. "I told you pale blue bows on the sleeves, at the elbows," she ~~said~~. "But to-day I don't see my blue bows at all. I don't know what has become of them. To-day I see pink—a tender pink. And then I pass through strange dull phases in which neither blue nor pink says anything to me. And yet I must have the bows."

"Have them green or yellow," ~~said~~ Newman.

"*Malheureux!*" the little Marquise would cry. ~~"Green bows would break your marriage—your children would be illegitimate!"~~

Madame de Cintré was calmly ~~happy~~ content before the world, ~~and Newman~~ had the felicity of ~~fancying~~ that before him,

earnest advances, he conceived, were usually much less direct

might be

at any rate,

he had done

not absolutely straight

would say

sort of cuisse de nymphe

sometimes suggested

then piercingly

but her lover

feeling

"I hope you're not going to pretend to dress your wife. Claire's an angel, yes; but her bows, already, are—well, are of another world."

when the world was absent, ~~she was almost agitatedly happy.~~ She said ~~very~~ tender things. "I take no pleasure in you. You never give me a chance to scold you, to correct you. I bargained for that; I expected to enjoy it. But you won't do anything dreadful; ~~you are dismally inoffensive.~~ It is very stupid; there is no excitement for me; I might as well be marrying some one else."

"I'm afraid it's the worst I can do," Newman would say in answer to this. "Kindly ~~overlook the deficiency.~~" He assured her that he, at least, would never ~~scold her~~; she was perfectly satisfactory. "If you only knew how exactly you're what I coveted! And I'm beginning to understand why I ~~coveted it~~; the having it makes all the difference that I expected. Never was a man so pleased with his good fortune. You've been holding your head for a week past just as I wanted my wife to hold hers. You say just the things I want her to say. You walk about the room just as I want her to walk. You've just the taste in dress ~~that~~ I want her to have. In short, you come up to the mark, and, I can tell you, my mark was high."

These observations ~~seemed to make Madame de Cintré rather~~ grave. At last she said: "Depend on it I don't come up to the mark; your mark's too high. I'm not all ~~that~~ you suppose; I'm a much smaller affair. She's a magnificent ~~woman, your ideal.~~ Pray, how did she come to such perfection?"

"She was never ~~anything else," Newman said.~~

"I really believe," ~~Madame de Cintré~~ went on, "that she's better than ~~my own ideal.~~ Do you know that's a very handsome compliment? Well, sir, I'll make her my own!"

Mrs. Tristram came to see her dear Claire after Newman had announced his engagement, and she ~~told~~ our hero the next day that his ~~good~~ fortune was simply absurd. "For the ridiculous part of it is [deleted]

[Manuscript revisions in the margins:]

charming and

her sense of security overflowed.

wrong or queer or

make the best of any inconvenience or any

visit on her any remonstrance;

tended to make his friend more

person, the image you cherish.

wanted

ed

all

myself

at all;

's much

his companion

observed to

any fond flight of my own ideal?

but perfection," Newman replied.

and yet you won't even look as if you were trying to do right. You're easier than we are, you're easier than I am, and I quite see that you've reasons, of some sort, that are as good as ours. It's dull for me, therefore," she smiled, "and it's rather disappointing, not to have anything to show you or to tell you or to teach you, that you don't seem already quite capable of knowing and doing and feeling. What's left of the good one was going to do you?"

[illegible] evidently going to be as happy as if you were marrying Miss Smith or Miss ~~Thompson~~. I call it a brilliant match for you, but you get brilliancy without paying any tax upon it. Those things are usually a compromise, but here you have everything, and nothing crowds anything else out. You will be brilliantly happy ~~as well~~." Newman thanked her for her pleasant encouraging way of saying things; no woman could encourage or discourage better. Tristram's way ~~of saying things~~ was different; he had been taken by his wife to call upon Madame de Cintré, and he gave an account of the expedition.

"You don't catch me ~~giving an opinion on your countess this time," he said;~~ I put my foot in it ~~once~~. That's a ~~damned~~ underhand thing to do, by the way—coming round to sound a fellow upon the woman you are going to marry. You deserve anything you get. Then of course you rush and tell her, and she takes care to make it pleasant for the poor spiteful wretch the first time he calls. I will do you the justice to say, however, that you don't seem to have told ~~Madame de Cintré; or, if you have, she's uncommonly magnanimous~~. She was very nice; she was tremendously polite. She and Lizzie sat on the sofa, pressing each other's hands and calling each other *chère belle*, and Madame de Cintré sent me with every third word a magnificent smile, as if to give me to understand that I too was a handsome dear. She quite made up for past neglect, I assure you; she was very pleasant and sociable. Only in an evil hour it came into her head to say that she must present us to her mother—her mother wished to know ~~your friends~~. I didn't want to know her mother, and I was on the point of telling Lizzie to go in alone and let me wait for her outside. But Lizzie, with her usual infernal ingenuity, guessed my purpose, and ~~reduced me by a glance of her eye~~. So they marched off arm-in-arm, and I followed as I could. We found the old lady in her armchair,

that you're

Brown.

with the rest of the brilliancy." "I consider really that I've done it for you, but it's almost more than I can bear."

tasting

a personal estimate this time, I guess—do you?

jolly

for you once.

your present friend—or if you did she let me down easy.

any good friends of yours.

looked me into obedience.

twiddling her aristocratic thumbs. She looked at Lizzie from head to foot; but at that game Lizzie, to do her justice, was a match for her. My wife told her we were great friends of Mr. Newman. The Marquise stared a moment, and then said: 'Oh, Mr. Newman? My daughter has made up her mind to marry a Mr. Newman.' Then Madame de Cintré began to fondle Lizzie again, and said it was this dear lady that had planned the match and brought them together. 'Oh, 'tis you I have to thank for my American son-in-law,' the old lady said to Mrs. Tristram. 'It was a very clever thought of yours. Be sure of my gratitude.' And then she began to look at me, and presently said: 'Pray, are you engaged in some species of manufacture?' I wanted to say that I manufactured broomsticks for old witches to ride on, but Lizzie got in ahead of me. 'My husband, Madame la Marquise,' [struck out] belongs to that unfortunate class of persons who have no profession, and no business, and do very little good in the world.' To get her poke at the old woman she didn't care where she shoved me. 'Dear me,' said the Marquise, 'we all have our duties.' 'I'm sorry mine compel me to take leave of you,' said Lizzie. And we bundled out again. But you have a mother-in-law, in all the force of the term."

"Oh," said Newman, "my mother-in-law desires nothing better than to let me alone!"

Betimes, on the evening of the 27th, he went to Madame de Bellegarde's ball. The old house in the Rue de l'Université looked strangely brilliant. In the circle of light projected from the outer gate a detachment of the populace stood watching the carriages roll in; the court was illumined with flaring torches, and the portico carpeted with crimson. When Newman arrived there were but a few people present. The Marquise and her two daughters were at the top of the staircase, where the sallow old nymph in the angle peeped out from a bower

hard, | eyed | who | had the first idea | it's | high appreciation!" | and his occupation | Madame de Bellegarde | who thereby | time-honoured term" | in | on | landing | made answer, | marble | shone strangely in his eyes.

of plants. Madame de Bellegarde, in purple and pearls and fine laces resembled some historic figure painted by Vandyke; she made her daughter, in comparative vaguenesses of white, splendid and pale, look, for his joy of possession, infinitely modern and near. His hostess greeted him with a fine cold urbanity and, looking round, called to several of the persons standing hard by. They were elderly gentlemen with faces as marked and featured and filled-in, for some science of social topography, as, to Newman's whimsical sense, any of the little towered and battered old towns, on high eminences, that his tour of several countries during the previous summer had shown him; they were adorned with strange insignia, cordons and ribbons and orders, as if the old cities were flying flags and streamers and hanging out shields for a celebration, and they approached with measured alertness while the Marquise presented them the good friend of the family who was to marry her daughter. The good friend heard a confused enumeration of titles and names that matched, to his fancy, the rest of the paraphernalia; the gentlemen bowed and smiled and murmured without reserve, and he indulged in a series of impartial handshakes, accompanied in each case by a "Very happy to meet you, sir." He looked at Madame de Cintré, but her attention was absent. If his personal self-consciousness had been of a nature to make him constantly refer to her as to the critic before whom in company he played his part, he might have found it a flattering proof of her confidence that he never caught her eyes resting on him. It is a reflection he didn't make, but we may nevertheless risk it, that in spite of this circumstance she probably saw every movement of his little finger. The Marquise Urbain was wondrously dressed in crimson crape bestrewn with huge silver moons — full disks and fine crescents, ~~in every phase of duration,~~ half the features of the firmament.

"You don't say anything about my *toilette*," she impatiently observed to him.

"Well, I feel as if I were looking at you through a

telescope. You put me in mind of some lurid comet, something grand and wild."

"Ah, if I'm grand and wild I match the occasion! But I'm not a heavenly body."

"I never saw the sky at midnight that particular shade of crimson," Newman said.

"That's just my originality: any fool could have chosen blue. My sister-in-law would have chosen a lovely shade of ~~blue~~, with a dozen little delicate moons. But I think crimson ~~is~~ much more amusing. And I give my idea, which is moonshine."

"Moonshine and bloodshed," said Newman.

"A murder by moonlight," ~~laughed Madame de Bellegarde~~. "What a delicious idea for a toilet! To make it complete, there is a dagger of diamonds, you see, stuck into my hair. But here comes Lord Deepmere," she added in a moment; "I must find out what he thinks of it." Lord Deepmere came up, ~~looking~~ very red in the face, and ~~laughing~~. "Lord Deepmere can't decide which he prefers, my sister-in-law or me," ~~said Madame de Bellegarde~~. "He likes Claire because she is his cousin, and me because I am not. But he has no right to make love to Claire, whereas I am perfectly *disponible*. It is very wrong to make love to a woman who is engaged, but it is very wrong not to make love to a woman who is married."

"Oh, it's very jolly making love to married women," ~~said Lord Deepmere~~, "because they can't ask you to marry them."

"Is that what the others do—the spinsters?" Newman inquired.

"Oh dear, yes, [illegible] England all the girls ask a fellow to marry them."

"And a fellow brutally refuses," said ~~Madame de Bellegarde~~.

"Why, really, you know, a fellow can't marry any girl that asks him," said his lordship.

"Your cousin won't ask you. She is going to marry Mr. Newman."

"Oh, that's a very different thing!" ~~laughed~~ Lord Deepmere.

"You would have accepted *her*, I suppose. That makes me hope that, after all, you prefer me."

"Oh, when things are nice I never prefer one to the other," said the young ~~Englishman~~. "I take them all."

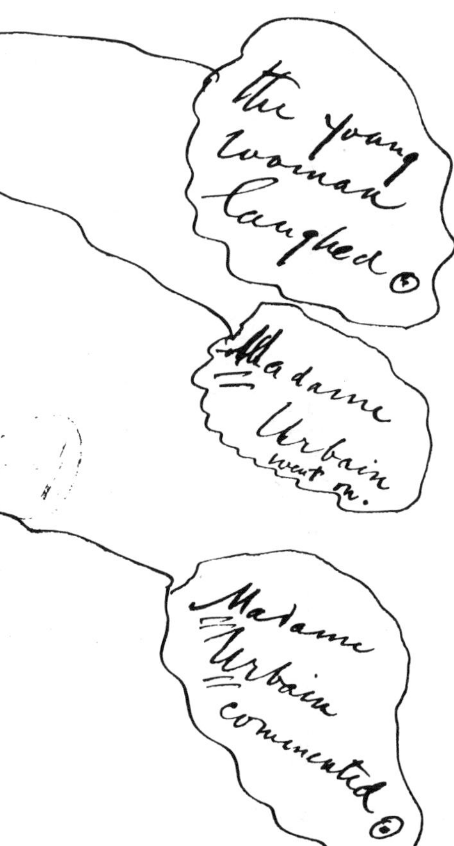

the young woman laughed
Madame Urbain went on.
Madame Urbain commented

36 THE AMERICAN. XVI.

"Ah, what a horror! I won't be taken in that way; I must be kept apart," cried Madame de Bellegarde. "Mr. Newman is much better; he knows how to choose. Oh, he chooses as if he were threading a needle. He prefers Madame de Cintré to any conceivable creature or thing."

"Well, you can't help my being her cousin," said Lord Deepmere to Newman, with candid hilarity.

"Oh no, I can't help that," said Newman, laughing back; "neither can she!"

"And you can't help my dancing with her," said Lord Deepmere, with sturdy simplicity.

"I could prevent that only by dancing with her myself," said Newman. "But unfortunately I don't know how to dance."

"Oh, you may dance without knowing how; may you not, milord?" said Madame de Bellegarde. But to this Lord Deepmere replied that a fellow ought to know how to dance if he didn't want to make an ass of himself; and at this same moment Urbain de Bellegarde joined the group, slow-stepping and with his hands behind him.

"This is a very splendid entertainment," said Newman, cheerfully. "The old house looks very bright."

"If *you* are pleased, we are content," said the Marquis, lifting his shoulders and bending them forward.

"Oh, I suspect every one is pleased," said Newman. "How can they help being pleased when the first thing they see as they come in is your sister, standing there as beautiful as an angel?"

"Yes, she is very beautiful," rejoined the Marquis, solemnly. "But that is not so great a source of satisfaction to other people, naturally, as to you."

"Yes, I am satisfied, Marquis, I am satisfied," said Newman, with his protracted enunciation. "And now tell me," he added, looking round, "who some of your friends are."

M. de Bellegarde looked about him in silence, with

his head bent and his hand raised to his lower lip, which he slowly rubbed. A stream of people had been pouring into the salon in which Newman stood with his host, the rooms were filling up, and the ~~spectacle had become brilliant~~. It borrowed its splendour ~~chiefly~~ from the shining shoulders and profuse jewels of the women, and from the ~~voluminous elegance of their dresses~~. There were ~~no~~ uniforms, as Madame de Bellegarde's door was inexorably closed against the myrmidons of the upstart power which then ~~ruled the fortunes~~ of France, and the great company of smiling and chattering faces was not graced by any very ~~frequent suggestions~~ of harmonious beauty. It ~~is a pity~~, nevertheless, that ~~Newman~~ had not been a physiognomist, for ~~a great many of the faces were irregularly agreeable, expressive, and suggestive.~~ If the occasion had been different they would hardly have pleased him; he would have thought the women not pretty enough and the men too smirking; but he was now in a humour to receive none but ~~agreeable~~ impressions, and he looked no more narrowly than to perceive that every one was ~~brilliant~~, and to feel that the sum of ~~their brilliancy was a~~ part of his credit. "I will present you to some people," said M. de Bellegarde after a while. "I will make a point of it, in fact. You will allow ~~me?~~"

"Oh, I will shake hands with any one you want," ~~said~~ Newman. "Your mother just introduced me to half a dozen old gentlemen. Take care you don't pick up the same parties again."

"Who are the gentlemen to whom my mother ~~presented~~ you?"

"Upon my word, I forget them," ~~said~~ Newman, ~~laughing. "The people here look very much alike."~~

"I suspect they have not forgotten you," said the Marquis, and he began to walk through the rooms. Newman, to keep near him in the crowd, took his arm; after which, for some time, the Marquis walked straight

place, all light and colour and fine resonance, looked rich and congressional ⊙

largely

rest of their festal array ⊙

but not many,

flourished on the soil

he

mere

was a pity for our friend,

fair

direct presentment

whole great

~~[struck out]~~ charged with ~~[struck out]~~ some vivacity or some solemnity

the faces about him were the picture of a world and the vivid translation, as might have seemed to him, of a text that had had otherwise its obscurities ⊙

~~[struck out]~~ character and confidence was

"I'm afraid I've got them rather mixed; and don't Chinamen—even great mandarins!—look very much the same to Occidentals???

had to confess.

returned.

presented

me? if I exercise my judgment ⊙?"

~~along~~ in silence. At last, reaching the farther end of the ~~suite of reception rooms,~~ Newman found himself in the presence of a lady of monstrous proportions, seated in a very capacious armchair, with several persons standing in a semicircle round her. This little group had divided as the Marquis came up, and ~~M. de Bellegarde~~ stepped forward and stood for an instant silent and obsequious, with his hat raised to his lips, as Newman had seen ~~some~~ gentlemen stand in churches as soon as they entered their pews. The lady, indeed, bore a very fair likeness to a reverend effigy in some idolatrous shrine. She was monumentally stout and imperturbably serene. Her aspect was to Newman almost formidable; he had a troubled consciousness of a triple chin, ~~a small piercing eye~~, a vast expanse of uncovered bosom, a nodding and twinkling tiara of plumes and gems and an immense circumference of satin petticoat. With her little circle of beholders this remarkable woman reminded him of the Fat Lady at a fair. She fixed her small, unwinking ~~eyes~~ at the newcomers.

"Dear Duchess," said the Marquis, "let me present you our good friend Mr. Newman, of whom you have heard us speak. Wishing to make Mr. Newman known to those who are dear to us, I could not possibly fail to begin with you."

"Charmed, dear friend; charmed, Monsieur," said the Duchess in a voice which, though small and shrill, was not disagreeable, while Newman ~~executed his~~ obeisance. "I came on purpose to see Monsieur. I hope he appreciates the compliment. You have only to look at me to do so, sir," she continued, sweeping her person with a much-encompassing glance. Newman hardly knew what to say, though it seemed that to a Duchess who joked about her corpulence one might say almost anything. On hearing ~~that the Duchess~~ had come on purpose to see ~~Newman,~~ the gentlemen who surrounded her turned a little and looked at him with sympathetic

on
the apartments
and
he
flattened
a pair of eyes that twinkled in her face like a pair of polished pin-heads in a cushion,
gaze
He always made his bow, as he wrote his name, very distinctly
performed with all his length his liberal
she
this object of interest

curiosity. The Marquis with supernatural gravity mentioned to him the name of each, while the gentleman who bore it bowed; they were all what are called in France *beaux noms*. "I wanted extremely to see you," the Duchess went on. "*C'est positif.* In the first place I am very fond of the person you are going to marry; she is the most charming creature in France. Mind you treat her well, or you shall hear some news of me. But you look as if you were good. I am told you are very remarkable. I have heard all sorts of extraordinary things about you. *Voyons*, are they true?"

"I don't know what you can have heard," said Newman.

"Oh, you have your *légende*. We have heard that you have had a career the most chequered, the most *bizarre*. What is that about your having founded a city some ten years ago in the great West, a city which contains to-day half a million of inhabitants? Isn't it half a million, Messieurs? You are exclusive proprietor of this flourishing settlement, and are consequently fabulously rich, and you would be richer still if you didn't grant lands and houses free of rent to all newcomers who will pledge themselves never to smoke cigars. At this game, in three years, we are told, you are going to be made President of America."

The Duchess recited this amusing "legend" with a smooth self-possession which gave the speech, to Newman's mind, the air of being a bit of amusing dialogue in a play delivered by a veteran comic actress. Before she had ceased speaking he had burst into loud, irrepressible laughter. "Dear Duchess, dear Duchess," the Marquis began to murmur soothingly. Two or three persons came to the door of the room to see who was laughing at the Duchess. But the lady continued with the soft, serene assurance of a person who, as a Duchess, was certain of being listened to, and, as a garrulous woman, was independent of the pulse of her auditors.

and these pronouncements again affected Newman as some enumeration of the titles of books, of the performers on playbills, of the items of indexes.

You'll have

on

the wonderful place

it,

ear the sound of an amusing passage in a play interpreted

great lady.

promptly pleaded

quaint fable

relieved himself, applausively, by laughter as frank as clapping or stamping

"But I know you are very remarkable. You must be, to have endeared yourself to this good Marquis and to his admirable mother. They don't bestow their esteem on all the world. They are very exacting. I myself am not very sure at this hour of really possessing it. Eh, Bellegarde? To please you, I see, one must be an American millionaire. But your real triumph, my dear sir, is pleasing the Countess; she is as difficult as a princess in a fairy-tale. Your success is a miracle. What is your secret? I don't ask you to reveal it before all these gentlemen, but come and see me some day and give me a specimen of your talents."

"The secret is with Madame de Cintré," said Newman. "You must ask her for it. It consists in her having a great deal of charity."

"Very pretty!" said the Duchess. "That's a very nice specimen to begin with. What, Bellegarde, are you already taking Monsieur away?"

"I have a duty to perform, dear friend," said the Marquis, pointing to the other groups.

"Ah, for you I know what that means. Well, I have seen Monsieur; that is what I wanted. He can't persuade me that he isn't very clever. Farewell."

As Newman passed on with his host, he asked who the Duchess was. "The greatest lady in France," said the Marquis. M. de Bellegarde then presented his prospective brother-in-law to some twenty other persons of both sexes, selected apparently for their typically august character. In some cases this character was written in a good round hand upon the countenance of the wearer; in others Newman was thankful for such help as his companion's impressively brief intimation contributed to the discovery of them. There were large, majestic men, and small, demonstrative men; there were ugly ladies in yellow lace and quaint jewels, and pretty ladies with white shoulders from which jewels and everything else were absent. Every one gave Newman extreme

Handwritten revisions:

- ones
- Urbain
- scatter
- enjoying their esteem—eh, Marquis?
- pronounced.
- Marquis,
- Au revoir, monsieur."
- He
- measured as to his scant capacity
- about.
- have resources to which we can't pretend.
- You must
- show me how you proceed.
- in
- in
- Urbain,
- might be.
- whereupon reservedly replied.
- insinuating extravagant ones,
- heavy, imperturbable gentlemen
- their honours were
- (recognised some) value of name or fame or attitude.
- reaches of white denudation that even their wealth of precious stones scarce availed to overtake.

attention, every one smiled, every one was charmed to make his acquaintance, every one looked at him with that soft hardness of good society which puts out its hand but keeps its fingers closed over the coin. If the Marquis was going about as a bear-leader, if the fiction of Beauty and the Beast was supposed to have found its companion-piece, the general impression appeared that the bear was a very fair imitation of humanity. Newman found his reception among the Marquis's friends very ; he could not have said more for it. It was pleasant to be treated with so much explicit politeness; it was pleasant to hear neatly-turned civilities, with a flavour of wit, uttered from beneath carefully-shaped moustaches; it was pleasant to see clever Frenchwomen—they all seemed clever—turn their backs to their partners to get a good look at the strange American whom Claire de Cintré was to marry, and reward the object of the exhibition with a charming smile. At last, as he turned away from a battery of smiles and other amenities, Newman caught the eye of the Marquis looking at him heavily, and thereupon, for a single instant, he checked himself. "Am I behaving like a d——d fool?" he asked himself. "Am I stepping about like a terrier on his hind legs?" At this moment he perceived Mrs. Tristram at the other side of the room, and he waved his hand in farewell to M. de Bellegarde and made his way toward her.

"Am I holding my head too high ? "Do I look as if I had the lower end of a pulley fastened to my chin?"

"You look like all happy men, very ridiculous," said Mrs. Tristram. "It's the usual thing, neither better nor worse. I have been watching you for the last ten minutes, and I have been watching M. de Bellegarde. He doesn't like it."

"The more credit to him for putting it through," replied Newman. "But I shall be generous. I sha'n't

fraudulent intensity

bountiful

show thus

in the charmed circle very handsome — he liked, handsomely himself, not to say less than that for it. It was handsome

handsome

syllabled and articulated that they were like handfuls of bank-notes pushed at you by a counting clerk;

handsome of

slightly gaunt outsider

vivid grimaces

fixed on him inscrutably;

wondered.

in order to make

they were saying 'Catch' and I were snapping down what they throw me and licking my lips?"

and opening my mouth too wide?" he demanded.

for such situations

what he has to do."

returned.

very successful men — fatuous without knowing it. Women triumph with more tact, just as they suffer with more grace. Therefore its trouble him any more. But I'm very happy. I can't stand still here. Please take my arm and we'll go for a walk."

He led Mrs. Tristram from one room to another, where, scattering wide glances and soft sharp comments, she reminded him of the pausing wayfarer who studies the contents of the confectioner's window, with platonic discriminations, through a firm plate of glass. But he made vague answers; he scarcely heard her; his thoughts were elsewhere. They were lost in the vastness of this attested truth of his having come out where he wanted. His momentary consciousness of possibly too broad a grin passed away, and he felt, the next thing, almost solemnly quiet. Yes, he had "got there," and now it was, all-powerfully, to stay. These prodigies of gain were in a general way familiar to him, but the sense of what he had "made" by an anxious operation had never been so deep and sweet. The lights, the flowers, the music, the "associations" vague and confused to him, yet hovering like some odour of dried spices, something far-away and Chinese; the splendid women, the splendid jewels, the strangeness even of the universal ease of a tongue that seemed the language of society as Italian was the language of opera: these things were all a gage of his having worked, from the old first years, under some better star than he knew. Yet if he showed again and again so many of his fine strong teeth it was not tickled vanity that pulled the exhibitory string: he had no wish to be pointed at with the finger or to be considered, by these people, for himself. If he could have looked down at the scene invisibly, as from a hole in the roof, he would have enjoyed it quite as much. It would have spoken to him of his energy and prosperity and deepened that view of his effective "handling" of life to which, sooner or later, he made all experience contribute. Just now the cup seemed full.

"It's all very fine and very funny, I mean very special and quite thrilling and almost interesting," said Mrs. Tristram while they circulated. ~~after they had walked a while.~~ "I've seen nothing objectionable except my husband leaning against that adorably faded strawberry damask of the other room and talking to an individual whom I suppose he takes for a prince, but whom I more than suspect to be the functionary taking care of the lamps.

~~ary who attends to the lamps.~~ Do you think you could separate them? ~~Knock~~ over a lamp!"

I doubt whether Newman, who saw no harm in Tristram's conversing with an ingenious mechanic, would have complied with this request; but at this moment Valentin de Bellegarde drew near. Newman, some weeks previously, had presented Madame de Cintré's youngest brother to Mrs. Tristram, ~~for whose merits Valentin professed a discriminating~~ relish, and to whom he had paid several visits.

"Did you ever ~~read~~ Keats's 'Belle Dame sans Merci'? ~~[struck out]~~ You remind me of the hero of the ballad:

"'Oh, what can ail thee, knight-at-arms,
Alone and palely loitering?'"

"If I am alone, it is because I have been deprived of your society," ~~said~~ Valentin. "Besides, it is good manners for no man except Newman to look happy. This is all to his address. It is not for you and me to go before the curtain."

"You promised me last spring," said Newman to Mrs. Tristram, "that six months from that time I should get into a ~~monstrous~~ rage. It seems to me the time's up, and yet the nearest I can come to doing anything rough now is to offer you a *café glacé*."

"I ~~told~~ you we should do things grandly," ~~said Valentin~~. "I don't allude to the *cafés glacés*. But every one is here, and my sister told me just now that Urbain had been adorable."

"He's a ~~good fellow, he's a good fellow," said Newman. "I love him~~ as a brother. That reminds me that I ought to go and say something ~~polite~~ to your mother."

"Let it be something very ~~polite~~ indeed," said Valentin. "It may be the last time you will feel so much ~~like it~~."

Handwritten revisions: Do Knock | read," she asked, | returned. | tearing | promised | for whose rather shy and subtle merit the young man promptly professed an intelligent | take the call | Valentin observed. | enthusiastic | real nice man—all the way through. | in the vein." | If I don't look out," Newman went on, "or if he doesn't—I shall begin to love him

Newman walked away almost disposed to clasp old Madame de Bellegarde round the waist. He passed through several rooms, and at last found the old Marquise in the first saloon, seated on a sofa, with her young kinsman, Lord Deepmere, beside her. The young man looked somewhat bored; his hands were thrust into his pockets and his eyes were fixed upon the toes of his shoes, his feet being thrust out in front of him. Madame de Bellegarde appeared to have been talking to him with some intensity, and to be waiting for an answer to what she had said, or for some sign of the effect of her words. Her hands were folded in her lap, and she was looking at his lordship's simple physiognomy with an air of politely suppressed irritation. Lord Deepmere looked up as Newman approached, met his eyes, and changed colour. "I'm afraid I disturb an interesting interview," said Newman.

Madame de Bellegarde rose, and her companion rising at the same time, she put her hand into his arm. She answered nothing for an instant, and then, as he remained silent, she said with a smile: "It would be polite for Lord Deepmere to say it was very interesting."

"Oh, I'm not polite!" cried his lordship. "But it *was* interesting."

"Madame de Bellegarde was giving you some good advice, eh?" said Newman: "toning you down a little?"

"I was giving him some excellent advice," said the Marquise, fixing her fresh cold eyes upon our hero. "It's for him to take it."

"Take it, sir, take it!" Newman exclaimed. "Any advice the Marquise gives you to-night must be good; for to-night, Marquise, you must speak from a cheerful, comfortable spirit, and that makes good advice. You see everything going on so brightly and successfully round you. Your party is magnificent; it was a very happy

Manuscript annotations: her; His hostess; now; considered; He; On which the latter; connect; said: "I'm; marked sharpness of attention; amiable; asked:; amiable; preaching you, with her high authority, the way you should go? In your place I'd go it then — blind!"; She; for soundness and sense."

thought. It's much better than that ~~thing~~ of mine would have been."

"If you're pleased I'm satisfied," ~~said Madame de Bellegarde~~. "My desire was to please you."

"Do you want to please me a little more?" ~~said Newman~~. "Just ~~drop our lordly friend; I am sure he wants to be off and shake his heels a little~~. Then take my arm and walk through the rooms."

"My desire was to please you," ~~the old lady repeated. And she liberated Lord Deepmere, Newman rather wondering~~ at her docility. "If this young man is wise," she added, "he'll go and find my daughter and ask her to dance."

"I've been endorsing your advice," said Newman, bending over her and laughing; "I suppose ~~he must swallow it~~."

Lord Deepmere wiped his forehead and departed, and Madame de Bellegarde took Newman's arm. "Yes, ~~it's a very pleasant, sociable entertainment~~," the latter declared, as they proceeded on their circuit. "Every one seems to know every one, and to be glad to see every one. The Marquis has made me acquainted with ever so many people, and I feel quite like one of the family. It's an occasion," Newman continued, wanting ~~to say something thoroughly kind and comfortable~~, "that I shall always remember, and remember very pleasantly."

"I think it's an occasion that we shall none of us forget," said the Marquise, with her pure, neat enunciation.

People made way for her as she passed, others turned round and looked at her, and she received a great many greetings and pressings of the hand, all of which she accepted with the most delicate dignity. But though she smiled ~~upon~~ on every one, she said nothing ~~until~~ she reached the last of the rooms, where she found her elder son. Then, "This is enough, sir," she ~~declared, with measured softness to Newman, and turned to the Marquis~~. He put out both his hands and took both hers, drawing

blow-out

she answered with rare accommodation

as much as possible

then?" Newman went on. "Just let Lord Deepmere digest your wisdom and take care of himself a little; and then

the Marquise rather stiffly repeated; and as she liberated her companion our friend wondered

still more to express appreciation without an afterthought,

Therefore I must let him cut in where I can neither lead nor follow."

it has been a real friendly, hearty, jolly idea;

ever

till

observed, with her dignity of distinctness, to Newman, turning at the same time to Urbain her to a seat with an air of the tenderest veneration. ~~It made a most harmonious family group~~, and Newman discreetly retired. He moved through the rooms for some time longer, circulating freely, overtopping most people by his great height, renewing acquaintance with some of the groups to which Urbain de Bellegarde had presented him, and expending generally the surplus of his equanimity. He continued to find it all extremely agreeable; but the most agreeable things have an end, and the revelry on this occasion began to deepen to a close. The music was sounding its ultimate strains, and people ~~were looking for the Marquise, to make their farewells~~. There seemed ~~to be~~ some difficulty in finding her, and Newman ~~heard~~ a report that she had left the ball, ~~feeling faint~~. "She has succumbed to the emotions of the evening," he heard ~~a~~ lady say. "Poor, dear Marquise; I can imagine all ~~that~~ they may have been for her!"

But he learned immediately afterwards that she had recovered herself and was seated in an armchair near the doorway, receiving ~~parting compliments from great ladies~~ who insisted upon her not rising. He himself set out in quest of Madame de Cintré, ~~He~~ had seen ~~her~~ move past him many times in the rapid circles of a waltz, but ~~in accordance with~~ her explicit instructions, he had exchanged no words ~~with her~~ since the beginning of the evening. The whole house having been thrown open the apartments of the *rez-de-chaussée* were also accessible, though a smaller number of persons had gathered there. Newman wandered through them, observing a few scattered couples to whom this comparative seclusion appeared grateful, and reached a small conservatory which opened into the garden. The end of the conservatory was formed by a clear sheet of glass, unmasked by plants, and admitting the winter starlight so directly that a person standing there would seem to have passed into the open air. Two persons stood there now, a lady and a gentleman; the lady Newman, from within the room,

Handwritten revisions:

- It appeared to (between them) attest ~~the~~ ~~[illegible]~~ the need of more intimate communion
- about to take their leave were looking for their hostess
- caught
- in an access of fatigue or of faintness
- a voluble lady
- whom
- the last honours from members of her own sex
- had
- with whom, also, conforming to

and although she had turned her back to it, immediately recognised as Madame de Cintré. He hesitated as to whether he would advance, but as he did so she looked round, feeling apparently that he was there. She rested her eyes on him a moment, and then turned again to her companion.

"It is almost a pity not to tell Mr. Newman," she said softly, but in a tone that Newman could hear.

"Tell him if you like!" the gentleman answered, in the voice of Lord Deepmere.

"Oh, tell me by all means!" said Newman, advancing.

Lord Deepmere, he observed, was very red in the face, and he had twisted his gloves into a tight cord as if he had been squeezing them dry. These, presumably, were tokens of violent emotion, and it seemed to Newman that the traces of a corresponding agitation were visible in Madame de Cintré's [illegible]. The two had been talking with much vivacity. "What I should tell you is only to my lord's credit," said Madame de Cintré, smiling frankly enough.

"He wouldn't [illegible] any better for that," said my lord, with his awkward laugh.

"Come; what's the mystery?" Newman demanded. "Clear it up. I don't like mysteries."

"We must have some things we don't like, and go without some we do," said the ruddy young nobleman, laughing still.

"It is to Lord Deepmere's credit, but it is not to every one's," said Madame de Cintré. "So I shall say nothing about it. You may be sure," she added; and she put out her hand to the Englishman, who took it half shyly, half impetuously. "And now go and dance!" she said.

"Oh yes, I feel awfully like dancing!" he answered. "I shall go and get tipsy." And he walked away with a gloomy guffaw.

"What has happened between you?" Newman asked.

"I can't tell you—now," said Madame de Cintré. "Nothing that need make you unhappy."

"Has ~~the little Englishman~~ been trying to make love to you?"

She hesitated, and then she uttered a grave "No! He's a ~~very honest little fellow~~."

"But ~~[illegible]~~. Something's the matter."

"Nothing, I repeat, that need make you unhappy. ~~[illegible]~~. Some day I'll tell you what it was; not now. I can't now."

"Well, I confess," ~~[illegible]~~ Newman, "I don't want to hear anything ~~[illegible]~~. I'm satisfied with everything—most of all with you. I've seen all the ladies and talked with a great many of them; but I'm satisfied with you." ~~Madame de Cintré~~ covered him for a moment ~~[illegible]~~, and then turned her eyes away into the starry night. So they stood silent a moment, side by side. "Say you are satisfied with *me*," said Newman.

He had to wait a moment for the answer; but it came at last, low yet distinct. "I'm very happy."

It was presently followed by a few words from another source which made them both turn round. "I am sadly afraid Madame ~~de Cintré~~ will take a chill. I've ventured to bring a shawl." Mrs. Bread stood there softly solicitous, holding a white drapery in her hand.

"Thank you," said Madame de Cintré; "the sight of those cold stars gives one a sense of frost. I won't take your shawl, but we'll go back into the house."

She passed back and Newman followed her, Mrs. Bread standing respectfully aside to make way for them. Newman paused an instant before the old woman, and she glanced up at him with a silent greeting. "Oh yes," he said, "you must come and live with us."

"Well then, sir, if you will," she answered; "you've not seen the last of me!"

that fellow

perfectly honest young man."

You've been somehow upset and are still worried.

I've completely recovered my balance if I had lost it: which I haven't!

out of key.

la Comtesse

with her bright mildness,

returned.

The charming woman

very

CHAPTER XVII.

NEWMAN was fond of music, and went often to the opera. A couple of evenings after Madame de Bellegarde's ball, he sat listening to "Don Giovanni," having in honour of this work, which he had never yet seen represented, come to occupy his orchestra chair before the rising of the curtain. Frequently he took a large box and invited a party of his compatriots; this was a mode of recreation to which he was much addicted. He liked making up parties of his friends and conducting them to the theatre, and taking them to drive on high drags or to dine at remote restaurants. He liked doing things which involved his paying for people; the vulgar truth is that he enjoyed "treating" them. This was not because he was what is called purse-proud; handling money in public was, on the contrary, positively disagreeable to him; he had a sort of personal modesty about it, akin to what he would have felt about making a toilet before spectators. But just as it was a gratification to him to be handsomely dressed, just so it was a private satisfaction to him (he enjoyed it very clandestinely) to have interposed, pecuniarily, in a scheme of pleasure. To set a large group of people in motion and transport them to a distance, to have special conveyances, to charter railway carriages and steamboats, harmonised with his relish for bold processes and made hospitality seem more active and more to the purpose. A few evenings before the occasion of which I speak he had invited several ladies and gentlemen to the opera to listen to Madame Alboni—a party which included Miss Dora Finch. It befell, however, that Miss Dora Finch, sitting near Newman in the box, discoursed brilliantly, not only during the entr'actes, but during many of the finest portions of the performance, so that Newman had really come away with an irritated

where, a group mail-coaches restaurants renowned, by what he could a trifle artlessly ascertaining for special dishes. that for he kept (the full flavour of it quite delicately to himself) to see people occupied and amused at his pecuniary expense and by his profuse interposition. To set a large body of them the potent thing it should ideally be. he the young and wondrous Adelina Patti—

sense that ~~Madame Alboni~~ had a thin, shrill voice, and that her musical phrase was much garnished with a laugh of the giggling order. After this he promised himself to go for a while to the opera alone.

When the curtain had fallen upon the first act of "Don Giovanni," he turned round in his place to observe the house. Presently, in one of the boxes, he perceived Urbain de Bellegarde and his wife. The little Marquise was sweeping the house very busily with a glass, and Newman, supposing ~~that~~ she saw him, determined to go and bid her good-evening. M. de Bellegarde ~~was lean-ing~~ against a column, motionless, looking straight in front of him, with one hand in the breast of his white waistcoat and the other resting his hat on his thigh. Newman was about to leave his place when he noticed in that obscure region devoted to the small boxes which in France are called, not inaptly, ~~bathing-tubs~~, a face which even the dim light and the distance could not make wholly indistinct. It was the face of a young and pretty woman, ~~and it was surmounted with a *coiffure* of~~ pink roses and diamonds. This person was looking round the house, and her fan ~~was moving~~ to and fro with ~~the most~~ practised grace; when she lowered it Newman perceived a pair of plump white shoulders and the edge of a rose-coloured dress. Beside her, very close to the shoulders, and talking, apparently with an earnestness which it ~~pleased~~ her scantly to heed, sat a young man with a red face and a very low shirt-collar. A moment's ~~gazing~~ left Newman with no doubts; the pretty young woman was Noémie Nioche. He looked hard into the depths of the box, thinking her father might perhaps be in attendance, but from what he could see the young man's eloquence had no other auditor. Newman at last made his way out, and in doing so he passed beneath the *baignoire* of ~~Mademoiselle Noémie~~. She saw him as he approached, ~~and gave~~ him a nod and smile which seemed meant as ~~an~~ ~~assurance~~ that ~~she was~~

Handwritten revisions:

- the new rare diva
- leaned
- bath-tubs, from their promoting at least immersion through the action of the pores,
- crowned with an arrangement of
- moved
- suited
- consideration
- a
- giving
- his former client.
- hint

still a good-natured girl, in spite of her enviable rise in the world. Newman passed into the *foyer* and walked through it. Suddenly he paused in front of a gentleman seated on one of the divans. The gentleman's elbows were on his knees; he was leaning forward and staring at the pavement, lost apparently in meditations of a somewhat gloomy cast. But in spite of his bent head Newman recognised him, and in a moment sat down beside him. Then the gentleman looked up and displayed the expressive countenance of Valentin de Bellegarde. connect

"What in the world are you thinking of so hard?" asked Newman.

"A subject that requires hard thinking to do it justice," said Valentin. "My immeasurable idiocy."

"What is the matter now?"

"The matter now is that, I am a man of sense again, more a fool than usual. But I came within an inch ace of taking that girl au sérieux."

"Newman the young lady below stairs, in a *baignoire*, in a pink dress?" said Newman.

"Did you notice what a brilliant kind of pink it was?" Valentin inquired, by way of answer. "It makes her look as white as new milk."

"White or black, as you please. But you have stopped going to see her?"

"Oh, bless you, no. Why should I stop? I have changed, but she hasn't," said Valentin. "I see she is a vulgar little wretch, after all. But she is as amusing as ever, and one *must* be amused."

"Well, I am glad she strikes you so unpleasantly," Newman rejoined. "I suppose you have swallowed all those fine words you used about her the other night. You compared her to a sapphire, or a topaz, or an amethyst—some precious stone; what was it?"

"I don't remember," said Valentin; "it may have been to a carbuncle! But she won't make a fool of me

had not made her inhuman ⊙

but suddenly to pause before

leaned forward and stared

had

promptly replied ⊙

rare

stopped them, at any rate,

For

as I'm a mad-man with lucid intervals, I'm having one of these now ⊙ But I came within an ace of entertaining a sentiment f a ——"

The more I see her the more sure I am—well, that I see her right ⊙ She

Newman had a stare of some wonderment and then: "Is she what you call the crème de la crème?" But as Valentin's face pronounced this a witticism below the Parisian standard he went on:

has awfully pretty arms, and other things; but she's not really a bit gentille. The

now. She has no real charm. It's an awfully low thing to make a mistake about a person of that sort."

"I congratulate you," Newman declared, "upon the scales having fallen from your eyes. It's a great triumph; it ought to make you feel better."

"Yes, it makes me feel better!" said Valentin, gaily. Then, checking himself, he looked askance at Newman. "I rather think you are laughing at me. If you were not one of the family I would take it up."

"Oh no, I'm not laughing, any more than I am one of the family. You make me feel badly. You are too clever a fellow, you are made of too good stuff, to spend your time in ups and downs over that class of goods. The idea of splitting hairs about Miss Nioche! It seems to me awfully foolish. You say you have given up taking her seriously; but you take her seriously so long as you take her at all."

Valentin turned round in his place and looked a while at Newman, wrinkling his forehead and rubbing his knees. "*Vous parlez d'or.* But she has wonderfully pretty arms. Would you believe I didn't know it till this evening?"

"But she is a vulgar little wretch, remember, all the same," said Newman.

"[struck out] other day she had the bad taste to begin to abuse her father, to his face, in my presence. I shouldn't have expected it of her; it was a disappointment. Heigho!"

"Why, she cares no more for her father than for her door-mat," ~~said~~ Newman declared. "I discovered that the first time I saw her."

"Oh, that's another affair; she may think of the poor old beggar what she pleases. But it was ~~low~~ base in her to call him bad names; it spoiled my reckoning and quite threw me off. It was about a frilled petticoat that he was to have fetched from the washerwoman's; he appeared to have ~~neglected this graceful duty~~ forgotten the frilled petticoat. She almost boxed his ears. He stood there staring at her with his little blank eyes and smoothing his old hat with his coat-tail. At last he turned round and went out without a word. Then I told her it was in very bad taste to speak so to one's papa. She said she should be so thankful to me if I would mention it to her whenever her taste was at fault; she had immense confidence in mine. I told her I couldn't have the ~~bother~~ of forming her manners; I had had an idea they were already formed, after the best models. She had ~~disappointed me.~~ But I shall get over it," said Valentin, gaily.

"Oh, time's a great consoler!" Newman answered, with humorous sobriety. He was silent a moment, and then he added in another tone: "I wish you ~~would~~ think of what I said to you the other day. Come over to America with us, and I ~~will~~ put you in the way of doing some business. You ~~have~~ got a very ~~good head~~ if ~~you will only use it.~~"

Valentin made a genial grimace. "My ~~head is~~ much obliged to you. Do you mean the place in a bank?"

"There are several places, but I suppose you ~~would~~ consider the bank the most aristocratic."

Valentin burst into a laugh. "My dear fellow, at night all cats are gray! When one ~~derogates there are no degrees.~~"

Newman answered nothing for a minute. Then, "I think you ~~will~~ find there are degrees in success," he said, with ~~a certain dryness.~~

Valentin had leaned forward again with his elbows on his knees, and ~~he~~ was scratching the pavement with his stick. At last, ~~he said,~~ looking up, "Do you really think I ought to do something?" he asked.

Newman laid his hand on his companion's arm and looked at him a moment through sagaciously-narrowed eyelids. "Try it and see. ~~You are not good enough for it, but we will stretch a point.~~"

inconscience

quite put me out.

fine brain if you'd only give it a chance."

brains

falls from such a height there are no degrees!"

his most exemplary mild distinctness.

You make it feel finer than ever. Would the 'chance' be that

I'm not sure you're not too bright to live; but why not find out how bright a man can afford to be?"

Once when I was a small boy I found a silver piece under a doormat I also

"Do you really think I can make some money? I should like to see how it feels to ~~have a lot~~."

"~~Do~~ what I tell you, and you ~~shall~~ ~~[blacked out]~~," said Newman. "Think of it." And he looked at his watch and prepared to resume his way to Madame de Bellegarde's box.

"Upon my ~~word~~ I will think of it," ~~said~~ Valentin. "I ~~will~~ go and listen to Mozart another half-hour—I can always think better to music—and profoundly meditate upon it."

The Marquis was with his wife when Newman entered their box; he was ~~bland, remote and correct as usual, or, as it seemed to Newman, [blacked out]~~. "~~[blacked out]~~ do you think of the opera?" ~~asked~~ our hero. "What do you think of the Don?"

"~~[blacked out]~~ all know what Mozart is; ~~[blacked out]~~ "our impressions don't date from this evening. Mozart is youth, freshness, brilliancy, facility—~~[blacked out] facility, perhaps~~. But the execution is here and there deplorably rough."

"I ~~am~~ very curious to see how it ends," ~~said~~ Newman.

"You speak as if it were a *feuilleton* in the *Figaro*," observed the Marquis. "You ~~have~~ surely seen the opera before?"

"Never. ~~[blacked out]~~ sure I should have remembered it. Donna Elvira reminds me of Madame de Cintré; I don't mean in her ~~circumstances~~, but in ~~the music she sings~~."

"It ~~is~~ a very nice distinction," ~~laughed~~ the Marquis ~~lightly~~. "There ~~is~~ no great possibility, I imagine, of ~~Madame de Cintré~~ being forsaken."

"~~Not much!~~" ~~said Newman~~. "But what becomes of the Don?"

"The devil comes down—or comes ~~[blacked out] de Bellegarde~~ and carries him off." I suppose Zerlina reminds you of me."

"I ~~will~~ go to the *foyer* for a few moments," ~~said the~~

awfully

find a gold one."

"Well, do

salvation,"

honour

"What

well."

cool old

returned.

"He doesn't remain so very cool; the Marquis amusedly replied. "But we

situation, neatly conceded.

up

said

Madame Urbain replied

as remotely bland as usual, but the great demonstration in which he had lately played his part appeared now to have been a drawbridge lowered and lifted again. Newman was once more outside the castle and its master was perched on the battlements.

facility perhaps a little too unbroken.

now the less artlessly demanded.

her coolly tone.

"That's right, sir," Newman said.

my sister's

less critically continued.

her husband,

Marquis, "and give you a chance to say that the Commander—the man of stone—resembles me." And he passed out of the box.

The little Marquise stared an instant at the velvet ledge of the balcony, and then murmured: "Not a man of stone, a man of wood." Newman had taken her husband's empty chair. She made no protest, and then she turned suddenly and laid her closed fan upon his arm. "I'm very glad you came in," she said. "I want to ask you a favour. I wanted to do so on Thursday, at my mother-in-law's ball, but you would give me no chance. You were in such very good spirits that I thought you might grant my little favour then; not that you look particularly doleful now. It's something you must promise me; now's the time to take you; after you're married you will be good for nothing. Come, promise!"

"I never sign a paper without reading it first," said Newman. "Show me your document."

"No, you must sign with your eyes shut; I'll hold your hand. Come, before you put your head into the noose. You ought to be thankful for me giving you a chance to do something amusing."

"If it's so amusing," said Newman, "it will be in even better season after I'm married."

"In other words," cried Madame de Bellegarde, "you will not do it at all. You will be afraid of your wife."

"Oh, if the thing is intrinsically improper," said Newman, "I won't go into it. If it is not, I will do it after my marriage."

"You talk like a treatise on logic, and English logic into the bargain," exclaimed Madame de Bellegarde. "Promise, then, after you're married. After all, I shall enjoy keeping you to it."

"Well, then, after I'm married," said Newman, serenely.

The little Marquise hesitated a moment, looking at

but

prayer

Allons,

Voyons,

she cried,

for then

the thing violates the moral law—pardon my strong language!—

She

she went on.

"Oh you people with your moral law—I wonder that with such big words in your mouth you don't all die of choking!" Madame Urbain declared.

Doesn't I shall be quite as ready for it

him, and he wondered what was coming. "I suppose you know what my life is," she presently said. "I have no pleasure, I see nothing, I do nothing. I live in Paris as I might live at Poitiers. My mother-in-law calls me—what is the pretty word?—a gad-about? accuses me of going to unheard-of places and thinks it ought to be joy enough for me to sit at home and count over my ancestors on my fingers. But why should I bother about my ancestors? I am sure they never bothered about me. I don't propose to live with a green shade on my eyes; I hold that things were made to look at. My husband, you know, has principles, and the first on the list is that the Tuileries are dreadfully vulgar. If the Tuileries are vulgar his principles are tiresome. If I chose I might have principles quite as well as he. If they grew on one's family tree I should only have to give mine a shake to bring down a shower of the finest. At any rate, I prefer clever Bonapartes to stupid Bourbons."

"Oh, I see; you want to go to court," said Newman, vaguely conjecturing that she might wish him to appeal to the United States Legation to smooth her way to the imperial halls.

The Marquise gave a little sharp laugh. "You are a thousand miles away. I will take care of the Tuileries myself; the day I decide to go they will be very glad to have me. Sooner or later I shall dance in an imperial quadrille. I know what you are going to say: 'How will you dare?' But I *shall* dare. I am afraid of my husband; he is soft, smooth, irreproachable, everything that you know; but I am afraid of him—horribly afraid of him. And yet I shall arrive at the Tuileries. But that will not be this winter, nor perhaps next, and meantime I must live. For the moment, I want to go somewhere else; it's my dream. I want to go to the Bal Bullier."

"To the Bal Bullier?" repeated Newman, for whom the words at first meant nothing.

bother

the best you can do with things arranged in a row before you is to look at them.

fantastically wondering if she mightn't

through some ingenious use of the American Legation.

"The ball in the Latin Quarter, where the students dance with their mistresses. Don't tell me you've not heard of it."

"Oh yes," said Newman; "I've heard of it; I remember now. I've even been there. And you want to go there?"

"It's silly, it's low, it is anything you please. But I want to go. Some of my friends have been, and they say it is awfully *drôle*. My friends go everywhere; it's only I who sit moping at home."

"It seems to me you're not at home now," said Newman, "and I shouldn't exactly say you were moping."

"I'm bored to death. I've been to the opera twice a week for the last eight years. Whenever I ask for anything my mouth is stopped with that: Pray, Madame, haven't you an opera-box? Could a woman of taste want more? In the first place, my opera-box was down in my *contrat;* they have to give it to me. To-night, for instance, I should have preferred a thousand times to go to the Palais Royal. But my husband won't go to the Palais Royal because the ladies of the court go there so much. You may imagine, then, whether he would take me to Bullier's; he says it is a mere imitation—and a bad one—of what they do at the Princess Kleinfuss's. But as I don't go to the Princess Kleinfuss's, the next best thing is to go to Bullier's. It's my dream, at any rate; it's a fixed idea. All I ask of you is to give me your arm; you are less compromising than any one else. I don't know why, but you are. I can arrange it. I shall risk something, but that's my own affair. Besides, fortune favours the bold. Don't refuse me; it is my dream!"

Newman gave a loud laugh. It seemed to him hardly worth while to be the wife of the Marquis de Bellegarde, a daughter of the crusaders, heiress of six centuries of glories and traditions, to have centred one's aspirations upon the sight of a couple of hundred young ladies kick-

in

your loge aux Italiens?

loge

in the imperial intimité.

traditions, only

I'm not yet for a little in the imperial intimité—which must be charming. Why shouldn't I look in where you can get the nearest notion of it?

ing off young men's hats. It struck him as a theme for the moralist, but he had no time to moralise upon it. The curtain rose again; M. de Bellegarde returned, and Newman went back to his seat.

He observed that Valentin de Bellegarde had taken his place in the *baignoire* of Mademoiselle Nioche, behind this young lady and her companion, where he was visible only if one carefully looked for him. In the next act Newman met him in the lobby and asked him if he had reflected upon possible emigration. "If you really meant to meditate," he said, "you might have chosen a better place for it."

"Oh, the place was not bad," said Valentin. "I was not thinking of that girl. I listened to the music and, without thinking of the play or looking at the stage, I turned over your proposal. At first it seemed quite fantastic. And then a certain fiddle in the orchestra—I could distinguish it—began to say as it scraped away: 'Why not, why not?' And then, in that rapid movement, all the fiddles took it up, and the conductor's stick seemed to beat it in the air: 'Why not, why not?' I'm sure I can't say! I don't see why not. I don't see why I shouldn't do something. It appears to me really a very bright idea. This sort of thing is certainly very stale. And then I could come back with a trunk full of dollars. Besides, I might possibly find it amusing. They call me a *raffiné;* who knows but that I might discover an unsuspected charm in shopkeeping? It would really have a certain romantic, picturesque side; it would look well in my biography. It would look as if I were a strong man, a first-rate man, a man who dominated circumstances."

"Never mind how it would look," said Newman. "It always looks well to have half a million of dollars. There's no reason why you shouldn't have them if you will mind what I tell you—I alone—and not talk to other parties." He passed his arm into that of his

the hats of five hundred young men ⊙

he

replied ⊙

handsome

an extravagant

rare and

not, why not?

not, why not?

an homme de premier ordre,

fool round with

"I guess you had better not

companion, and the two walked for some time up and down one of the less frequented corridors. Newman's imagination began to glow with the idea of converting his bright, impracticable friend into a first-class man of business. He felt for the moment a sort of spiritual zeal, the zeal of the propagandist. Its ardour was in part the result of that general discomfort which the sight of all uninvested capital produced in him; so fine an intelligence as Bellegarde's ought to be dedicated to high uses. The highest uses known to Newman's experience were certain transcendent sagacities in the handling of railway stock. And then his zeal was quickened by his personal kindness for Valentin; he had a sort of pity for him which he was well aware he never could have made the Comte de Bellegarde understand. He never lost a sense of its being pitiable that Valentin should think it a large life to revolve in varnished boots between the Rue d'Anjou and the Rue de l'Université, taking the Boulevard des Italiens on the way, when over there in America one's promenade was a continent, and one's boulevard stretched from New York to San Francisco. It mortified him, moreover, to think that Valentin lacked money; there was a painful grotesqueness in it. It affected him as the ignorance of a companion, otherwise without reproach, touching some rudimentary branch of learning would have done. There were things that one knew about as a matter of course, he would have said in such a case. Just so, if one pretended to be easy in the world, one had money as a matter of course; one had made it! There was something almost ridiculously anomalous to Newman in the sight of lively pretensions unaccompanied by large investments in railroads; though I may add that he would not have maintained that such investments were in themselves a proper ground for pretensions. "I will make you do something," he said to Valentin; "I will put you through. I know half a dozen things in which we can make a place for you.

- friend
- this irresistible idler
- charming
- fine
- finest
- operations in ferocious markets.
- he entertained a form of pity
- so bright a figure
- have to understand
- one great world-sea to another.
- advantages
- see
- "I'll put you into
- at any rate;
- a considerable control of Western railroads;
- wanted for
- wasn't business, exactly, as he would have said; it was unpractical, unsuitable, unsightly — very much as if he hadn't known how to spell as to ride.

You will see some lively work. It will take you a little while to get used to the life, but you will work in before long, and at the end of six months—after you have done a thing or two on your own account—you will like it. And then it will be very pleasant for you, having your sister over there. It will be pleasant for her to have you, too. Yes, Valentin," continued Newman, pressing his friend's arm genially, "I think I see just the opening for you. Keep quiet, and I'll push you right in."

Newman pursued this favouring strain for some time longer. The two men strolled about for a quarter of an hour. Valentin listened and questioned, many of his questions making Newman laugh loud at [illegible] his ignorance of the vulgar processes of money-getting; smiling himself, too, half ironical and half curious. And yet he was fascinated by Newman's plain prose version of the legend of El Dorado. It is true, however, that though to accept an "opening" in an American mercantile house might be a bold, original, and in its consequences extremely agreeable thing to do, he did not quite see himself objectively doing it. So that when the bell rang to indicate the close of the entr'acte, there was a certain mock-heroism in his saying, with his [illegible]: "Well, then, put me through; push me [illegible] I make myself over to you. Dip me into the pot and turn me into gold."

They had passed into the corridor which encircled the row of *baignoires*, and Valentin stopped in front of the dusky little box in which Mademoiselle Nioche had bestowed herself, laying his hand on the door-knob. "Oh, come, are you going back there?" asked Newman.

"*Mon Dieu, oui*," said Valentin.

"Haven't you another place?"

"Yes, I have my usual place, in the stalls."

"You had better go and occupy it [illegible]."

"I see her very well from there, too," added Valentin, serenely; "and to-night she is worth seeing. But," he added, in a moment, "I have a particular reason for going back just now."

"Oh, I give you up," said Newman. "You're sunk in depravity and don't know the right when you see it!"

"No, it is only this. There is a young man in the box whom I shall worry by going in, and I want to worry him."

"Can't you leave the poor creature alone?"

"No, he has given me cause. The box is not his; Noémie came in alone and installed herself. I went and spoke to her, and in a few moments she asked me to go and get her fan from the pocket of her cloak, which the *ouvreuse* had carried off. In my absence this gentleman came in and took the chair beside Noémie in which I had been sitting. My reappearance disgusted him, and he had the grossness to show it. He came within an ace of being impertinent. I don't know who he is — a big red-faced animal! I can't think where she picks up such acquaintances. He has been drinking, too, but he knows what he is about. Just now, in the second act, the brute showed an intention. I shall put in another appearance for ten minutes—time enough to give him an opportunity to commit himself, if he feels inclined. I really can't let him suppose he is keeping me out of the box."

"My poor dear boy," said Newman, remonstrantly, "why shouldn't he have his good time? You are not going to pick a quarrel about such a girl as that, I hope."

"The nature of the girl has nothing to do with it, and I have no intention of picking a quarrel. I am not a bully nor a fire-eater. I simply wish to make a point that a gentleman must."

"Oh, damn your point!" Newman impatiently returned. "That is the trouble with you Frenchmen; you must be always making points. Well," he added, "be lively, or I shall pack you off to a decenter country first!"

"Why, you cold-blooded calculating wretch!" Newman cried.

"Very good," Valentin answered, "whenever you please. But if I go to America, I must not let this gentleman suppose that it is to run away from him."

And they separated. At the end of the act Newman observed that Valentin was still in the *baignoire*. He strolled into the corridor again, expecting to meet him, and when he was within a few yards of Mademoiselle Nioche's box, saw his friend pass out, accompanied by the young man who had been seated beside its fair occupant. The two gentlemen walked with some quickness of step to a distant part of the lobby, where Newman perceived them stop and stand talking. The manner of each was perfectly quiet, but the stranger, who looked flushed, had begun to wipe his face very emphatically with his pocket-handkerchief. By this time Newman was abreast of the *baignoire*; the door had been left ajar, and he could see a pink dress inside. He immediately went in. Mademoiselle Nioche turned and greeted him with a brilliant smile.

"Ah, you have at last decided to come and see me," she exclaimed. "You just save your politeness. You find me in a fine moment. Sit down." There was a very becoming little flush in her cheek, and her eye had a noticeable spark. You would have said that she had received some very good news.

"Something has happened here!" said Newman, without sitting down.

"You find me in a very fine moment," she repeated. "Two gentlemen—one of them is M. de Bellegarde, the pleasure of whose acquaintance I owe to you—have just had words about your humble servant. Very big words too. They can't come off without crossing swords. A duel—that will give me a push!" cried Mademoiselle Noémie, clapping her little hands. "*C'est ça qui pose une femme!*"

"You don't mean to say that Bellegarde is going to fight about *you!*" exclaimed Newman, disgustedly.

the fellow

interesting occupant

was

Strikingly

Noémie

've

me you but

said

while he kept his feet

meeting and a big noise

said Noémie, clapping with a soft thud her little pearl-coloured hands

cried.

it's going further!

She looked, it had to be owned, exceedingly pretty and perverse and animated and elegant and quite as if she had had some very good news.

"Nothing less!" and she looked at him with a hard little smile. "No, no, you are not *galant!* And if you prevent this affair I shall owe you a grudge—and pay my debt!"

Newman uttered an imprecation which, though brief it consisted simply of the interjection "Oh!" followed by a geographical, or more correctly, perhaps, a theological noun in four letters—had better not be transferred to these pages. He turned his back without more ceremony upon the pink dress, and went out of the box. In the corridor he found Valentin and his companion walking towards him. The latter was thrusting a card into his waistcoat pocket. Mademoiselle Noémie's jealous votary was a tall robust young man with a thick nose, a prominent blue eye, a Germanic physiognomy and a massive watch-chain. When they reached the box, Valentin with an emphasised bow made way for him to pass in first. Newman touched Valentin's arm as a sign that he wished to speak with him, and Bellegarde answered that he would be with him in an instant. Valentin entered the box after the robust young man, but a couple of minutes afterwards he reappeared, hardly smiling.

"She is immensely tickled," he said. "She says we will make her fortune. I don't want to be fatuous, but I think it is very possible."

"So you are going to fight?" said Newman.

"My dear fellow, don't look so mortally disgusted. It was not my own choice. The thing is all arranged."

"I told you so!" groaned Newman.

"I told *him* so," said Valentin, smiling.

"What did he do to you?"

"My good friend, it doesn't matter what. He used an expression—I took it up."

"But I insist upon knowing; I can't, as your elder brother, have you rushing into this sort of nonsense."

"I am very much obliged to you," said Valentin.

"I have nothing to conceal, but I can't go into particulars now and here."

"We will leave this place, then. You can tell me outside."

"Oh no, I can't leave this place; why should I hurry away? I will go to my orchestra-stall and sit out the opera."

"You will not enjoy it; you will be preoccupied."

Valentin looked at him a moment, coloured a little, smiled, and patted him on the arm. "[illegible] fully simple! Before an affair a man is quiet. The quietest thing I can do is to go straight to my place."

"Ah," said Newman, "you want her to see you there—you and your quietness. [illegible] simple! It is a poor business."

Valentin remained, and the two men, in their respective places, sat out the rest of the performance, which was also enjoyed by Mademoiselle Nioche and her truculent admirer. At the end Newman joined Valentin again, and they went into the street together. Valentin shook his head at his friend's proposal that he should get into Newman's own vehicle, and stopped on the edge of the pavement. "I must go off alone; [illegible] I must look up a couple of friends who will take charge of this matter."

"I will take charge of it," Newman declared. "Put it into my hands."

"You are very kind, but that is hardly possible. In the first place, you are, as you said just now, almost my brother; you are about to marry my sister. That alone disqualifies you; it casts doubts on your impartiality. And if it didn't it would be enough for me that I strongly suspect you of disapproving of the affair. You would try to prevent a meeting."

"Of course I should," said Newman. "Whoever your friends are, [illegible] they will do that."

"Unquestionably they will. They will urge that ex-

his

his friend

"You'd have been an ornament to the Golden Age."

be so good as to act for me."

"I'll be so good as to act for you,"

I'm not so undeveloped. It's the damnedest foolery."

The case

then they'll do it."

they'll be ruffians if they don't

'd only try to prevent a meeting."

The young man

You haven't, as I say, God forgive you, the delineation of certain shades.

cuses be made, proper excuses. But you would be too good natured. You won't do."

Newman was silent a moment. He was keenly annoyed, but he saw it was useless to attempt interference. "When is this precious performance to come off?" he asked.

"The sooner the better, [illegible] The day after to-morrow, I hope."

"Well," said Newman, "I have certainly a claim to know the facts. I can't consent to shut my eyes to the matter."

"I shall be most happy to tell you [illegible] They are very simple, and it will be quickly done. But now everything depends on my putting my hand on my friends without delay. I will jump into a cab; you had better drive to my room and wait for me there. I will turn up at the end of an hour."

Newman assented protestingly, let his friend go, and then betook himself to the picturesque little apartment in the Rue d'Anjou. It was more than an hour before Valentin returned, but when he did so he was able to announce that he had found one of his desired friends, and that this gentleman had taken upon himself the care of securing an associate. Newman had been sitting without lights by Valentin's faded fire, upon which he had thrown a log; the blaze played over the richly-encumbered little sitting-room and produced fantastic gleams and shadows. He listened in silence to Valentin's account of what had passed between him and the gentleman whose card he had in his pocket—M. Stanislas Kapp, of Strasbourg—after his return to Mademoiselle Nioche's box. This hospitable young lady had espied an acquaintance on the other side of the house, and had expressed her displeasure at his not having the civility to come and pay her a visit. "Oh, let him alone!" M. Stanislas Kapp had hereupon exclaimed. "There are too many people in the box already." And he had fixed

in presence, it seemed to him of a vain and grotesque parade, restricted, indirect & poor is a salve to an insult & a righting of a wrong; and yet pretentious & pompous as an accommodation. Yet

the most

You'd be much too coulant.

went on

could only ask

them all then.

a single one of them.

him

the

encumbered

accessories

the other

acute young woman

rich multifarious properties of the place and

the society of their common hostess.

66 THE AMERICAN. XVII.

his eyes with a demonstrative stare upon M. de Bellegarde. Valentin had promptly retorted that if there were too many people in the box it was easy for M. Kapp to diminish the number. "I shall be most happy to open the door for *you!*" M. Kapp exclaimed. "I shall be delighted to fling you into the pit!" Valentin had answered. "Oh, do make a rumpus and get into the papers!" Miss Noémie had gleefully ejaculated. "M. Kapp, turn him out; or, M. de Bellegarde, pitch him into the pit, into the orchestra—anywhere! I don't care who does which, so long as you make a scene." Valentin answered that they would make no scene, but that the gentleman would be so good as to step into the corridor with him. In the corridor, after a brief further exchange of words, there had been an exchange of cards. M. Stanislas Kapp was very stiff. He evidently meant to force his offence home.

"The man, no doubt, was insolent," Newman said; "but if you hadn't gone back into the box the thing wouldn't have happened."

"Why, don't you see," Valentin replied, "that the event proves the extreme propriety of my going back into the box? M. Kapp wished to provoke me; he was awaiting his chance. In such a case—that is, when he has been, so to speak, notified—a man must be on hand to receive the provocation. My not returning would simply have been tantamount to my saying to M. Stanislas Kapp: 'Oh, if you are going to be disagreeable'—!"

"'You must manage it by yourself; damned if I'll help you!' That would have been a thoroughly sensible thing to say. The only attraction for you seems to have been the prospect of M. Kapp's impertinence," Newman went on. "You told me that you were not going back for that girl."

"Oh, don't mention that girl any more," murmured Valentin. "She's a bore."

"With all my heart. But if that is the way you feel about her, why couldn't you let her alone?"

Valentin shook his head with a fine smile. "I don't think you quite understand, and I don't believe I can make you. She understood the situation; she knew what was in the air; she was watching us."

"A cat may look at a king! What difference does that make?"

"Why, a man can't back down before a woman."

"I don't call her a woman. You said yourself she was a stone," cried Newman.

"Well," Valentin rejoined, "there is no disputing about tastes. It's a matter of feeling; it's measured by one's sense of honour."

"Oh, confound your sense of honour!" cried Newman.

"It is vain talking," said Valentin; "words have passed, and the thing is settled."

Newman turned away, taking his hat. Then pausing, with his hand on the door, "What are you going to use?" he asked.

"That is for M. Stanislas Kapp, as the challenged party, to decide. My own choice would be a short, light sword. I handle it well. I am an indifferent shot."

Newman had put on his hat; he pushed it back, gently scratching his forehead high up. "I wish it were pistols," he said. "I could show you how to lodge a bullet!"

Valentin broke into a laugh. "What is it some English poet says about consistency? It's a flower, or a star, or a jewel. Yours has the beauty of all three!" But he agreed to see Newman again on the morrow, after the details of his meeting with M. Stanislas Kapp should have been arranged.

In the course of the day Newman received three lines from him, saying that it had been decided that he should cross the frontier, with his adversary, and that he was to take the night express to Geneva. He should have time, however, to dine with Newman. In the afternoon New-

"I'm doing it for myself, and you must let me judge of what concerns my honour." "Well, I'll let you judge if you'll let me quite impartially kick somebody!"

"Then you are doing it for her," Newman wailed.

as if with interest

Replied to this words

"You're going to use knives?"

guns,"

hold on

"Murderer!" he cried with some intensity, but

him

the

together

him to the effect

They

accordingly

gave him a hard look and then

---

man called on Madame de Cintré for the single daily hour of reinvoked and reasserted confidence — a solemnity but the more exquisite with repetition — to which she had, a little strangely, given him to understand it was convenient, important, in fact vital to her, that their communion should, for their strained interval, be restricted, even though this reduced him for so many other recurrent hours, the hours of evening in particular, the worst of the probation, to the state of a restless prowling, time-keeping ghost, a taker of long night-walks through streets that affected him at moments as the alleys of a great darkened bankrupt bazaar. But his visit to-day had a worry to reckon with — all the more that it had as well so much of one to conceal. She shone upon him, as always, with that light of her gentleness which might have been figured, in the heat-thickened air, by a sultry harvest moon; but she was visibly bedimmed, and she confessed, on his charging her with her red eyes, that she had been, for a vague vain reason, crying them half out. Valentin had been with her a couple of hours before and had somehow troubled her without in the least intending it. He had laughed and gossiped, had brought her no bad news, had only been, in taking leave, of her, rather "dearer," poor boy, than usual. A certain extravagance of tenderness in him had in fact touched her to positive pain, so that on his departure she had burst into miserable tears. She had felt as if something strange and wrong were hanging about them — ah, she had had that feeling in other connections too; nervous, always nervous, she had tried to reason away the fear, but the effort had only given her a headache. Newman was of course tongue-tied on what he himself knew, and, his power of simulation and his general art of optimism breaking down on this occasion as if some needle-point had suddenly passed, to make him wince, through the sole crevice of his armour, he could, to his high chagrin, but cut his call short. Before he retreated, however, he asked if Valentin had seen his mother.

"Yes; but he didn't make her cry."

It was in Newman's own apartments that the young man dined, having sent his servant and his effects to await him at the railway. M. Stanislas Kapp had positively declined to make excuses, and he on his side had obviously none to offer. Valentin had found out with whom he was dealing, and that his adversary was the son and heir of a rich brewer of Strasbourg, a youth sanguineous, brawny, bull-headed, and lately much occupied in making ducks and drakes of the paternal brewery. Though passing in a general way for a good companion he had already been noted as apt to quarrel after dinner and to be disposed then to charge with his head down. "Que voulez-vous?" said Valentin: "brought up on beer how could he stand such champagne as Noemie, cup-bearer to the infernal gods, had poured out for him?" He had chosen the weapon known to Newman as the gun. Valentin had an excellent appetite: he made a point, in view of his long journey, of eating more than usual: one of the points, no doubt, that his friend had accused him of always needing to make. He took the liberty of suggesting to the latter ~~a slight modification~~ the difference of the suspicion of a shade in the ~~mixture~~ composition of a fish-sauce; he thought it worth hunting with precautions to the cook. But Newman had no mind for sauces; there was more in the dish itself, the mixture now presented to him, than he could swallow; he was in short "nervous" to a tune of which he felt almost ashamed as he watched his inimitable friend go through their superior meal without skipping a step or missing a savour, the exposure, the possible sacrifice, of so charming a life on the altar of a stupid tradition struck him as an intolerable wrong. He exaggerated the perversity of Noémie, the ferocity of M. Kapp, the grimness of M. Kapp's friends, and only knew that he did yearn now as a brother.

"This sort of thing may be all very well," he broke out at last, "but I'll be blowed if I see it. I can't stop you perhaps, but at least I can swear at you handsomely. Take me as doing so in the most awful terms."

"My dear fellow, don't make a scene," — Valentin was almost sententious. "Scenes in these cases are in very bad taste."

"Your duel itself is a scene," Newman said; "a scene of the most flagrant description. It's a wretched theatrical affair. Why don't you take a band of music with you outright? It's G—— d—— barbarous, and yet it's G—— d—— effete."

"Oh, I can't begin at this time of day to defend the theory of duelling," the young man blandly reasoned. "It's our only resource at given moments, and I hold it a good thing. Quite apart from the merit of the cause in which a meeting may take place, it strikes a romantic note that seems to me in this age of vile prose greatly to recommend it. It's a remnant of a higher-tempered time; one ought to cling to it. It's a way of more decently testifying. Testify when you can!"

"I don't know what you mean by a higher-tempered time," Newman retorted. "Because your great-grandfather liked to prance, is that any reason for you, who have got beyond it? For my part I think we had better let our temper take care of itself; it generally seems to me quite high enough; I'm not more of a fire-eater than most, but I'm not afraid of being too mild. If your great grand-father were to make himself unpleasant to me I think I could tackle him yet."

"My dear friend" — Valentin was perfectly patient with him — "you can't invent anything that will take the place of satisfaction for an insult. To demand it and to give it are equally excellent arrangements."

"Do you call this sort of thing satisfaction?" Newman roared. "Does it satisfy you to put yourself at the disposal of a bigger fool even than yourself? I'd see him somewhere first! Does it satisfy you that he should set up this ridiculous relation with you? I'd like to see him try anything of the sort with me! If a man has a bad intention on you it's his own affair till it takes effect; but when it does, give him one in the eye. If you don't know how to do that — straight — you're not fit to go round alone. But I'm talking of those who claim they are, and that they don't require some one to take care of them."

"Well," Valentin smiled, "it would be interesting truly to go round with _you._ But to get the full good of that, alas, I should have begun earlier!"

Newman could scarcely bear even the possible pertinence of his "alas." "See here," he said at the last: "if any one ever hurts you again — !"

"Well, mon ~~bo...~~ bon ?" — and Valentin, with his eyes on his friend's, might now have been much moved.

"Come straight to me about it. _I'll_ go for him."

"_Matamore!_" the young man laughed as they parted.

CHAPTER XVIII.

Newman went the next morning to see Madame de Cintré, timing his visit so as to arrive after the noonday breakfast. In the court of the *hôtel*, before the portico, stood Madame de Bellegarde's old square carriage. The servant who opened the door answered Newman's inquiry with a slightly embarrassed and hesitating murmur, and at the same moment Mrs. Bread appeared in the background, dim-visaged as usual, and wearing a large black bonnet and shawl.

"What is the matter?" asked Newman. "Is Madame la Comtesse at home, or not?"

Mrs. Bread advanced, fixing her eyes upon him; he observed that she held a sealed letter, very delicately, in her fingers. "The Countess has left a message for you, sir; she has left this," said Mrs. Bread, holding out the letter, which Newman took.

"Left it? Is she out? Is she gone away?"

"She is going away, sir; she is leaving town," said Mrs. Bread.

"Leaving town!" exclaimed Newman. "What has happened?"

"It is not for me to say, sir," said Mrs. Bread, with her eyes on the ground. "But I thought it would come."

"What would come, pray?" Newman demanded. He had broken the seal of the letter, but he still questioned. "She is in the house? She is visible?"

"I don't think she expected you this morning," the old waiting-woman replied. "She was to leave immediately."

"Where is she going?"

"To Fleurières."

"To Fleurières? But surely I can see her?"

That, by exception, Newman went to see

his

It was

he asked.

And the good woman held

missive, which he

he

And

in the world

cast

to

his venerable friend

Away off there?

Mrs. Bread hesitated, a moment, and then clasping together her two hands, "I will take you!" she said. And she led the way upstairs. At the top of the staircase she paused and fixed her dry, sad eyes upon Newman. "Be very easy with her, [illegible]" Then she went on to Madame de Cintré's apartment; Newman, perplexed and alarmed, followed her [illegible] threw open the door, and Newman pushed back the curtain at the farther side of its deep embrasure. In the middle of the room stood Madame de Cintré; her face was pale, and she was dressed for travelling. Behind her, before the fireplace, stood Urbain de Bellegarde, looking at his finger-nails; near the Marquis sat his mother, buried in an armchair, and with her eyes immediately fixing themselves upon Newman. He felt, as soon as he entered, the room, that he was in the presence of something evil; he was startled and pained, as he would have been by a threatening cry in the stillness of the night. He walked straight to Madame de Cintré and seized her by the hand.

"What is the matter?" he asked, commandingly; "what is happening?"

Urbain de Bellegarde stared, then left his place and came and leaned upon his mother's chair, behind. Newman's sudden irruption had evidently discomposed both mother and son. Madame de Cintré stood silent, with her eyes resting upon Newman's. She had often looked at him with all her soul, as it seemed to him; but in this present gaze there was a sort of bottomless depth. She was in distress; it was the most touching thing he had ever seen. His heart rose into his throat, and he was on the point of turning to her companions with an angry challenge; but she checked him, pressing the hand that held her own.

"Something very grave has happened," she said. "I cannot marry you."

but then,

rather desperately

on him

Nobody else is it?

[as to she]

flushed and marked

himself,

on her friends

— monstrously, and was somehow, to her own sense, helpless. It would have been

black= gloard

/however,/

he

and looked

on the invader, as he felt them pronounce him.

them both.

if it hadn't been the most absurd.

brought out.

of which she had possessed herself.

can't

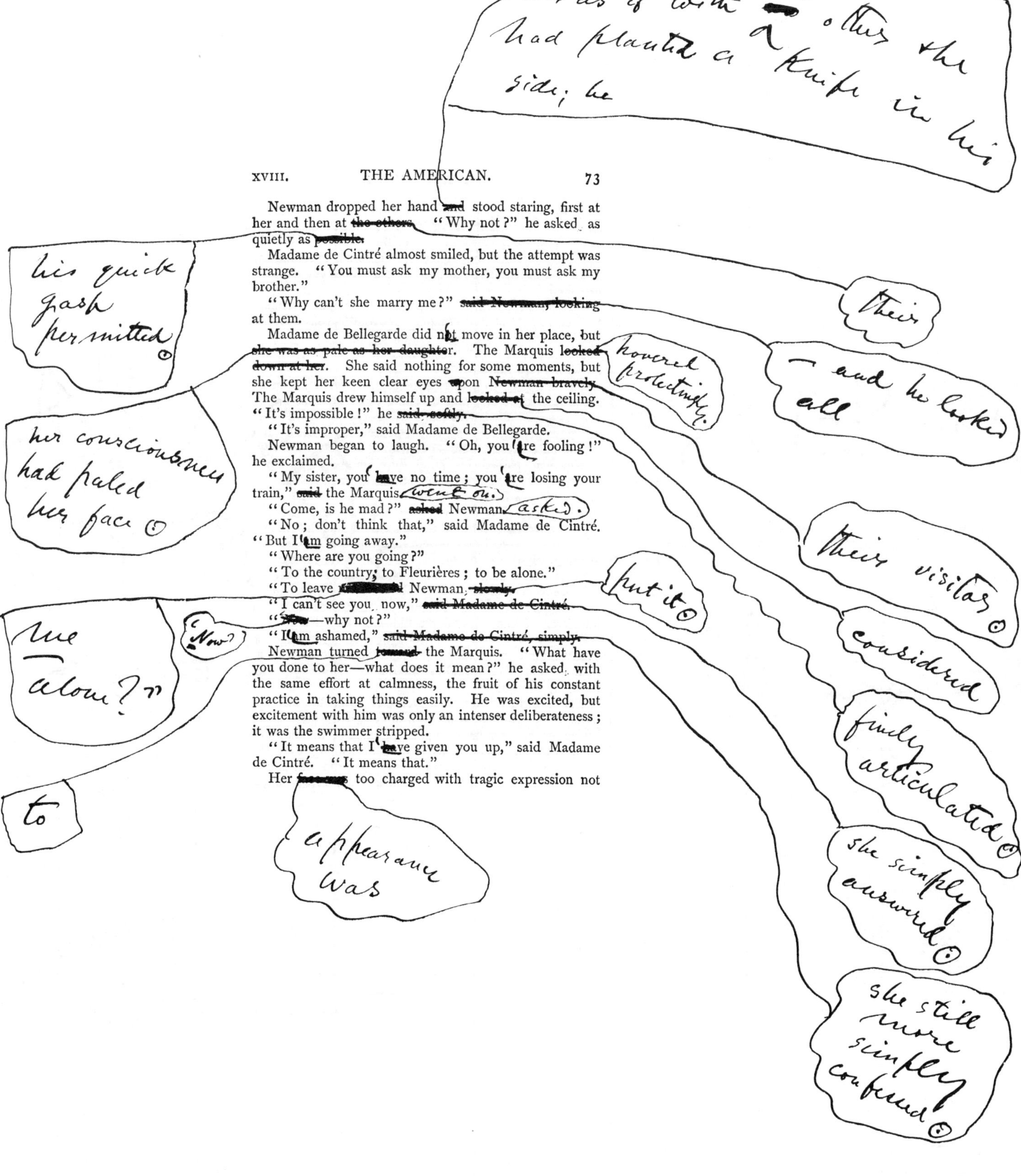

XVIII. THE AMERICAN. 73

Newman dropped her hand and stood staring, first at her and then at the others. "Why not?" he asked, as quietly as possible.

Madame de Cintré almost smiled, but the attempt was strange. "You must ask my mother, you must ask my brother."

"Why can't she marry me?" said Newman, looking at them.

Madame de Bellegarde did not move in her place, but she was as pale as her daughter. The Marquis looked down at her. She said nothing for some moments, but she kept her keen clear eyes upon Newman bravely. The Marquis drew himself up and looked at the ceiling. "It's impossible!" he said, softly.

"It's improper," said Madame de Bellegarde.

Newman began to laugh. "Oh, you are fooling!" he exclaimed.

"My sister, you have no time; you are losing your train," said the Marquis.

"Come, is he mad?" asked Newman.

"No; don't think that," said Madame de Cintré. "But I am going away."

"Where are you going?"

"To the country; to Fleurières; to be alone."

"To leave [illegible] Newman, slowly.

"I can't see you, now," said Madame de Cintré.

"Now—why not?"

"I am ashamed," said Madame de Cintré, simply.

Newman turned toward the Marquis. "What have you done to her—what does it mean?" he asked, with the same effort at calmness, the fruit of his constant practice in taking things easily. He was excited, but excitement with him was only an intenser deliberateness; it was the swimmer stripped.

"It means that I have given you up," said Madame de Cintré. "It means that."

Her face was too charged with tragic expression not

fully to confirm her words. Newman was profoundly shocked, but he felt as yet no resentment against her. He was amazed, bewildered, and the presence of the old Marquise and her son seemed to smite his eyes like the glare of a watchman's lantern. "Can't I see you alone?" he asked.

"It would be only more painful. I hoped I should not see you—I should escape. I wrote to you. Good-bye." And she put out her hand again.

Newman put both his own into his pockets. "I will go with you," he said.

She laid her two hands on his arm. "Will you grant me a last request?" and as she looked at him, urging this, her eyes filled with tears. "Let me go alone—let me go in peace. I can't call it peace—it's death. But let me bury myself. So—good-bye."

Newman passed his hand into his hair and stood slowly rubbing his head and looking through his keenly-narrowed eyes from one to the other of the three persons before him. His lips were compressed, and the two lines which had formed themselves beside his mouth might have made it appear at a first glance that he was smiling. I have said that his excitement was an intenser deliberateness, and now he looked grimly deliberate. "It seems very much as if you had interfered, Marquis," he said, slowly. "I thought you said you wouldn't interfere. I know you don't like me; but that doesn't make any difference. I thought you promised me you wouldn't interfere. I thought you swore on your honour that you wouldn't interfere. Don't you remember, Marquis?"

The Marquis lifted his eyebrows, but he was apparently determined to be even more urbane than usual. He rested his two hands upon the back of his mother's chair and bent forward, as if he were leaning over the edge of a pulpit or a lecture-desk. He did not smile, but he looked softly grave. "Excuse me, sir, [illegible]

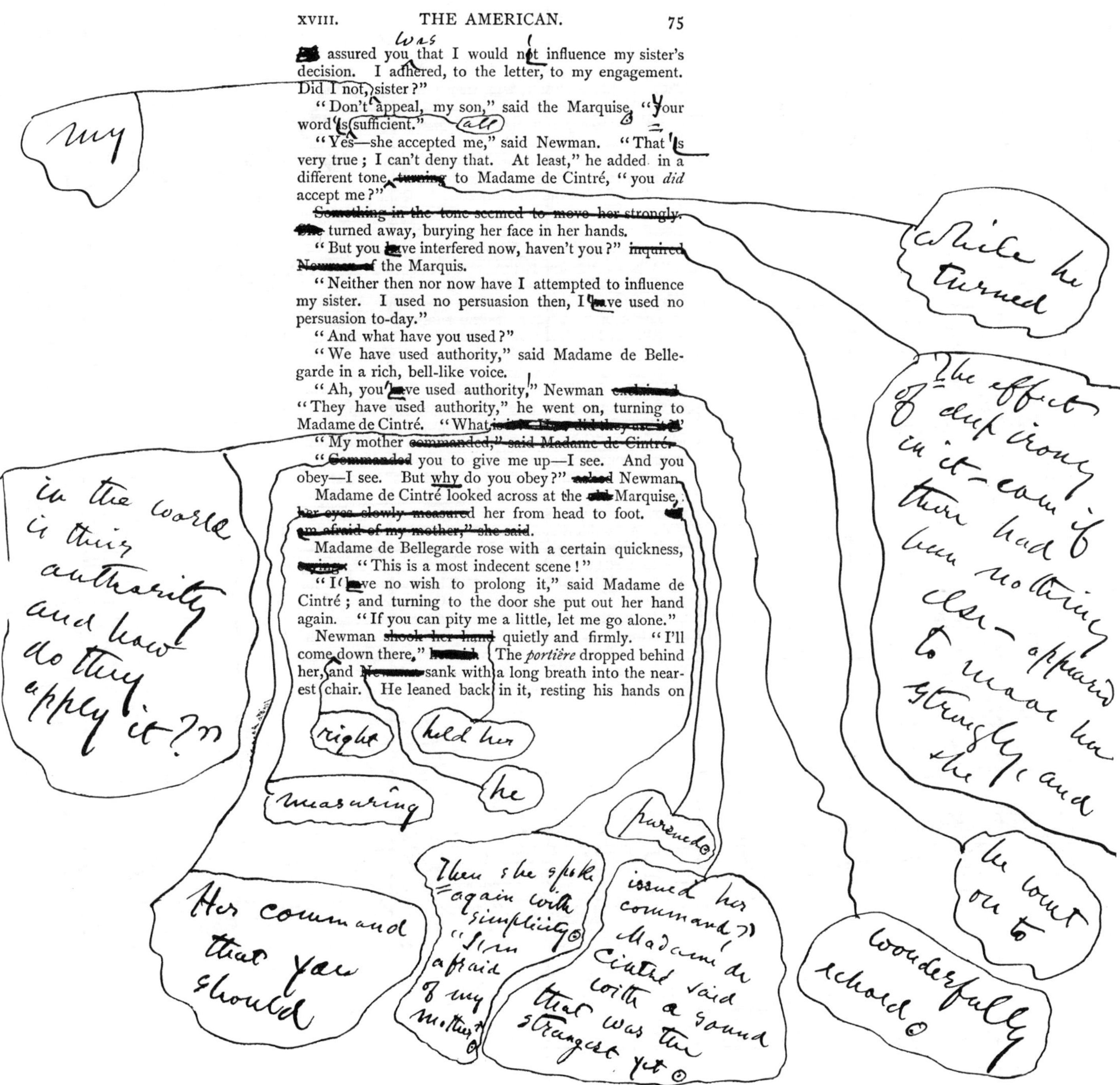

XVIII. THE AMERICAN. 75

"I assured you that I would not influence my sister's decision. I adhered, to the letter, to my engagement. Did I not, sister?"

"Don't appeal, my son," said the Marquise, "your word is sufficient."

"Yes—she accepted me," said Newman. "That is very true; I can't deny that. At least," he added in a different tone, turning to Madame de Cintré, "you *did* accept me?"

Something in the tone seemed to move her strongly. She turned away, burying her face in her hands.

"But you have interfered now, haven't you?" inquired Newman of the Marquis.

"Neither then nor now have I attempted to influence my sister. I used no persuasion then, I have used no persuasion to-day."

"And what have you used?"

"We have used authority," said Madame de Bellegarde in a rich, bell-like voice.

"Ah, you have used authority," Newman exclaimed. "They have used authority," he went on, turning to Madame de Cintré. "What is it? How did they use it?"

"My mother commanded," said Madame de Cintré.

"Commanded you to give me up—I see. And you obey—I see. But why do you obey?" asked Newman.

Madame de Cintré looked across at the old Marquise; her eyes slowly measured her from head to foot. "I am afraid of my mother," she said.

Madame de Bellegarde rose with a certain quickness, crying, "This is a most indecent scene!"

"I have no wish to prolong it," said Madame de Cintré; and turning to the door she put out her hand again. "If you can pity me a little, let me go alone."

Newman shook her hand quietly and firmly. "I'll come down there," he said. The *portière* dropped behind her, and Newman sank with a long breath into the nearest chair. He leaned back in it, resting his hands on the knobs of the arms and looking at Madame de Bellegarde and Urbain. There was a long silence. They stood side by side, with their heads high and their handsome eyebrows arched.

"So you make a distinction?" Newman said at last. "You make a distinction between persuading and commanding? It's very neat. But the distinction is in favour of commanding. That rather spoils it."

"We have not the least objection to defining our position," said M. de Bellegarde. "We understand that it should not at first appear to you quite clear. We rather expect, indeed, that you should not do us justice."

"Oh, I'll do you justice," said Newman. "Don't be afraid. Please proceed."

The Marquise laid her hand on her son's arm, as if to deprecate the attempt to define their position. "It is quite useless," she said, "to try and arrange this matter so as to make it agreeable to you. It can never be agreeable to you. It is a disappointment, and disappointments are unpleasant. I thought it over carefully and tried to arrange it better: but I only gave myself a headache and lost my sleep. Say what we will, you will think yourself ill-treated, and you will publish your wrongs among your friends. But we are not afraid of that. Besides, your friends are not our friends, and it will not matter. Think of us as you please. I only beg you not to be violent. I have never in my life been present at a violent scene of any kind, and at my age I can't be expected to begin."

"Is *that* all you have got to say?" asked Newman, slowly rising out of his chair. "That's a poor show for a clever lady like you, Marquise. Come, try again."

"My mother goes to the point, with her usual honesty and intrepidity," said the Marquis, toying with his watch-guard. "But it is perhaps well to say a little more. We, of course, quite repudiate the charge of having broken faith with you. We left you entirely at liberty to make

commit

commit

he went on

quite

's

altogether

Only give me a chance!

bad

our necessity over — that of letting you know that we don't after all see our way! —

to Marshal reasons or to meet this friend again, on any ground, too intimately.

add another word.

any sort of roughness, and I think my age should now protect me."

by so much the less.

— I grant it — sometimes odious things.

like — You don't really know us."

from

yourself agreeable to my sister. We left her quite at liberty to entertain your proposal. When she accepted you we said nothing. We therefore ~~quite~~ observed our promise. It was only at a later stage of the affair, and on quite a different basis, as it were, that we determined to speak. It would have been better, perhaps, if we had spoken before. But really, you see, nothing has yet been done."

"Nothing has yet been done?" Newman repeated the words, unconscious of their comical effect. He had lost the sense of what the Marquis was saying; M. de Bellegarde's superior style was a mere humming in his ears. All ~~that~~ he understood, in his deep and simple ~~indignation~~, was that the matter was not a violent joke, and that the people before him were perfectly serious. "Do you suppose I can take ~~this [illegible]~~ you suppose it can matter to me what you say? Do you suppose I can seriously listen to you? ~~You are simply crazy!~~"

Madame de Bellegarde gave a rap with her fan in the palm of her hand. "If you don't take it you can leave it, sir. It matters very little what you do. ~~My~~ daughter has given you up."

"She doesn't mean it," Newman declared after a moment.

"I think I can assure you that she does," ~~said~~ the Marquis rectified.

"Poor ~~woman~~, what damnable thing have you done to her?" ~~cried~~ Newman demanded.

"Gently, gently!" murmured M. de Bellegarde.

"She told you," ~~said the old lady. "I commanded her."~~

Newman shook his head heavily. "This sort of thing can't be, you know," he said. "A man can't be used in this fashion. ~~You have got no right; you have got no power.~~"

"My power," ~~said~~ Madame de Bellegarde, "is in my children's obedience."

Wholly

—

as if

wrath

this from you?" he wonderingly asked. "Do

stricken woman, poor bleeding heart,

due

observed.

Do you suppose I'm an idiot that you can so put off?"

You not only have no right that isn't a preposterous pretension, but you haven't a pennyworth of power."

his mother said. "I expressed my final wish."

as he rocked on his neat foundations.

The simple fact is that my

"In their fear your daughter said. There is something very strange in it. Why should your daughter be afraid of you?" added Newman, after looking a moment at the old lady. "There [illegible]" The Marquise met his gaze without flinching and as if she did not hear or heed what he said. "I did my best," she said quietly. "I could endure it no longer."

"It was a bold experiment!" said the Marquis.

Newman felt disposed to walk to him, clutch his neck with his fingers, and press his windpipe with his thumb. "I needn't tell you how you strike me," he said, "of course you know that. But I should think you would be afraid of your friends—all those people you introduced me to the other night. There were some very nice people among them; you may depend upon it there were some honest men and women."

"Our friends approve us," said M. de Bellegarde; "there is not a family among them that would have acted otherwise. And however that may be we take the cue from no one. The Bellegardes have been used to set the example, not to wait for it."

"You would have waited long before any one would have set you such an example as this," exclaimed Newman. "Have I done anything wrong?" he demanded. "Have I given you reason to change your opinion? Have you found out anything against me? I can't imagine."

"Our opinion," said Madame de Bellegarde, "is quite the same as at first—exactly. We have no ill-will towards yourself; we are very far from accusing you of misconduct. Since your relations with us began you have been, I frankly confess, less—less peculiar than I expected. It is not your disposition that we object to, it is your antecedents. We really cannot reconcile ourselves to a commercial person. We fancied in an evil hour that we could; it was a great misfortune. We determined to persevere to the end and to give you every advantage. I was resolved that you should have no reason to accuse me of a want of loyalty. We let the thing certainly go very far—we introduced you to our friends. To tell the truth, it was that, I think, that broke me down. I succumbed to the scene that took place on Thursday night in these rooms. You must excuse me if what I say is disagreeable to you, but we cannot release ourselves without an explanation."

"There can be no better proof of our good faith," said the Marquis, "than our committing ourselves to you in the eyes of the world the other evening. We endeavoured to bind ourselves—to tie our hands, as it were."

"But it was that," added his mother, "that opened our eyes and broke our bonds. We should have been most uncomfortable! You know," she added in a moment, "that you were forewarned. [illegible]"

Newman took up his hat aud began mechanically to smooth it; the very fierceness of his scorn kept him from speaking. "You are not proud enough," he observed at last.

"In all this matter," said the Marquis, smiling, "I really see nothing but our humility."

"Let us have no more discussion than is necessary," resumed Madame de Bellegarde. "My daughter told you everything when she said she gave you up."

"I am not satisfied about your daughter," said Newman; "I want to know what you did to her. It is all very easy talking about authority, and saying you commanded her. She didn't accept me blindly, and she wouldn't have given me up blindly. Not that I believe yet she has really given me up; she will talk it over with me. But you have frightened her, you have bullied her, you have *hurt* her. What was it you did to her?"

"I did very little!" said Madame de Bellegarde, in a tone which gave Newman a chill when he afterwards remembered it.

"Let me remind you that we offered you these explanations," the Marquis observed, "with the express understanding that you should abstain from violence of language."

"I am not violent," Newman answered, "it is you who are violent! But I don't know that I have much more to say to you. What you expect of me, apparently, is to go my way, thanking you for favours received and promising never to trouble you again."

"We expect of you to act like a clever man," said Madame de Bellegarde. "You have shown yourself that already, and what we have done is altogether based upon your being so. When one must submit, one must. Since my daughter absolutely withdraws, what will be the use of your making a noise?"

"It remains to be seen whether your daughter absolutely withdraws. Your daughter and I are still very good friends; nothing is changed in that. As I say, I will talk it over with her."

"That will be of no use," said the old lady. "I know my daughter well enough to know that words spoken as she just now spoke to you are final. Besides, she has promised me."

"I have no doubt her promise is worth a good deal more than your own," said Newman; "nevertheless I don't give her up."

"Just as you please! But if she won't even see you —and she won't—your constancy must remain purely Platonic."

Poor Newman was feigning a greater confidence than he felt. Madame de Cintré's strange intensity had, in fact, struck a chill to his heart; her face, still impressed upon his vision, had been a terribly vivid image of renunciation. He felt sick, and suddenly helpless. He turned away and stood for a moment with his hand on the door; then he faced about, and after the briefest hesitation broke out with a different accent. "Come, think of what this must be to me, and ~~let her alone~~! Why should you object to me so—what's the matter with me? I can't hurt you, I wouldn't if I could. I'm the most unobjectionable ~~fellow~~ in the world. What if I am a commercial person? What under the sun do you mean? A commercial person? I'll be any sort of person you want. I never talk to you about business. Let her go, and I'll ask no questions. I'll take her away, and you shall never see me or hear of me again. I'll stay in America if you like. I'll sign a paper promising never to come back to Europe. All I want is not to lose her!"

~~Madame de Bellegarde and her son~~ exchanged a glance of lucid irony, and Urbain said: "My dear sir, what you propose is hardly an improvement. We have not the slightest objection to seeing you, as an amiable foreigner, and we have every reason for not wishing to be eternally separated from my sister. We object to ~~the~~ marriage; and in that way," and M. de Bellegarde gave a small, thin laugh, "she would be more married than ever."

"Well, then," ~~said~~ Newman, "where is this place of yours—Fleurières? I know it is near some old city on a hill."

"Precisely. Poitiers is on a hill," ~~said Madame de Bellegarde~~. "I don't know how old it is. We are not afraid to tell you."

"It is Poitiers, is it? Very good," said Newman. "I shall immediately follow Madame de Cintré."

"The trains after this hour won't serve you," ~~said~~ Urbain.

"I shall hire a special train."

"That will be a very ~~silly~~ waste of money," said Madame de Bellegarde.

"It will be time enough to talk about waste three days hence," Newman answered; and, clapping his hat on his head, he departed.

leave her to herself and to the man whom, before God I believe, she loves!

man

—where on earth does it come in?

His companion

her

presently broke out again.

then

interesting

appeared to judge it his duty to mention.

the Marquise admitted.

foolish

He did not immediately start for Fleurières; he was too stunned and wounded for consecutive action. He simply walked; he walked straight before him, following the river, till he got out of the *enceinte* of Paris. He had a burning, tingling sense of personal outrage. He had never in his life received so absolute a check; he had never been pulled up, or, as he would have said, "let down," so short, and he found the sensation intolerable; he strode along tapping the trees and lamp-posts fiercely with his stick and inwardly raging. To lose Madame de Cintré after he had taken such jubilant and triumphant possession of her was as great an affront to his pride as it was an injury to his happiness. And to lose her by the interference and the dictation of others, by an impudent old woman and a pretentious fop stepping in with their "authority"! It was too preposterous, it was too pitiful. Upon what he deemed the unblushing treachery of the Bellegardes, Newman wasted little thought; he consigned it, once for all, to eternal perdition. But the treachery of Madame de Cintré herself amazed and confounded him; there was a key to the mystery, of course, but he groped for it in vain. Only three days had elapsed since she stood beside him in the starlight, beautiful and tranquil as the trust with which he had inspired her, and told him that she was happy in the prospect of their marriage. What was the meaning of the change? of what infernal potion had she tasted? Poor Newman had a terrible apprehension that she had really changed. His very admiration for her attached the idea of force and weight to her rupture. But he did not rail at her as false, for he was sure she was unhappy. In his walk he had crossed one of the bridges of the Seine, and he still followed, unheedingly, the long, unbroken quay. He had left Paris behind him, and he was almost in the country; he was in the pleasant suburb of Auteuil. He stopped at last, looked around him without seeing or caring for its pleasantness, and then slowly turned, and at a slower pace retraced his steps. When he came abreast of the fantastic embankment known as the Trocadero he reflected, through his throbbing pain, that he was near Mrs. Tristram's dwelling, and that Mrs. Tristram, on particular occasions, had much of a woman's kindness in her utterance. He felt that he needed to pour out his ire, and took the road to her house. Mrs. Tristram was at home and alone, and as soon as she had looked at him, on his entering the room, she told him that she knew what he had come for. Newman sat down heavily, in silence, looking at her.

"They have backed out!" she said. "Well, you may think it strange, but I felt something the other night in the air." Presently he told her his story; she listened with her eyes fixed on him. When he had finished she said quietly: "They want her to marry Lord Deepmere." Newman stared. He did not know that she knew anything about Lord Deepmere. "But I don't think she will," Mrs. Tristram added.

"*She* marry that poor little cub!" cried Newman. "Oh Lord! And yet, why did she refuse me?"

"But that isn't the only thing," said Mrs. Tristram. "They really couldn't endure you any longer. They had overrated their courage. I must say, to give the devil his due, that there is something rather fine in that. It was your commercial quality in the abstract they couldn't swallow. That is really aristocratic. They wanted your money, but they have given you up for an idea."

Newman frowned most ruefully, and took up his hat again. "I thought you would encourage me!" he said, with almost childlike sadness.

"Excuse me," she answered, very gently. "I feel none the less sorry for you, especially as I am at the bottom of your troubles. I have not forgotten that I suggested the marriage to you. I don't believe that

he

in her chords.

She

He

with his eyes on her.

while her whole face took it in.

without his even needing to tell her.

gave her his account;

he didn't

Save us!

"Pardon my trying to understand — of course it doesn't concern *you* to understand!"

consistent the inconsistency had been the other way.

and the mere historic fact of your washtubs and other lucrative wares that

Live with

Madame de Cintré has any intention of marrying Lord Deepmere. It is true he is not younger than she, as he looks. He is thirty-three years old; I looked in the Peerage. But no—I can't believe her so horribly, cruelly false."

"Please say nothing against her," said Newman.

"Poor woman, she *is* cruel. But of course you will go after her and you will plead powerfully. Do you know that as you are now," Mrs. Tristram pursued with characteristic audacity of comment, "you are extremely eloquent, even without speaking? To resist you a woman must have a very fixed idea in her head. I wish I had done you a wrong, that you might come to me in that fine fashion! But go to Madame de Cintré, at any rate, and tell her that she is a puzzle even to me. I am very curious to see how far family discipline will go."

Newman sat a while longer, leaning his elbows on his knees and his head in his hands, and Mrs. Tristram continued to temper charity with philosophy, and compassion with criticism. At last she inquired: "And what does the Count Valentin say to it?" Newman started; he had not thought of Valentin and his errand on the Swiss frontier since the morning. The reflection made him restless again, and he took his leave. He went straight to his apartment, where, upon the table of the vestibule, he found a telegram. It ran (with the date and place) as follows: "I am seriously ill; please to come to me as soon as possible. V. B." Newman groaned at this miserable news, and at the necessity of deferring his journey to the Château de Fleurières. But he wrote to Madame de Cintré these few lines; they were all he had time for:

"I don't give you up, and I don't really believe you give me up. I don't understand it, but we shall clear it up together. I can't follow you to-day, as I am called to see a friend at a distance who is very ill, perhaps

Claire

consenting

might pass for being.

strangely cried.

She looked at him an instant; she had one of her odd little outbreaks. "You're lamentable—you're splendid! Go to

and make me so fine is—and fine, you, just you.

a clever woman like me, who so greatly admires her.

the time allowed him.

speak your intention.

broke away on a promise that his hostess should have without delay his next news.

He had a savage groan for

in a fine old case like this, dear, go on

waiting

reason

Page for Copy

426

~~425~~

~~XIX. THE AMERICAN. 85~~

~~dying. But I shall come to you as soon as I can leave my friend. Why shouldn't I say that he is your brother?—C. N."~~

~~After this he had only time to catch the night-express to Geneva.~~

tell you

426

XIX.

He had a rare gift

~~Newman possessed a remarkable talent~~ for sitting still when ~~it was necessary, and he had an~~ opportunity to use it on his journey to Switzerland. The successive hours of the night brought him no sleep; but he ~~sat~~ kept motionless in his corner of the railway-carriage, with his eyes closed, and the most observant of his fellow-travellers might have envied him his apparent ~~slumber~~ rest. Toward morning ~~slumber~~ rest really came, as an effect of mental rather than of physical fatigue. He slept for a couple of hours, and at last, waking, found his eyes ~~resting upon~~ attaching themselves to one of the snow-powdered peaks of the Jura, behind which the sky was just reddening with the dawn. But he saw neither the cold mountain nor the warm ~~sky~~ light: his consciousness began to throb again, on the very instant, with a sense of his wrong. He got out of the train half an hour before it reached Geneva, in the ~~cold morning twilight~~ pale early glow and at the station indicated in Valentin's telegram. A drowsy station-master was on the platform with a lantern, and the hood of his overcoat over his head, and near him stood a gentleman who advanced to meet Newman. This personage was a man of forty, with a tall lean figure, a ~~sallow~~ long brown face, ~~a dark eye, a neat moustache, and a pair of fresh~~ marked eyebrows, high moustaches and fresh light gloves. He took off his hat, looking very grave, and ~~pronounced Newman's name~~ articulated "Monsieur!" ~~Our hero assented, and said~~ To which our hero replied: "You've ~~are M. de Bellegarde's friend?~~" been acting, in this tragedy, for the Count?"

Marginal balloons:

nothing else would serve,

and rare was his

rest

light

"I unite with you in claiming that sad honour," said the gentleman. "I had placed myself at M. de Bellegarde's service in this melancholy affair, together with M. de Grosjoyaux, who is now at his bedside. M. de Grosjoyaux, I believe, has had the honour of meeting you in Paris, but as he is a better nurse than I he remained with our poor friend. Bellegarde has been eagerly expecting you."

"And how is Bellegarde?" said Newman. "He was badly hit?"

"The doctor has condemned him; we brought a surgeon with us. But he will die in the best sentiments. I sent last evening for the curé of the nearest French village, who spent an hour with him. The curé was quite satisfied."

"Heaven forgive us!" groaned Newman. "I would 'd rather the doctor were satisfied! And can he see me—shall he know me?"

Surgeon were so!

"When I left him, half an hour ago, he had fallen asleep, after a feverish, wakeful night. But we shall see." And Newman's companion proceeded to lead the way out of the station to the village, explaining as he went that the little party was lodged in the humblest of Swiss inns, where, however, they had succeeded in making M. de Bellegarde much more comfortable than could at first have been expected. "We are old companions-in-arms," said Valentin's second; "it is not the first time that one of us has helped the other to lie easily. It is a very nasty wound, and the nastiest thing about it is that Bellegarde's adversary was no shot. He put his bullet where he could. It took it into his head to walk straight into Bellegarde's left side, just below the heart."

its

As they picked their way in the gray, deceptive dawn, between the manure-heaps of the village street Newman's new acquaintance narrated the particulars of the duel. The conditions of the meeting had been that

meeting

if the first exchange of shots should fail to satisfy one of the two gentlemen, a second should take place. Valentin's first bullet had done exactly what Newman's companion was convinced he had intended it to do; it had grazed the arm of M. Stanislas Kapp, just scratching the flesh. M. Kapp's own projectile, meanwhile, had passed at ten good inches from the person of Valentin. The representatives of M. Stanislas had demanded another shot, which was granted. Valentin had then fired aside, and the young Alsatian had done effective execution. "I saw, when we met him on the ground," said Newman's informant, "that he was not going to be *commode*. ~~It is a kind of bovine temperament.~~" Valentin had immediately been installed at the inn, and M. Stanislas and his friends had withdrawn to regions unknown. The police authorities of the canton had waited upon the party at the inn, had been extremely majestic, and had drawn up a long *procès-verbal;* but ~~it was probable that they would wink at so very gentlemanly a bit of bloodshed.~~ Newman asked ~~whether~~ a message had not been sent to Valentin's family, and learned that up to a late hour of the ~~preceding evening~~ Valentin had opposed it. He had refused to believe his wound was dangerous. But after his interview with the curé he had consented, and a telegram had been despatched to his mother. "But the Marquise ~~had better hurry," said Newman's conductor.~~

"Well, it's an ~~abominable~~ affair!" ~~said Newman. "That's all I have got to say!" To say this, at least, in a tone of infinite disgust, was an irresistible need.~~

"Ah, you don't approve?" ~~questioned his conductor, with curious urbanity.~~

"Approve?" cried Newman. "I wish that when I had him there, night before last, I had locked him up in my *cabinet de toilette!*"

Valentin's ~~late second~~ opened his eyes, and shook his head up and down two or three times, ~~gravely~~, with a

A mixture of the ass and the buffalo — with no sense of proportion."

as the wine had been drawn — alas! — Justice would have to drink it.

if

previous night

will scarcely have time," so judged Newman's conductor.

So judged Newman himself.

atrocious

his friend ~~[illegible]~~ gravely questioned, while he was passionately careless of the ~~[illegible]~~ involved reflection on this gentleman's partial management of the encounter.

supporter

portentously

little flute-like whistle. But they had reached the inn, ~~and~~ a stout maid-servant in a night-cap was ~~at the door~~ with a lantern, to take ~~Newman's travelling-bag~~ from the porter who trudged behind him. Valentin was lodged on the ground-floor at the back of the house, and Newman's companion went along a stone-faced passage and softly opened a door. Then he beckoned to Newman, who advanced and looked into the room, which was lighted by a single shaded candle. Beside the fire sat M. de Grosjoyaux asleep in his dressing-gown—a ~~little plump fair man~~ whom Newman had seen several times in Valentin's company. On the bed lay Valentin, pale and still, with his eyes closed—a figure very shocking to Newman, who had ~~seen~~ it hitherto awake to its finger-tips. M. de Grosjoyaux's colleague pointed to an open door beyond, and whispered that the doctor was within, ~~keeping~~ guard. So long as Valentin slept, or seemed to sleep, of course ~~Newman~~ could not approach him; so our hero withdrew for the present, committing himself to the care of the half-waked *bonne*. She took him to a room above-stairs, and introduced him to a bed on which a magnified bolster, in yellow calico, figured as a counterpane. Newman lay down, and, in spite of his counterpane, slept for three or four hours. When he awoke the morning was advanced and the sun ~~was~~ filling his window, ~~and~~ he heard [illegible] the clucking of hens. While he was dressing there came to his door a messenger from M. de Grosjoyaux and his companion, ~~proposing that~~ he should breakfast with them. Presently he went downstairs to the little stone-paved dining-room, where the maid-servant, who had taken off her night-cap, was serving the repast. M. de Grosjoyaux was there, surprisingly fresh for a gentleman who had been playing sick-nurse half the night; ~~rubbing~~ his hands and watch~~ing~~ the breakfast-table attentively. Newman renewed acquaintance with him, and learned that Valentin was ~~still sleeping~~; the ~~surgeon~~, who had had a fairly tranquil

Handwritten revisions:

- But he had evidently been prepared, in respect to this outer barbarian, for some oddity of emotion and expression. They had in any case
- where
- the traveller's bag
- on the threshold
- stout fair man, with an air of gay surprise,
- known
- short
- his visitor
- message
- where he kept guard,
- who proposed
- and most other things,
- outside of which
- still in a doze;
- doctor,
- he now rubbed his hands very constantly and very hard and watched

night, was at present sitting with him. Before M. de Grosjoyaux's associate reappeared, Newman learned that his name was M. Ledoux, and that Bellegarde's acquaintance with him dated from the days when they served together in the Pontifical Zouaves. M. Ledoux was the nephew of a distinguished Ultramontane bishop. At last the bishop's nephew came in with a toilet in which an ingenious attempt at harmony with the peculiar situation was visible, and with a gravity tempered by a decent deference to the best breakfast that the Croix Helvétique had ever set forth. Valentin's servant, who was allowed only in scanty measure the honour of watching with his master, had been lending a light Parisian hand in the kitchen. The two Frenchmen did their best to prove that if circumstances might overshadow, they could not really obscure the national talent for conversation, and M. Ledoux delivered a neat little eulogy on poor Bellegarde, whom he pronounced the most charming Englishman he had ever known.

"Do you call him an Englishman?" Newman asked.

M. Ledoux smiled a moment and then made an epigram. "*C'est plus qu'un Anglais—c'est un Anglomane!*" Newman said soberly that he had never noticed it, and M. de Grosjoyaux remarked that it was really too soon to deliver a funeral oration upon poor Bellegarde. "Evidently," said M. Ledoux. "But I couldn't help observing this morning to Mr. Newman that when a man has taken such excellent measures for his salvation as our dear friend did last evening, it seems almost a pity he should put it in peril again by returning to the world." M. Ledoux was a great Catholic, and Newman thought him a queer mixture. His countenance, by daylight, had a sort of amiably saturnine cast; he had a very large thin nose, and looked like a Spanish picture. He appeared to think duelling a very perfect arrangement, provided, if one should get hit, one could promptly see the priest. He seemed to take a great satisfaction in

[Handwritten revisions:]
an effect of dress
adjustment at once to a confirmed style and to
attending
but with reserve
gift
good talk,
returned, sturdily and handsomely, that any country might have been proud to claim him,
took clearly
might
an old
an
lean
the use of pistols at thirty paces
coming back to the world

Valentin's interview with that functionary, and yet his general tone was far from indicating a sanctimonious habit of mind. M. Ledoux had evidently a high sense of propriety and was furnished, in respect to everything, with an explanation and a grave grin which combined to push his moustache up under his nose. *Savoir-vivre* — knowing how to live — was his strong point, in which he included knowing how to die; but, as Newman reflected with a good deal of dumb irritation, he seemed disposed to delegate to others the application of his mastery of this latter resource. M. de Grosjoyaux was quite of another complexion and appeared to regard his friend's theological unction as the sign of an inaccessibly superior spirit. His surprise was so bright that it made him look amused; as if, under the impression of M. Kapp's mere mass, he couldn't recover from the oddity of these hazards, that of the translation of so much large looseness into a thing so fine as a direction — even, as it were, a wrong one. He could have understood the *coup* if it had been his own indeed, and he kept looking through the window, over the shoulder of M. Ledoux, at a slender tree by the end of a lane opposite the inn, as if measuring its distance from his extended arm and secretly wishing that, since the association of ideas was so close, he might indulge in a little speculative practice.

Newman found his company depressing,

He could neither eat nor talk; his soul was sore with grief and anger, and the weight of his double sorrow was intolerable. He sat with his eyes fixed upon his plate, counting the minutes, wishing at one moment that Valentin would see him and leave him free to go in quest of Madame de Cintré and his lost happiness, and mentally calling himself a vile brute the next, for the impatient egotism of the wish. He was very poor company, himself, and even his acute preoccupation, and his general lack of the habit of pondering the impression he produced, did not prevent him from reflecting that his companions must be puzzled to see how poor Bellegarde came to take such a fancy to this taciturn Yankee that he must needs have him at his deathbed. After breakfast he strolled forth alone into the village and looked at the fountain, the geese, the open barn doors, the brown, bent old women showing their hugely-darned stocking-heels at the end of their slowly-clicking sabots, and the beautiful view of snowy Alp and purple Jura at either end of the little street. The day was brilliant; early spring was in the air and sunshine, and the winter's damp was trickling out of the cottage eaves. It was birth and brightness for all nature, even for chirping chickens and waddling goslings, and it was to be death and burial for poor, foolish, generous, delightful Bellegarde. Newman walked as far as the village church, and went into the small graveyard beside it, where he sat down and looked at the awkward tablets which were planted around. They were all sordid and hideous, and Newman could feel nothing but the hardness and coldness of death. He got up and came back to the inn, where he found M. Ledoux having coffee and a cigarette at a little green table which he had caused to be carried into the small garden. Newman, learning that the doctor was still sitting with Valentin, asked Mr. Ledoux if he might not be allowed to relieve him; he had a great desire to be useful to his poor friend. This was easily arranged; the doctor was very glad to go to

almost irritating
enough
his impatience.
his guessing to the others
at
who showed
as well as at
a dull barbarian as to desire
taking
hanging across
rude
he
trickled
only
precious Valentine
was, through M. Ledoux

92 THE AMERICAN. XIX.

bed. He was a youthful and rather jaunty practitioner, but he had a clever face, and the ribbon of the Legion of Honour in his button-hole; Newman listened attentively to ~~the~~ instructions ~~he gave him before retiring~~, and took mechanically from his hand ~~a small volume which the surgeon~~ recommended as a help to wakefulness, and which ~~turned out to be an old copy~~ of "Les Liaisons Dangereuses."

Valentin ~~was still lying~~ with his eyes closed, and ~~there was no~~ visible change ~~in his~~ condition. Newman sat down near him, and for a long time narrowly watched him. Then ~~his eyes wandered away with his thoughts upon~~ his own situation, ~~and rested upon~~ the chain of the Alps, disclosed by the drawing of the scant white cotton curtain of the window, through which the sunshine passed and lay in squares ~~upon~~ on the red-tiled floor. He tried to interweave his ~~reflections with~~ hope, but ~~he~~ only half succeeded. What had happened to him ~~seemed to have in its violence and audacity, the force of a real calamity — the strength and insolence of Destiny herself. It was unnatural and monstrous, and~~ he had no arms against it. At last a sound struck ~~upon~~ on the stillness, and he heard Valentin's voice.

"It can't be about *me* you are pulling that long face!" He found, when he turned, that ~~Valentin was lying in~~ the same position; but ~~his eyes were open, and he was even trying to smile~~. It was with a very slender strength that ~~he returned~~ the pressure of ~~Newman's~~ his hand. "I've been watching you for a quarter of an hour," Valentin went on; "you've been looking as ~~black as thunder~~. You're greatly disgusted with me, I see. Well, of course! So am I!"

"Oh, I ~~shall not scold~~ you," said Newman. "I feel too badly. And how are you getting on?"

"Oh, I'm getting off! They have quite settled that ~~haven't they?~~"

"That's for you to settle; you can get well if you try," ~~said~~ Newman, with ~~resolute cheerfulness.~~

an old book from the window-seat of the inn,

his

proved

by him

without

of

still lay

he let his vision stray with his consciousness of

an odd volume

gloom with strains of

range away and rest

with eyes now open and showing the glimmer of a smile.

he felt

declared

answered

his hating lay in

a queer strained quaver

Aren't you here to see me off?"

if you too had had to swallow some vile drug

shan't abuse

was violent and insolent, but, like all great strokes of evil, unnatural and monstrous, it showed the hard hand of the Fate that rejoices in the groans of men and the blood and the terrors of women, and

"My dear fellow, how can I try? Trying is violent exercise, and that sort of thing isn't in order for a man with a hole in his side as big as your hat, that begins to bleed if he moves a hair's-breadth. I knew you would come," he continued; "I knew I should wake up and find you here; so I'm not surprised. But last night I was very impatient. I didn't see how I could keep still until you came. It was a matter of keeping still, just like this; as still as a mummy in his case. You talk about trying; I tried that! Well, here I am yet—these twenty hours. It seems like twenty days." Bellegarde talked slowly and feebly, but distinctly enough. It was visible, however, that he was in extreme pain, and at last he closed his eyes. Newman begged him to remain silent and spare himself; the doctor had left urgent orders. "Oh," said Valentin, "let us eat and drink, for to-morrow—to-morrow ——" he paused again. "No, not to-morrow, perhaps, but to-day. I can't eat and drink, but I can talk. What's to be gained, at this pass, by renun—renunciation? I mustn't use such big words. I was always a chatterer; Lord, how I have talked in my day!"

"That's a reason for keeping quiet now," said Newman. "We know how well you talk, you know."

But Valentin, without heeding him, went on in the same weak dying drawl. "I wanted to see you because you have seen my sister. Does she know—will she come?"

Newman was embarrassed. "Yes, by this time she must know."

"Didn't you tell her?" Valentin asked. And then, in a moment: "Didn't you bring me any message from her?" His eyes rested upon Newman's with a certain soft keenness.

"I didn't see her after I got your telegram," said Newman. "I wrote to her."

"And she sent you no answer?"

Handwritten revisions:

which

'd

without you

It's more

again closed his eyes

—!" And

'd

've

Valentin's speech was slowly taken, with strange punctuations, but it had, however faint, the flicker of his gaiety; and he seemed almost to say what he wanted

against worry

gabbled

make no effort—just, as he called it, to take his ease;

with the same effect of trouble and of pluck

said

felt himself the poorest of deceivers

now covered his friend like lifted lamps

94 THE AMERICAN. XIX.

~~Newman~~ He was obliged to reply that Madame de Cintré had left Paris. "She went yesterday to Fleurières."

"Yesterday—to Fleurières? Why did she go to Fleurières? What day is this? What day was yesterday? Ah, then, I sha'n't see her," ~~said Valentin, sadly.~~ "Fleurières is too far!" And ~~then he closed his eyes again.~~ Newman sat silent, summoning pious invention to his aid, but he was relieved at ~~finding that Valentin was apparently too weak to reason or to~~ be curious. ~~Bellegarde, however, presently went on.~~ "And my mother—and my brother—will they come? Are they at Fleurières?

"They were in Paris, but I didn't see them either," Newman answered. "If they received your telegram in time, they ~~will~~ 'll have started this morning. Otherwise they ~~will~~ 'll be obliged to wait for the night-express, and [struck out] arrive at the same hour ~~as~~ I did."

"They won't thank me—they won't thank me," Valentin murmured. "They ~~will~~ 'll pass an atrocious night, and Urbain doesn't like the early morning air. I don't remember ever in my life to have seen him before noon—before breakfast. No one ever saw him. We don't know how he is then. Perhaps he's different. Who knows? Posterity, perhaps, will know. That's the time he works, in his *cabinet*, at the history of the Princesses. But I had to send for them—hadn't I? And then I want to see my mother sit there where you sit, and say good-bye to her. Perhaps, after all, I don't know her, and she ~~will~~ have some surprise for me. Don't think you know her yet, yourself; perhaps she may surprise *you*. But if I can't see Claire, I don't care ~~for anything. I have been thinking of it—and in my dreams too.~~ Why did she go to Fleurières to-day? She never told me. What has happened? Ah, she ought to have guessed I ~~was~~ 'm here—this way. It's the first time in her life she ever disappointed me. Poor Claire!"

He

Valentin moaned.

He did, however, at last break out again.

will

he became dark and dumb again, only breathing a little harder.

— hear her above all say hers to me.

'm

poor

being at being able [?] to believe him really so weak to

may

— what do you call it? — a red cent. Have you green ones or blue ones or any other colour? Ah vous, mon cher, vous en avez de toutes les couleurs! But what's the matter — while I've been dreaming of her?

XIX. THE AMERICAN. 95

"You know we are not man and wife quite yet—your sister and I," said Newman. "She doesn't yet account to me for all her actions." And, after a fashion, he smiled.

Valentin looked at him a moment. "Have you quarrelled?"

"Never, never, never!" Newman exclaimed.

"How happily you say that!" said Valentin. "You are going to be happy—very!" In answer to this stroke of irony, none the less powerful for being so unconscious, all poor Newman could do was to give a helpless and transparent stare. Valentin continued to fix him with his own rather over-bright gaze, and presently he said: "But something *is* the matter with you. I watched you just now; you haven't a bridegroom's face."

"My dear fellow," said Newman, "how can I show *you* a bridegroom's face? If you think I enjoy seeing you lie there and not being able to help you——"

"Why, you are just the man to be cheerful; don't forfeit your rights. I'm a proof of your wisdom. When was a man ever gloomy when he could say 'I told you so'? You told me so, you know. You did what you could about it. You said some very good things; I have thought them over. But, my dear friend, I was right, all the same. This is the regular way."

"I didn't do what I ought," said Newman. "I ought to have done something else."

"For instance?"

"Oh, something or other. I ought to have treated you as a small boy."

"Well, I'm a very small boy now," said Valentin, "rather less than an infant. An infant is helpless, but it's generally voted promising. I'm not promising, eh? Society can't lose a less valuable member."

Newman was strongly moved. He got up and turned his back upon his friend and walked away to the window, where he stood looking out but only vaguely seeing.

unimaginably

two

He tried to throw off this statement with grace, but felt as if the muscles of his face didn't serve him.

re

la-la!

ridiculous grin for the conscious failure of which he then more ridiculously blushed.

harder.

've

the light of fever,

and have locked you up!

jolly and—what do you call it?—to crow,

to it!"

carefully aver.

naughty

better."

Valentin softly wailed, "and God knows I've been naughty enough! I'm

"No, I don't like the look of your back," Valentin continued. "I ~~ha~~ve always been an observer of backs; yours is quite out of sorts."

Newman returned to his bedside and begged him to be quiet. "Be quiet and get well[illegible]; that's what you must do. Get well and help me."

"I told you you were in trouble! How can I help you?" Valentin asked.

"I'll let you know when you are better. You were always ~~curious~~; there is something to get well for!" Newman answered, with resolute animation.

Valentin ~~closed his eyes~~ and lay a long time without speaking. He seemed even to have fallen asleep. But at the end of half an hour he ~~began to talk again.~~ "I am rather sorry about that place in the bank. Who knows but ~~that~~ I might have become another Rothschild? But I wasn't meant for a banker; bankers are not so easy to kill. Don't you think I have been very easy to kill? It's not like a serious man. It's really very mortifying. It's like telling your hostess you must go, when you count upon her begging you to stay, and then finding she does no such thing. 'Really—so soon? You've only just come!' Life doesn't make me any such polite little speech."

Newman for some time said nothing, but at last he broke out. "It's a bad case—it's a bad case—it's the worst case I ever met. I don't want to say anything unpleasant, but I can't help it. I've seen men dying before—and I've seen men shot. But it always seemed more natural; they ~~were not so clever as you.~~ Damnation,—damnation! You might have done something ~~better than this~~. It's about the meanest winding-up of a man's ~~affairs that~~ I can imagine!"

Valentin feebly waved his hand to and fro. "Don't insist—don't insist! ~~It is mean—decidedly mean.~~ For you see at the bottom—down at the bottom, in a little place as small as the end of a wine-funnel—I agree with you!"

give yourself the very best chance. That's what you want and

awfully inquiring;

was again conversing.

relapsed once more

I've seen men in the worst kind of holes—worse even than yours.

were of no account compared to you—and at any rate I didn't care. But now—

business

It's taking a mean advantage.

more to the purpose.

XIX. THE AMERICAN. 97

A few moments after this the doctor put his head through the half-opened door, and, perceiving ~~that Valentin~~ was awake, came in and felt his pulse. He shook his head and declared ~~that~~ he had talked too much—ten times too much. "Nonsense!" ~~said~~ Valentin, "a man sentenced to death ~~can never talk too much.~~ Have you never read an account of an execution in a newspaper?" ~~Don't~~ they always set a lot of people at the prisoner—lawyers, reporters, priests—to make him talk? But it's not ~~M.~~ Newman's fault; he sits there as mum as a death's-head."

The doctor observed that it was time ~~his patient's~~ wound should be dressed again; MM. de Grosjoyaux and Ledoux, who had already witnessed this delicate operation, taking Newman's place as assistants. Newman withdrew, ~~and learned~~ from his fellow-watchers that they had received a telegram from ~~Urbain de Bellegarde~~ to the effect that their message had been delivered in the Rue de l'Université too late to allow him to take the morning train, but that he would start with his mother in the evening. Newman wandered away into the village again, and walked about restlessly for two or three hours. The day ~~seemed terribly long~~. At dusk he came back and dined with the doctor and M. Ledoux. The dressing of Valentin's wound had been a very critical operation; ~~the doctor didn't really see how he was to endure~~ a repetition of it. He then declared that he must beg of Mr. Newman to deny himself for the present the satisfaction of sitting with M. de Bellegarde; more than any one else, apparently, he had the flattering but ~~inconvenient privilege~~ of exciting him. M. Ledoux, at this, swallowed a glass of wine in silence; he must have been wondering what the deuce Bellegarde found so exciting in the American.

Newman, after dinner, went up to his room, where ~~he sat for a long time staring at his~~ lighted candle and thinking that Valentin was dying downstairs. Late,

his charge
protested;
he went on. "Don't
the
and learned
is allowed to get in first all he can? He can't talk after, and if he was ever a talker—!
the Marquis
had the length of some interminable tragedy
in the other room
for black weariness, at the
flinging himself too on his bed, at his grim length, he lay staring,
but fatal gift
the question was definitely if he could bear

when the candle had burnt low, there came a soft tap at his door. The doctor stood there with a candlestick and a shrug.

"He must amuse himself still! He insists upon seeing you, and I am afraid you must come. I think, at this rate, that he will hardly outlast the night."

Newman went back to Valentin's room, which he found lighted by a taper on the hearth. Valentin begged him to light a candle. "I want to see your face. They say you excite me," he went on, as Newman complied with this request, "and I confess I do feel excited; but it isn't you—it's my own thoughts. I have been thinking—thinking. Sit down there and let me look at you again." Newman seated himself, folded his arms, and bent a heavy gaze upon his friend. He seemed to be playing a part, mechanically, in a lugubrious comedy. Valentin looked at him for some time. "Yes, this morning I was right; you have something on your mind heavier than Valentin de Bellegarde. Come, I'm a dying man, and it's indecent to deceive me. Something happened after I left Paris. It was not for nothing that my sister started off at this season of the year for Fleurières. Why was it? It sticks in my crop. I have been thinking it over, and if you don't tell me I shall guess."

"I had better not tell you," said Newman. "It won't do you any good."

"If you think it will do me any good not to tell me, you are very much mistaken. There is trouble about your marriage."

"Yes," said Newman. "There is trouble about my marriage."

"Good!" And Valentin was silent again. "They have stopped it."

"They have stopped it," said Newman. Now that he had spoken out, he found a satisfaction in it which

another light and a motion of despair.
for something brighter.
work me up?
feel worked-up;
felt as if he were now
great cleverness, of which you've such an opinion.
faced him thus for some time
I've
stopped it off."
admitted.
it off?"
reasoned.
relief
than any flare had.

deepened as he went on. "Your mother and brother have broken faith. They have decided that it can't take place. They have decided that I am not good enough, after all. They have taken back their word. Since you insist, there it is!"

Valentin gave a sort of groan, lifted his hands a moment, and then let them drop.

"I am sorry not to have anything better to tell you about them," Newman pursued. "But it's not my fault. I was, indeed, very unhappy when your telegram reached me; I was quite upside down. You may imagine whether I feel any better now."

Valentin moaned gaspingly, as if his wound were throbbing. "Broken faith, broken faith!" [illegible].

"And my sister—my sister?"

"Your sister is very unhappy; she has consented to give me up. I don't know why. I don't know what they have done to her; it must be something pretty bad. In justice to her you ought to know it. They have made her suffer. I haven't seen her alone, but only before them. We had an interview yesterday morning. They came out flat, in so many words. They told me to go about my business. It seems to me a very bad case. I'm angry, I'm sore, I'm sick."

Valentin lay there staring, with his eyes more brilliantly lighted, his lips soundlessly parted, and a flush of colour in his pale face. Newman had never before uttered so many words in the plaintive key, but now, in speaking to Valentin in the poor fellow's extremity, he had a feeling that he was making his complaint somewhere within the presence of the power that men pray to in trouble; he felt his outgush of resentment as a sort of spiritual privilege.

"And Claire," said Bellegarde, "Claire? She has given you up?"

"I don't really believe it," said Newman.

"No, don't believe it, don't believe it. She is gaining time; excuse her."

when they come to think of it.

want to know,

count

cannot

uttered a strange sound,

what it is they must have put her through!

bewildered enough when

I'm sorry to have such a report to make of them.

let me have it full in the face.

his friend in that friend's extremity, he had a sense of making his lament

spiritual act, an appeal to higher protection.

the young man breathed;

believe that!

"I pity her!" said Newman.

"Poor Claire!" murmured Valentin. "But they—but they—" and he paused again. "You saw them; they dismissed you, face to face?"

"Face to face. They were very explicit." — rather (?)

"What did they say?"

"They said they couldn't stand a commercial person."

Valentin put out his hand and laid it upon Newman's arm. "And about their promise—their engagement with you?"

"They made a distinction. They said it was to hold good only until Madame de Cintré accepted me."

Valentin lay staring a while, and his flush died away. "Don't tell me any more; [illegible] I'm ashamed."

"You? You are the soul of honour," said Newman, simply.

Valentin groaned and turned away [averted] his head. For some time nothing more was said. Then Valentin turned back again and found a certain force to press Newman's arm. "It's very bad—very bad. When my people—when my race—come to that, it is time for me to withdraw. I believe in my sister; she will explain. Excuse her. If she can't—if she can't, forgive her. She has suffered. But for the others it is very bad—very bad. You take it very hard? No, it's a shame to make you say so." He closed his eyes, and again there was a silence. Newman felt almost awed; he had evoked a more solemn spirit than he expected. Presently Valentin looked at him again, removing his hand from his arm. "I apologise, [illegible] Do you understand? Here on my deathbed. I apologise for my family. For my mother. For my brother. For the ancient house of Bellegarde. *Voilà!*" he added softly.

Newman for all answer took his hand, and pressed it with a world of kindness. Valentin remained quiet, and at the end of half an hour the doctor softly came in.

immensely

sighed

//Poor

And

—

very

he

to pass away

Pardon her, allow for her, wait for that

fixed him again, releasing his arm

kept it in his own

make her conduct clear: we'll forgive her somehow, at any rate don't curse her. She'll pay — she has paid, with her own chance of happiness

noiselessly returned

name I was proud of

stirred his companion to depths into which now he shrank from looking

Behind him, through the half-open door, Newman saw the two questioning faces of MM. de Grosjoyaux and Ledoux. The doctor laid ~~his hand on Valentin's~~ wrist and sat looking at him. He gave no sign, and the two gentlemen came in, M. Ledoux having first beckoned to some one outside. This was M. le Curé, who carried in his hand an object unknown to Newman, and covered with a white napkin. M. le Curé was short, round, and red: he advanced, pulling off his little black cap to Newman, and deposited his burden on the table; and then he sat down in the best armchair, ~~with~~ his hands ~~folded~~ across his person. The other gentlemen had exchanged glances which expressed unanimity as to the timeliness of their presence. But for a long time Valentin neither spoke nor moved. It was Newman's belief, afterwards, that M. le Curé ~~went~~ to sleep. At last, abruptly, ~~Valentin~~ pronounced Newman's name. ~~His friend~~ went to him, and he said in French: "You are not alone. I want to speak to you alone." Newman looked at the doctor, and the doctor looked at the curé, who looked back at him; and then the doctor and the curé, together, gave a shrug. "Alone—for five minutes," Valentin repeated. "Please leave us."

The curé took up his burden again and led the way out, followed by his companions. Newman closed the door behind them and came back to Valentin's bedside. Bellegarde had watched all this intently.

"It's very bad, it's very bad," he said, after Newman had seated himself close ~~to him~~. "The more I think of it the worse it is."

"Oh, don't think of it," ~~said~~ Newman.

But Valentin went on, without heeding him. "Even if they should come round again, the shame—the baseness—is there."

"Oh, they won't come round!" said Newman.

"Well, you can make them."

"Make them?"

a hand on the patient's

folding

their friend

had gone

This visitor

begged.

"I can tell you something—a great secret—an immense secret. You can use it against them—frighten them, force them."

"A secret!" Newman repeated. The idea of letting Valentin, on his deathbed, confide to him an "immense secret" shocked him, for the moment, and made him draw back. It seemed an illicit way of arriving at information, and even had a vague analogy with listening at a keyhole. Then, suddenly, the thought of "forcing" Madame de Bellegarde and her son became attractive, ~~and Newman bent his head closer to Valentin's lips.~~ For some time, however, ~~the dying man said nothing more. He only lay and looked at his friend with his~~ kindled, expanded, troubled eyes, and Newman began to believe ~~that~~ he had spoken in delirium. But at last he ~~said:~~ began again.

"There was something done—something done at Fleurières. It was ~~foul play~~. My father—something happened to him. I don't know; I've been ashamed—afraid to know. But ~~I know there~~ My mother knows—Urbain knows."

"Something happened to your father?" ~~said Newman, urgently.~~

Valentin looked at him, still more wide-eyed. "He didn't get well."

"Get well of what?"

But the immense effort which Valentin had made, first to decide to utter these words, and then to bring them out, appeared to have taken his last strength. He lapsed again into silence, and Newman sat watching him. "Do you understand?" he began again presently. "At Fleurières. You can find out. Mrs. Bread knows. Tell her I ~~begged you to ask her~~. ~~Then tell them that, and see.~~ It may ~~help you~~. If ~~not~~, tell every one. It will—it will"—here Valentin's voice sank to the feeblest murmur—"it will ~~avenge you!~~" vague wail.

The words died away in a long ~~sob~~ Newman

he

nothing more came. Valentin but covered him with

and, as to lose in any case no last breath of the spirit for which he had felt such a kindness, he brought his head nearer.

"Pay them?" "Pay them?" Newman wondered. "What you owe them?"

—some wrong, some violence, ~~I believe~~ some cruelty. It may have been—God forgive me now!—some crime.

permitted himself to ask

come to your aid.

it

made this point—at this hour—of your asking her.

a bad business—a worse one than yours—there was that.

She'll give you the truth—and then you'll show it. You know it...

stood up, deeply impressed, not knowing what to say; his heart was beating ~~violently~~. "Thank you," he said at last. "I'm much obliged." But Valentin seemed not to hear him; he remained silent and his silence continued. At last Newman went and opened the door. M. le Curé re-entered, bearing his sacred vessel, and followed by the three gentlemen and by Valentin's servant. It was ~~almost~~ processional.

~~CHAPTER~~ XX.

VALENTIN DE BELLEGARDE died tranquilly, just as the cold faint March dawn began to illumine the faces of the little knot of friends gathered about his bedside. An hour afterwards Newman left the inn and drove to Geneva; he was naturally unwilling to be present at the arrival of Madame de Bellegarde and her first-born. At Geneva, for the moment, he remained. He was like a man who has had a fall and wants to sit still and count his bruises. He instantly wrote to Madame de Cintré, ~~relating~~ to her the circumstances of her brother's death—with certain exceptions—and asking her what was the earliest moment at which he might hope that she would consent to see him. M. Ledoux had told him ~~that~~ he had reason to know that Valentin's will—~~Bellegarde~~ had a great deal of elegant personal property to dispose of—contained a request that he should be buried near his father in the churchyard of Fleurières, and Newman intended that the state of his own relations with the family should not deprive him of the satisfaction of helping to pay the last earthly honours to the ~~best fellow in the world~~. He reflected that Valentin's friendship was older than Urbain's enmity, and that at a funeral it was easy to escape notice. Madame de Cintré's answer to his letter enabled him to time his arrival at Fleurières. This answer was very brief; it ran as follows:

"I thank you for your letter and for your being with Valentin. It is a most inexpressible sorrow to me that I was not. To see you will be nothing but a distress to me; there is no need, therefore, to wait for what you call brighter days. It is all one now, and I shall have no brighter days. Come when you please; only notify me first. My brother is to be buried here on Friday, and my family is to remain.—C. DE C."

As soon as he received this letter Newman went straight to Paris and to Poitiers. The journey took him far southward, through green Touraine and across the far-shining Loire, into a country where the early spring deepened about him as he went; but he had never made a journey during which he heeded less what he would have called the lay of the land. He ~~obtained lodging at an inn at Poitiers~~, and the next morning drove in a couple of hours to the village of Fleurières. But here, ~~preoccupied though he was, he could not fail to notice the picturesqueness of the place. It was what the French call a~~ *petit bourg* it lay at the base of a ~~sort of~~ huge mound, on the summit of which stood the crumbling ruins of a feudal castle, much of whose sturdy material, as well as that of the wall ~~which~~ dropped along the hill to enclose the clustered houses defensively, had been absorbed into the very substance of the village. The church was simply the former chapel of the castle, fronting upon its grass-grown court, which, however, was of generous enough width to have given up its quaintest corner to a ~~little~~ graveyard. Here the very headstones themselves seemed to sleep as they slanted into the grass; the patient elbow of the rampart held them together on one side, and in front, far beneath their mossy lids, the green plains and blue distances stretched away. The

alighted at an hotel in respect to which he scarce knew whether the wealth of its provincial note honoured or shamed it;

for all his melancholy, he could not resist the intensity of an impression. The

that

small

~~way to~~ church, up the hill, ~~was impracticable to vehicles.~~ It was lined with peasants two or three rows deep, who stood watching old Madame de Bellegarde slowly ~~ascend~~ ~~it~~ on the arm of her elder son, behind the pall-bearers of the other. Newman chose to lurk among the common mourners, who murmured "Madame la Comtesse" as a ~~tall figure veiled in black~~ passed before them. He stood in the dusky little church while the service was going forward, but at the dismal tomb-side he turned away and walked down the hill. He went back to Poitiers, and spent two days in which patience and ~~impatience were singularly commingled~~. On the third day he sent Madame de Cintré a note, ~~saying~~ that he would call upon her in the afternoon, and in accordance with this he again took his way to Fleurières. He left his vehicle at the tavern in the village street, and obeyed the simple instructions ~~which were~~ given him for finding the château.

"It is just beyond there," said the landlord, and pointed to the tree-tops of the ~~park~~ above the opposite houses. Newman followed the first cross-road to the right—it was bordered with mouldy cottages—and in a few moments saw before him the peaked roofs of the towers. Advancing farther he found himself before a vast iron gate, rusty and closed; here he paused a moment, looking through the bars. The ~~château~~ was near the road; ~~this was at once its merit and its defect; but its aspect was extremely impressive~~. Newman learned afterwards, from a guide-book of the province, that it dated from the ~~time of Henry IV~~. It presented to the wide-paved area which preceded it, and which was edged with shabby farm-buildings, an immense façade of dark time-stained brick, flanked by two low wings, each of which terminated in a little Dutch-looking pavilion, capped with a fantastic roof. Two towers rose behind, and behind the towers was a mass of elms and beeches, now just faintly green.

But the great feature was a wide green river, which

[Manuscript annotations: "approach to the"; "defied all wheels"; "ascend"; "and"; "almost bowed beneath its ladings of woe"; "yearning were commingled in a single ache"; "to the effect"; "u"; "parc"; "residence"; "reign of Henry III."; "as if the very highway belonged to it; this gave it a fine old masterly air"] washed the foundations of the château. The building rose from an island in the circling stream, so that this formed a perfect moat, spanned by a two-arched bridge without a parapet. The dull brick walls, which here and there made a grand straight sweep, the ugly little cupolas of the wings, the deep-set windows, the long steep pinnacles of mossy slate, all mirrored themselves in the quiet water. Newman rang at the gate, and was almost frightened at the tone with which a big rusty bell above his head replied to him. An old woman came out from the gate-house and opened the creaking portal just wide enough for him to pass, and he went in, across the dry bare court and the little cracked white slabs of the causeway on the moat. At the door of the château he waited for some moments, and this gave him a chance to observe that Fleurières was not "kept up" and to reflect that it was a melancholy place of residence. "It looks," said Newman to himself—and I give the comparison for what it is worth—"like a Chinese penitentiary." At last the door was opened by a servant whom he remembered to have seen in the Rue de l'Université. The man's dull face brightened as he perceived our hero, for Newman, for indefinable reasons, enjoyed the confidence of the liveried gentry. The footman led the way across a great central vestibule, with a pyramid of plants in tubs in the middle and glass doors all around, to what appeared to be the principal drawing-room of the château. Newman crossed the threshold of a room of superb proportions, which made him feel at first like a tourist with a guide-book and a cicerone awaiting a fee. But when his guide had left him alone, with the observation that he would call Madame la Comtesse, Newman perceived that the salon contained little that was remarkable, save a dark ceiling with curiously-carved rafters, some curtains of elaborate antiquated tapestry and a dark oaken floor polished like a mirror. He waited some minutes, walking up and down; but at length, as he turned at the end of the room, he saw that Madame de Cintré had come in by a distant door. She wore a black dress, and she stood looking at him. As the length of the immense room lay between them he had time to look at her before they met in the middle of it.

He was dismayed at the change in her appearance. Pale, heavy-browed, almost haggard, with a sort of monastic rigidity in her dress, she had little but her pure features in common with the woman whose radiant good grace he had hitherto admired. She let her eyes rest on his own and she let him take her hand; but her eyes looked like two rainy autumn moons, and her touch was portentously lifeless.

"I was at your brother's funeral," Newman said. "Then I waited three days. But I could wait no longer."

"Nothing can be lost or gained by waiting," said Madame de Cintré. "But it was very considerate of you to wait, wronged as you have been."

"I'm glad you think I have been wronged," said Newman, with that oddly humorous accent with which he often uttered words of the gravest meaning.

"Do I need to say so?" she asked. "I don't think I have wronged, seriously, many persons; certainly not consciously. To you, to whom I have done this hard and cruel thing, the only reparation I can make is to say: 'I know it, I feel it!' The reparation is pitifully small!"

"Oh, it's a great step forward!" said Newman, with a gracious smile of encouragement. He pushed a chair towards her and held it, looking at her urgently. She sat down mechanically, and he seated himself near her; but in a moment he got up, restlessly and stood before her. She remained seated, like a troubled creature who had passed through the stage of restlessness.

"I say nothing is to be gained by my seeing you," she went on, "and yet I am very glad you came. Now I can tell you what I feel. It is a selfish pleasure, but it is one of the last I shall have." And she paused, with her great misty eyes fixed upon him. "I know how I have deceived and injured you; I know how cruel and cowardly I have been. I see it as vividly as you do—I feel it to the ends of my fingers." And she unclasped her hands, which were locked together in her lap, lifted them, and dropped them at her side. "Anything that you may have said of me in your angriest passion is nothing to what I have said to myself."

"In my angriest passion," said Newman, "I have said nothing hard of you. The very worst thing I have said of you yet is that you are the loveliest of women." And he seated himself before her again abruptly.

She flushed a little, but even her flush was pale. "That is because you think I will come back. But I will not come back. It is in that hope you have come here, I know; I am very sorry for you. I would do almost anything for you. To say that, after what I have done, seems simply impudent; but what can I say that will not seem impudent? To wrong you and apologise—that is easy enough. I should not have wronged you." She stopped a moment, looking at him, and motioned him to let her go on. "I ought never to have listened to you at first; that was the wrong. No good could come of it. I felt it, and yet I listened; that was your fault. I liked you too much; I believed in you."

"And don't you believe in me now?"

"More than ever. But now it doesn't matter. I have given you up."

Newman gave a powerful thump with his clenched fist upon his knee. "Why, why, why?" he cried. "Give me a reason—a decent reason. You are not a child—you are not a minor, nor an idiot. You are not obliged to drop me because your mother told you to. Such a reason isn't worthy of you."

"I know that; it's not worthy of me. But it's the only one I have to give. After all," said Madame de Cintré, throwing out her hands, "think me an idiot and forget me! That will be the simplest way."

Newman got up and walked away with a crushing sense that his cause was lost, and yet with an equal inability to give up fighting. He went to one of the great windows and looked out at the stiffly-embanked river and the formal gardens which lay beyond it. When he turned round Madame de Cintré had risen; she stood there silent and passive. "You are not frank," said Newman; "you are not honest. Instead of saying that you are imbecile, you should say that other people are wicked. Your mother and your brother have been false and cruel; they have been so to me, and I am sure they have been so to you. Why do you try to shield them? Why do you sacrifice me to them? I'm not false; I'm not cruel. You don't know what you give up; I can tell you that—you don't. They bully you and plot about you; and I—I——" And he paused, holding out his hands. She turned away and began to leave him. "You told me the other day that you were afraid of your mother," he said, following her. "What did you mean?"

Madame de Cintré shook her head. "I remember; I was sorry afterwards."

"You were sorry when she came down and put on the thumbscrews. In God's name, what *is* it she does to you?"

"Nothing. Nothing that you can understand. And now that I have given you up, I must not complain of her to you."

"That's no reasoning!" cried Newman. "Complain of her, on the contrary. Tell me all about it, frankly and trustfully, as you ought, and we will talk it over so satisfactorily that you won't give me up."

Madame de Cintré looked down some moments, fixedly; and then, raising her eyes, she said: "One good at least has come of this: I have made you judge me more fairly. You thought of me in a way that did me great honour; I don't know why you had taken it into your head. But it left me no loophole for escape—no chance to be the common weak creature I am. It was not my fault; I warned you from the first. But I ought to have warned you more. I ought to have convinced you that I was doomed to disappoint you. But I *was*, in a way, too proud. You see what my superiority amounts to, I hope!" she went on, raising her voice with a tremor which even then and there Newman thought beautiful. "I am too proud to be honest, I am not too proud to be faithless. I am timid and cold and selfish. I am afraid of being uncomfortable."

"And you call marrying me uncomfortable!" said Newman, staring.

Madame de Cintré blushed a little, and seemed to say that if begging his pardon in words was impudent, she might at least thus mutely express her perfect comprehension of his finding her conduct odious. "It is not marrying you; it is doing all that would go with it. It's the rupture, the defiance, the insisting upon being happy in my own way. What right have I to be happy when—when——" And she paused.

"When what?" said Newman.

"When others have been most unhappy."

"What others?" Newman asked. "What have you to do with any others but me? Besides, you said just now that you wanted happiness, and that you should find it by obeying your mother. You contradict yourself."

"Yes, I contradict myself; that shows you that I am not even intelligent."

"You are laughing at me!" cried Newman. "You are mocking me!"

She looked at him intently, and an observer might have said that she was asking herself whether she might not most quickly end their common pain by confessing

that

he found strangely sweet.

She flushed as with the sense of being only shut up in her pain,

he stands.

he demanded. "What?

I'm

he cried.

had that effect of an easy condition for her

if she ~~might~~ shouldn't

So suffer."

believed her to be

It's as if you were horribly mocking!"

Yet

to some such monstrosity.

that she was mocking him. "No; I am not," she presently said.

"Granting that you are not intelligent," he went on, "that you are weak, that you are common, that you are nothing that I have believed you were—what I ask of you is not an heroic effort, it is a very common effort. There is a great deal on my side to make it easy. The simple truth is that you don't care enough about me to make it."

was what

to be—

possible

for

"I am cold," said Madame de Cintré. "I am as cold as that flowing river."

Newman gave a great rap on the floor with his stick and a long grim laugh. "Good, good!" he cried. "You go altogether too far—you overshoot the mark. There isn't a woman in the world as bad as you would make yourself out. I see your game; it's what I said. You are blackening yourself to whiten others. You don't want to give me up at all; you like me—you like me, I know you do; you have shown it, and I have felt it. After that you may be as cold as you please! They have bullied you, I say; they have tortured you. It's an outrage, and I insist upon saving you from the extravagance of your own generosity. Would you chop off your hand if your mother requested it?"

You ?

heaven help you!

and adored you for it!

Madame de Cintré looked a little frightened. "I spoke of my mother too blindly the other day. I am my own mistress, by law and by her approval. She can do nothing to me; she has done nothing. She has never alluded to those hard words I used about her."

"She gave at this the long sigh of a creature too hard pressed ⊙*

has made you feel them, I'll promise you!" said Newman.

"It's my conscience that makes me feel them."

"Your conscience seems to me rather mixed!" exclaimed Newman, passionately.

"It has been in great trouble, but now it is very clear," said Madame de Cintré. "I don't give you up for any worldly advantage or for any worldly happiness."

extraordinarily

returned ⊙

she nevertheless persisted ⊙

"Oh, you don't give me up for Lord Deepmere, I know," said Newman. "I won't pretend, even to provoke you, that I think that. But that's what your mother and your brother wanted, and your mother, at that villainous ball of hers—I liked it at the time, but the very thought of it now makes me rabid—tried to push him on to make up to you."

"Who told you this?" said Madame de Cintré, softly.

"Not Valentin. I observed it. I guessed it. I didn't know at the time that I was observing it, but it stuck in my memory. And afterwards, you recollect, I saw Lord Deepmere with you in the conservatory. You said then that you would tell me at another time what he had said to you."

"That was before—before *this*," said Madame de Cintré.

"It doesn't matter," said Newman; "and, besides, I think I know. He's an honest little Englishman. He came and told you what your mother was up to—that she wanted him to supplant me; not being a commercial person. If he would make you an offer she would undertake to bring you over and give me the slip. Lord Deepmere isn't very intellectual, so she had to spell it out to him. He said he admired you 'no end,' and that he wanted you to know it; but he didn't like being mixed up with that sort of underhand work, and he came to you and told tales. That was about the amount of it, wasn't it? And then you said you were perfectly happy."

"I don't see why we should talk of Lord Deepmere," said Madame de Cintré. "It was not for that you came here; and about my mother, it doesn't matter what you suspect and what you know. When once my mind has been made up, as it is now, I should not discuss these things. Discussing anything, now, is very idle. We must try and live each as we can. I believe you will be happy again; even, sometimes, when you

he agreed.
is a bath of fire!
she asked with her strange, stricken mildness.
She immediately pleaded.
treachery.
size
she returned.
very vain and only a fresh torment.

think of me. When you do so, think this—that it was not easy, and that I did the best I could. I have things to reckon with that you don't know. I mean I have feelings. I must do as they force me—I must, I must. They would haunt me otherwise," she cried, with vehemence; "they would kill me!"

"I know what your feelings are: they are superstitions! They are the feeling that, after all, though I *am* a good fellow, I have been in business; the feeling that your mother's looks are law and your brother's words are gospel; that you all hang together and that it's a part of the everlasting proprieties that they should have a hand in everything you do. It makes my blood boil. That *is* cold; you are right. And what I feel here," and Newman struck his heart and became more poetical than he knew, "is a glowing fire!"

A spectator less preoccupied than Madame de Cintré's distracted wooer would have felt sure from the first that her appealing calm of manner was the result of violent effort, in spite of which the tide of agitation was rapidly rising. On these last words of Newman's it overflowed, though at first she spoke low, for fear of her voice betraying her. "No, I was not right—I am not cold! I believe that if I am doing what seems so bad, it is not mere weakness and falseness. Mr. Newman, it's like a religion. I can't tell you—I can't! It's cruel of you to insist. I don't see why I shouldn't ask you to believe me—and pity me. It's like a religion. There's a curse upon the house; I don't know what—I don't know why—don't ask me. We must all bear it. I have been too selfish; I wanted to escape from it. You offered me a great chance—besides my liking you. It seemed good to change completely, to break, to go away. And then I admired you. But I can't—it has overtaken and come back to me." Her self-control had now completely abandoned her, and her words were broken with long sobs. "Why do such dreadful things happen to

"they would give me no rest and

perversities and

might

ity.

My dear friend, my best of friends,

"I admired you," she nobly repeated.

"I liked you more than I ever liked any one," she insisted to him with a beauty and purity of clearness; and yet with the sad fallacy of thinking apparently that she made the case less tragic for him by making it more tragic for herself.

us—why is my brother Valentin killed, like a beast, in the midst of his youth and his gaiety and his brightness and all that we loved him for? Why are there things I can't ask about—that I am afraid to know? Why are there places I can't look at, sounds I can't hear? Why is it given to me to choose, to decide, in a case so hard and so terrible as this? I am not meant for that—I am not made for boldness and defiance. I was made to be happy in a quiet natural way." At this Newman gave a most expressive groan, but Madame de Cintré went on: "I was made to do gladly and gratefully what is expected of me. My mother has always been very good to me; that's all I can say. I must not judge her; I must not criticise her. If I did, it would come back to me. I can't change!"

"No," said Newman, bitterly; "*I* must change—if I break in two in the effort!"

"You are different. You are a man; you will get over it. You have all kinds of consolation. You were born—you were trained, to changes. Besides, besides, I shall always think of you."

"I don't care for that!" cried Newman. "You are cruel—you are terribly cruel. God forgive you! You may have the best reasons and the finest feelings in the world; that makes no difference. You are a mystery to me; I don't see how such hardness can go with such loveliness."

Madame de Cintré fixed him a moment with her swimming eyes. "You believe I am hard, then?"

Newman answered her look, and then broke out: "You are a perfect faultless creature! Stay by me!"

"Of course I am hard," she went on. "Whenever we give pain we are hard. And we *must* give pain; that's the world—the hateful miserable world! Ah!" and she gave a long deep sigh, "I can't even say I am glad to have known you—though I am. That too is to wrong you. I can say nothing that is not cruel. There-

beauty

for my life?

she quavered heartbreakingly on:

You'll live, you'll do things, you can't not do good, therefore you can't not be happy: you'll find

dreadfully

anything so divine!"

a sigh as sharp as the shudder of an ague,

priceless

He glared as if at her drowning beyond help; then he

"I'm hard in effect," she pitifully reasoned, "though if ever a creature was innocent in intention

For God's sake, stay

fore let us part, without more of this. Good-bye!" And she put out her hand.

Newman stood and looked at it without taking it, and then raised his eyes to her face. He felt himself like shedding tears of rage. "What are you going to do? Where are you going?"

"Where I shall give no more pain and suspect no more evil. I'm going out of the world."

"Out of the world?"

"I'm going into a convent."

"Into a convent!" Newman repeated the words with the deepest dismay; it was as if she had said she was going into an hospital. "Into a convent—*you!*"

"I told you that it was not for my worldly advantage or pleasure I was leaving you."

But still Newman hardly understood. "You are going to be a nun," he went on, "in a cell—for life—with a gown and white veil?"

"A nun—a Carmelite nun," said Madame de Cintré. "For life, with God's leave."

The idea struck Newman as too dark and horrible for belief, and made him feel as he would have done if she had told him that she was going to mutilate her beautiful face, or drink some potion that would make her mad. He clasped his hands and began to tremble visibly.

"Madame de Cintré, don't, don't! I beseech you! On my knees, if you like, I'll beseech you."

She laid her hand upon his arm, with a tender, pitying, almost reassuring gesture. "You don't understand," she said. "You have wrong ideas. It's nothing horrible. It is only peace and safety. It is to be out of the world, where such troubles as this come to the innocent, to the best. And for life—that's the blessing of it! They can't begin again."

Newman dropped into a chair and sat looking at her with a long inarticulate murmur. That this superb

in them the rising

do you mean

He

a black

and mercy

for incurables.

he

come

cannot

I

You're

The image rose there, at her words,

He

wail.

afflicted him as

woman, in whom he had seen all human grace and household force, should turn from him and all the brightness that he offered her—him and his future and his fortune and his fidelity—to muffle herself in ascetic rags and entomb herself in a cell, was a confounding combination of the inexorable and the grotesque. As the image deepened before him the grotesque seemed to expand and overspread it; it was a reduction to the absurd of the trial to which he was subjected. "You—you a nun ; "you with your beauty defaced—you behind locks and bars! Never, never, if I can prevent it!" And he sprang to his feet with a violent laugh.

"You can't prevent it," said Madame de Cintré, "and it ought—a little—to satisfy you. Do you suppose I will go on living in the world, still beside you, and yet not with you? It is all arranged. Good-bye, good-bye."

This time he took her hand, took it in both his own. "For ever?" he said. Her lips made an inaudible movement and his own uttered a deep imprecation. She closed her eyes as if with the pain of hearing it; then he drew her towards him and clasped her to his breast. He kissed her white face; for an instant she resisted and for a moment she submitted; then, with force, she disengaged herself and hurried away over the long shining floor. The next moment the door closed behind him. Newman made his way out as he could.

CHAPTER XXI.

THERE is a pretty public walk at Poitiers, laid out upon the crest of the high hill around which the little city clusters, planted with thick trees, and looking down upon the fertile fields in which the old English princes

vision spread before him the impossibility turned to the monstrous:

merciless and the impossible.

beauty defaced and your nature wasted—

she returned,

he had

her, and after another

in loud derision.

on

that threw him back panting,

as to leave less of it for his loss;

fought for their right and held it. Newman paced up and down this quiet ~~promenade~~ for the greater part of the next day, and let his eyes wander over the historic prospect; but he would have been sadly at a loss to tell you afterwards ~~whether the latter was~~ made up of coal-fields or of vineyards. He was wholly ~~given up to his grievance~~, of which reflection by no means diminished the ~~weight~~. He feared ~~that Madame de Cintré was irretrievably lost; and yet, as he would have said himself, he didn't see his way clear to giving her up.~~ ~~He~~ found it impossible to turn his back upon Fleurières and its inhabitants; it seemed to him ~~that~~ some germ of hope or reparation must lurk there somewhere if he could only stretch his arm out far enough to pluck it. It was as if he had his hand on a door-knob and were closing his clenched fist upon it: he had thumped, he had called, he had pressed the door with his powerful knee, and shaken it with all his strength, and dead damning silence had answered him. And yet something held him there —something hardened the grasp of his fingers. ~~Newman's~~ satisfaction had been too intense, his whole plan too deliberate and mature, his prospect of happiness too rich and comprehensive, for this fine moral fabric to crumble at a stroke. The very foundation seemed fatally injured, and yet he felt a stubborn desire still to try to save the edifice. He was filled with a sorer sense of wrong than he had ever known, or than he had supposed it possible he should know. To accept his injury and walk away without looking behind him was a stretch of ~~good nature~~ of which he found himself incapable. He looked behind him intently and continually, and what he saw there did n't assuage his resentment. He saw himself trustful, generous, liberal, patient, easy, pocketing frequent irritation and furnishing unlimited modesty. To have eaten humble pie, to have been snubbed and patronised and satirised, and have consented to take it as one of the conditions of the bargain—to have done

precinct

if the latter

possessed by his pang;

Wholly unused to giving up in difficulties, he

ache

His

~~his~~ accommodation

the creature he had thus learned to adore was irretrievably lost; and yet ~~when~~ in what case of ~~[illegible]~~ straight violation of his right of property had he ever merely sat down and groaned? In what case had he not made some attempt at recovery?

this, and done it all for nothing, surely gave one a right to protest. And to be turned off because one was a commercial person! As if he had ever talked or dreamt of the commercial since his connection with the Bellegardes began—as if he had made the least circumstance of the commercial—as if he would not have consented to confound the commercial fifty times a day, if it might have increased by a hair's-breadth the chance of ~~the Bellegardes not playing him a trick!~~ Granted ~~that~~ being commercial was fair ground for ~~having a trick played upon one,~~ how little they knew about the class so designated and its enterprising way of not standing upon trifles! It was in the light of his injury that the weight of ~~Newman's~~ past endurance seemed so heavy; his ~~actual~~ irritation had not been so great, merged as it was in his vision of the cloudless blue that overarched ~~his immediate wooing.~~ But now his sense of outrage was deep, rancorous, and ever-present; he felt ~~that he was a good fellow wronged.~~ As for ~~Madame de Cintré's conduct~~ it struck him with a kind of awe, and the fact that he was powerless to understand it or feel the reality of its motives only ~~deepened the force with which he had attached himself to her.~~ He had never let the fact of her ~~Catholicism~~ trouble him; Catholicism ~~to him was nothing but a name,~~ and to express a mistrust of ~~the form in which her religious feelings had moulded themselves would have seemed to him on his own part a rather pretentious affectation of Protestant zeal.~~ If such superb white flowers as that could bloom in Catholic soil, ~~the soil was not insalubrious.~~ But it was one thing to be a Catholic, and another to turn nun—on your hands! There was something lugubriously comical in the way Newman's thoroughly contemporaneous optimism was confronted with this dusky old-world expedient. To see a woman made for him and for motherhood to his children juggled away in this tragic travesty—it was a thing to rub one's eyes over, a nightmare, an illusion, a

ones

one's being cleverly "sold,"

his not suffering this so much more than commercial treachery!

his

current

his friend's spiritual position, it but moved him to ~~[illegible]~~ dismal mystification

his more intimate relation

they attested its richness

religious faith

her forms of worship would have implied that he had other and finer ones to offer; which was as little as possible be might

was only a name to him

swindled himself ~~[illegible]~~ as he had been confiding

hoax. But the hours passed away without disproving the thing, and leaving him only the after-sense of the vehemence with which he had embraced Madame de Cintré. He remembered her words and her looks; he turned them over and tried to shake the mystery out of them, and to infuse them with an endurable meaning. What had she meant by her feeling being a kind of religion? It was the religion simply of the family laws, the religion of which her implacable little mother was the high priestess. Twist the thing about as her generosity would, the one certain fact was that they had used force against her. Her generosity had tried to screen them, but Newman's heart rose into his throat at the thought that they should go scot-free.

The twenty-four hours wore themselves away, and the next morning Newman sprang to his feet with the resolution to return to Fleurières and demand another interview with Madame de Bellegarde and her son. He lost no time in putting it into practice. As he rolled swiftly over the excellent road in the little calèche furnished him at the inn at Poitiers, he drew forth, as it were, from the very safe place in his mind to which he had consigned it, the last information given him by poor Valentin. Valentin had told him he could do something with it, and Newman thought it would be well to have it at hand. This was of course not the first time, lately, that Newman had given it his attention. It was information in the rough—it was dark and puzzling; but Newman was neither helpless nor afraid. Valentin had evidently meant to put him in possession of a powerful instrument, though he could not be said to have placed the handle very securely within his grasp. But if he had not really told him the secret, he had at least given him the clue to it—a clue of which that queer old Mrs. Bread held the other end. Mrs. Bread had always looked to Newman as if she knew secrets; and as he apparently enjoyed her esteem, he suspected she might be induced to share her knowledge with him. So long as there was only Mrs. Bread to deal with he felt easy. As to what there was to find out, he had only one fear—that it might not be bad enough. Then, when the image of the Marquise and her son rose before him again, standing side by side, the old woman's hand in Urbain's arm, and the same cold ~~unsociable fixedness~~ in the eyes of each, he cried out to himself that the fear was groundless. There was ~~blood in the secret~~ at the very least! He arrived at Fleurières almost in a state of elation; he had satisfied himself, logically, that in the presence of his threat of ~~exposure~~ they would, as he mentally phrased it, rattle down like unwound buckets. He remembered, indeed, that he must first catch his hare—first ascertain what there was to ~~expose~~; but after that, why shouldn't his happiness be as good as new again? Mother and son would drop ~~their lovely victim in terror~~ and take to hiding, and Madame de Cintré, left to herself, would surely come back to him. Give her a chance and she would rise to the surface, return to the light. How could she fail to perceive that his house would ~~be much the most comfortable sort of convent?~~

Newman, as he had done before, left his conveyance at the inn and walked the short remaining distance to the château. When he reached the gate, however, a singular feeling took possession of him—a feeling which, strange as it may seem, had its source in his unfathomable good-nature. He stood there a while, looking through the bars ~~of~~ the large time-stained face ~~of the edifice~~ and wondering to what ~~crime~~ it was that the dark old ~~house, with its~~ flowery name, had given convenient occasion. It had given occasion, first and last, to tyrannies and sufferings enough, Newman said to himself; it was an evil-looking place to live in. Then suddenly, came the reflection: What a horrible rubbish-heap of iniquity to fumble ~~in~~! The attitude of inquisitor turned its ignoble face, and with the same movement

guarded glare

crime in the air

penetration

penetrate;

in terror the soft victim they had mauled

have all the security of a convent and none of the dampness?

at

dwelling, with its

through!

misdeed

beyond

~~Newman~~ declared that the Bellegardes should have another chance. He would appeal once more directly to their sense of fairness, and not to their fear; and if they should be accessible to reason, he need know nothing worse about them than what he already knew. That was bad enough.

The gate-keeper let him in through the same ~~stiff~~ crevice as before, and he passed through the court and over the ~~little~~ rustic bridge on the moat. The door was opened before he had reached it, and, as if to put his clemency to rout with the suggestion of a richer opportunity, Mrs. Bread stood there awaiting him. Her face, as usual, looked as hopelessly blank as the tide-smoothed sea-sand, and her black garments ~~seemed of an intense sable.~~ Newman had already learned ~~that her strange inexpressiveness could be a vehicle for emotion, and he was not surprised at the~~ [illegible] "I thought you would try again, sir. I was looking out for you."

"I'm glad to see you," ~~said Newman~~; "I think you're my friend."

Mrs. Bread looked at him opaquely. "I wish you well, sir; but it's vain wishing now."

"You know, then, how they've treated me?"

"Oh, sir," ~~said Mrs. Bread, drily~~, "I know everything."

~~Newman hesitated a moment.~~ "Everything?"

~~Mrs. Bread gave him a glance somewhat more lucent.~~ "I know at least too much, sir."

"One can never know too much. I congratulate you. I've come to see Madame de Bellegarde and her son," Newman added. "Are they at home? If they're not, I'll wait."

"My lady's always at home," Mrs. Bread replied, "and the Marquis is mostly with her."

"Please, then, tell them—one or the other, or both—that I'm here, and that I ~~desire~~ to see them."

Handwritten revisions:

he

"mean"

of aperture — for so he qualified it —

hung as heavy as if soaked in salt tears.

he answered;

she drily returned,

how interesting she could make the expression of nothing, and he ~~[illegible]~~ scarce knew whether the note struck him as almost dumb or as almost effusive.

Her eyes just visibly lighted.

He frankly enough wondered.

on every scrap of it.

should like

Mrs. Bread hesitated. "May I take a great liberty, sir?"

"You have never taken a liberty but you have justified it," said Newman, with diplomatic urbanity.

Mrs. Bread dropped her wrinkled eyelids as if she were curtsying; but the curtsy stopped there; the occasion was too grave. "You have come to plead with them again, sir? Perhaps you don't know this—that Madame de Cintré returned this morning to Paris."

"Ah, she's gone!" And Newman, groaning, smote the pavement with his stick.

"She has gone straight to the convent—the Carmelites, they call it. I see you know, sir. My lady and the Marquis take it very ill. It was only last night she told them."

"Ah, she had kept it back, then?" cried Newman. "Good, good! And they are very fierce?"

"They are not pleased, [struck out] But they may well dislike it. They tell me it's most dreadful, sir; of all the nuns in Christendom the Carmelites are the worst. You may say they are really not human, sir; they make you give up everything—for ever. And to think of *her* there! If I was one that cried, sir, I could cry."

Newman looked at her an instant. "We mustn't cry, Mrs. Bread; we must act. Go and call them!" And he made a movement to enter farther.

But Mrs. Bread gently checked him. "May I take another liberty? I am told you were with my dearest Mr. Valentin, in his last hours. If you would tell me a word about him! The poor Count was my own boy, sir; for the first year of his life he was hardly out of my arms; I taught him to speak. And the Count spoke so well, sir! He always spoke well to his poor old Bread. When he grew up and took his pleasure he always had a kind word for me. And to die in that wild way! They have a story that he fought with a wine-mer-

Handwritten revisions:

the poor Countess

you know, [struck out] is the sad name.

he cried.

certainly

in the world You have—

highly worked up?"

and ever.

in that destitution!

sat down and

could [struck out] give way at this moment?

poor [struck out] Count Valentine heaven forgive him in his last hours, and I should bless you, sir, if you could tell me

the first words he spoke—and he spoke so beautifully, didn't he, sir?

dear

He

took a forward step.

and still less must we sit down. We must stand up and act. Please let them know?

chant. I can't believe that, sir! And was he in great pain?"

"You are a wise kind old woman, Mrs. Bread," said Newman. "I hoped I might see you with my own children in your arms. Perhaps I shall yet." And he put out his hand. Mrs. Bread looked for a moment at his open palm, and then, as if fascinated by the novelty of the gesture, extended her own ladylike ~~fingers.~~ Newman held ~~her hand~~ firmly and deliberately, fixing his eyes [redacted]pon her. "You want to know all about [redacted] ~~Valentin~~?" [redacted]d.

"It would be a [redacted] pleasure, sir."

"I can tell you everything. Can you sometimes leave this place?"

"The château, sir? I really don't know. I never tried."

"Try, then; try hard. Try this evening, at dusk. Come to me in the old ruin there on the hill, in the court before the church. I will wait for you there; I [redacted] something very important to tell you. An old woman like you can do as she pleases."

Mrs. Bread stared, wondering, with parted lips. "Is it from the Count, sir?" ~~she asked.~~

"From the Count—from his deathbed," ~~said Newman.~~

"I will come, then. I will be bold, for once, for *him*."

She led Newman into the great drawing-room with which he had already made acquaintance, and retired to ~~execute his commands. Newman~~ waited a long time; at last he was on the point of ringing and repeating his request. He was looking round him for a bell when the Marquis came in with his mother on his arm. It will be seen that Newman had a logical mind when I say that he declared to himself, in perfect good faith, as a result of Valentin's [redacted], that his adversaries looked grossly wicked. "There is no mistake about it now," he said to himself as they advanced. "They're a bad

it

member ⊙

the Count?"

terrible

I've

dear

grand

dear

damnable

and capable of the blackest evil ⊙

supreme communication,

carry his message ⊙ He

lot; they have pulled off the mask." Madame de Bellegarde and her son certainly bore in their faces the signs of extreme perturbation; they ~~looked like~~ people who had passed a sleepless night. Confronted, moreover, with an annoyance which they hoped they had disposed of, it was not natural ~~that~~ they should have ~~any very tender glances to bestow upon Newman.~~ He stood before them, and ~~such eyebeams as they found available they levelled at him~~; Newman feeling as if the door of a sepulchre had suddenly been opened. and the damp darkness were being exhaled.

"You see I have come back," he ~~said~~. "I have come to try again."

"It would be ridiculous," ~~said M. de Bellegarde~~, "to pretend that we are glad to see you or that we don't question the taste of your visit."

"Oh, don't talk about taste," ~~said Newman with a laugh, "or~~ that will bring us round to yours! If I consulted my taste I certainly shouldn't come to see you. Besides, I will make as short work as you please. ~~Promise me to~~ raise the blockade—~~to~~ set Madame de Cintré at liberty—and ~~I will retire instantly~~."

"We hesitated as to whether we would see you," said Madame de Bellegarde; "and we were on the point of declining the honour. But it seemed to me ~~that~~ we should act with civility, as we have always done, and I wished to have the satisfaction of informing you that there are certain weaknesses ~~that~~ people of our way of feeling can be guilty of but once."

"You may be weak but once, but you will be audacious many times, Madam," Newman ~~answered~~. "I didn't come, however, for conversational purposes. I came to say this simply: that if you will write immediately to your daughter that you withdraw your opposition to her marriage, ~~I will~~ take care of the rest. You don't want ~~her to turn nun~~—you know more about the horrors of it than I do. Marrying a commercial person is better

bad

varnished mask

were plainly

of the coldest glare they could command he had the full benefit;

met their visitor with conciliatory looks

he said, however, with a tentative freshness

the Marquis returned,

rang out

to me you'll

to make of her a cloistered nun—

I'll retire on the spot."

Give me a guarantee that you'll

that you'll

and Newman permitted himself perhaps the harshest laugh into which he had ever broken; " that would

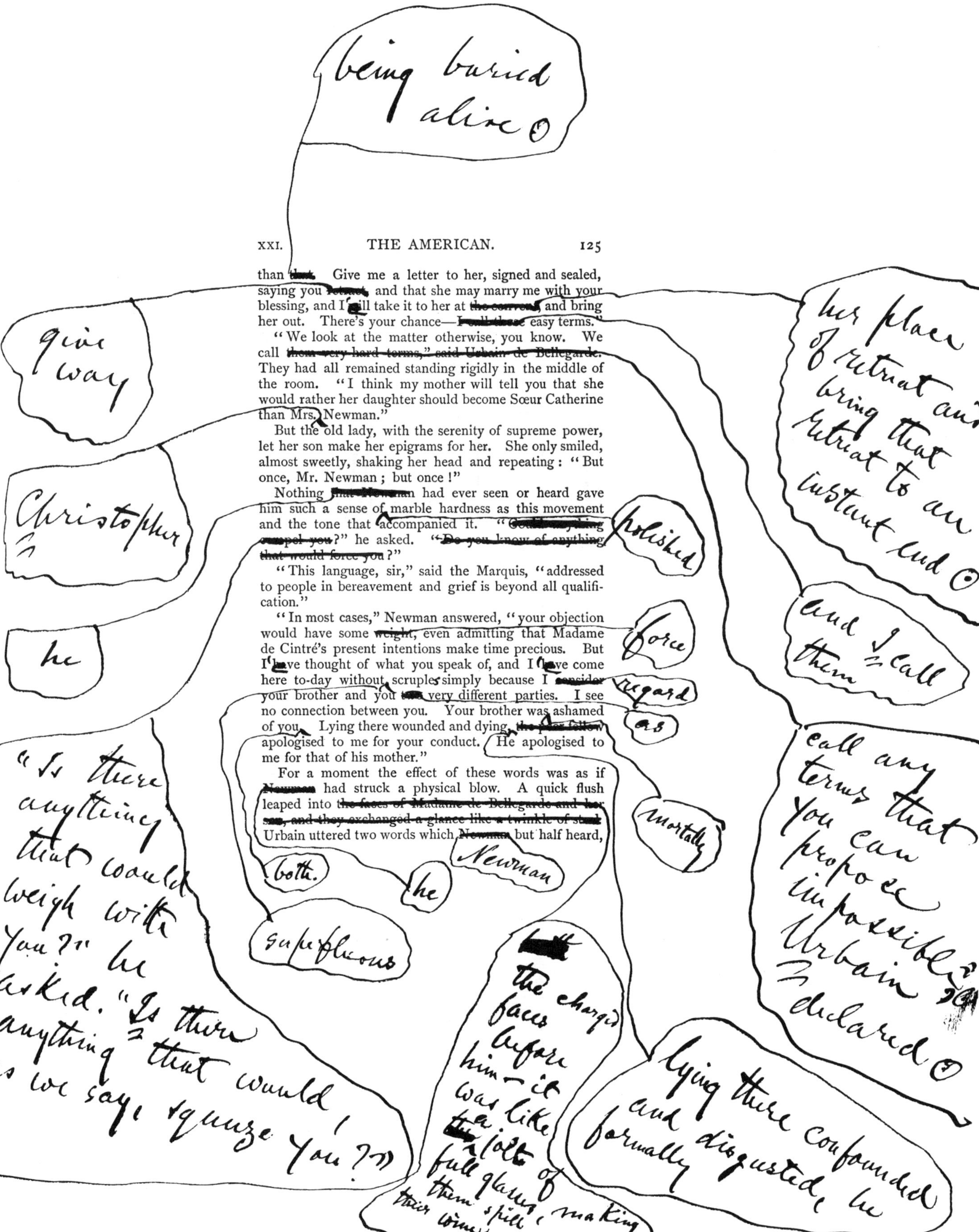

XXI. THE AMERICAN. 125

than that. Give me a letter to her, signed and sealed, saying you retract, and that she may marry me with your blessing, and I will take it to her at the convent and bring her out. There's your chance—I call these easy terms."

"We look at the matter otherwise, you know. We call them very hard terms," said Urbain de Bellegarde. They had all remained standing rigidly in the middle of the room. "I think my mother will tell you that she would rather her daughter should become Sœur Catherine than Mrs. Newman."

But the old lady, with the serenity of supreme power, let her son make her epigrams for her. She only smiled, almost sweetly, shaking her head and repeating: "But once, Mr. Newman; but once!"

Nothing that Newman had ever seen or heard gave him such a sense of marble hardness as this movement and the tone that accompanied it. "Could anything compel you?" he asked. "Do you know of anything that would force you?"

"This language, sir," said the Marquis, "addressed to people in bereavement and grief is beyond all qualification."

"In most cases," Newman answered, "your objection would have some weight, even admitting that Madame de Cintré's present intentions make time precious. But I have thought of what you speak of, and I have come here to-day without scruple simply because I consider your brother and you two very different parties. I see no connection between you. Your brother was ashamed of you. Lying there wounded and dying, the poor fellow apologised to me for your conduct. He apologised to me for that of his mother."

For a moment the effect of these words was as if Newman had struck a physical blow. A quick flush leaped into the faces of Madame de Bellegarde and her son, and they exchanged a glance like a twinkle of steel. Urbain uttered two words which Newman but half heard,

but of which the aftersense came to him in the reverberation of the sound. "*Le misérable!*"

"You show little respect for the afflicted living," said Madame de Bellegarde, "but you might at least respect the helpless dead. Don't profane — don't touch with your unholy hands — the memory of my innocent son."

"I speak the simple sacred truth," Newman now imperturbably proceeded, "and, speaking it for a purpose, I desire you shall have no genuine doubt of it. You made Valentine's last hour an hour of anguish, and my friend's generous spirit repudiates your abominable act."

Urbain de Bellegarde had, from whatever emotion, turned so pale that it might have been at the evoked spectre of his brother; but not for an appreciable instant did his mother lower her crest. "You have *beau jeu*, as we say, before the silence of the grave, for every calumny and every insult. But I don't know," she admirably wound up, "that it in the least matters."

"Ah, I don't know that poor Valentine's apology particularly does either," Newman reflectively conceded. "I pitied him certainly more for having to utter it than I felicitate myself even now for your having to hear it."

The Marquise wrapt herself for a minute in a distinction so entire, so of her whole being, as he could feel, that she fairly appeared rather to contract than to expand with the intensity and dignity of it; and out of the heart of this withdrawn extravagance her final estimate of their case sounded clear. "To have broken with you, sir, almost consoles me; and you can judge how much that says! Urbain, open the door." She turned away with an imperious motion to her son and passed rapidly down the length of the room. The Marquis went with her and held the door open. Newman was left standing.

He lifted ~~his~~ finger, as a sign to M. de Bellegarde, who closed the door behind his mother and stood waiting. Newman slowly advanced, more silent, for the moment, ~~than~~ life. The two men stood face to face. Then ~~Newman~~ had a singular sensation; he felt his sense of ~~injury~~ almost brimming over into ~~jocularity~~. "Come," he said, "you don't treat me well, ~~at~~ least, admit that."

M. de Bellegarde looked at him from head to foot, and then, in the most delicate best-bred voice, "I ~~detest~~ you personally," ~~he said~~.

"That's the way I feel to you, but for politeness' sake I don't say it, ~~said Newman.~~ It's singular I should want so much to be your brother-in-law, but I can't give it up. Let me try once more." And ~~he~~ paused a moment. "You ~~have a secret—you have a skeleton in the closet.~~" M. de Bellegarde continued to look at him hard, but ~~Newman could not see whether~~ his eyes betrayed anything; the ~~look~~ of his eyes was always so strange. Newman paused again, and then went on. "~~You and your mother have committed a crime.~~" At this M. de Bellegarde's eyes certainly did change; they ~~seemed to~~ flicker, like blown candles. Newman could ~~see that he was profoundly startled; but there was something admirable in his self-control.~~

"Continue," ~~said M. de Bellegarde.~~

Newman lifted a finger and made it waver a little in the air. "Need I continue? You ~~are trembling.~~"

"Pray, where did you obtain this interesting information?" ~~M. de Bellegarde asked very softly.~~

"I shall be strictly accurate," said Newman. "I won't pretend to know more than I do. At present that ~~is~~ all I know. You ~~have~~ done something ~~that you must hide,~~ something that would damn you if it were known, something that would disgrace the name you ~~are~~ so proud of. I don't know what it is, but I've reason to believe I can find out -- though of course I had much rather not. Persist in your present course, however, and I will find out. Depart from that course, let your sister go in peace, and then fancy how I'll leave you alone. It's a bargain?"

M. de Bellegarde's face looked to him now like a mirror, very smooth fine glass, breathed upon and blurred; but what he would have liked still better to see was a spreading, disfiguring crack. There was something of that, it was true, in the grimace with with the Marquis brought out: "My brother regaled you with this infamy?"

Newman scantly hesitated. "Yes -- it was a treat!"

The grimace, if anything, deepened. "He must at the last have raved then horribly."

"He raved if I find nothing out. If I find -- what you know I may find -- he was beautifully inspired."

M. de Bellegarde's shoulders declined even a shrug. "Eh, sir, find what you please!"

"What I say has no weight with you?" Newman was thus reduced to asking.

"That's for you to judge."

"No, it's for *you* to judge -- at your leisure. Think it over; feel yourself all round; I'll give you an hour or two. I can't give you more, for how do we know how tight they mayn't be locking your sister up? Talk it over with your mother; let her judge what weight *she* attaches. She's constitutionally less accessible to pressure than you, I think; but *enfin*, as you say, you'll see. I'll go and wait in the village, at the inn; where I beg you to let me know as soon as possible. Say by three o'clock. A simple *yes* or *no* on paper will do. That will refer to your attaching or not attaching what we call weight; or better still, to your consenting or refusing to take your hands off Madame de Cintré. Only you understand that if you do engage again I shall expect you this time to stick to your bargain." And with this Newman opened the door to let himself out. The Marquis made no motion, and Newman paused but for a last emphasis. "I can give you, let me add, no *more* than the time." Then he turned away altogether and passed out of the house.

He was extremely excited by what he had been doing, for it was inevitable that there should be a certain emotion in calling up the spectre of dishonour before a family a thousand years old. But he went back to the inn and contrived to wait there, deliberately, for the next two hours. He thought it more than probable that Urbain de Bellegarde would give no sign; for an answer to his challenge, in either sense, would be a confession of guilt. What he most expected was silence—in other words, defiance. But he prayed that, as he imaged it, his shot might bring them down. It did bring, by three o'clock, a note, delivered by a footman; a note addressed in Urbain de Bellegarde's handsome English hand. It ran as follows:—

"I cannot deny myself the satisfaction of letting you know that I return to Paris to-morrow, with my mother, in order that we may see my sister and confirm her in the resolution which is the most effectual reply to your audacious pertinacity.

"HENRI-URBAIN DE BELLEGARDE."

Newman put the letter into his pocket, and continued his walk up and down the inn parlour. He had spent most of his time, for the past week, in walking up and down. He continued to measure the length of the little *salle* of the Armes de France until the day began to wane, when he went out to keep his rendezvous with Mrs. Bread. The path which led up the hill to the ruin was easy to find, and Newman in a short time had followed it to the top. He passed beneath the rugged arch of the castle-wall, and looked about him in the early dusk for an old woman in black. The castle yard was empty, but the door of the church was open. Newman went into the little nave, and of course found a deeper dusk than without. A couple of tapers, however, twinkled on the altar, and just enabled him to perceive a figure seated

an emotion should attach to

would

since

Urbain's

a recognition of his reference

a delirium extravagant even as a result of your wound

forth

He

leading

helped him to distinguish

by one of the pillars. Closer inspection helped him to recognise Mrs. Bread, in spite of the fact that she was dressed with unwonted splendour. She wore a large black silk bonnet with imposing bows of crape, and an old black satin dress disposed itself in vaguely lustrous folds about her person. She had judged it proper to the occasion to appear in her stateliest apparel. She had been sitting with her eyes fixed upon the ground, but when Newman passed before her she looked up at him and then she rose.

"Are you a Catholic, Mrs. Bread?" he asked.

"No, sir; I'm a good Church of England woman, very Low," she answered. But I thought I should be safer in here than outside. I was never out in the evening before, sir."

"We shall be safer," said Newman, "where no one can hear us." And he led the way back into the castle court and then followed a path beside the church, which he was sure must lead into another part of the ruin. He was not deceived. It wandered along the crest of the hill and terminated before a fragment of wall pierced by a rough aperture which had once been a door. Through this aperture Newman passed, and found himself in a nook peculiarly favourable to quiet conversation, as probably many an earnest couple, otherwise assorted than our friends, had assured themselves. The hill sloped abruptly away, and on the remnant of its crest were scattered two or three fragments of stone. Beneath, over the plain, lay the gathered twilight, through which, in the near distance, gleamed two or three lights from the château. Mrs. Bread rustled slowly after her guide, and Newman, satisfying himself that one of the fallen stones was steady, proposed to her to sit upon it. She cautiously complied, and he placed himself, upon another, near her.

led

gown

invoked for

the highest dignity of dress.

of this faith,

indeed,

She said.

he returned,

to find

on another.

XXII.

"I AM very much obliged to you for coming," Newman said. "I hope it won't get you into trouble."

"I don't think I shall be missed. My lady, in these days, is not fond of having me about her." This was said with a certain fluttered eagerness which increased Newman's sense of having inspired the old woman with confidence.

"From the first, you know," he answered, "you took an interest in my prospects. You were on my side. That gratified me, I assure you. And now that you know what they have done to me, I am sure you are with me all the more."

"They have not done well—I must say it," said Mrs. Bread. "But you mustn't blame the poor Countess; they pressed her hard."

"I would give a million of dollars to know what they did to her!" cried Newman.

Mrs. Bread sat with a dull, oblique gaze fixed upon the lights of the château. "They worked on her feelings; they knew that was the way. She is a delicate creature. They made her feel wicked. She is only too good."

"Ah, they made her feel wicked," said Newman, slowly; and then he repeated it. "They made her feel wicked—they made her feel wicked." The words seemed to him for the moment a vivid description of infernal ingenuity.

"It was because she was so good that she gave up—poor sweet lady!" added Mrs. Bread.

"But she was better to them than to me," said Newman.

"She was afraid," said Mrs. Bread, very confidently; "she has always been afraid, or at least for a long time.

Handwritten revisions:

he began with observing

dry lucidity which added to his

his friend

he remarked, "to know the secret of such successful pressure as that."

represented

cruelly

and quite as to the point of high interest, a wondrous triumph of infernal art.

Her fear was there—it was always like a pit that yawned for her.

rejoined

That was the real trouble, sir. She was a fair peach, I may say, with just one little speck. She had one little sad spot. You pushed her into the sunshine, sir, and it almost disappeared. Then they pulled her back into the shade, and in a moment it began to spread. Before we knew it she was gone. She was a delicate creature."

This singular attestation of Madame de Cintré's delicacy, for all its singularity, set Newman's wound aching afresh. "I see knew something bad about her mother."

"No, sir, she knew nothing," Mrs. Bread ing her head very stiff and her eyes the glimmering windows of the château.

"She guessed something then, or suspected it."

"She was afraid to know," said Mrs. Bread.

"But *you* know, at any rate."

She slowly turned her vague eyes squeezing her hands together in her lap. "You are not quite faithful, sir. I thought it was to tell me about you asked me to come

"Oh, the more we talk of the better," "That's exactly what I want. I was with him, as I told you, in his last hour. He was in a great deal of pain, but he was quite himself. You know what that means; he was bright and and clever."

"Oh, he would always be clever, sir," said Mrs. Bread. "And did he know of your trouble?"

"Yes he guessed it of himself."

"And what did he say to it?"

"He said it was a disgrace to his name—but it was not the first."

"Lord, Lord!" murmured Mrs. Bread.

"He said his mother and his brother had once put their heads together

"You shouldn't have listened to that, sir."

"Perhaps not. But I *did* listen, and I don't forget it. Now I want to know what it is they did."

Mrs. Bread gave a soft moan. "And you ~~have~~ enticed me up into this strange place to tell you?"

"Don't be alarmed," said Newman. "I won't say a word that shall be disagreeable to you. Tell me as it suits you and when it suits you. Only remember that it was ~~Mr. Valentin's~~ last wish that you should."

"Did he say that?"

"He said it with his last breath: 'Tell Mrs. Bread I told you to ask her.'"

"Why didn't he tell you himself?"

"It was too long a story for a dying man; he ~~had no breath left in his body.~~ He could only say that he wanted me to know—that, wronged as I was, it was my right to know."

"But how will it help you, sir?" ~~said Mrs. Bread.~~

"That's for me to decide. ~~Mr. Valentin~~ believed it would, and that's why he told me. Your name was almost the last word he spoke."

~~Mrs. Bread was evidently awestruck by this statement~~; she shook her clasped hands slowly up and down. "~~Excuse me, sir,~~ [illegible] if I take a great liberty. Is it the solemn truth you are speaking? I *must* ask you that; must I not, sir?"

"There's no offence. It *is* the solemn truth; I solemnly swear it. ~~Mr. Valentin~~ himself would certainly have told me more if he had been able."

"Oh, sir, if he ~~knew~~ more!"

"Don't you suppose [illegible]"

"There's no saying what he knew about anything," ~~said Mrs. Bread with a mild head-shake.~~ "He was ~~so mightily clever.~~ He could make you believe he knew things ~~that~~ he didn't, and that he didn't know others ~~that~~ he had better not have known."

"I suspect he knew something about his brother that ~~kept~~ the Marquis ~~civil to him~~," Newman propounded;

- tell me
- the Count's
- The Count
- was incapable of the effort and the pain ⊙
- she asked ⊙
- This statement ~~produced~~ in her a sharp checked convulsion;
- Pardon me
- made
- mind his eye (")
- wailingly (almost wailingly) she conceded ⊙
- he did know?")
- clever to that grand extent ⊙
- The Count

"he made the Marquis feel him. What he wanted now was to put me in his place; he wanted to give me a chance to make the Marquis feel *me*."

"Mercy on us," cried the old waiting-woman, "how wicked we all are!"

"I don't know," said Newman; "some of us are wicked, certainly. I am very angry, I am very sore, and I am very bitter, but I don't know that I am wicked. I have been cruelly injured. They have hurt me and I want to hurt them. I don't deny that; on the contrary, I tell you plainly that that is the use I want to make of [illegible]."

Mrs. Bread seemed to hold her breath. "You want to publish them—you want to shame them?"

"I want to bring them down—down, down, down! I want to turn the tables upon them—I want to mortify them as they mortified me. They took me up into a high place and made me stand there for all the world to see me, and then they stole behind me and pushed me into this bottomless pit, where I lie howling and gnashing my teeth! I made a fool of myself before all their friends; but I shall make something worse of them."

This passionate sally, which Newman uttered with the greater fervour that it was the first time he had had a chance to say all this aloud, kindled two small sparks in Mrs. Bread's fixed eyes. "I suppose you have a right to your anger, sir; but think of the dishonour you will draw down on Madame de Cintré."

"Madame de Cintré is buried alive," cried Newman. "What is honour or dishonour to her? The door of the tomb is at this moment closing behind her."

"Yes, it is most awful," moaned Mrs. Bread.

"She has moved off, like her brother Valentin, to give me room to work. It's as if it were done on purpose."

"Surely," said Mrs. Bread, apparently impressed by the ingenuity of this reflection. She was silent for some moments; then she added: "And would you bring my lady before the courts?"

"The courts care nothing for my lady," Newman replied. "If she has committed a crime, she will be nothing for the courts but a wicked old woman."

"And will they hang her, sir?"

"That depends upon what she has done." And Newman eyed Mrs. Bread intently.

"It would break up the family most terribly, sir!"

"It's time such a family should be broken up!" said Newman, with a laugh.

he outrageously declared.

"And me at my age out of place, sir!" sighed Mrs. Bread.

"Oh, I will take care of you! You shall come and live with me. You shall be my housekeeper, or anything you like. I will pension you for life."

You shall sit and be waited on and twiddle your thumbs.

high

He

"Dear, dear, sir, you think of everything." And she seemed to fall a-brooding.

Newman watched her a while, and then he said suddenly: "Ah, Mrs. Bread, you are too fond of my lady!"

be

such great

an extraordinary place,

bent on her his large benevolence while she nursed

h

She looked at him as quickly. "I wouldn't have you say that, sir. I don't think it any part of my duty to be fond of my lady. I have served her faithfully this many a year; but if she were to die to-morrow, I believe, before Heaven, I shouldn't shed a tear for her." Then after a pause, "I have no reason to love her!" Mrs. Bread added. "The most she has done for me has been not to turn me out of the house." Newman felt that decidedly his companion was more and more confidential—that, if luxury is corrupting, Mrs. Bread's conservative habits were already relaxed by the spiritual comfort of this preconcerted interview, in a remarkable locality, with a free-spoken millionaire. All his native shrewdness admonished him that his part was simply to let her take her time—let the charm of the occasion work. So he said nothing; he only looked at her

~~kindly. Mrs. Bread sat nursing~~ her lean elbows. "My lady once did me a great wrong," she went on at last. "She has a terrible tongue when she ~~[illegible]~~. It was many a year ago, but I have never forgotten it. I have never mentioned it to a human creature; I have kept my grudge to myself. I daresay I have been wicked, but my grudge has grown old with me. It has grown good for nothing, too, I daresay; but it has lived ~~along~~ as I have lived. It will die when I die—not before!"

"And what *is* your grudge?" Newman asked.

Mrs. Bread dropped her eyes and hesitated. "If I were a foreigner, sir, I should make less of telling you; it comes harder to a decent Englishwoman. But I sometimes think I have picked up too many foreign ways. What I was telling you belongs to a time when I was much younger and ~~very~~ different ~~looking~~ to what I am now. I had a very high colour, sir, if you can believe it; indeed I was a very smart ~~lass~~. My lady was younger, too, and the late Marquis was youngest of all—I mean in the way he went on, sir; he had a very high spirit; ~~he was a magnificent man~~. He was fond of his pleasure, like most foreigners, and it must be owned ~~that~~ he sometimes went rather below him to take it. My lady was often jealous, and, if you'll believe it, sir, she did me the honour to ~~be jealous of me~~. One day I had a red ribbon in my cap, and ~~my lady~~ flew out at me and ordered me to take it off. She accused me of putting it on to make the Marquis look at me. I don't know that I was impertinent, but I spoke up like an honest girl, and didn't count my words. A red ribbon indeed! As if it was my ribbons the Marquis looked at! My lady knew afterwards that I was perfectly respectable, but she never said a word to show ~~that~~ she believed it. But the Marquis did ~~!~~ Mrs. Bread presently added; ~~I~~ took off my red ribbon and put it away in a drawer, where I have kept it to this day. It's faded, now, it's a very pale pink; but there it lies. My grudge has faded too; the red has all gone out of it; but it lies here yet." And Mrs. Bread stroked her black satin bodice.

Newman listened with interest to this decent narrative, which seemed to have opened up the deeps of memory to his companion. Then, as she remained silent, and seemed ~~to be losing~~ herself in retrospective meditation upon her perfect respectability, he ventured upon a short cut to his goal. "So Madame de Bellegarde was jealous; I see. And ~~M. de Bellegarde~~ admired pretty women, without distinction of class. I suppose one mustn't be hard upon him, for they probably didn't all behave so properly as you. But years afterwards it could hardly have been jealousy that turned ~~Madame de Bellegarde~~ into a criminal."

Mrs. Bread gave a weary sigh. "We are using dreadful words, sir, but I don't care now. I see you have your idea, and I have no will of my own. My will was the will of my children, as I called them; but I have lost my children now. They are dead—I may say it of both of them; and what should I care for the living? What is any one in the house to me now—what am I to them? My lady objects to me—she has objected to me these thirty years. I should have been glad to be something to young Madame ~~de Bellegarde~~, though I never was nurse to the present Marquis. When he was a baby I was too young; they wouldn't trust me with him. But his wife told her own maid, Mamselle Clarisse, the opinion she had of me. Perhaps you would like to hear it, sir."

"Oh, ~~immensely," said Newman.~~

"She said that if I would sit in her children's school-room I should do very well for a penwiper! When things have come to that I don't think I need stand upon ceremony."

"~~Decidedly not," said Newman.~~ "Go on, Mrs. Bread."

rather to love

yet vivid

the Marquis

the Marquise

Urbain

"I never heard of anything so vicious!" Newman declared.

"Wouldn't I?" Newman almost panted.

Mrs. Bread, however, relapsed again into troubled ~~dumbness~~, and all ~~Newman~~ could do was to fold his arms and wait. But at last she appeared to have set her memories in order. "It was when the late Marquis was an old man and his eldest son had been two years married. It was when the time came on for marrying Mademoiselle Claire; that's the way they talk of it here, you know, sir. The Marquis's health was bad; he was ~~very much~~ broken down. My lady had picked out M. de Cintré, for no good reason that I could see. But there are reasons, I very well know, that are beyond me, and you must be high in the world to ~~understand them~~. Old M. de Cintré was very high, and my lady thought him almost as good as herself; that's saying ~~a good deal~~. Mr. Urbain took sides with his mother, as he always did. The trouble, I believe, was that my lady would give ~~very little money~~, and all the other gentlemen asked more. It was only M. de Cintré ~~that was satisfied~~. The Lord willed it he should have that one soft spot; it was the only one he had. He may have ~~been~~ very grand ~~in his birth~~, and he certainly ~~was very~~ grand ~~in his bows and speeches; but that was all the grandeur he had~~. I think he was like what I have heard of comedians; not that I have ever seen one. But I know he painted his face. He might paint it all he would; he could never make me like it! The Marquis couldn't abide him, and declared that sooner than take such a husband as that, Mademoiselle Claire should take none at all. He and my lady had a great scene; it came even to our ears in the servants' hall. It was not their first quarrel, if the truth must be told. They were not a loving couple, but they didn't often come to words, because ~~I think~~ neither ~~of~~ them ~~thought the other's doings worth the trouble~~. My lady had long ago got over ~~her jealousy, and she had taken to indifference~~. In this, I must say, they were well matched. The Marquis ~~was very easy going; he had a most gentlemanly temper~~.

Reserve

he

, as you might talk of sending a heifer to market.

catch what's under and behind.

Sadly

very little money—to go with the young lady,

was content.

as much as you please.

had

'minding'—minding, I mean, the worst, for she had had plenty of assistance.

to waste; they had too much use for them otherwise.

Who

connections,

after a while

I think, was the measure of his honour.

made grand bows and ~~compliments~~ speeches and flourishes; but that,

He got angry ~~only~~ once a year, but then it was very bad. He always took to bed directly afterwards. This time I speak of he took to bed as usual, but he never got up again. I'm afraid ~~the poor gentleman~~ was paying for ~~his dissipation~~; isn't it true they mostly do, sir, when they get old? My lady and Mr. Urbain kept quiet, but I know my lady wrote letters to M. de Cintré. The Marquis got worse, and the doctors gave him up. My lady ~~she~~ gave him up too, and if the truth must be told she gave him up ~~gladly.~~ When once he was out of the way she could do what she ~~pleased~~ with her daughter, and it was all arranged that my poor ~~innocent child~~ should be handed over to M. de Cintré. You don't know what Mademoiselle was in those days, sir; she was the sweetest ~~young creature in France, and knew as~~ little of what was going on around her as the lamb ~~does~~ ~~of~~ the butcher. I used to nurse ~~the Marquis, and I~~ was always in his room. It was here at Fleurières, in the autumn. We had a doctor from Paris, who came and stayed two or three weeks in the house. Then there came two others, and there was a consultation, and these two others, as I said, declared ~~that~~ the Marquis couldn't ~~recover~~. After this they went off, pocketing their fees, but the other one ~~stayed~~ and did what he could. ~~The~~ ~~Marquis~~ himself kept crying out that he ~~wouldn't die,~~ ~~that he didn't want to die~~, that he would live and look after his daughter. Mademoiselle Claire and the ~~Vicomte~~ —that was Mr. Valentin, you know—were both in the house. The doctor was a clever man—that I could see myself—and I think he believed that the Marquis might ~~get well~~. We took good care of him, he and I, between us, and one day, when my lady had almost ordered her mourning, my patient suddenly began to mend. He ~~got better and better, till~~ the doctor said he was out of danger. What was killing him was the dreadful fits of pain in his stomach. But little by little they stopped, ~~and the poor Marquis began to make his jokes again.~~

was one who would but too easily go as you please—he had the temper of the perfect gentleman.

the free life he had led;

he was

— he kept to that;

wished

child and treasure.

as I've seen her clap together sharp enough to make you jump the covers of a book she has read enough of

come round.

gentlest, fairest!—and guessed as

my unhappy master and

took a better turn and came up so that

recover with the right things done.

stopped over

M. de Bellegarde

Vicomte

refused to be given up, that he insisted on getting better.

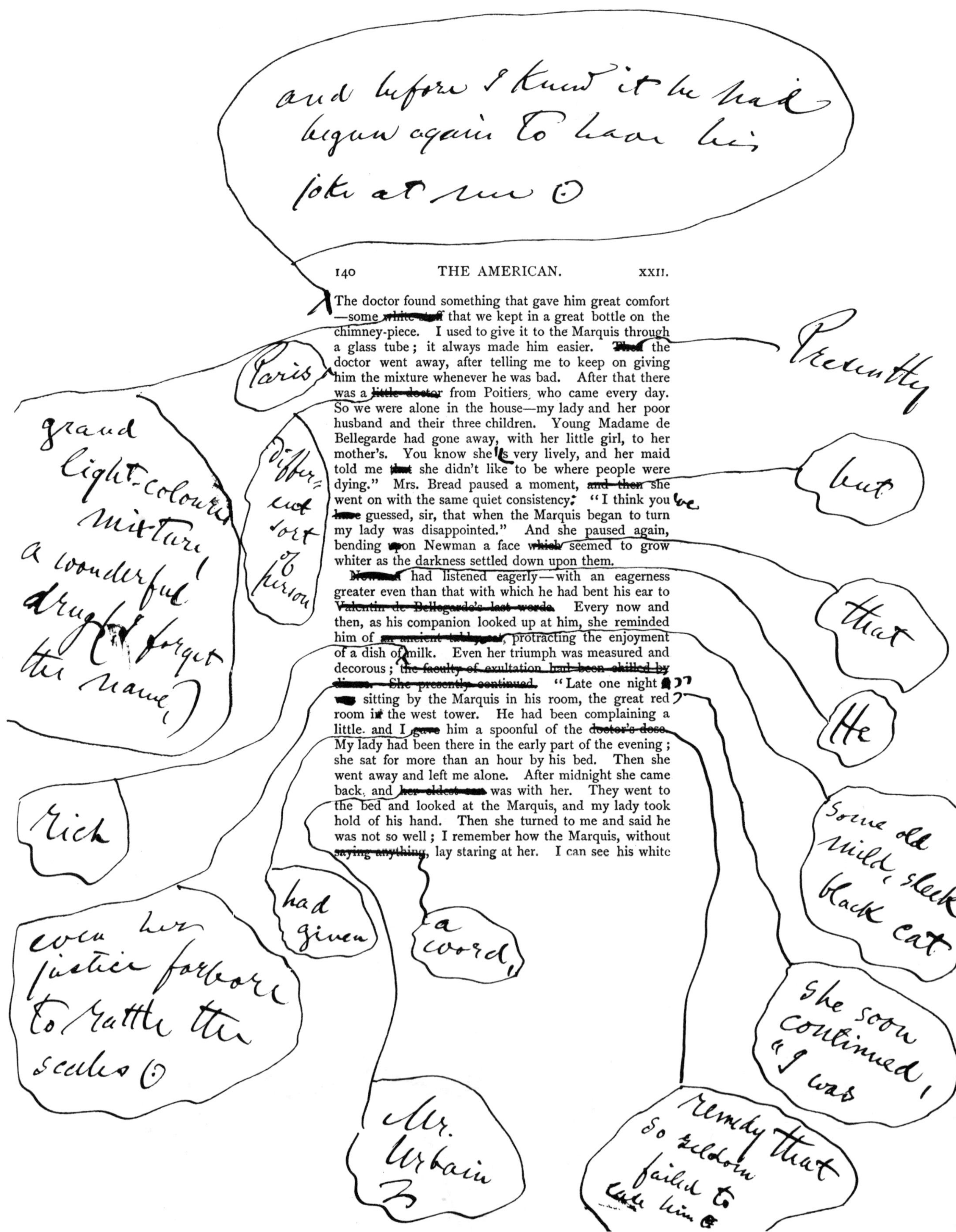

140 THE AMERICAN. XXII.

The doctor found something that gave him great comfort —some white stuff that we kept in a great bottle on the chimney-piece. I used to give it to the Marquis through a glass tube; it always made him easier. Then the doctor went away, after telling me to keep on giving him the mixture whenever he was bad. After that there was a little doctor from Poitiers, who came every day. So we were alone in the house—my lady and her poor husband and their three children. Young Madame de Bellegarde had gone away, with her little girl, to her mother's. You know she's very lively, and her maid told me that she didn't like to be where people were dying." Mrs. Bread paused a moment, and then she went on with the same quiet consistency. "I think you have guessed, sir, that when the Marquis began to turn my lady was disappointed." And she paused again, bending upon Newman a face which seemed to grow whiter as the darkness settled down upon them.

and before I knew it he had begun again to have his joke at me.
Paris
Presently
grand light-coloured mixture, a wonderful drug (I forget the name)
different sort of person
but
've
that
He
Rich
Some old mild, sleek black cat
had given
a word,
even her justice forbore to rattle the scales.
She soon continued, "I was
Mr. Urbain
remedy that so seldom failed to ease him.

Newman had listened eagerly—with an eagerness greater even than that with which he had bent his ear to Valentin de Bellegarde's last words. Every now and then, as his companion looked up at him, she reminded him of an ancient tabby cat, protracting the enjoyment of a dish of milk. Even her triumph was measured and decorous; the faculty of exultation had been chilled by disuse. She presently continued. "Late one night I was sitting by the Marquis in his room, the great red room in the west tower. He had been complaining a little, and I gave him a spoonful of the doctor's dose. My lady had been there in the early part of the evening; she sat for more than an hour by his bed. Then she went away and left me alone. After midnight she came back, and her eldest son was with her. They went to the bed and looked at the Marquis, and my lady took hold of his hand. Then she turned to me and said he was not so well; I remember how the Marquis, without saying anything, lay staring at her. I can see his white face, at this moment, in the great black square between the bed-curtains. I said I didn't think he was very bad; and she told me to go to bed—she would sit a while with him. When ~~the Marquis~~ saw me going he gave a ~~sort of groan~~, and called out to me not to leave him; but Mr. Urbain opened the door for me and pointed the way out. The present Marquis—perhaps you have noticed, sir—has a very ~~proud~~ way of giving orders, and I was there to take orders. I went to my room, but I wasn't easy; I couldn't tell you why. I didn't undress; I sat there waiting and listening. For what would you have said, sir? I couldn't have told you; ~~for~~ surely a poor gentleman might be ~~comfortable~~ with his wife and his son. It was as if I expected to hear ~~the Marquis~~ moan~~ing~~ after me again. I listened, but I heard nothing. It was a very still night; I never knew a night so still. At last the very stillness itself seemed to frighten me, and I came out of my room and went very softly down-stairs. In the anteroom, outside of ~~the Marquis's~~ chamber, I found ~~Mr. Urbain~~ walking up and down. He asked me what I wanted, and I said I ~~came back~~ to relieve my lady. He said *he* would relieve my lady, and ordered me back to bed; but as I stood there, unwilling to turn away, the door of the room opened and my lady came out. I noticed she was very pale; she was ~~very~~ strange. She looked a moment at the Count and at me, and then ~~she~~ held out her arms to the Count. He went to her, and she fell upon him and hid her face. ~~I went~~ quickly past her into the room, and to the Marquis's bed. He was lying there, very white, with his eyes shut, ~~like~~ a corpse. I took hold of his hand and spoke to him, ~~and he felt to me like a dead man~~. Then I turned round; my lady and Mr. Urbain were there. 'My poor Bread,' said my lady, 'M. le Marquis is gone.' Mr. Urbain knelt down by the bed, and said softly '*Mon père, mon père.*' I thought it ~~wonderful strange~~, and asked my lady what in the world had happened, and why

he

sound like a scared child

high

since

in safety at such a crisis

him

his father's

the Count, as he then was,

come

most extraordinary

I brushed

had returned

You could have taken him for

altogether

but it was as if I had been dealing with death.

she hadn't called me. She said nothing had happened; that she had only been sitting there with ~~the Marquis, very quiet~~. She had closed her eyes, thinking she might sleep, and she had slept she didn't know how long. When she woke up he was dead. 'It's death, my son, it's death,' she said to the Count. Mr. Urbain said they must have the doctor immediately from Poitiers, and that he would ride off and fetch him. He kissed his father's face and then he kissed his mother and went away. My lady and I stood there at the bedside. As I looked at ~~the poor Marquis~~ it came ~~into my head that he was not~~ dead, that he was ~~in a kind of swoon~~. And then my lady repeated: 'My poor Bread, it's death, it's death;' and I said, 'Yes, my lady, it's certainly death.' I said just the opposite to what I believed; it was my notion. Then my lady said we must wait for the doctor, and we sat there and waited. It was a long time; the poor Marquis neither stirred nor changed. 'I ~~have~~ seen death before,' said my lady, 'and it's terribly like this.' 'Yes, please, my lady,' said I~~, and I kept thinking~~. The night wore away without the Count's coming back, and ~~my lady~~ began to be frightened. She was afraid he had had an accident in the dark, or met with some ~~wild~~ people. At last she got so restless that she went below to watch in the court for her son's return. I sat there alone, and the Marquis never stirred."

Here Mrs. Bread paused again, and the most ~~artistic of romancers could not have~~ been more effective. Newman made ~~a movement as if he were turning over the~~ page of a novel. "So he *was* dead!" he exclaimed.

"Three days ~~afterwards~~ he was in his grave," said Mrs. Bread sententiously. "In a little while I went away to the front of the house and looked out into the court, and there, before long, I saw Mr. Urbain ride in alone. I waited a bit, to hear him come upstairs with his mother, but they ~~stayed~~ below, and I ~~went back~~ to the ~~Marquis's~~ room. I went to the bed and held up the

him in perfect stillness

my poor master

to me ever so sharply that he wasn't

only in a stupor of weakness

particular

the Marquise

and I thought things I didn't say

later

the other

almost the motion of turning the

stopped

returned

prowling

expert story-teller couldn't have

light to him, but I don't know why I didn't let the candlestick fall. The Marquis's eyes were open—open wide! they were staring at me. I knelt down beside him and took his hands, and begged him to tell me, in the name of wonder, whether he was alive or dead. Still he looked at me a long time, and then he made me a sign to put my ear close to him. 'I am dead,' he said, 'I am dead. The Marquise has killed me.' I was all in a tremble. I didn't understand him. I didn't know what had become of him. He seemed both a man and a corpse, if you can fancy, sir. 'But you'll get well now, sir,' I said. And then he whispered again, ever so weak: 'I wouldn't get well for a kingdom. I wouldn't be that woman's husband again.' And then he said more; he said she had murdered him. I asked him what she had done to him, but he only replied: 'Murder, murder. And she'll kill my daughter,' he said; 'my poor unhappy child.' And he begged me to prevent that, and then he said that he was dying, that he was dead. I was afraid to move or to leave him; I was almost dead myself. All of a sudden he asked me to get a pencil and write for him; and then I had to tell him that I couldn't manage a pencil. He asked me to hold him up in bed while he wrote himself, and I said he could never, never do such a thing. But he seemed to have a kind of terror that gave him strength. I found a pencil in the room and a piece of paper and a book, and I put the paper on the book and the pencil into his hand, and moved the candle near him. You will think all this very strange, sir; and very strange it was. The strangest part of it was that I believed he was dying, and that I was eager to help him to write. I sat on the bed and put my arm round him and held him up. I felt very strong. I believe I could have lifted him and carried him. It was a wonder how he wrote, but he did write, in a big scratching hand; he almost covered one side of the paper. It seemed a long time; I suppose it was three or four minutes. He was groaning, terribly, all the while. Then he said it was ended, and I let him down upon his pillows, and he gave me the paper and told me to fold it and hide it, and to give it to those who would act upon it. 'Whom do you mean?' I said. 'Who are those who will act upon it?' But he only groaned, for an answer; he couldn't speak for weakness. In a few minutes he told me to go and look at the bottle on the chimney-piece. I knew the bottle he meant, the white stuff that was good for his stomach. I went and looked at it, but it was empty. When I came back his eyes were open and he was staring at me; but soon he closed them and he said no more. I hid the paper in my dress; I didn't look at what was written upon it, though I can read very well, sir, if I haven't any handwriting. I sat down near the bed, but it was nearly half an hour before my lady and the Count came in. The Marquis looked as [illegible] when they left him, and I never said a word about his having been otherwise. Mr. Urbain said that the doctor had been called to a person in childbirth, but that he promised to set out for Fleurières immediately. In another half-hour he arrived, and as soon as he had examined the Marquis he said that we had had a false alarm. The poor gentleman was very low, but he was still living. I watched my lady and her son, when he said this, to see if they looked at each other, and I'm obliged to admit that they didn't. The doctor said there was no reason he should die; he had been going on so well. And then he wanted to know how he had suddenly fallen off; he had left him so very hearty. My lady told her little story again—what she had told Mr. Urbain and me—and the doctor looked at her and said nothing. He stayed all the next day at the château, and hardly left the Marquis. I was always there. Mademoiselle and Mr. Valentin came and looked at their father, but he never stirred. It was a strange deathly stupor. My lady was always about; her face was as white as her husband's, and she looked very proud, as I had seen her look when her orders or her wishes had been disobeyed. It was as if the poor Marquis had defied her; and the way she took it made me afraid of her. The apothecary from Poitiers kept the Marquis along through the day, and we waited for the other doctor from Paris, who, as I told you, had been staying at Fleurières. They had telegraphed for him early in the morning, and in the evening he arrived. He talked a bit outside with the doctor from Poitiers, and then they came in to see the Marquis together. I was with him, and so was Mr. Urbain. My lady had been to receive the doctor from Paris, and she didn't come back with him into the room. He sat down by the Marquis—I can see him there now, with his hand on the Marquis's wrist, and Mr. Urbain watching him with a little looking-glass in his hand. 'I'm sure he's better,' said the little doctor from Poitiers; 'I'm sure he'll come back.' A few moments after he had said this the Marquis opened his eyes, as if he were waking up, and looked at us, from one to the other. I saw him look at me very softly, as you'd say. At the same moment my lady came in on tiptoe; she came up to the bed and put in her head between me and the Count. The Marquis saw her and gave a long, most wonderful moan. He said something we couldn't understand, and he seemed to have a kind of spasm. He shook all over, and then closed his eyes, and the doctor jumped up and took hold of my lady. He held her for a moment a bit roughly. The Marquis was stone dead! This time there were those there that knew."

Newman felt as if he had been reading by starlight the report of highly important evidence in a great murder case. "And the paper—the paper!" he said excitedly. "What was written upon it?"

"I can't tell you, sir," answered Mrs. Bread. "I couldn't read it; it was in French."

"But could no one else read it?"

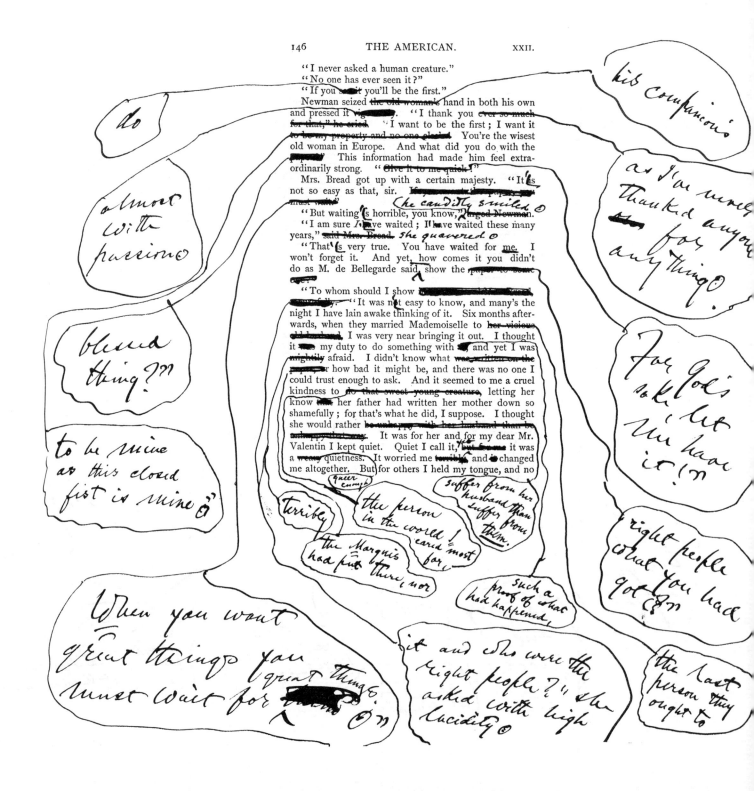

"I never asked a human creature."

"No one has ever seen it?"

"If you see it you'll be the first."

Newman seized the old woman's hand in both his own and pressed it vigorously. "I thank you ever so much for that," he cried. "I want to be the first; I want it to be my property and no one else's. You're the wisest old woman in Europe. And what did you do with the paper?" This information had made him feel extraordinarily strong. "Give it to me quick!"

Mrs. Bread got up with a certain majesty. "It is not so easy as that, sir. If you want the paper, you must wait."

"But waiting is horrible, you know," urged Newman.

"I am sure I have waited; I have waited these many years," said Mrs. Bread.

"That is very true. You have waited for me. I won't forget it. And yet, how comes it you didn't do as M. de Bellegarde said, show the paper to some one?"

"To whom should I show it?" "It was not easy to know, and many's the night I have lain awake thinking of it. Six months afterwards, when they married Mademoiselle to her vicious old husband, I was very near bringing it out. I thought it was my duty to do something with it, and yet I was mightily afraid. I didn't know what was written on the paper or how bad it might be, and there was no one I could trust enough to ask. And it seemed to me a cruel kindness to do that sweet young creature, letting her know that her father had written her mother down so shamefully; for that's what he did, I suppose. I thought she would rather be unhappy with her husband than be unhappy that way. It was for her and for my dear Mr. Valentin I kept quiet. Quiet I call it, but for me it was a weary quietness. It worried me terribly, and it changed me altogether. But for others I held my tongue, and no one, to this hour, knows what passed between the poor Marquis and me."

"But evidently there were suspicions," said Newman. "Where did Mr. Valentin get his ideas?"

"I mean the little doctor from Poitiers. He was very ill-satisfied, and he made a great talk. He was a sharp Frenchman, and coming to the house, as he did, day after day, I suppose he saw more than he seemed to see. And indeed the way the poor Marquis went off as soon as his eyes fell on my lady was a most shocking sight for any one. The medical gentleman from Paris was much more accommodating, and he hushed up the other. But for all he could do Mr. Valentin and Mademoiselle heard something; they knew their father's death was somehow against nature. Of course they couldn't accuse their mother, and, as I tell you, I was as dumb as that stone. Mr. Valentin used to look at me sometimes, and his eyes seemed to shine, as if he were thinking of asking me something. I was dreadfully afraid he would speak, and always looked away and went about my business. If I were to tell him, I was sure he would hate me afterwards, and that I could never have borne. Once I went up to him and took a great liberty; I kissed him, as I had kissed him when he was a child. 'You oughtn't to look so sad, sir,' I said; 'believe your poor old Bread. Such a gallant, handsome young man can have nothing to be sad about.' And I think he understood me; he understood that I was begging off, and he made up his mind in his own way. He went about with his unasked question in his mind, as I did with my untold tale; we were both afraid of bringing dishonour on a great house. And it was the same with Mademoiselle. She didn't know what had happened; she wouldn't know. My lady and Mr. Urbain asked me no questions, because they had no reason. I was as still as a mouse. When I was younger my lady thought me saucy, and now she thought me a fool. How should I have any ideas?"

Handwritten revisions:

urged.

Count Z

great man

kind person.

he didn't care who knew it. He had a very good opinion of his own sharpness, as Frenchmen mostly have.

"From our little local man – who has yet never been in the house, as you may imagine, since.

he had more ideas – as a consequence – than he had had, before, any call to put about.

decent

her ladyship

which was what

my dear young lady.

may have known, after he had taken things in, what to think but he also what not to say.

The Vicomte and I

stopped clock.

fear of knowing. The Marquis and I

some question he could ask me.

false, and now she thought me stupid.

"But you say the little doctor from Poitiers made a talk, [illegible]. Did no one take it up?"

"I heard nothing of it, sir. They're always talking scandal in these foreign countries—you may have noticed—and I suppose they shook their heads over Madame de Bellegarde. But after all what could they say? The Marquis had been ill and the Marquis had died; he had as good a right to die as any one. The doctor couldn't say he had not come honestly by his cramps. The next year the little doctor left the place and bought a practice in Bordeaux, and if there had been any gossip it died out. And I don't think there could have been much gossip about my lady that any one would listen to. My lady is so very respectable."

Newman, at this last affirmation, broke into an immense resounding laugh. Mrs. Bread had begun to move away from the spot where they were sitting, and he helped her through the aperture in the wall and along the homeward path. "Yes, [illegible] my lady's respectability, [illegible]!" They reached the empty space in front of the church, where they stopped a moment, looking at each other with something of an air of closer fellowship—like two sociable conspirators. "But what was it," said Newman, "what was it she did to her husband? She didn't stab him or poison him."

"I don't know, sir; no one saw it."

"Unless it was Mr. Urbain. You say he was walking up and down outside the room. Perhaps he looked through the keyhole. But no; I think that with his mother he would take it on trust."

"You may be sure I've often thought of it," said Mrs. Bread. "I'm sure she didn't touch him with her hands. I saw nothing on him anywhere. I believe it was in this way. He had a fit of his great pain, and he asked her for his medicine. Instead of giving it to him she went and poured it away, before his eyes. Then he

A woman turned it all grandly down
That
What he suffered
at
a
Don't know how far they went
had stories about my lady
ugly tales the worst of them were among ugly people. There couldn't have been any bad ones that those who were believed. My lady is so very respectable."
he
insisted
not speaking, only looking at him, so that he might have the scare
almost cheerfully returned
a pair of
the miserable man?
throttle him or
a Treasure; I shall have a great deal of use for my lady's respectability"

149

and the shock and the horror of it. Then he saw what she meant, and weak and helpless, he took fright, was terrified. 'You want to kill me,' he must have said – do you see? 'Yes, Mr. le Marquis, I want to kill you,' says my lady, and sits down and keeps her dreadful eyes on him. You know my lady's eyes. I think it was with them she killed him; it was with the terrible strong will and all the cruelty she put into them. It was if she

149a ~~[illegible]~~

out of her boat

had pushed him overboard and sunk into the cold sea, and remained there to push him again should he try to scramble back; making him feel he was lost by her intention and watching him awfully sink and drown. It was enough indeed to take the heart out of him, and that, in his state, was enough for a death-stroke.

Newman rendered this vivid image, which in truth ~~[illegible]~~ did great honour to the old woman's haunted

144b

sensibility, the tribute of a comprehensive gasp. "Well, you've got right hold of it — you make me see it and hate it and want to go for it. But I've got to keep right hold of you too, you know."

They had begun to descend the hill, and she said nothing till they reached the foot. He moved beside her as on air, his hands in his pockets, his head thrown back while he gazed at the stars; he seemed to himself to be

149c

riding his vengeance along the Milky Way. "So you're serious about that?" she sighed.

"About your living with me? Why, you don't suppose I've turned you inside out this way not to want to get you into shape again? You're in no kind of shape for these people now if they come in any face; after your seeing what they've done to her. You and

next give me thing I'm after? 149 d & 149 e
and then you quit."

"I never thought I should
have had to take a new place
unless," Mrs. Bread made moan
"I should have gone some day
to ~~the~~ Mr. Valentin or, in her own establishment, to my young
lady."

"Come to me and you'll come
to *her* establishment yet, I guess—
you'll come at least to where
~~[illegible]~~
both those names will be cherished and revered."

She considered a little, a ~~[illegible]~~ rest,
then replied: "Oh, I should like
to pronounce them to you, sir!"

And if you're going to pull the "house down" she added, "I had surely better be clear of it."

"Oh," said Newman almost with the gaiety of a dozzle of alternatives, "it won't be quite my idea to appeal, if that's what you mean, to the police. The meanest and the damnedest things are always beyond their ken, and out of their hands. Which has the merit in this case, however, that it leaves the whole story in mine. And to mine," he declared, "you're a great power!"

"Ah, you're bolder than I ever

1499

was:) the exceedingly righted; and he felt himself now, to shatters end, possessed of her.

He walked back with her to the château; the curfew—it couldn't have been anything but the curfew, he was sure—had tolled for the weary serfs and ~~the~~ villains (as he could also quite have believed) and the small street of Fleurières was unlighted and empty. She promised he should have ~~the Marquis's manuscript~~ in half an hour. Mrs. Bread choosing not to go in by the great gate, they passed round by a winding lane to a door in the wall of the park, of which she had the key, and which would enable her to the château from behind. Newman arranged with her that he should await outside the wall her return with ~~the assured document~~ *his prize* ⊙

She went in, and his half-hour in the dusky lane seemed very long. But he had plenty to think about. At last the door in the wall opened and Mrs. Bread stood there, with one hand on the latch and the other holding out a scrap of white paper. In a moment he was master of it, and it had passed into his waistcoat pocket. "Come and see me in Paris," he said; "we to settle your future, you know; and I ill translate poor M. de Bellegarde's French to you." Never had he felt so grateful as at this moment for M. Nioche's instructions.

Mrs. Bread's eyes had followed the disappearance of ~~the paper~~, and she gave a heavy sigh. "Well, you done what you would with me, sir, and I suppose do it again. You *must* take care of me now. You re a terribly positive gentleman."

"Just now," said Newman, "I'm a terribly impatient !" And he bade her good night, and walked rapidly back to the inn. He ordered his vehicle to be prepared for return to Poitiers, and then he shut the door of the common salle and strode towards the solitary lamp on the chimney-piece. He pulled out the paper and quickly unfolded it. It was covered with pencil-marks, which at first, in the feeble light, seemed indistinct. But fierce curiosity forced a meaning from the tremulous signs. ~~The English of them was as follows:~~

"My wife has tried to kill me, and has done it; I am ~~dying, dying~~ horribly. It s to marry my ~~dear~~

folded small and dearer to his sight than any love-token ever brought of old by bribed duenna to lurking cavalier ⊙

her treasure

what he was after as he had called it. ⊙

re-enter

one I'm

the

for the English of which might have been: ⊙

his   helplessly dying ⊙   beloved

daughter to M. de Cintré. With all my soul I protest—I forbid it. I am not insane—ask the doctors, ask Mrs. B——. It was alone with me here to-night; she attacked me and put me to death. It is murder, if murder ever was. Ask the doctors, tell everyone, show everyone this.

"HENRI-URBAIN DE BELLEGARDE."

and then go on herself all the same.

CHAPTER XXIII.

NEWMAN returned to Paris the second day after his interview with Mrs. Bread. The morrow he had spent at Poitiers, reading over and over again the little document which he had lodged in his pocket-book, and thinking what he would do in the circumstances, and how he would do it. He would not have said that Poitiers was an amusing place; yet the day seemed very short. Domiciled once more in the Boulevard Haussmann, he walked over to the Rue de l'Université and inquired of Madame de Bellegarde's portress whether the Marquise had come back. The portress told him that she had arrived, with M. le Marquis, on the preceding day, and further informed him that if he desired to enter, Madame de Bellegarde and her son were both at home. As she said these words the little white-faced old woman who peered out of the dusky gate-house of the Hôtel de Bellegarde gave a small wicked smile—a smile which seemed to Newman to mean, "Go in if you dare!" She was evidently versed in the current domestic history; she was placed where she could feel the pulse of the house. Newman stood a moment, twisting his moustache and looking at her; then he abruptly turned away. But this was not because he was afraid to go in—though he doubted whether, if he did so, he should be able to make his way, unchallenged, into the presence of

the signed warrant

persuading himself more than more that it had, as he put it to himself a social value,

answered

now do

h

that

had much to hold him,

He

for all his courage

should he wish to see them they

Madame de Cintré's relatives. Confidence, excessive confidence, perhaps, quite as much as timidity, prompted his retreat. He was nursing his thunderbolt; he loved it; he was unwilling to part with it. He seemed to be holding it aloft in the rumbling, vaguely-flashing air, directly over the heads of his victims, and he fancied he could see their pale upturned faces. Few specimens of the human countenance had ever given him such pleasure as these, lighted in the lurid fashion I have hinted at, and he was disposed to sip the cup of contemplative revenge in a leisurely fashion. It must be added, too, that he was at a loss to see exactly how he could arrange to witness the operation of his thunder. To send in his card to Madame de Bellegarde would be a waste of ceremony; she would certainly decline to receive him. On the other hand, he could not force his way into her presence. It annoyed him keenly to think that he might be reduced to the blind satisfaction of writing her a letter; but he consoled himself in a measure with the reflection that a letter might lead to an interview. He went home, and, feeling rather tired—nursing a vengeance was, it must be confessed, a rather fatiguing process; it took a good deal out of one—flung himself into one of his brocaded fauteuils, stretched his legs, thrust his hands into his pockets, and, while he watched the reflected sunset fading from the ornate house-tops on the opposite side of the Boulevard, began mentally to compose a cool epistle to Madame de Bellegarde. While he was so occupied his servant threw open the door and announced ceremoniously, "Madame Brett!"

Newman roused himself, expectantly, and in a few moments perceived upon his threshold the worthy woman with whom he had conversed to such good purpose on the starlit hill-top of Fleurières. Mrs. Bread had made for this visit the same toilet as for her former expedition. Newman was struck with her distinguished appearance. His lamp was not lit, and as her large grave face gazed at him through the light dusk from under the shadow of her ample bonnet, he felt the incongruity of such a person presenting herself as a servant. He greeted her with high geniality, and bade her come in and sit down and make herself comfortable. There was something which might have touched the springs both of mirth and of melancholy in the ancient maidenliness with which Mrs. Bread endeavoured to comply with these directions. She was not playing at being fluttered, which would have been simply ridiculous; she was doing her best to carry herself as a person so humble, that, for her, even embarrassment would have been pretentious; but evidently she had never dreamed of its being in her horoscope to pay a visit, at nightfall, to a friendly single gentleman who lived in theatrical-looking rooms on one of the new boulevards.

"I truly hope I am not forgetting my place, sir," she murmured.

"Forgetting your place? Why, you are remembering it. This is your place, you know. You are already in my service; your wages, as housekeeper, began a fortnight ago. I can tell you my house wants keeping! Why don't you take off your bonnet and stay?

"Take off my bonnet?" said Mrs. Bread, with timid literalness. "Oh sir, I haven't my cap. And with your leave, sir, I couldn't keep house in my best gown."

"Never mind your gown," said Newman, cheerfully. "You shall have a better gown than that."

Mrs. Bread stared solemnly, and then stretched her hands over her lustreless satin skirt, as if the perilous side of her situation was defining itself. "Oh sir, I am fond of my own clothes," she murmured.

"I hope you have left those wicked people, at any rate," said Newman.

"Well, sir, here I am! That's all I can tell you. Here I sit, poor Catherine Bread.

clear

her pretending to any servile stamp ⊙

that

spirit of formal accommodation

anxiously pleaded ⊙

right now?"

with which she endeavoured to meet this new conception of her duty ⊙

as a good woman remembers her promises ⊙

She

might be flushing into view ⊙

went on.

She gave it her gravest consideration ⊙

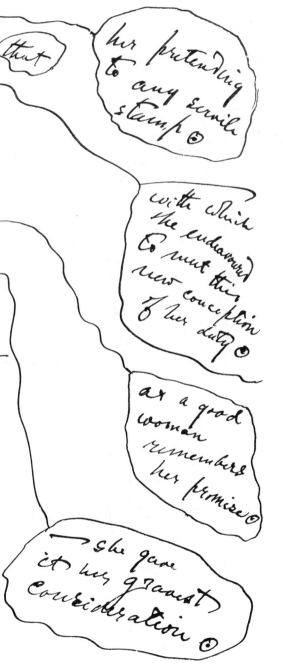

It's a strange place for me to be. I don't know myself; I never supposed I was so bold. But indeed, sir, I have gone as far as my own strength will bear me."

"Oh, come, Mrs. Bread!" said Newman, almost caressingly, "don't make yourself uncomfortable. Now's the time to feel lively, you know!"

She began to speak again with a trembling voice. "I think it would be more respectable if I could—if I could——" and her voice trembled to a pause.

"If you could give up this sort of thing altogether?" said Newman kindly, trying to anticipate her meaning, which he supposed might be a wish to retire from service.

"If I could give up everything, sir! All I should ask is a decent Protestant burial."

"Burial!" cried Newman, with a burst of laughter. "Why, to bury you now would be a sad piece of extravagance. It's only rascals who have to be buried to get respectable. Honest folks like you and me can live our time out—and live together. Come! did you bring your baggage?"

"My box is locked and corded; but I haven't yet spoken to my lady."

"Speak to her, then, and have done with it. I should like to have your chance!" cried Newman.

"I would gladly give it you, sir. I have passed some weary hours in my lady's dressing-room; but this will be one of the longest. She will tax me with ingratitude."

"Well," said Newman, "so long as you can tax her with murder——"

"Oh, sir, I can't; not I," sighed Mrs. Bread.

"You don't mean to say anything about it? So much the better. Leave that to me."

"If she calls me a thankless old woman," said Mrs. Bread, "I shall have nothing to say. But it is better so," she softly added. "She shall be my lady to the last. That will be more respectable."

"And then you will come to me and I shall be your

But she quavered

two boxes are

Bread stout on.

with supreme mildness.

he returned

Why, you're going to have now the time of your life over

he cried

base

it all

she

gentleman," said Newman; "that will be more respectable still!"

Mrs. Bread rose, with lowered eyes, and stood a moment; then, looking up, she rested her eyes upon Newman's face. The disordered proprieties were somehow settling to rest. She looked at Newman so long and so fixedly, with such a dull intense devotedness, that he himself might have had a pretext for embarrassment. At last she said gently: "You're not looking well, sir."

"That's natural enough," said Newman. "I have nothing to feel well about. To be very indifferent and very fierce, very dull and very jovial, very sick and very lively, all at once—why, it rather mixes one up."

Mrs. Bread gave a noiseless sigh. "I can tell you something that will make you feel duller still, if you want to feel all one way. About Madame de Cintré."

"What can you tell me?" Newman demanded. "Not that you have seen her?"

She shook her head. "No, indeed, sir, nor ever shall. That's the dulness of it. Nor my lady. Nor M. de Bellegarde."

"You mean that she is kept so close?"

"Close, close," said Mrs. Bread, very softly.

These words, for an instant, seemed to check the beating of Newman's heart. He leaned back in his chair, staring up at the old woman. "They have tried to see her, and she wouldn't—she couldn't?"

"She refused—for ever! I had it from my lady's own maid," said Mrs. Bread, "who had it from my lady. To speak of it to such a person my lady must have felt the shock. Madame de Cintré won't see them now, and now is her only chance. A while hence she will have no chance."

"You mean the other women—the mothers, the daughters, the sisters; what is it they call them?—won't let her?"

- + his
- She
- gaze
- her friend
- "Why, Mrs. Bread," he answered, "~~you're~~ not my natural balance. You mean don't look sunny guess I look as I feel ☉
- "You're not your natural appearance tir ☉"
- fine
- Violent
- queerer
- choice.
- the Countess declines to receive
- the poor Countess"
- "The closest ~~they~~ they kut any ☉"
- dead weight
- quickly asked ☉

"It is what they call the rule of the house—or of the order, I believe. There is no rule so strict as that of the Carmelites. The bad women in the reformatories are fine ladies to them. They wear old brown cloaks—so the *femme de chambre* told me—that you wouldn't use for a horse-blanket. And the poor Countess was so fond of soft-feeling dresses; she would never have anything stiff! They sleep on the ground," Mrs. Bread went on; "they are no better, no better"—and she hesitated for a comparison—"they are no better than tinkers' wives. They give up everything, down to the very name their poor old nurses called them by. They give up father and mother, brother and sister—to say nothing of other persons," Mrs. Bread delicately added. "They wear a shroud under their brown cloaks and a rope round their waists, and they get up on winter nights and go off into cold places to pray to the Virgin Mary. The Virgin Mary is a hard mistress!"

Mrs. Bread, dwelling on these terrible facts, sat dry-eyed and pale, with her hands clasped in her satin lap. Newman gave a melancholy groan and fell forward, leaning his head in his hands. There was a long silence, broken only by the ticking of the great gilded clock on the chimney-piece.

"Where is this place—where is the convent?" Newman asked at last, looking up.

"There are two houses," said Mrs. Bread. "I found out; I thought you would like to know—though it's poor comfort, I think. One is the Avenue de Messine; they have learned that Madame de Cintré is there. The other is in the Rue d'Enfer. That's a terrible name; I suppose you know what it means."

Newman got up and walked away to the end of his long room. When he came back Mrs. Bread had got up and stood by the fire with folded hands. "Tell me this. Can I get near her—even if I don't see her? Can I look through a grating, or some such thing, at the place where she is?"

It is said that all women love a lover, and Mrs. Bread's sense of the pre-established harmony which kept servants in their "place," even as planets in their orbits (not that Mrs. Bread had ever consciously likened herself to a planet), barely availed to temper the maternal melancholy with which she leaned her head on one side and gazed at her new employer. She probably felt for the moment as if, forty years before, she had held him also in her arms. "That wouldn't help you, sir. It would only make her seem farther away."

"I want to go there, at all events," ~~said Newman~~. "Avenue de Messine, you say? And what is it they call themselves?"

"Carmelites," said Mrs. Bread.

"I shall remember that."

~~Mrs. Bread~~ hesitated a moment, and then: "It's my duty to tell you ~~this, sir," she went on. "The~~ convent has a chapel, and ~~some people~~ are admitted on Sunday to the mass. You don't see the poor creatures ~~that are shut up there~~, but I'm told you can hear them sing. It's a wonder they have any heart for singing! Some Sunday I shall make bold to go. It seems to me I should know *her* voice in fifty."

Newman ~~looked at his visitor very gratefully; then he held out his hand and shook hers. "Thank you," he said~~. "If any one can get in, I will." A moment later Mrs. Bread proposed, deferentially, to retire, but he checked her and put a lighted candle into her hand. "There are half a dozen rooms there I don't use," ~~he said, pointing~~ through an open door. "Go and look at them and take your choice. You can live in the one you like best." From this bewildering ~~opportunity Mrs. Bread~~ at first recoiled; but finally, yielding to [illegible], she wandered off into the dusk with her tremulous taper. She remained absent a

Handwritten revisions:

ll

The

he returned

She

Whatever it means!"

that persons

her friend's almost fraternal pat of reassurance

privilege she

this, that the

and he pointed

in their prison or their tomb,

thanked her, while he held her hand, with a stare through which he bore a good reason. [illegible] failed to see her quarter of an hour, during which Newman paced up and down, stopped occasionally to look out of the window at the lights on the Boulevard, and then resumed his walk. Mrs. Bread's relish for her investigations apparently increased as she proceeded; but at last she reappeared and deposited her candlestick on the chimney-piece.

"Well, have you picked one out?" asked Newman.

"A room, sir? They are all too fine for a dingy old body like me. There isn't one that hasn't a bit of gilding."

"It's only tinsel, Mrs. Bread," said Newman. "If you stay there a while it will all peel off of itself." And he gave a dismal smile.

"Oh, sir, there are things enough peeling off already!" rejoined Mrs. Bread, with a head-shake. "Since I was there I thought I would look about me. I don't believe you know, sir. The corners are most dreadful. You do want a housekeeper, that you do; you want a tidy Englishwoman that isn't above taking hold of a broom."

Newman assured her that he suspected, if he had not measured, his domestic abuses, and that to reform them was a mission worthy of her powers. She held her candlestick aloft again and looked round the salon with compassionate glances; then she intimated that she accepted the mission, and that its sacred character would sustain her in her rupture with Madame de Bellegarde. With this she curtsied herself away.

She came back the next day with her worldly goods, and Newman, going into his drawing-room, found her upon her aged knees before a divan, sewing up some detached fringe. He questioned her as to her leave-taking with her late mistress, and she said it had proved easier than she feared. "I was perfectly civil, sir, but the Lord helped me to remember that a good woman has no call to tremble before a bad one."

"I should think so!" cried Newman. "And does she know you have come to me?"

XXIII. THE AMERICAN. 159

"She asked me where I was going, and I mentioned your name," said Mrs. Bread.

"What did she say to that?"

"She looked at me very hard, and she turned very red. Then she bade me leave her. I was all ready to go, and I had got the coachman, who is an Englishman, to bring down my poor box and to fetch me a cab. But when I went down myself to the gate I found it closed. My lady had sent orders to the porter not to let me pass, and by the same orders the porter's wife—she is a dreadful sly old body—had gone out in a cab to fetch home M. de Bellegarde from his club.

Newman slapped his knee. "She *is* scared! she *is* scared!" he cried, exultantly.

"I was frightened too, sir," said Mrs. Bread, "but I was also mightily vexed. I took it very high with the porter, and asked him by what right he used violence to an honourable Englishwoman who had lived in the house for thirty years before he was heard of. Oh, sir, I was very grand, and I brought the man down. He drew his bolts and let me out, and I promised the cabman something handsome if he would drive fast. But he was terribly slow; it seemed as if we should never reach your blessed door. I am all of a tremble still; it took me five minutes, just now, to thread my needle."

Newman told her, with a gleeful laugh, that if she chose she might have a little maid on purpose to thread her needles; and he went away murmuring to himself again that the old woman *was* scared—she *was* scared!

He had not shown Mrs. Tristram the little paper that he carried in his pocket-book, but since his return to Paris he had seen her several times, and she had told him that he seemed to her to be in a strange way—an even stranger way than his sad situation made natural. Had his disappointment gone to his head? He looked like a man who was going to be ill, and yet she had never seen him more restless and active. One day he

returned.

thank goodness

boxes

them

those terrible great gates

thank the I felt my powers temper rise.

's face lighted almost with the candour of childhood.

blest

Some days he

not disguised from him that he struck her as

in munificent mirth,

document

nursing this sketch of the scene in the Rue de l'Université and rejoicing in the belief that he had produced there what he had called the impression of his life.

would ~~sit hanging~~ his head and ~~looking as if he were firmly resolved~~ never to smile again; ~~another~~ he would indulge in laughter that was almost ~~unseemly~~ jokes that were bad even for him. If he was trying to carry off his ~~sorrow, he~~ at such times really ~~went~~ too far. She begged him of all things not to be "strange." Feeling in a measure ~~responsible as she did~~ for the ~~affair which~~ had turned out so ill for him, she could ~~endure~~ anything but his strangeness. He might be ~~melancholy~~ if he would, or he might ~~be stoical, he might be cross and cantankerous with her~~ why she had ever dared to meddle with his destiny: to this she would submit; for this she would make allowances. Only, ~~for Heaven's sake,~~ let him not be incoherent. That would ~~be extremely unpleasant.~~ It was like people talking in their sleep; they always frightened her. And Mrs. Tristram intimated that, taking very high ground as regards the moral obligation which events had laid upon her, she proposed not to rest quiet until she should have confronted him with the least inadequate substitute for ~~Madame de Cintré~~ that the two hemispheres contained.

"~~Oh," said Newman, "~~ and we had better not open a new account! You may bury me some day, but you shall never marry me. It's too rough. I hope, at any rate," he added, "that there is nothing incoherent in this—that I want to go next Sunday to the Carmelite chapel in the Avenue de Messine. You know one of the Catholic ~~ministers~~—an abbé, is that it?—I've seen him here; that motherly old gentleman with the big waist-band. Please ask him if I need a special leave to go in, and if I do, beg him to obtain it for me."

Mrs. Tristram gave expression to the liveliest joy. "I'm so glad you've asked me to do something! You shall get into the chapel if the abbé is disfrocked for his share in it." And two days afterwards she told him that it was all arranged; the abbé

hang

fold his brow and

Get his teeth wish to appear to give out that he would

on others

rude and make

humiliation he count

adventure that

answerable

put up with

tragic

be terribly touching and pierce her to the heart with silent sorrow; he might be violent and summon her to say

if he loved her,

with you I think, on some errand for his poor;

You see—it's worse than a free fight in Arkansaw

his lost

to this, "Ah, he replied: square now I think we're

quite break down her nerves

clergymen—

was enchanted to serve him, and if he would present himself civilly at the convent gate there would be no ~~difficulty.~~ obstacle.

~~CHAPTER~~ XXIV.

SUNDAY was as yet two days off; but meanwhile, to beguile his impatience, Newman took his way to the Avenue de Messine and got what comfort he could in staring at the blank outef wall of Madame de Cintré's present ~~residence.~~ abode. The street in question, as some travellers will remember, adjoins the Parc Monceau, which is one of the ~~prettiest corners~~ finest quarters of reconstructed Paris. ~~The quarter~~ It has an air of modern opulence and convenience ~~which seems at variance with the ascetic institution~~ that makes a false note of any temple of sacrifice, and the impression made ~~upon Newman's~~ on his gloomily-irritated gaze by the fresh-looking, windowless expanse behind which the woman he loved was perhaps even then pledging herself to pass the rest of her days was less exasperating than he had feared. The place suggested a convent with the modern improvements—an asylum in which privacy, though unbroken, might be not quite identical with privation, and meditation, though monotonous, might be ~~of a cheerful cast.~~ sufficiently placid. And yet he knew the case was otherwise; only at present it was not a reality to him. It was too strange and too mocking to be real; it was like a page torn ~~out of a romance~~ out of some superannuated unreadable book, with no context in his own experience.

On Sunday morning, at the hour ~~which~~ Mrs. Tristram had indicated, he rang at the gate in the blank wall. It instantly opened and admitted him into a clean, cold-looking court, ~~from~~ beyond which a dull, plain edifice ~~looked down upon him~~ met his view in the manner of some cold blank party to an introduction. A robust lay sister with a cheerful complexion emerged from a porter's lodge and, on his stating his errand, pointed to the open door of the chapel, an edifice which occupied the right side of the court and was preceded by a high flight of steps. Newman ascended the steps and immediately entered the open door. Service had not yet begun; the ~~place~~ was dimly lighted, and it was some moments before he could distinguish ~~its~~ features. Then he saw ~~it was~~ divided by a large close iron screen into two unequal ~~portions~~. The altar was on the hither side of the screen, and between it and the entrance were disposed several benches and chairs. Three or four of these were occupied by vague, motionless figures—figures that he presently perceived to be women, deeply absorbed in their devotion. The ~~place~~ seemed to Newman very cold; the smell of the incense itself was cold. ~~Besides this there~~ was a twinkle of tapers, and here and there a glow of coloured glass. ~~Newman~~ seated himself; the praying women kept still, with their backs turned. He saw they were visitors like himself, and he would have liked to see their faces; for he believed that they were the mourning mothers and sisters of other women who had had the same pitiless courage as ~~Madame de Cintré~~. But they were better off than he, for they at least shared the faith to which the others had sacrificed themselves. Three or four persons came in, two of them ~~were elderly~~ gentlemen. Every one was very quiet. ~~Newman~~ fastened his eyes ~~upon~~ the screen behind the altar. That was the convent, the real convent, the place where she was. But he could see nothing; no light came through the crevices. He got up and approached the partition very gently, trying to look through. But behind it there was darkness, with ~~nothing stirring~~. He went back to his place, and after that a priest and two altar-boys came in and began to say mass.

Newman watched their genuflexions and gyrations with a grim, still enmity; they seemed ~~aids~~ and abettors of ~~Madame de Cintré's desertion~~; they were mouthing and droning out their triumph. The priest's long, dis-

interior; the [illegible] scene; mixed with in this impression; parts.; place; He; important and mature; the person in whom he was interested; with a perverse effect of submission; prompters; no sign even of despair; the wrong he had suffered; He [illegible] mal intonings acted upon his nerves and deepened his wrath; there was something defiant in his unintelligible drawl ~~; it seemed meant for Newman himself.~~ Suddenly there arose from the depths of the chapel, from behind the inexorable grating, a sound ~~which~~ drew his attention from the altar—the sound of a strange, lugubrious chant uttered by women's voices. It began softly, but it presently grew louder, and as it increased it became more of a wail and a dirge. It was the chant of the Carmelite nuns, their only human utterance. It was their dirge over their buried affections and over the vanity of earthly desires. At first ~~Newman~~ was bewildered—almost stunned—by the strangeness of the sound; then, as he comprehended its meaning, he listened intently and his heart began to throb. He listened for Madame de Cintré's voice, and in the very heart of the tuneless harmony he imagined he made it out. We are obliged to believe that he was wrong, ~~inasmuch~~ as she had obviously not yet had time to become a member of the invisible sister~~hood. The chant~~ kept on, mechanical and monotonous, with dismal repetitions and despairing cadences. It was hideous, it was horrible; as it continued, ~~Newman~~ felt ~~that~~ he needed all his self-control. He was growing more agitated; ~~he felt tears~~ in his eyes. At last, as in its full force the thought came over him that this confused, impersonal wail was all that he or the world she had deserted ~~should ever~~ hear of the ~~voice he had found so sweet, he felt that~~ he could bear it no longer. He rose abruptly and made his way out. On the threshold he paused, listened again to the dreary strain, and then hastily descended into the court. As he did so he saw that the good sister with the high-coloured cheeks and the fan-like frill to her ~~coiffure,~~ who had admitted him, was in conference at the gate with two persons who had just come in. A second glance ~~informed~~ him that these ~~persons~~ were Madame de Bellegarde and her son, and that they were about to avail themselves of that method

as if it had been meant for his own swindled self

that

he

hood;

since

But the chant, at any rate

he

the tears were hot

were ever again to

breath of those lips of which his own held still the pressure, he knew

visitors

showed

head-dress

their lost victim

of approach to ~~Madame de Cintré~~ which ~~Newman~~ had
found but a mockery of consolation. As he crossed the
court ~~Mr. de Bellegarde~~ recognised him; ~~the Marquis
was coming to the steps, leading~~ his mother. ~~The old
lady gave Newman a look~~, and it resembled that of
~~Newman~~. Both faces expressed a ~~further~~ perturbation,
something more akin to the ~~humbleness of~~ dismay than
Newman had yet seen in them. Evidently he ~~startled
the Bellegardes, and they had not their grand behaviour
immediately in hand~~. Newman hurried past them, guided
only by the desire to get out of the convent walls into the
street. The gate opened itself at his approach; he strode
over the threshold and it closed behind him. A carriage,
which appeared to have been standing there, was just
turning away from the ~~sidewalk. Newman~~ looked at it
for a moment blankly; then he became conscious,
through the dusky mist that swam before his eyes, that
a lady seated in it was bowing to him. The vehicle had
~~turned away~~ before he recognised her; it was an ancient
landau with one half the cover lowered. The lady's bow
was very ~~positive~~, and accompanied with a smile; a little
girl was seated beside her. He raised his hat, and then
the lady bade the coachman stop. *drew up again*
The carriage ~~halted again beside the pavement~~, and
she sat there and beckoned to Newman—beckoned with
the demonstrative grace of ~~Madame Urbain de Bellegarde~~.
Newman hesitated a moment before he obeyed her sum-
mons; during this moment he had time to curse his stu-
pidity for letting the others escape him. He had been
wondering how he could get at them; fool that he was
for not stopping them then and there! What better
place than beneath the very prison walls to which they
had consigned the promise of his joy? He had been too
bewildered ~~to stop~~ them, but now he felt ready to ~~wait
for~~ them at the gate. Madame Urbain, with a certain
attractive petulance, ~~beckoned to him again~~, and this
time he went over to the carriage. She leaned out

the Marquis

he

Urbain

*he was on
the way
to the
steps and
was supporting*

*From Madame
de Bellegarde
he also received
a look,*

*less
guarded*

*pavement
He*

*publicly to
fall on*

await

immediate

*got into
motion*

the Marquis

*made
a sign
of
insistance*

expressive

*Was
disconcerting
and neither
mother nor
you had quite
her presence
of mind*

and gave him her hand, looking at him kindly, and smiling.

"Ah, Monsieur, you don't include me in your wrath? I had nothing to do with it."

"Oh, I don't suppose *you* could have prevented it," answered in a tone which was not that of studied gallantry.

"What you say is too true for me to resent the small account it makes of my influence. I forgive you, at any rate, because you look as if you had seen a ghost."

"I have seen a ghost,"

"I am glad, then, I didn't go in with and my husband. You must have seen them, eh? Was the meeting affectionate? Did you hear the chanting? They say it's like the lamentations of the damned. I wouldn't go in: one is certain to hear that soon enough. Poor Claire—in a white shroud and a big brown cloak! That's the *toilette* of the Carmelites, you know. Well, she was always fond of long, loose things. But I must not speak of her to you; I must say I am very sorry for you, that if I could have helped you I would, and that I think every one has. I was afraid of it, you know; I felt it in the air for a fortnight before it came. When I saw you at my mother-in-law's ball, felt as if you were dancing on your grave. But what could I do? I wish you all the good I can think of. You will say that isn't much! Yes; they have been; I am not a bit afraid to say it; I assure you every one thinks so. We are not all like that. I sorry I am not going to see you again; you know I think you very good company. I prove it by asking you to get into the carriage and drive with me for a quarter of an hour wait for my mother-in-law. Only if we were seen—considering what has passed, and every one knows you have been —it might be thought I was going a little too far, even for me.

m

he

only

abominable;

the

joué

Newman *darkly* *returned ⊙*

my belle=mère

behaved infernally ⊙

*take it all in
such good faith*

that I shall

But I shall see you sometimes—somewhere, eh? You know"—this was said in English—"we have a plan for a little amusement."

Newman stood there with his hand on the carriage door, listening to this consolatory murmur with an unlighted eye. He hardly knew what Madame de Bellegarde was saying; he was only conscious that she was chattering ineffectively. But suddenly it occurred to him that, with her pretty professions, there was a way of making her effective; she might help him to get at the old woman and the Marquis. "They are coming back soon—your companions? [illegible] You are waiting for them?"

"They will hear the mass out; there is nothing to keep them longer. Claire has refused to see them."

"I want to speak to them," said Newman, "and you can help me, you can do me a favour. Delay your return for five minutes, and give me a chance at them. I will wait for them here."

Madame de Bellegarde clasped her hands with a tender grimace. "My poor friend, what do you want to do to them? To beg them to come back to you? It will be wasted words. They will never come back!"

"I want to speak to them, all the same. Pray do what I ask you. Stay away and leave them to me for five minutes; you needn't be afraid; I shall not be violent; I am very quiet."

"Yes, you look very quiet! If they had *le cœur tendre* you would move them. But they haven't! However, I will do better for you than what you propose. The understanding is not that I shall come back for them. I am going into the Parc Monceau with my little girl to give her a walk, and my mother-in-law, who comes so rarely into this quarter, is to profit by the same opportunity to take the air. We are to wait for her in the park, where my husband is to bring her to us. Follow me now; just within the gates I shall get out of my carriage. Sit down on a chair in some quiet corner and I will bring them near you. There's devotion for you! *Le reste vous regarde.*"

This proposal seemed to Newman extremely felicitous; it revived his drooping spirit, and he reflected that Madame Urbain was not [illegible] she seemed. He promised immediately to overtake her, and the carriage drove away.

The Parc Monceau is a very pretty piece of landscape-gardening, but Newman, passing into it, bestowed little attention upon its elegant vegetation, which was full of the freshness of spring. He found Madame de Bellegarde promptly, seated in one of the quiet corners of which she had spoken, while before her, in the alley, her little girl, attended by the footman and the lap-dog, walked up and down as if she were taking a lesson in deportment. Newman sat down beside the mamma, and she talked a great deal, apparently with the design of convincing him that—if he would only see it—poor dear Claire did not belong to the most fascinating type of woman. She was too tall and thin, too stiff and cold; her mouth was too wide and her nose too narrow. She had no dimples anywhere. And then she was eccentric, eccentric in cold blood; she was an Anglaise, after all. Newman was very impatient; he was counting the minutes until his victims should reappear. He sat silent, leaning upon his cane, looking absently and insensibly at the little Marquise. At length Madame de Bellegarde said she would walk toward the gate of the park and meet her companions; but before she went she dropped her eyes, and, after playing a moment with the lace of her sleeve, looked up again at Newman.

"Do you remember, [illegible] the promise you made me three weeks ago?" And then, as Newman, vainly consulting his memory, was obliged to confess that the promise had escaped it, she declared that he had made her at the time a very queer answer—an answer at which, viewing it in the light of the sequel, she had fair ground for taking offence. "You promised to take me to Bullier's after your marriage. After your marriage—you made a great point of that. Three days after that your marriage was broken off. Do you know, when I heard the news, the first thing I said to myself? 'Oh heaven, now he won't go with me to Bullier's!' And I really began to wonder if you had not been expecting the rupture."

"Oh, my dear lady," murmured Newman, looking down the path to see if the others were not coming.

"I shall be good-natured," said Madame de Bellegarde. "One must not ask too much of a gentleman who is in love with a cloistered nun. Besides, I can't go to Bullier's while we are in mourning. But I haven't given it up for that. The *partie* is arranged; I have my cavalier. Lord Deepmere, if you please! He has gone back to his dear Dublin; but a few months hence I am to name any evening, and he will come over from Ireland on purpose. That's what I call gallantry!"

Shortly after this Madame de Bellegarde walked away with her little girl. Newman sat in his place; the time seemed terribly long. He felt how fiercely his quarter of an hour in the convent chapel had raked over the glowing coals of his resentment. Madame de Bellegarde kept him waiting, but she proved as good as her word. At last she reappeared at the end of the path, with her little girl and her footman; beside her slowly walked her husband, with his mother on his arm. They were a long time advancing, during which Newman sat unmoved. Tingling as he was with passion, it was extremely characteristic of him that he was able to moderate his expression of it, as he would have turned down a flaring gas-burner. His native coolness, shrewdness, and deliberateness, his lifelong submissiveness to the sentiment that words were acts and acts were steps in life, and that in this matter of taking steps curveting and prancing were

— ! he merely murmured — his friend. feeling for a woman very much jet. ion sense shrewdness, coolness, clearness, t

Aching as he fairly did now with his passion — the passion of his wrath at the impudence, on the part of such a pair, of an objection to *him* in the name of clean hands —

exclusively reserved for quadrupeds and foreigners—all this admonished him that rightful wrath had no connection with being a fool and indulging in spectacular violence. So as he rose, when old Madame de Bellegarde and her son were close to him, he only felt very tall and ~~light.~~ He had been sitting beside some shrubbery in such a way as not to be noticeable at a distance; but ~~M. de Bellegarde~~ had ~~evidently already~~ perceived him. ~~His mother and he were holding their course, but Newman stepped in front of them, and~~ they were obliged to pause. He lifted his hat slightly, and looked at them ~~for a moment~~; they were pale with amazement and disgust.

"~~Excuse me~~ for stopping you," he ~~said in a low tone~~, "but I must profit by the occasion. I have ten words to say to you. Will you listen to them?"

The Marquis glared ~~at him, and~~ then turned to his mother. "Can Mr. Newman possibly have anything to say that is worth our listening to?"

"I assure you I ~~have~~ something," ~~said~~ Newman "besides, it is my duty to say it. ~~It's a notification or warning.~~"

"Your duty?" said ~~old Madame de Bellegarde~~, her ~~thin lips curving like a cracked paper~~. "That is your affair, not ours."

Madame Urbain meanwhile had seized her little girl by the hand, with a gesture of surprise and impatience which struck Newman, intent as he was upon his own words, with its dramatic effectiveness. "If Mr. Newman is going to make a scene in public," she exclaimed, "I ~~will~~ take my poor child out of the *mêlée*. She is too young to see such naughtiness!" ~~and~~ she instantly resumed her walk.

"You had much better listen to me," ~~Newman went on~~. "Whether you do or not, ~~things will be disagreeable for you; but at any rate you will be prepared." "I have already heard something of your threats,"~~

Handwritten revisions:

unencumbered and alert.

the Marquis, at hand,

The couple were then for holding their course, at sight of which Newman stepped so straight in front of them that

hard;

"Pardon my

quickly enough

went on;

drily said;

"It concerns you so closely."

he persisted with his diffident ease.

shall

your gain will be small;

the Marquise,

small fine mouth contracting in its odd way as for a whistle.

170

["Whether you do or not your gain will be small,] but at least perhaps you'll be prepared."

"If you mean prepared for your preposterous threat," the Marquis replied, "there's nothing grotesque from you, certainly, for which we're not prepared, and of the idea of which you don't perfectly know what we think."

"You think a great deal more than you yet admit. A moment!" Newman added in reply to a sharp exclamation from Madame de Bellegarde. "I don't at all forget that we're in a

170a

public place, and you see I'll be very quiet. I'm not going to tell your secret to the passers-by; I shall keep it, to begin with, for certain picked listeners. They only who observe us will think we're having a friendly chat and that I'm complimenting you, Madame, on your venerable virtues."

The Marquis gave a hiss that fairly evoked for our friend some vision of a hunched back and a pair of shining evil eyes. "I demand of you to step out of our path!"

Newman instantly complied

170b

and his interlocutors proceeded. But he was still beside them. (and was still distinct.)
"Half an hour hence Madame de Bellegarde will regret that she didn't learn exactly what I mean."

The Marquise had taken a few steps, but at these words she pulled up again, as if not to have the appearance of not facing some monstrous possibilities — monstrous, that is, as a monster of rudeness might make them. "Oh you're like a pedlar with something trumpery to sell," she said, and accompanied it with a strange, small, cold laugh — a demonstration so inconsequent that it meant nothing. He quickly

170c

fell, if it didn't mean a "lovely" "lovely" introduction.

"Oh no, not to sell; I give it to you for nothing." And he had never in his life, no matter under what occasion for it, spoken so completely and so gratefully to the point as now. "You cruelly killed your helpless husband, you know; and I'm in possession of all the facts. That is you did your best, first, and failed and then succeeded—by which I mean finished him—at a stroke and almost without trying."

The Marquise closed her eyes and gave a small dry cough which, as a piece of dissimulation and of self-possession,

170d

seemed to her adversary consummate. "Dear mother," said Urbain as if she had been moved to hilarity, "does this stuff amuse you so much?"

"The rest is more amusing," Newman went on. "You had better not lose it."

The eyes she fixed on him might well have been, he recognized, those with which, according to Mrs. Bread, she had done her husband to death; and they had somehow nothing to do with the stifled shrillness of her spoken retort. "Amusing? Have I killed some one else?"

But she smiled superbly, with her narrow little lips, and repeated Newman's word. "Amusing? Have I killed some one else?"

"I don't count your daughter," said Newman, "though I might! Your husband knew what you were doing. I have a proof of it, whose existence you have never suspected." And he turned to the Marquis, who was terribly white—whiter than Newman had ever seen any one out of a picture. "A paper written by the hand, and signed with the name of Henri-Urbain de Bellegarde. Written after you, Madame, had left him for dead, and while you, sir, had gone—not very fast—for the doctor."

The Marquis looked at his mother; she turned away, looking vaguely round her. "I must sit down," she said in a low tone, going toward the bench on which Newman had been sitting.

"Couldn't you have spoken to me alone?" said the Marquis to Newman, with a strange look.

"Well, yes, if I could have been sure of speaking to your mother alone, too," Newman answered. "But I have had to take you as I could get you."

Madame de Bellegarde, with a movement very eloquent of what he would have called her "grit," her steel-cold pluck and her instinctive appeal to her own personal resources, drew her hand out of her son's arm and went and seated herself upon the bench. There she remained, with her hands folded in her lap, looking straight at Newman. The expression of her face was such that he fancied at first that she was smiling; but he went and stood in front of her, and saw that her elegant features were distorted by agitation. He saw, however, equally, that she was resisting her agitation with all the rigour of her inflexible will, and there was nothing like either fear or submission in her stony stare. She had been startled, but she was not terrified. Newman had an exasperating feeling that she would get the better of him still; he would not have believed it possible that he could so

Handwritten revisions: I've; you've; the; of which; whose face was beyond any he had ever seen dis-composed, decomposed—what did they call it?; madam; and dated; turned to; seated; don't you see?; But her answer to his appeal fell after an instant, rather short; her; fine front she presented; on his drawing nearer felt this movement to be strange and convulsive; extravagantly; with her head erect and; moved, averting herself and; simply said and went back to; in a manner; her companion then asked, all remarkably of their purpose, who wondered if it meant that there was suddenly, all amazingly, a basis for discussion utterly fail to be touched by the sight of a woman (criminal or other) in so tight a place. Madame de Bellegarde gave a glance at her son which seemed tantamount to an injunction to be silent and leave her to her own devices. The Marquis stood beside her, with his hands behind him, looking at Newman.

"What paper is this you speak of?" asked the old lady, with an imitation of tranquillity which would have been applauded in a veteran actress.

"Exactly what I have told you, [illegible] A paper written by your husband after you had left him for dead, and during the couple of hours before you returned. You see he had the time; you shouldn't have stayed away so long. It declares distinctly his wife's murderous intent."

"I should like to see it," Madame de Bellegarde observed.

"I thought you might," said Newman, "and I have taken a copy." And he drew from his waistcoat pocket a small folded sheet.

"Give it to my son," said Madame de Bellegarde. Newman handed it to the Marquis, whose mother, glancing at him, said simply, "Look at it." M. de Bellegarde's eyes had a pale eagerness which it was useless for him to try to dissimulate; he took the paper in his light-gloved fingers and opened it. There was a silence, during which he read it. He had more than time to read it, but still he said nothing; he stood staring at it.

"Where is the original?" asked Madame de Bellegarde, in a voice which was really a consummate negation of impatience.

"In a very safe place. Of course I can't show you that," said Newman. "You might want to take hold of it," he added, with conscious quaintness. "But that's a very correct copy—except, of course, the handwriting. I am keeping the original to show some one else."

M. de Bellegarde at last looked up, and his eyes

She had been upset, but she could think. He felt the pang of a conviction that she would get the better of him still, and he wouldn't — he couldn't so

He

She

connect

connect

the Marquise asked as if confessing to an interest in any possible contribution to the family archives.

him, that evening,

in the most convincing way

she returned

looking at it hard

she observed as with the most natural concern for a manifesto so compromising to the — already in his day, alas, so painfully compromised — author of it.

took it in.

While she simply added

irrepressible

with decision, on which

quite making up in attitude, as our observer noted, for what he failed of in utterance. It was to remain rather a burden on Newman's mind to the end, this irritating, perplexing illustration he afforded of the positive virtue and the incalculable force even in the unholy of "attitude" "as such."

(172a)

"Where is the original?" his mother meantime asked in a voice of the most disinterested curiosity.

"In a very safe place. Of course I can't show you *that*," Newman went on—"a thing the value of which makes it sacred to me. You might want to grab it," he added with conversational quaintness, "and *I've* too much other use for it. But this is a very correct copy—except of course the handwriting. *I'll* get it properly certified for you if you wish. *That* ought to suit you

173

–ity's being properly certified."

The Marquis at last raised a countenance deeply and undisguisedly flushed. "It will require," he nevertheless lightly remarked, "a vast deal of certification!"

"Well," Newman returned, "we can always fall back on the original."

"I'm speaking," said the Marquis, "of the original."

"Oh that, I think, will speak for itself. Still, we can easily get as many persons as possible — as many of those who knew the writer's hand — to speak for it. Think of the number it will interest — if I begin, myself, say, with the Duchess, that amiable very stout lady whose name I forget but who was pleasant to me at your party. She asked me to come and see her, and I've been thinking that in that case I should have much to say to her. But such a matter as this gives me plenty at this rate!"

"You had better keep what you have there, my son," the old woman answered with a strained gaiety.

"By all means," said Newman. "Keep it and show it to your mother when you get home."

1736

"And after enlisting the Duchess?" asked the Marquis, folding the paper and putting it away.

"Well, there are all the other people you had the cruelty to introduce me to in a character of which you were capable, at the next turn, of rudely divesting me. Many of them immediately afterwards left cards on me, so that I have their names correctly and shall know how to find them."

For a moment, on this, neither of Newman's friends spoke; the Marquise sat looking down very hard, while her son's blanched pupils were fixed on her face. "Is that all you have to say?" she finally asked.

173c

"No, I want to say a few words more. I want to say this: I hope you quite understand what I'm about. This is my vindication, you know, of my claim that I've been cruelly wronged. You've treated me before the world, convened for the express purpose, as if I were not good enough for you. I mean to show the world that however bad I may be, you're not quite the proper to say it."

Madame de Bellegarde was silent again and then, with a return of her power to face him, she dealt with his point. Her coolness continued to affect him as extraordinary; otherwise of what alarms, what effronteries, what suspicions and what precautions had she not had from far back, to make her life? "I needn't ask you who has been your accomplice in this clumsy fraud? Catherine Bread told me you had purchased her services."

"Don't accuse Mrs. Bread of venality," Newman returned. "She has kept your secret all these years. She has [given you a long]

given you a long respite. It was beneath her eyes your husband wrote that paper; he put it into her hands with a solemn injunction that she was to make it public. She was too good-hearted to make use of it."

The old lady appeared for an instant to hesitate, and then, "She was my husband's mistress," she said, softly. This was the only concession to self-defence that she condescended to make.

"I doubt that," said Newman.

Madame de Bellegarde got up from her bench. "It was not to your opinions I undertook to listen, and if you have nothing left but them to tell me I think this remarkable interview may terminate." And turning to the Marquis she took his arm again. "My son," she said, "say something!"

[illegible] looked down at his mother, passing his hand over his forehead, and then, tenderly, caressingly, "What shall I say?" he asked.

"There is only one thing to say, [illegible]. [illegible] really not worth while to have interrupted our walk."

But the Marquis thought he could improve this. "Your paper's a forgery," he said to Newman.

Newman shook his head a little, with a tranquil smile. "M. de Bellegarde," [illegible] your mother does better. She has done better all along, from the first of my knowing you. You're a mighty plucky woman, Madame," he continued. "It's a great pity you have made me your enemy. I should have been one of your greatest admirers."

"*Mon pauvre ami,*" said Madame de Bellegarde to her son, in French, and as if she had not heard these words, "you must take me immediately to my carriage."

Newman stepped back and let them leave him; he watched them a moment and saw Madame Urbain, with her little girl, come out of a by-path to meet them. The elderly stooped and kissed her grandchild. "Damn it,

beliefs—however interesting in themselves—

You have had the benefit of her merciful delay."

Marquis

"I believe in her decency!"

charming

very much

too uncertainly inquired.

= that it was really not worth while, on such a showing, to have pulled us up in the street like a pair of pickpockets."

Marquis

surpass

"My husband for years, what he most remarkably liked, with her," she declared drily enough: "She was the meanest of his many mistresses." then oddly resumed,

all amusedly.

of course the crudest of forgeries."

to the position displacement of his hat; with which,

she *is* plucky!" said Newman, and he walked home with a slight sense of being balked. She was so inexpressively defiant! But on reflection he decided that what he had witnessed was no real sense of security, still less a real innocence. It was only a very superior style of brazen assurance. "Wait till she reads the paper!" he said to himself; and he concluded that he should hear from her soon.

He heard sooner than he expected. The next morning, before midday, when he was about to give orders for his breakfast to be served, M. de Bellegarde's card was brought to him. "She has read the paper and she has passed a bad night," said Newman. He instantly admitted his visitor, who came in with the air of the ambassador of a great power meeting the delegate of a barbarous tribe whom an absurd accident had enabled for the moment to be abominably annoying. The ambassador, at all events, had passed a bad night, and his faultlessly careful toilet only threw into relief the frigid rancor in his eyes and the mottled tones of his refined complexion. He stood before Newman a moment, breathing quickly and softly, and shaking his forefinger curtly as his host pointed to a chair.

"What I have come to say is soon said, [illegible] [illegible] can only be said without ceremony."

"I am good for as much or for as little as you desire," said Newman.

The Marquis looked round the room a moment, and then: "On what terms will you part with your scrap of paper?"

"On none!" And while Newman, with his head on one side and his hands behind him, sounded the Marquis's turbid gaze with his own, he added: "Certainly, that is not worth sitting down about."

M. de Bellegarde hesitated a moment, as if he had not heard Newman's refusal. "My mother and I, last evening, [illegible] talked over your story. [illegible]

he sighed,

a sense of having been almost worsted

quite heroically impenetrable

of what M. Nioche called l'usage du monde and Mrs. Tristram the grand manner

has seen how he puts it!

seen

also

he promptly inferred

at any rate,

there

and

painfully

array

sick rancour of his eyes and the mottled spots on his fine skin that resembled, to his host's imagination, the hard finger-prints of fear

What you call your original?

"Ah, on

You'll

Newman

went on, however, as without having heard him

his visitor's depth of detestation,

176 THE AMERICAN. XXIV.

be surprised to learn that we think your little document is—a"—and he held back his word a moment—~~"so garnished."~~

"You forget that with you I'm used to surprises!" ~~exclaimed Newman, with a laugh.~~

"~~The very smallest amount of respect that we owe to my father's~~ memory," the Marquis continued, "makes us desire ~~that~~ he should not be held up to the world as the author of ~~an infamous~~ an attack upon the reputation of a wife whose only fault was that she had been submissive to ~~accumulated injury~~."

"Oh, I see," ~~said Newman.~~ It's for your father's sake." And ~~he~~ laughed the laugh in which he indulged when he was ~~most amused—a noiseless laugh, with his lips closed.~~

But M. de Bellegarde's gravity held good. "There are a few of ~~my father's~~ particular friends for whom the knowledge of so—so unfortunate an—inspiration—would be a real grief. Even say we firmly established by medical evidence the presumption of a mind disordered by fever, *il en resterait quelque chose.* At the best it would look ill in him. Very ill!"

"Don't try medical evidence," said Newman. "Don't touch the doctors and they won't touch you. I don't mind your knowing that I have not written to ~~them~~."

~~Newman fancied that he saw~~ signs in ~~M. de Bellegarde's~~ discoloured mask that this information was extremely pertinent. ~~But it may have been merely fancy, for the Marquis remained majestically argumentative.~~ "For instance, Madame d'Outreville," ~~[struck]~~ of whom you spoke yesterday. I can imagine nothing that would shock her more."

"Oh, I'm quite prepared to shock Madame d'Outreville, ~~you know. That's [struck]. I'm prepared to shock a great many~~ people."

M. de Bellegarde examined for a moment the stitching on ~~the back of~~ one of his gloves. Then, without look-

Characteristic. Newman laughed out as it came. "Of your mother and you I mean?" "Of my deplorable father."

Newman gaily pursued.

an elaborately malignant

his

repeated outrage.

Newman

He flattered himself he saw

his visitor's

"The very scantest consideration we owe his

if not most amused, at any rate most pleased—an intimate noiseless laugh with closed lips.

either of the gentlemen present at the court.

fine white

black

singularly want to shock

That's just what's the matter with me.

The Marquis however remained irreducibly argumentative.

ing up, "We don't offer you money," he said. "That we suppose to be useless."

Newman, turning away, took a few turns about the room, and then came back. "What *do* you offer me? By what I can make out the generosity is all to be on my side."

The Marquis dropped his arms at his side and held his head a little higher. "What we offer you is a chance—a chance that a gentleman should appreciate. A chance to abstain from inflicting a terrible blot upon the memory of a man who certainly had his faults, but who, personally, had done you no wrong."

"There are two things to say to that," said Newman. "The first is, as regards appreciating your 'chance,' that you don't consider me a gentleman. That's your great point, you know. It's a poor rule that won't work both ways. The second is that—well, in a word, you are talking great nonsense!"

Newman, who in the midst of his bitterness had, and have said, kept well before his eyes a certain ideal of saying nothing rude, was immediately somewhat regretfully conscious of the sharpness of these words. But he speedily observed that the Marquis took them more quietly than might have been expected. Mr de Bellegarde, like the stately ambassador that he was, continued the policy of ignoring what was disagreeable in his adversary's replies. He gazed at the gilded arabesques on the opposite wall, and then presently transferred his glance to Newman, as if he too were a large grotesque in a rather vulgar system of chamber-decoration. "I suppose you know that, as regards yourself, it won't do at all."

"How do you mean it won't do?"

"Why, of course you damn yourself. But I suppose that's in your programme. You propose to throw mud at us; you believe, you hope, that some of it may stick. We know, of course, it can't," explained the Marquis in

sides

returned.

felt a quick scruple for the too easy impatience

Sublime

his host

sad nonsense!

as I have ~~said~~ noted,

that

he

had been

naturally,

this horrible ordure

that you've raked together; and

a course so confoundly vindictive vindictive in respect to your discomfiture a tone of conscious lucidity; "but you take the chance and are willing at any rate to show that you yourself have dirty hands."

"That's a good comparison; at least half of it is," said Newman. "I take the chance of something sticking. But as regards my hands, they are clean. I have taken the matter up with my finger-tips."

M. de Bellegarde looked a moment into his hat. "All our friends are quite with us, [illegible] They would have done exactly as we have done."

"I shall believe that when I hear them say it. Meanwhile I shall think better of human nature."

The Marquis looked into his hat again. "Madame de Cintré was extremely fond of her father. If she knew of the existence of the few written words of which you propose to make this scandalous use, she would demand of you, proudly, for his sake, to give it up to her, and she would destroy it without reading it."

"Very possibly," Newman rejoined. "But she will [illegible]. I was in that convent yesterday, and I know what *she* is doing. Lord deliver us! You can guess whether it made me feel forgiving!"

M. de Bellegarde appeared to have nothing more to suggest; but he continued to stand there, rigid and elegant, as a man who believed that his mere personal presence had an argumentative value. Newman watched him, and without yielding an inch on the main issue, felt an incongruously good-natured impulse to help him to retreat in good order.

"Your visit's a failure, you see," he said. "You offer too little."

"Propose something yourself," said the Marquis.

"Give me back Madame de Cintré in the same state in which you took her from me."

M. de Bellegarde threw back his head and his pale face flushed. "Never!" he said.

"You can't!"

awful thing

"My poor perverse sister

require

them

destroy them on the spot!"

it's exactly what she wouldn't know!

hideous place

of mercy!

flush darkly spread

relieved of the blight and free of the poison that are all of your producing!

idea, you see, though ingenious in its way—doesn't work!

at last brought out

"We wouldn't if we could! In the sentiment which led us to deprecate her marriage nothing is changed."

"'Deprecate' is good!" cried Newman. "It was hardly worth while to come here only to tell me that you are not ashamed of yourselves. I could have guessed that!"

The Marquis slowly walked toward the door, and Newman, following, opened it for him. "What you propose to do will be very disagreeable," M. de Bellegarde said. "That is very evident. But it will be nothing more."

"As I understand it," Newman answered, "that will be quite enough!"

M. de Bellegarde stood a moment looking on the ground, as if he were ransacking his ingenuity to see what else he could do to save his father's reputation. Then, with a little cold sigh, he seemed to signify that he regretfully surrendered the late Marquis to the penalty of his turpitude. He gave a hardly perceptible shrug, took his neat umbrella from the servant in the vestibule, and, with his gentlemanly walk, passed out. Newman stood listening till he heard the door close; then he slowly exclaimed: "Well, I ought to begin to be satisfied now!"

XXV.

Newman called upon the comical Duchess, and found her at home. An old gentleman with a high nose and a gold-headed cane was just taking leave of her; he made Newman a protracted obeisance as he retired, and our hero supposed that he was one of the mysterious grandees with whom he had shaken hands at Madame de Bellegarde's ball. The Duchess, in her armchair, from which she did not move, with a great flower-pot on one side of her, a pile of pink-covered novels on the other and a large piece of tapestry depending from her lap, presented an expansive and imposing front; but her aspect was in the highest degree gracious, and there was nothing in her manner to check the effusion of his confidence. She talked to him ~~about~~ flowers and books, getting launched with marvellous promptitude; about the theatres, about the peculiar institutions of his native country, about the humidity of Paris, about the pretty complexions of the American ladies, about his impressions of France and his opinion of its female inhabitants. All this ~~was a brilliant monologue~~ on the part of the Duchess, who, like many of her countrywomen, was a person of an affirmative rather than an interrogative cast ~~of mind~~, who ~~made mots~~ and put them herself into circulation, and who was apt to offer you a present of a convenient little opinion neatly enveloped in the gilt paper of a happy Gallicism. Newman had come to her with a grievance, but he found himself in an atmosphere in which apparently no cognisance was taken of ~~grievances~~; an atmosphere into which the chill of discomfort had never penetrated, and which seemed exclusively made up of mild, sweet, stale intellectual perfumes. The feeling with which he had watched Madame d'Outreville at the treacherous festival of the Bellegardes came back to him; she struck him as a wonderful old lady in a comedy, particularly well up in her part. He ~~observed~~ before long that she asked him no questions about their common friends; she made no allusion to the circumstances under which he had been presented to her. She neither feigned ignorance of a change in these circumstances nor pretended to condole with him upon it; but she smiled and discoursed and compared the tender-tinted wools of her tapestry as if the Bellegardes and their wickedness were not of this world. "She's fighting shy!" ~~said Newman~~ to himself; and, having ~~made the observation, he was prompted to observe~~, further, how ~~the Duchess would carry off her indifference.~~ She did so in a masterly

of

had a large free flow

uttered "good things"

such matters;

noticed

he said

drawn the inference,

was curious to see,

if this were a policy, she would carry it off.

manner. There was not a gleam of disguised consciousness in those small, clear, demonstrative eyes which constituted her nearest claim to personal loveliness; there was not a symptom of apprehension ~~that Newman~~ would trench ~~upon the~~ ground she proposed to avoid. "Upon my word, she does it very well," he tacitly commented. "They all hold together bravely, and, whether any one else can trust them or not, they can certainly trust each other."

Newman, at this juncture ~~fell~~ to admiring the Duchess for her fine manners. He felt, most accurately, that she was not a grain less urbane than she would have been if his marriage were still in prospect; but he felt also that she ~~was not a particle more urbane~~. He had come, so reasoned ~~the Duchess~~—Heaven knew why he had come after what had happened; and for the half hour, therefore, she would be *charmante*. But she would never see him again. Finding no ready-made opportunity to tell his story, ~~Newman~~ pondered these things more dispassionately than might have been expected; he stretched his legs, as usual, and even chuckled a little, appreciatively and noiselessly. And then as ~~the Duchess~~ went on relating a *mot* with which her mother had snubbed the great Napoleon, it occurred to ~~Newman~~ that her evasion of a chapter of French history more interesting to himself might possibly be the result of an extreme consideration for his feelings. Perhaps it was delicacy ~~on the Duchess's part—not policy~~. He was on the point of saying something himself, to make the chance which he had determined to give her still better, when the servant announced another visitor. The Duchess on hearing the name—it was that of an Italian prince—gave a little imperceptible pout, and said to ~~Newman~~ rapidly: "I beg you to remain; I desire this visit to be short." ~~Newman said to himself, at this, that Madame d'Outreville intended, after all, that they should discuss the Bellegardes together.~~

he

on any

fell

led him on single inch further.

this eminent lady—

h

he

rather than diplomacy

his hostess

him

him

He wondered, at this,

then if they mightn't after all get round to the Bellegardes.

The Prince was a short stout man, with a head disproportionately large. He had a dusky complexion and bushy eyebrows, beneath which his eye wore a fixed and somewhat defiant expression; he seemed to be challenging you to insinuate that he was top-heavy. The Duchess, judging from her charge to Newman, regarded him as a bore; but this was not apparent from the unchecked flow of her conversation. She made a fresh series of *mots*, characterised with great felicity the Italian intellect and the taste of the figs at Sorrento, predicted the ultimate future of the Italian kingdom (disgust with the brutal Sardinian rule and complete reversion, throughout the peninsula, to the sacred sway of the Holy Father) and, finally, gave a history of the love affairs of the Princess X—. This narrative provoked some rectifications on the part of the Prince, who, as he said, pretended to know something about that matter; and having satisfied himself that Newman was in no laughing mood, either with regard to the size of his head or anything else, he entered into the controversy with an animation for which the Duchess, when she set him down as a bore, could not have been prepared. The sentimental vicissitudes of the Princess X— led to a discussion of the heart history of the Florentine nobility in general; the Duchess had spent five weeks in Florence, and had gathered much information on the subject. This was merged, in turn, in an examination of the Italian heart *per se*. The Duchess took a brilliantly heterodox view—thought it the least susceptible organ of its kind that she had ever encountered, related examples of its want of susceptibility, and at last declared that for her the Italians were a people of ice. The Prince became flame to refute her, and his visit really proved charming. Newman was naturally out of the conversation; he sat with his head a little on one side watching the interlocutors. The Duchess, as she talked, frequently looked at him with a smile, as if to intimate, in the charming

stare;

so

glowered

hint that he might be hydrocephalic.

mild

our own friend,

abundance of her speech. She caused it to frisk hither and yon and then pull up on a *mot* as a ballerina whirls, for breath, into an ecstatic balance; she

took up the heart-history of things friend cette pauvre Princesse, a lady unknown to Newman, who had notoriously so much heart. This record exposed itself to a considerable contrail from the Prince, who was apparently not related to the heroine in question otherwise than by her intimate annals, familiarity with

the authenticity of his facts,

and rhetoric

pray

race were half arithmetic and half ice.

Machiavellian power to calculate its perils and profits,

The often so oddly-directed passions of their friend led Newman's companions to

côté

côté passionel of the body and the very bosom of that

who had arrived at highly original conclusions,

lately spent several weeks in

manner of her nation, that it lay only with him to say something very much to the point. But he said nothing at all, and at last his thoughts began to wander. A singular feeling came over him—a sudden sense of the folly of his errand. What under the sun had he to say to the Duchess, ~~after all~~? Wherein would it profit him ~~to tell her that~~ the Bellegardes ~~were traitors and that the old lady,~~ into the bargain ~~was~~ a murderess? He seemed morally to have turned ~~a sort of~~ somersault, and to find things looking differently in consequence. He felt ~~a sudden stiffening of his will and quickening of his reserve.~~ What in the world had he been thinking of when he fancied the Duchess could help him, and that it would conduce to his comfort to make her think ill of the Bellegardes? What did her opinion of the Bellegardes matter to him? It was only a shade more important than the opinion the Bellegardes entertained of ~~her.~~ The Duchess help him—that cold, stout, soft, artificial woman help him?—she who in the last twenty minutes had built up between them a wall of polite conversation in which she evidently flattered herself that he would never find a gate. Had it come to that—that he was asking favours of ~~conceited people~~, and appealing for sympathy where he had no sympathy to give? He rested his arms on his knees and sat for some minutes staring into his hat. As he did so his ears tingled—~~he had come very near being an ass.~~ Whether or no the Duchess would hear his story he wouldn't tell it. Was he to sit there another half-hour for the sake of exposing the Bellegardes? The Bellegardes be ~~hanged!~~ He got up abruptly and advanced to shake hands with his hostess.

"You can't stay longer?" she ~~asked, very~~ graciously.

"~~I am afraid not," he said.~~

She hesitated, ~~a moment~~, and then, "I had an idea you had something particular to say to me," she ~~declared.~~

Newman ~~looked at her~~; he felt a little dizzy; for the

after all

for

a sudden

for traitors and the Marquise

herself

false gods

as by the effect of some colder current of the air his will stiffen in another direction and the mantle of his reserve draw closer

Was he to have brayed like that animal whose ears are longest?

met her eyes;

returned

deeply damned!

"If you'll pardon me, no"

asked

184 THE AMERICAN. XXV.

moment he seemed to be turning his somersault again. The little Italian prince came to his help: "Ah, Madame, who has not that?" he softly sighed.

"Don't teach Mr. Newman to say *fadaises*," said the Duchess. "It is his merit that he doesn't know how."

"Yes, I don't know how to say *fadaises*," said Newman, "and I don't want to say anything unpleasant."

"I am sure you are very considerate," said the Duchess with a smile; and she gave him a little nod for good-bye, with which he took his departure.

Once in the street he stood for some time on the pavement, wondering whether after all he was not an ass not to have discharged his pistol. And then he decided that to talk to any one whomsoever about the Bellegardes would be extremely disagreeable to him. The least disagreeable thing, under the circumstances, was to banish them from his mind, and never think of them again. Indecision had not hitherto been one of Newman's weaknesses, and in this case it was not of long duration. For three days after this he did not, or at least he tried not to, think of the Bellegardes. He dined with Mrs. Tristram and on her mentioning their name he begged her almost severely to desist. This gave Tom Tristram a much-coveted opportunity to offer his condolences.

He leaned forward, laying his hand on Newman's arm, compressing his lips and shaking his head. "The fact is, my dear fellow, you see that you ought never to have gone into it. It was not your doing, I know—it was all my wife. If you want to come down on her I'll stand off: I give you leave to hit her as hard as you like. You know she has never had a word of reproach from me in her life, and I think she's in need of something of the kind. Why didn't you listen to me? You know I didn't believe in the thing. I thought it at the best an amiable delusion. I don't profess to be a Don Juan or a gay Lothario—that class of man, you know; but I

was conscious of the high—or at least the higher—air in which he performed gymnastic revolutions

admitted,

smiled;

of

all

had,

had not

however,

been most of an ass not to have offered to the great lady's inhalation his nosegay of strange flowers.

austerity

decided, he quite had the sense of discovering that he should simply hate to talk of the Bellegardes with any one. The thing he most wanted to do, it suddenly appeared,

a high jump in which you might bruise a shin

a flick of the whip

requested

+ shin

he applied all his thought to not thinking—thinking that is, of the Marquise and her son

do think she wants to be a bit touched up

do pretend to know something about the harder sex. I have never disliked a woman in my life that she has not turned out badly. I was not at all deceived in Lizzie for instance; I always had my doubts about her. Whatever you may think of my present situation, I must at least admit that I got into it with my eyes open. Now suppose you had got into something like this box with Madame de Cintré. You may depend upon it she would have turned out a stiff one. And upon my word I don't see where you could have found your comfort. Not from the Marquis, my dear Newman; he wasn't a man you could go and talk things over with in a sociable, common-sense way. Did he ever seem to want to have you on the premises—did he ever try to see you alone? Did he ever ask you to come and smoke a cigar with him of an evening, or step in, when you had been calling on the ladies, and take something? I don't think you would have got much encouragement out of *him*. And as for the old lady, she struck one as an uncommonly strong dose. They have a great expression here, you know; they call it 'sympathetic.' Everything is sympathetic—or ought to be. Now Madame de Bellegarde is about as sympathetic as that mustard-pot. They're a d——d cold-blooded lot, any way; I felt it awfully at that ball of theirs. I felt as if I were walking up and down in the Armoury in the Tower of London. My dear boy, don't think me a vulgar brute for hinting at it, but, you may depend upon it, all they wanted was your money. I know something about that; I can tell when people want one's money. Why they stopped wanting yours I don't know; I suppose because they could get some one else's without working so hard for it. It isn't worth finding out. It may be that it was not Madame de Cintré that backed out first; very likely the old woman put her up to it. I suspect she and her mother are really as thick as thieves, eh? You're well out of it, my boy, make up your mind to that. If I express myself strongly

have been a tremendous homme à femmes, as they say here, but I've instincts

about the rest that, hang it, I've honestly come by. I've never mistrusted

your grand old Countess.

She'd

an easy and natural

that daughter of a hundred earls his mother,

that is when it isn't it ought to be.

stony-faced

any damned thing

with your Countess, Lizzie's and yours, that the idea of chucking you originated;

at any rate old man;

every one cased in ancestral steel, every one perched up in a panoply.

it is all because I love you so much; and from that point of view I may say I should as soon have thought of making up to that piece of pale high-mightiness as I should have thought of making up to the Obelisk in the Place de la Concorde."

Newman sat gazing at Tristram during this harangue with a lack-lustre eye; never yet had he seemed to himself to have outgrown so completely the phase of equal comradeship with Tom Tristram. Mrs. Tristram's glance at her husband had more of a spark; she turned to Newman with a slightly lurid smile. "You must at least do justice," she said, "to the felicity with which Mr. Tristram repairs the indiscretions of a too zealous wife."

But even without the aid of Tom Tristram's conversational felicities, Newman would have begun to think of the Bellegardes again. He could cease to think of them only when he ceased to think of his loss and privation, and the days had as yet but scantily lightened the weight of this incommodity. In vain Mrs. Tristram begged him to cheer up; she assured him that the sight of his countenance made her miserable.

"How can I help it?" he demanded with a trembling voice. "I feel like a widower—and a widower who has not even the consolation of going to stand beside the grave of his wife—who has not the right to wear so much mourning as a weed on his hat. I feel," he added in a moment, "as if my wife had been murdered and her assassins were still at large."

Mrs. Tristram made no immediate rejoinder, but at last she said, with a smile which, in so far as it was a forced one, was less successfully simulated than such smiles, on her lips, usually were: "Are you very sure that you would have been happy?"

Newman stared a moment, and then shook his head. "That's weak [struck out]; that won't do."

"Well," said Mrs. Tristram, with a more triumphant

peculiarity

he

lash of his friend's loud tongue Newman would have waked again into his bitterest consciousness. He could keep it at bay only when he could cease to miss what he had lost and each day, for the present, but added a ton of weight to that quantity.

se faire, as she put it, une raison;

wretched.

— how can I help it when the sight of everything makes me so?

He

She persisted as with an idea,

bravery, "I don't believe you would have been happy."

Newman gave a little laugh. "Say I should have been miserable, then; it's a misery I should have preferred to any happiness."

Mrs. Tristram began to muse. "I should have been curious to see; it would have been very strange."

"Was it from curiosity that you urged me to try and marry her?"

"A little," said Mrs. Tristram, growing still more audacious. Newman gave her the one angry look he had been destined ever to give her, turned away and took up his hat. She watched him a moment, and then she said, "That sounds very cruel, but it is less so than it sounds. Curiosity has a share in almost everything I do. I wanted very much to see, first, whether such a marriage could actually take place; second, what would happen if it should take place."

"So you didn't believe," said Newman resentfully.

"Yes, I believed—I believed that it would take place, and that you would be happy. Otherwise I should have been, among my speculations, a very heartless creature. *But*," she continued, laying her hand upon Newman's arm, and hazarding a grave smile, "it was the highest flight ever taken by a tolerably bold imagination!"

Shortly after this she recommended him to leave Paris and travel for three months. Change of scene would do him good, and he would forget his misfortune sooner in absence from the objects which had witnessed it. "I really feel," Newman rejoined, "as if to leave *you*, at least, would do me good—and cost me very little effort. You are growing cynical; you shock me and pain me."

"Very good," said Mrs. Tristram, good-naturedly or cynically, as may be thought most probable. "I shall certainly see you again."

Newman was very willing to get away from Paris; the brilliant streets he had walked through in his happier

He gave a sound of irritation.

She took it in her musing way.

union

to it afterwards.

really done."

then it would have damnably failed. Failure for failure I should have preferred that one to this."

put myself forward?"

she still more boldly answered.

He was ready enough to get quite away;

she said,

come through;

if

he replied,

had n't faith?" he said resentfully.

"Yes, I had faith—faith that

hours, and which then seemed to wear a higher brilliancy in honour of his happiness, appeared now to be in the secret of his defeat and to look down upon it in shining mockery. He would go somewhere; he cared little where; and he made his preparations. Then, one morning, at haphazard, he drove to the train that would transport him to Boulogne and despatch him thence to the shores of Britain. As he rolled along in the train he asked himself what had become of his revenge, and he was able to say that it was provisionally pigeon-holed in a very safe place; it would keep till called for.

He arrived in London in the midst of what is called "the season," and it seemed to him at first that he might here put himself in the way of being diverted from his heavy-heartedness. He knew no one in all England, but the spectacle of the mighty metropolis roused him somewhat from his apathy. Anything that was enormous usually found favour with [illegible], and the multitudinous energies and industries of England stirred within him a dull vivacity of contemplation. It is on record that the weather, at that moment, was of the finest English quality; he took long walks and explored London in every direction; he sat by the hour in Kensington Gardens and beside the adjoining Drive, watching the people and the horses and the carriages; the rosy English beauties, the wonderful English dandies. and the splendid flunkeys. He went to the opera and found it better than in Paris; he went to the theatre and found a surprising charm in listening to dialogue the finest points of which came within the range of his comprehension. He made several excursions into the country, recommended by the waiter at his hotel, with whom, on this and similar points, he had established confidential relations. He watched the deer in Windsor Forest and admired the Thames from Richmond Hill; he ate whitebait and brown bread and butter at Greenwich, and strolled in the grassy shadow of the cathedral of Canterbury. He also visited the

Tower of London and Madame Tussaud's exhibition. One day he thought he would go to Sheffield, and then, thinking again, he gave it up. Why should he go to Sheffield? He had a feeling that the link which bound him to a possible interest in the manufacture of cutlery was broken. He had no desire for an "inside view" of any successful enterprise whatever, and he would not have given the smallest sum for the privilege of talking over the details of the most "splendid" business with the ~~shrewdest of overseers~~.

One afternoon he had walked into ~~Hyde~~ Park and was slowly threading his way through the human maze which ~~edges the Drive. The~~ stream of carriages ~~was no~~ less dense, and Newman, as usual, marvelled at the strange dingy figures ~~which~~ he saw taking the air in some of the ~~stateliest vehicles~~. They reminded him of what he had read of eastern and southern countries, in which grotesque idols and fetiches were sometimes taken out of their temples and carried abroad in golden chariots to be ~~displayed to the multitude~~. He ~~saw~~ a great many pretty cheeks beneath high-plumed hats as he squeezed his way through serried waves of crumpled muslin; and, sitting on little chairs at the base of the great serious English trees, he observed a number of quiet-eyed maidens, who seemed only to remind him afresh that the magic of beauty had gone out of the world with ~~Madame de Cintré~~: to say nothing of other damsels whose eyes were not quiet and who struck him still more as a satire on possible consolation. He had been walking for some time, when, directly in front of him, borne ~~back~~ by the summer breeze, he heard a few words uttered in ~~that~~ bright Parisian idiom ~~from which~~ his ears had begun to ~~alienate themselves~~. The voice in which the words were spoken ~~made them seem even more like a thing with which he had once been familiar~~, and as he bent his eyes it lent an identity to the commonplace elegance of the back ~~hair and shoulders~~ of a young lady walking in the

the

most original of managers.

fringes the

This stream was no

seen of the people

most shining conveyances

the

noted

forget

was a peculiar recall

view

toward him

the woman wrenched from him:

same direction as himself. Mademoiselle Nioche, apparently, had come to seek a more rapid advancement in London, and another glance led Newman to suppose that she had found it. A gentleman was strolling beside her, lending a most attentive ear to her conversation and too entranced to open his lips. Newman did not hear his voice, but perceived that he presented the dorsal expression of a well-dressed Englishman. Mademoiselle Nioche was attracting attention: the ladies who passed her turned round to survey the Parisian perfection of her toilet. A great cataract of flounces rolled down from the young lady's waist to Newman's feet; he had to step aside to avoid treading upon them. He stepped aside, indeed, with a decision of movement which the occasion scarcely demanded; for even this imperfect glimpse of Miss Noémie had excited his displeasure. She seemed an odious blot upon the face of nature; he wanted to put her out of his sight. He thought of Valentin de Bellegarde still green in the earth of his burial—his young life clipped by this flourishing impudence. The perfume of the young lady's finery sickened him; he turned his head and tried to deflect his course; but the pressure of the crowd drove him near her a few minutes longer, so that he heard what she was saying.

"Ah, I'm sure he will miss me," she murmured. "It was very cruel in me to leave him; I'm afraid you will think me a very heartless creature. He might perfectly well have come with us. I don't think he is very well," she added; "it seemed to me to-day that he was not very gay."

Newman wondered whom she was talking about, but just then an opening among his neighbours enabled him to turn away, and he said to himself that she was probably paying a tribute to British propriety and playing at tender solicitude about her papa. Was that miserable old man still treading the path of vice in her train? Was he still giving her the benefit of his experience of

seeking her fortune had apparently thought she might find it faster in London

him to wonder if she might now have lighted on it

beguiled

strolled

as with a sense of the Parisian finish

caught no sound of him but had the impression of "English shoulders" an "English" fit, an English silence

held

'll

he was rather down

parent

fragrance

sharpened again his constant soreness

keep his distance;

think I'm a very little heart

affairs, and had he crossed the sea to serve as her interpreter? Newman walked some distance farther, and then began to retrace his steps, taking care not to ~~traverse~~ again the orbit of Mademoiselle Nioche. At last he looked for a chair under the trees, but he had some difficulty in finding an empty one. He was about to give up the search when he saw a gentleman rise from the seat he had been occupying, leaving ~~Newman~~ to take it without looking at his neighbours. ~~He~~ sat there for some time without heeding them; his attention was lost in the ~~irritation and bitterness produced by his recent glimpse of Miss Noémie's iniquitous vitality~~. But at the end of a quarter of an hour, dropping his eyes, he perceived a small pug dog squatted upon the path near his feet—a diminutive but very perfect specimen of its interesting species. The pug was sniffing at the fashionable world, as it passed him, with his little black muzzle, and was kept from extending his investigation by a large blue ribbon attached to his collar with an enormous rosette, and held in the hand of a person seated next to Newman. To this person ~~Newman~~ transferred his attention, and immediately ~~perceived that he was~~ the object of all that of his neighbour, who was staring up at him from a pair of little fixed white eyes. These eyes ~~Newman~~ instantly recognised; he had been sitting for the last quarter of an hour beside M. Nioche. He had vaguely felt ~~that some one was staring at him~~. M. Nioche continued to stare; he appeared afraid to move, even to the extent of ~~evading Newman's glance~~.

"Dear me!" said Newman; "are you here too?" And he looked at his neighbour's helplessness more grimly than he knew. M. Nioche had a new hat and a pair of kid gloves; his clothes, too, seemed to belong ~~to a more recent antiquity~~ than of yore. Over his arm was suspended a lady's mantilla—a light and brilliant tissue, fringed with white lace—which had apparently been committed to his keeping; and the little dog's blue

w/

cross

Newman

our friend

our hero

found himself

he

rage of his renewed vision of the little horrid fact of Noémie

to a less hoary old

himself in range of some gaze

saving by flight what might have been left of his honour

ribbon was wound tightly round his hand. There was no ~~expression~~ hint of recognition in his face—~~or~~ nor of anything ~~indeed, but a sort of~~ save a feeble fascinated dread. Newman looked at the pug and the lace mantilla, and then he met the old man's eyes again. "You know me, I see," he pursued. "You might have spoken to me before." M. Nioche still said nothing, but it seemed to ~~Newman~~ his ex-patron that his eyes began faintly to water. "I didn't expect," ~~our hero~~ he went on, "to meet you so far from—from the Café de la Patrie." ~~The old man~~ the latter remained silent, but decidedly Newman had touched the source of tears. His neighbour sat staring, and ~~Newman~~ He added: "What's the matter, M. Nioche? You used to talk, to talk very ~~prettily~~. Don't you remember you even gave lessons in conversation?" — What did you call it? — very sentiment

At this M. Nioche decided to change his attitude. He stooped and picked up the pug, lifted it to his face and wiped his eyes on its little soft back. "I'm afraid to speak to you," he presently said, looking over the puppy's shoulder. "I hoped you wouldn't notice me. I should have moved away, but I was afraid that if I moved ~~you would notice me~~ it would strike you. So I sat very still."

"I suspect you've a bad conscience, sir," ~~said~~ he pronounced Newman.

The old man put down the little dog and held it carefully in his lap. Then he shook his head, with his eyes still ~~fixed upon his interlocutor~~ shining and pleading. "No, Mr. Newman, I've a good conscience," he ~~murmured~~ weakly wailed.

"Then why should you want to slink away from me?"

"Because—because you don't understand my position."

"Oh, I think you once explained it to me," said Newman. "But it seems improved."

"Improved!" ~~exclaimed M. Nioche, under his breath~~ his companion quavered. "Do you call this improvement?" And he ~~glanced at~~ ~~gracefully~~ embraced the treasures in his arms.

"Why, you're on your travels," Newman rejoined.

superior

inane

dig

if he were

his critic

for his base accommoda= tion

an affected failure of reason

his face gave out a peculiar convulsion (?)

pestilent

appealed

Je ne lui ai pas trouvé trouvé d'excuses (?)

public

vaguely inquired

had

have

returned with mild portentousness

"A visit to London in the season is certainly a sign of prosperity."

M. Nioche, in answer to this piece of irony, lifted the puppy up to his face again, peering at Newman with his small blank eye-holes. There was something almost imbecile in the movement, and Newman hardly knew whether he was taking refuge in a convenient affectation of unreason, or whether he had in fact paid for his dishonour by the loss of his wits. In the latter case, just now, he felt little more tenderly to the foolish old man than in the former. Responsible or not, he was equally an accomplice of his detestably mischievous daughter. Newman was going to leave him abruptly when a ray of entreaty appeared to disengage itself from the old man's misty gaze. "Are you going away?" he asked.

"Do you want me to stay?" said Newman.

"I should have left you—from consideration. But my dignity suffers at your leaving me—that way."

"Have you got anything particular to say to me?"

M. Nioche looked round him to see that no one was listening, and then he said, very softly, but distinctly, "I have not forgiven her!"

Newman gave a short laugh, but the old man seemed for the moment not to perceive it; he was gazing away, absently, at some metaphysical image of his implacability. "It doesn't much matter whether you forgive her or not," said Newman. "There are other people who won't, I assure you."

"What has she done?" M. Nioche softly questioned, turning round again. "I don't know what she does, you know."

"She has done a devilish mischief; it doesn't matter what. She's a nuisance; she ought to be stopped."

M. Nioche stealthily put out his hand and laid it very gently upon Newman's arm. "Stopped, yes," he whispered. "That's it. Stopped short. She is running away—she must be stopped." Then he paused a moment and looked round him. "I mean to stop her," he went on. "I am only waiting for my chance."

"I see," said Newman, laughing briefly again. "She is running away and you are running after her. You have run a long distance."

But M. Nioche stared insistently. "I shall stop her!" he softly repeated.

He had hardly spoken when the crowd in front of them separated, as if by the impulse to make way for an important personage. Presently, through the opening, advanced Mademoiselle Nioche, attended by the gentleman whom Newman had lately observed. His face being now presented to our hero, the latter recognised the irregular features, the hardly more regular complexion, and the amiable expression of Lord Deepmere. Noémie, on finding herself suddenly confronted with Newman, who, like M. Nioche, had risen from his seat, faltered for a barely perceptible instant. She gave him a little nod, as if she had seen him yesterday, and then, with a good-natured smile, "*Tiens*, how we keep meeting!" she said. She looked consummately pretty, and the front of her dress was a wonderful work of art. She went up to her father, stretching out her hands for the little dog, which he submissively placed in them, and she began to kiss it and murmur over it: "To think of leaving him all alone,—what a wicked, abominable creature he must believe me! He has been very unwell," she added, turning and affecting to explain to Newman, with a spark of infernal impudence, fine as a needle-point, in her eye. "I don't think the English climate agrees with him."

"It seems to agree wonderfully well with his mistress," said Newman.

"Do you mean me? I have never been better, thank you," Miss Noémie declared. "But with *milord*," and she gave a brilliant glance at her late companion, "how can one help being well?" She seated herself in the chair from which her father had risen and began to arrange the little dog's rosette.

Lord Deepmere carried off such embarrassment as might be incidental to this unexpected encounter with the inferior grace of a male and a Briton. He blushed a good deal, and greeted the object of his late momentary aspiration to rivalry in the favour of a person other than the mistress of the invalid pug with an awkward nod and a rapid ejaculation—an ejaculation to which Newman, who often found it hard to understand the speech of English people, was able to attach no meaning. Then the young man stood there with his hand on his hip and with a conscious grin, staring askance at Miss Nioche. Suddenly an idea seemed to strike him and he said, turning to Newman, "Oh, you know her?"

"Yes," said Newman, "I know her. I don't believe you do."

"Oh dear, yes, I do!" said Lord Deepmere with another grin. "I knew her in Paris—by my poor cousin Bellegarde, you know. He knew her, poor fellow, didn't he? It was she, you know, who was at the bottom of his affair. Awfully sad, wasn't it?" continued the young man, talking off his embarrassment as his simple nature permitted. "They got up some story about its being for the Pope; about the other man having said something against the Pope's morals. They always do that, you know. They put it on the Pope because Bellegarde was once in the Zouaves. But it was about *her* morals—*she* was the Pope!" Lord Deepmere pursued, directing an eye illumined by this pleasantry toward Mademoiselle Nioche, who was bending gracefully over her lap-dog, apparently absorbed in conversation with it. "I daresay you think it rather odd that I should—ah—keep up the acquaintance," the young man resumed; "but she couldn't help it, you know, and

Bellegarde was only my twentieth cousin. I daresay you think ~~her~~ rather cheeky, my showing with her in [struck out]; but you see she isn't known yet, and she's ~~in such a very good form——" And Lord Deepmere's conclusion was lost in the~~ attesting glance ~~which he again directed toward the young lady~~.

Newman turned away; he was having ~~more of her than he relished~~. M. Nioche had stepped aside on his daughter's approach, and he stood there, within a very small compass, looking down hard at the ground. It had never yet, as between him and ~~Newman~~, been so apposite to place on record ~~the fact that he had not forgiven his daughter~~. As Newman ~~was moving away he looked up and drew near to him, and Newman~~, seeing the old ~~man~~ had something particular to say, bent his head ~~for~~ an instant.

"You'll see it some day ~~in the papers," murmured M. Nioche~~.

Our hero ~~departed to hide his smile~~, and to this day, though the newspapers form his principal reading, his eyes have not been arrested by any paragraph forming a sequel to this announcement.

~~[struck out]~~ XXVI.

IN that uninitiated observation of the great spectacle of English life ~~upon~~ which I have touched, it might be supposed that ~~Newman~~ passed a great many dull days. But the dulness ~~of his days pleased him~~; his melancholy, which was settling ~~into~~ a secondary stage, like a healing wound, had in it a certain acrid, palatable sweetness. He had company ~~of~~ his thoughts and for the present ~~he~~ wanted ~~no~~ other. He had no desire to make acquaintances and ~~he~~ left untouched a couple of notes of intro-

it

their place;

so remarkably, thoroughly nice—!" With which his

too much of her niceness ⊙

returned to the young lady ⊙

who had drawn so near,

late protector,

decidedly

he

the

turned off he felt himself held, and,

was as grateful as a warm, fragrant bath, and

none

that, for his vindication, he was only waiting to strike ⊙

broke away ~~[struck out]~~ for impatience of the whole connection,

Dans les feuilles ⊙")

feuilles.

197

-duction which had been sent him by Tom Tristram. He mused a great deal on Madame de Cintré—sometimes with a dull despair that might have seemed a near neighbour to detachment. He lived over again the happiest hours he had known—that silver chain of numbered days in which his afternoon visits, strained so sensibly to the ideal end, had come to figure for him a flight of firm marble steps where the ascent from one to the other was a distinct occasion, giving a nearer view of the chamber of confidence at the top, a white tower that flushed more and more as with a light of dawn. He had yet held in his cheated arms, he felt the full experience and when he closed them together round the void that was all they now possessed, he might have been some solitary & spare athlete practising restlessly in the corridor of the circus. He came back to reality's mind, after such reveries, with a shock somewhat muffled; he had begun to know the need of accepting the absolute. At other times, however, the truth was again an infamy and the actual a lie, and he could only pace and rage and remember till

1976

he was weary. Passion in him by habit was hotter, burned clear rather than thick, and in the clearness he saw things, common things not gross and close things, having never the excuse that anything could make him blind. Without quite knowing it at first, he began to read a moral into his strange adventure. He asked himself in his quieter hours whether he perhaps *had* been more commercial than was decent. We know that it was in reaction against questions exclusively commercial that he had come out to pick up for a while or otherwise a critical an intellectual living in Europe: it may therefore be

197c

understand that he was able to conceive of a votary of the mere market smelling too strong for true good company. He was willing to grant in a given case that unpleasant effect, but he couldn't bring it home to himself that he had reeked. He believed there had been as few reflections of his smugness caught during all those weeks in the high polish of surrounding surfaces as there were monuments of his meanness scattered about the world. No one had ever unprovokedly suffered by him — as provokedly was another matter: he liked to remember that and to repeat it, and to defy himself to bring up a case. If moreover there was any reason in the nature of things why his connection with

business should have cast a
shadow on a connection even a
connection broken with a woman
justly proud, he was willing to
sponge it out of his life forever.
The thing seemed a possibility; he
couldn't feel it doubtless as keenly
as some people, and it scarce
struck him as worth while to flap
his wings very —

hard to rise to the idea; but he could feel it enough to make any sacrifice that still remained to be made. As to what such sacrifice ~~was now to be made to~~ [illegible] stopped short before a blank wall over which there sometimes played ~~a shadowy imagery~~. ~~He had a fancy~~ of carrying out his life as he would have directed it [illegible] Madame de Cintré had been left to him [illegible] making it a religion to do nothing [illegible] she would have disliked. In this, certainly, there was no sacrifice; but there was a pale, oblique ray of inspiration. It would be lonely entertainment—a good deal like a [illegible] talking to himself ~~in the mirror for want of~~ better company. Yet the idea yielded [illegible] several half-hours' dumb exaltation as he sat, ~~with~~ his hands in his pockets and his legs ~~stretched~~, over the relics of an expensively [illegible] dinner, in the undying English twilight. If, however, his commercial imagination was dead, he felt no contempt for the surviving actualities begotten by it. He was glad he had been prosperous and had been a great ~~man of business~~ ~~rather than a small~~ one; he was extremely glad he was rich. He felt no impulse to sell all he had and give to the poor, or to retire into meditative economy and asceticism. He was glad he was rich and tolerably young; if it was possible to ~~think too much about buying and selling~~ it was ~~a gain to have a good slice of life left in which not to think about them. Come, what should he think about now? Again and again Newman could only think of one thing; his thoughts always came back to it, and as they did so, with an emotional rush~~ which seemed physically to express itself in a sudden upward choking, he leaned forward—the waiter having left the room—and, resting his arms on the table, buried his troubled face.

He remained in England till midsummer, and spent a month in the country, wandering ~~about~~ among cathedrals, castles and ruins. Several times, taking a walk from his inn ~~into meadows and~~ parks, he stopped by a well-worn

- strange shadows and confused signs
- Was now to be made to, here he
- Was it a thinkable plan, that
- man's
- him
- had
- operating
- that of
- Yet again still to have time for experiments in other air. Come then, what air should it now be?
- outstretched
- bad
- hanging about
- swept across field-paths and through great
- Ah, again and again, he could taste but one sweetness, that came back to him and back; and as this happened, with a force
- have inhaled too fondly the reek of the market,

stile, looked across through the early evening at a gray church tower, with its dusky nimbus of thick-circling swallows, and remembered that this might have been part of the entertainment of his honeymoon. He had never been so much alone or indulged so little in accidental dialogue. The period of recreation appointed by Mrs. Tristram had at last expired and he asked himself what he should do now. Mrs. Tristram had written to him, proposing to him that he should join her in the Pyrenees, but he was not in the humour to return to France. The simplest thing was to repair to Liverpool and embark on the first American steamer. Newman made his way to the great seaport and secured his berth; and the night before sailing he sat in his room at the hotel staring down vacantly and wearily, at an open portmanteau. A number of papers were lying upon it, which he had been meaning to look over; some of them might conveniently be destroyed. But at last he shuffled them roughly together and pushed them into a corner of the valise; they were business papers and he was in no humour for sifting them. Then he drew forth his pocket-book and took out a paper of smaller size than those he had dismissed. He did not unfold it; he simply sat looking at the back of it. If he had momentarily entertained the idea of destroying it the idea quickly expired. What the paper suggested was the feeling that lay in his innermost heart and that no reviving cheerfulness could long quench—the feeling that, after all and above all, he was a good fellow wronged. With it came a hearty hope that the Bellegardes were enjoying their suspense as to what he would do yet. The more it was prolonged the more they would enjoy it. He had hung fire once, yes; perhaps in his present queer state of mind he might hang fire again. But he restored the little paper to his pocket-book very tenderly, and felt better for thinking of the suspense of the Bellegardes. He felt better every time he thought of it after that, as he sailed the summer seas.

Handwritten revisions:

- such
- intimacy
- nor
- chance talk.
- next [blotted] do ⊙ She had written to propose
- He proceeded accordingly to that
- and stared
- sorting
- lay
- bag
- leaf
- this possibility at last quickly dropped
- the thing
- while
- safe scrap
- hope as intense as a pang.

He landed in New York and journeyed across the continent to San Francisco, and nothing that he observed by the way contributed to mitigate his sense of being a good fellow wronged.

He saw a great many other good fellows—his old friends—but he told none of them of the trick that had been played him. He said simply that the lady he was to have married had changed her mind, and when he was asked if he had changed his own himself "Suppose we change the subject." He told his friends that he had brought home no "new ideas" from Europe, and his conduct probably struck them as an eloquent proof of failing invention. He took no interest in chatting about his affairs, and manifested no desire to look over his accounts. He asked half a dozen questions which, like those of an eminent physician inquiring for particular symptoms, showed that he still knew what he was talking about; but he made no comments and gave no directions. He not only puzzled [illegible] Stock [illegible] himself surprised at the extent of his indifference. As it seemed only to increase he made an effort to combat it; he tried to interest himself and [illegible] occupations. But they appeared [illegible]; do what he would he somehow could not believe in them. Sometimes he began to fear that there was something the matter with [illegible] brain, [illegible] softened, and that the end of his strong activities had come. This idea came back to him with an exasperating force. A hopeless, helpless loafer, useful to no one and detestable to himself—this was what the treachery of the Bellegardes had made of him. In his restless idleness he came back from San Francisco to New York, and sat for three days in the lobby of his hotel looking out through a huge wall of plate-glass at the unceasing stream of pretty girls in Parisian-looking dresses, undulating past with little parcels nursed against their neat figures. At the end of three days he returned

simply answering

discussing business and showed no desire to go into anything whatever.

proud he was master of his subject;

take hold and to recover as they said his 'spring.' But the ground was inelastic and the issues dead;

all the prominent men but was

him, that he had suffered unwittingly, some small horrid cerebral lesion or nervous accident;

for a while hung about him and haunted him.

and looked

who

where he

anxious

to San Francisco, and having arrived there he wished he had stayed away. He had nothing to do, his occupation was gone and it seemed to him that he should never find it again. He had nothing to do *here*, he sometimes said to himself; but there was something beyond the ocean that he was still to do; something that he had left undone experimentally and speculatively, to see if it could content itself to remain undone. But it was not content; it kept pulling at his heart-strings and thumping at his reason; it murmured in his ears and hovered perpetually before his eyes. It interposed between all new resolutions and their fulfilment; it seemed like a stubborn ghost dumbly entreating to be laid. Till that was done he should never be able to do anything else.

One day toward the end of the winter, after a long interval, he received a letter from Mrs. Tristram, who apparently was animated by a charitable desire to amuse and distract her correspondent. She gave him much Paris gossip, talked of General Packard and Miss Kitty Upjohn, enumerated the new plays at the theatre and enclosed a note from her husband, who had gone down to spend a month at Nice. Then came her signature, and after this her postscript. The latter consisted of these few lines: "I heard three days since from my friend the Abbé Aubert that Madame de Cintré last week took the veil at the Carmelites. It was on her twenty-seventh birthday, and she took the name of her patroness, St. Veronica. Sister Veronica has a lifetime before her!"

This letter came to Newman in the morning; in the evening he started for Paris. His wound began to ache with its first fierceness, and during his long bleak journey the thought of Madame de Cintré's "lifetime," passed within prison walls on whose outer side he might stand, kept him perpetual company. Now he would fix himself in Paris for ever; he would extort a sort of happiness from the knowledge that if she was not there at

had gone, had simply strayed and lost itself in the great desert of life

couldn't

itself;

was

appeared to have been moved

On the doing of that all other doing depended

reached him

received

wring a hard

Claire

the new Sister's "lifetime" — every one's sister but his! —

Soeur Véronique

least the stony sepulchre that held her was. He descended, unannounced, upon Mrs. Bread, whom he found keeping lonely watch in his great empty saloons on the Boulevard Haussmann. They were as neat as a Dutch village; Mrs. Bread's only occupation had been removing individual dust-particles. She made no complaint, however, of her loneliness, for in her philosophy a servant was but a mysteriously projected machine, and it would be as fantastic for a housekeeper to comment upon a gentleman's absences as for a clock to remark upon not being wound up. No particular clock, Mrs. Bread supposed, kept all the time, and no particular servant could enjoy all the sunshine diffused by the career of an exacting master. She ventured, nevertheless, to express a modest hope that Newman meant to remain a while in Paris. Newman laid his hand on hers and shook it gently. "I mean to remain for ever," [illegible].

He went after this to see Mrs. Tristram, to whom he had telegraphed and who expected him. She looked at him a moment and shook her head. "This won't do," she said; "you've come back too soon." He sat down and asked about her husband and her children, tried even to inquire about Miss Dora Finch. In the midst of this, "Do you know where she is?" he asked abruptly.

Mrs. Tristram hesitated [illegible]; of course he couldn't mean Miss Dora Finch. Then she answered, properly: "She has gone to the other house—in the Rue d'Enfer." After Newman had sat a while longer looking very sombre, she went on: "You're not so good a man as I thought. You're more—you're more——"

"More what?" Newman asked.

"More unforgiving."

"Good God!" cried Newman; "do you expect me to forgive?"

"No, not that. I've not forgiven, so of course you can't. But you might forget! You've a worse temper about it than I should have expected. You look wicked —you look dangerous."

"I may be dangerous," he said; "but I am not wicked. No, I am not wicked." And he got up to go. Mrs. Tristram asked him to come back to dinner, but he answered that he did not feel like pledging himself to be present at an entertainment, even as a solitary guest. Later in the evening, if he should be able, he would come.

He walked away through the city, beside the Seine and over it, and took the direction of the Rue d'Enfer. The day had the softness of early spring, but the weather was gray and humid. Newman found himself in a part of Paris which he little knew—a region of convents and prisons, of streets bordered by long dead walls and traversed by few wayfarers. At the intersection of two of these streets stood the house of the Carmelites—a dull, plain edifice, with a high-shouldered blank wall all round it. From without Newman could see its upper windows, its steep roof and its chimneys. But these things revealed no symptoms of human life; the place looked dumb, deaf, inanimate. The pale, dead, discoloured wall stretched beneath it far down the empty side-street—a vista without a human figure. Newman stood there a long time; there were no passers; he was free to gaze his fill. This seemed the goal of his journey; it was what he had come for. It was a strange satisfaction, and yet it was a satisfaction; the barren stillness of the place seemed to be his own release from ineffectual longing. It told him that the woman within was lost beyond recall, and that the days and years of the future would pile themselves above her like the huge immovable slab of a tomb. These days and years, in this place, would always be just so gray and silent. Suddenly, from the thought of their seeing him stand there, again the charm utterly departed. He would never stand there again; it was gratuitous dreariness. He turned away with a heavy heart, b[illegible] a heart lighter than the one he had brought.

Everything was over, and he too at last could rest. He walked down through narrow, winding streets to the edge of the Seine again, and there he saw, close above him, the [illegible] towers of Notre Dame. He crossed one of the bridges and stood a moment in the empty place before the great cathedral; then he went in beneath the grossly-imaged portals. He wandered some distance up the nave and sat down in the splendid dimness. He sat a long time; he heard far-away bells chiming off, at long intervals, [illegible]. He was very tired; this was the best place he could be in. He said no prayers; he had no prayers to say. He had nothing to be thankful for and he had nothing to ask; nothing to ask because now he must take care of himself. But a great cathedral offers a very various hospitality, and Newman sat in his place, because while he was there he was out of the world. The most unpleasant thing that had ever happened to him had reached its formal conclusion, as it were; he could close the book and put it away. He leaned his head for a long time on the chair in front of him; when he took it up he felt that he was himself again. Somewhere in his [illegible] loosened. He thought of the Bellegardes; he had almost forgotten them. He remembered them as people he had meant to do something to. He gave a groan as he remembered what he had meant to do; he was annoyed at having meant to do it; the bottom, suddenly, had fallen out of his revenge. Whether it was Christian charity or unregenerate good nature—what it was, in the background of his soul—I don't pretend to say; but Newman's last thought was that of course he would let the Bellegardes go.

If he had spoken it aloud he would have said that he didn't want to hurt them. He was ashamed of having wanted to hurt them. They had hurt him, but such

Yet
back
high and wild and grey, the twin
makes square that the great front clear;
into space,
he
church
but such a place was a kingdom of rest.
the big bronze syllables of the Word.
mere human weakness of will—
spirit
he had learnt his lesson—not indeed that he the least understand it—and could put away the book.
and yet partly incredulous, at this
soul a tight constriction had loosened.

things were really not his game. At last he got up and came out of the darkening church; not with the elastic step of a man who has won a victory or taken a resolve, but strolling soberly, like a good-natured man who is still a little ashamed.

Going home, he said to Mrs. Bread that he must trouble her to put back his things into the portmanteau she had had unpacked the evening before. His gentle stewardess looked at him through eyes a trifle bedimmed. "Dear me, sir," she exclaimed, "I thought you said that you were going to stay for ever."

"I meant that I was going to stay away for ever," said Newman, kindly. And since his departure from Paris on the following day he has certainly not returned. The gilded apartments I have so often spoken of stand ready to receive him, but they serve only as a spacious sinecure for Mrs. Bread, who wanders eternally from room to room, adjusting the tassels of the curtains, and keeps her wages, which are regularly brought her by a banker's clerk, in a great pink Sèvres vase on the drawing-room mantel-shelf.

Late in the evening Newman went to Mrs. Tristram's, and found Tom Tristram by the domestic fireside. "I'm glad to see you back in Paris," this gentleman declared. "You know it's really the only place for a white man to live." Mr. Tristram made his friend welcome, according to his own rosy light, and offered him a convenient résumé of the Franco-American gossip of the last six months. Then at last he got up and said he would go for half an hour to the club. "I suppose a man who has been for six months in California wants a little intellectual conversation. I'll let my wife have a go at you."

Newman shook hands heartily with his host, but did not ask him to remain; and then he relapsed into his place on the sofa, opposite to Mrs. Tristram. She presently asked him what he had done after leaving her. "Nothing particular," said Newman.

He ~~was puzzled by the idea~~ quite failed, of a sudden, to recognise the fact of his having cultivated any such link with them. It was a link for themselves perhaps, their having so hurt him; but that side of it was now not his affair.

rather to the quiet measure of a discreet escape, of a retreat with appearances preserved.

It was therefore as if she had looked at him on this through bedimmed eyes, with the conviction of a value, so far as she could see, quite extravagantly wasted.

him

he was obliged a little awkwardly to explain

telling

its

in

far, you know.

patched up gaps in the latter

's solitary straightness which

the more jovial member of the pair

205 a

repaired in free remarks, with a free tongue, the too visible and too innocent deficiencies in Newman's acquaintance with current history. Then, having made him gape with strange information — all as to what had been going on in "notre monde à nous," you know — Tristram got up to go and resume his own budget at the club.

To this Newman replied

2056

that Mrs. Tristram was his club and that he had never wanted a better: a statement he felt the truth of when he was presently alone with her and came or perhaps all the more when she asked him what he had done on leaving her in the afternoon. "Well," then replied, "I worked it off."

"Worked off the afternoon?"

2052

"Yes, and a lot of other troublesome stuff."

"You struck me," she confessed, "as a man filled with some rather uncanny idea. I wondered if I were right to leave you to the prey of it, and whether I ought not to have had you followed and watched."

This appeared to strike him with surprise. "Surely I didn't look as if I wanted to take life." "I might have feared,

206

if I had let myself go a little that you were thinking of taking your own ⊙"

He breathed a long sigh of such apparent indifference to his own as would have ended that aunt. "Well," he now the less after a moment went on, "I have got rid of about nine tenths of something that had become the biggest part of me. But I did that only by walking over

2062

to see the Carmelites."

"You've been there," she stared – "at the Carmelites?" And as he only met her eyes: "Trying to scale the wall?"

"Well, I thought of that – I measured the wall. I looked at it a long time. But it's too high – it's beyond me."

"That's right," she said. "Give it up."

"I have given it up. But, on the spot there, I took it all in."

2066

She rested now her kindest eyes on him. "On the spot then you didn't happen to meet M. de Bellegarde—also taking it all in? I'm told his sister's course doesn't suit him the least little bit."

Newman had a moment's gravity of silence. "No, luckily—I didn't meet either of *them*. In that case I *might* have fired."

"Ah, it isn't they're

206c

not been keeping quiet; she said: "I mean in the country"

207

"You struck me," she rejoined, "as a man with a plot in his head. You looked as if you were bent on some sinister errand, and after you had left me I wondered whether I ought to have let you go."

"I only went over to the other side of the river—to the Carmelites," said Newman.

Mrs. Tristram looked at him a moment and smiled. "What did you do there? Try to scale the wall?"

"I did nothing. I looked at the place for a few minutes and then came away."

Mrs. Tristram gave him a sympathetic glance. "You didn't happen to meet M. de Bellegarde," she asked, "staring hopelessly at the convent wall as well? I am told he takes his sister's conduct very hard."

"No, I didn't meet him, I am happy to say," Newman answered, after a pause.

"They are in the country," Mrs. Tristram went on; "at—what is the name of the place?—Fleurières. They returned there at the time you left Paris, and have been spending the year in extreme seclusion. The little Marquise must enjoy it; I expect to hear that she has eloped with her daughter's music-master!"

Newman was looking at the light wood-fire; but he listened to this with extreme interest. At last he spoke: "I mean never to mention the name of those people again, and I don't want to hear anything more about them." And then he took out his pocket-book and drew forth a scrap of paper. He looked at it an instant, then got up and stood by the fire. "I am going to burn them up," he said. "I am glad to have you as a witness. There they go!" And he tossed the paper into the flame.

Mrs. Tristram sat with her embroidery-needle suspended. "What is that paper?" she asked.

Newman, leaning against the fireplace, stretched his arms and drew a longer breath than usual. Then after a moment, "I can tell you now," he said. "It was a

at

far from human eye

had gazed

and

Then

an apparent admission of its irrelevance; but he spoke in another sense

in the world is that?"

chimney-piece, he seemed to grasp its ledge with force and to draw his breath a moment in pain; for that after that,

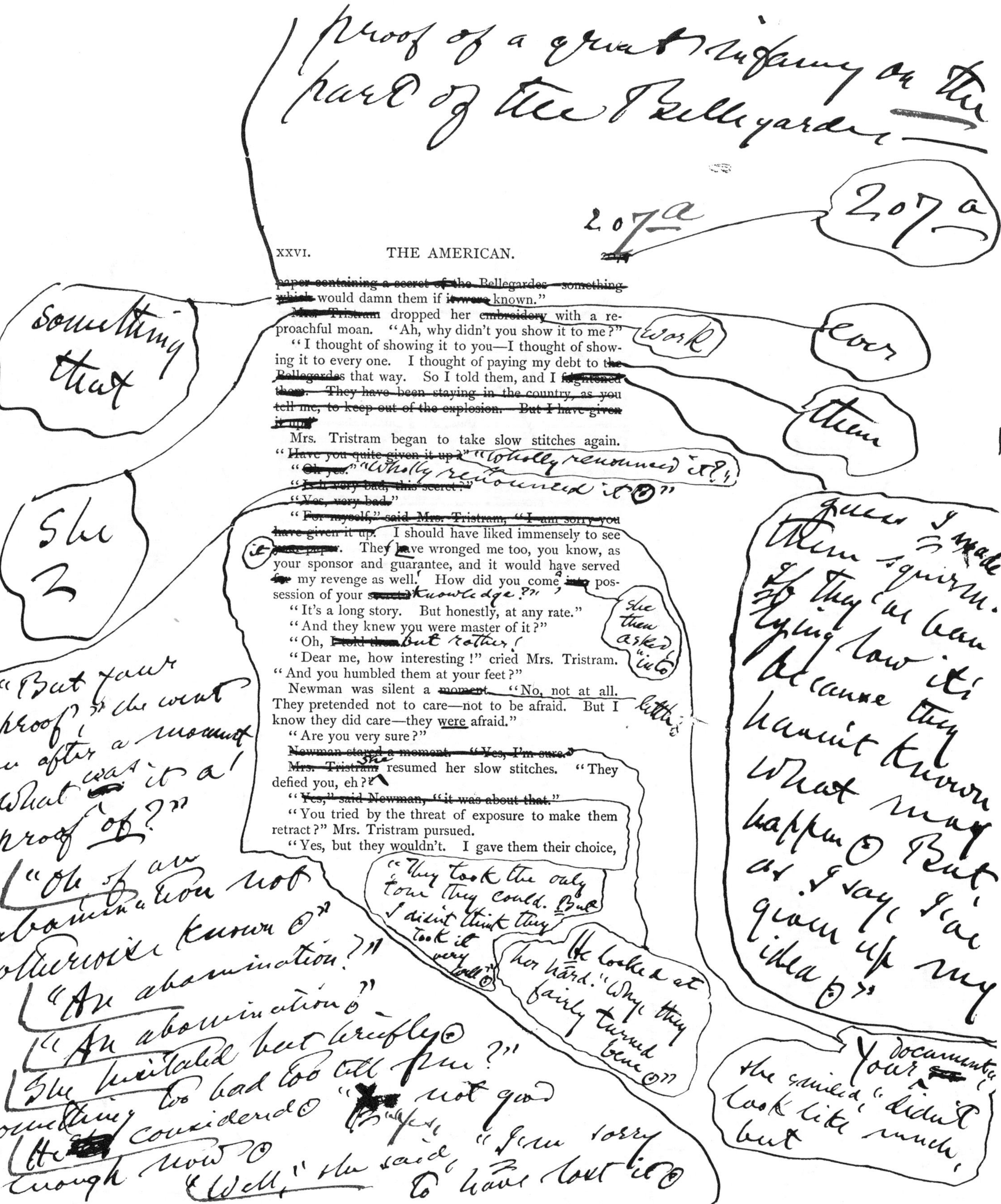

XXVI. THE AMERICAN.

paper containing a secret of the Bellegardes—something which would damn them if it were known."

Mrs. Tristram dropped her embroidery with a reproachful moan. "Ah, why didn't you show it to me?"

"I thought of showing it to you—I thought of showing it to every one. I thought of paying my debt to the Bellegardes that way. So I told them, and I frightened them. They have been staying in the country, as you tell me, to keep out of the explosion. But I have given it up."

Mrs. Tristram began to take slow stitches again. "Have you quite given it up?"

"Oh yes."

"Is it very bad, this secret?"

"Yes, very bad."

"For myself," said Mrs. Tristram, "I am sorry you have given it up. I should have liked immensely to see your paper. They have wronged me too, you know, as your sponsor and guarantee, and it would have served for my revenge as well. How did you come into possession of your secret?"

"It's a long story. But honestly, at any rate."

"And they knew you were master of it?"

"Oh, I told them."

"Dear me, how interesting!" cried Mrs. Tristram. "And you humbled them at your feet?"

Newman was silent a moment. "No, not at all. They pretended not to care—not to be afraid. But I know they did care—they were afraid."

"Are you very sure?"

Newman stared a moment. "Yes, I'm sure."

Mrs. Tristram resumed her slow stitches. "They defied you, eh?"

"Yes," said Newman, "it was about that."

"You tried by the threat of exposure to make them retract?" Mrs. Tristram pursued.

"Yes, but they wouldn't. I gave them their choice,

and they chose to take their chance of bluffing off the charge and convicting me of fraud~~. But they were frightened," Newman added, "and I have had all the vengeance I want."~~

"It is most provoking," ~~said Mrs. Tristram,~~ "to hear you talk of the 'charge' when the charge is burned up. Is it quite consumed?" she asked, glancing at the fire. ~~Newman~~ He assured her ~~that~~ there was nothing left of it. ~~"Even then," she said, "I suppose there is no harm in saying that you probably did not make them so very uncomfortable. My impression would be that since, as you say, they defied you, it was because they believed that, after all, you would never really come to the point. Their confidence, after counsel taken of each other, was not in their innocence, nor in their talent for bluffing things off; it was in your remarkable good nature! You see they were right."~~

~~Newman instinctively turned to see if the little paper was in fact consumed, but there was nothing left of it.~~

that is of having procured and paid for a forgery. Forgery of course is an easy word — but they didn't and don't matter. They're a pair of sick cats poisoned and I don't want any more 'revenge.'"

She returned

and at this, dropping her embroidery, she got up and came near him. "I made it tell you at this hour how I've felt for you. But I like you as you are," she said.

"As I am —?"

"As you are." She stood before him and put out her hand as for his arm, which he a little blankly let her take. "Just exactly as you are," she repeated. With which, bending her head, she raised his hand and very tenderly and beautifully kissed it. Then "Ah, poor Claire!" she sighed as she went back to her place. It drew from him, while his flushed face followed her, a strange inarticulate sound, but this made her say again: "Yes, poor, poor Claire!"

THE END.

Printed by R. & R. Clark, *Edinburgh.*